PRAISE FOR THE LORD OF THE ISLES

The Fortress of Glass

"Drake possesses every skill necessary to make this story a thoroughly absorbing one, even to new readers. Those who have sailed with him through the preceding two Isles trilogies ought to eagerly demand it." —*Booklist*

Master of the Cauldron

"Drake's grasp of large-scale action, as well as small dramas, makes him a superb storyteller. The sixth addition to his Lord of the Isles series belongs in most fantasy collections." —*Library Journal*

"Drake writes this kind of fantasy adventure as well as anyone active in the field and has a real gift for the intricacies of court intrigues." —*Science Fiction Chronicle*

"Great, gritty realism on both material and magical planes, and Hell quite literally breaks loose on occasion. The audience for this kind of fantasy saga should prove large and ongoing." —*Booklist*

Goddess of the Ice Realm

"With *Goddess of the Ice Realm*, Drake once again shows that originality is possible in the fantasy realm. . . . The ensemble cast of characters continues to charm and, at the same time, to change. Serious issues of choice and moral responsibility face them along with the ghouls and spells. All in all, a solid addition to an outstanding fantasy series, showing once again that Drake is among the most versatile of authors in the SF/fantasy genres."

—S. M. Stirling, author of *The Sky People*

Tor Books by David Drake

The Mirror of Worlds

THE SECOND VOLUME OF
The Crown of the Isles

DAVID DRAKE

TOR®
fantasy

A TOM DOHERTY ASSOCIATES BOOK
NEW YORK

This is a work of fiction. All the characters, organizations, and events portrayed in this novel are either products of the author's imagination or are used fictitiously.

THE MIRROR OF WORLDS: THE SECOND VOLUME OF THE CROWN OF THE ISLES

Copyright © 2007 by David Drake

All rights reserved.

Edited by David G. Hartwell

A Tor Book
Published by Tom Doherty Associates, LLC
175 Fifth Avenue
New York, NY 10010

www.tor-forge.com

Tor® is a registered trademark of Tom Doherty Associates, LLC.

ISBN-13: 978-0-7653-5117-3
ISBN-10: 0-7653-5117-X

First Edition: July 2007
First Mass Market Edition: November 2008

Printed in the United States of America

0 9 8 7 6 5 4 3 2 1

TO LUCILE CARTER

Acknowledgments

Dan Breen continues as my first reader, catching the sort of grammatical errors which creep in when I'm writing fast or heavily editing chunks that just didn't come out right the first time. (Or the second time and third time, often enough. My roughs are sometimes a mass of arrows, brackets, scribblings, and overstrikes by the time they get to Dan.) He's also very good on size issues. As an aside, he was hugely amused when he saw that the counterpart in the Isles of Saxo Grammaticus was the Scribe of Breen.

My webmaster, Karen Zimmerman, and Dorothy Day archived my texts in widely separated parts of the country. If an asteroid destroys the Triangle region of North Carolina, it will still be possible to reconstruct my drafts. (I won't be the person reconstructing them in that event, of course.)

In addition, Dorothy acted as my continuity person (for example, "What the dickens was the name of the Minister of Supply?"), and Karen provided research on all manner of questions that cropped up while I was writing (for example, "I need more information on the Great Tar Lake of Jamaica"— which, lest anyone be misled, turned out to be the Great Pitch Lake of Trinidad). Their efforts made the book better and my life easier.

It's traditional that each of my novels involves a computer problem. This time the power supply of my desktop unit (hooked up to my laser printer) went out as I started the first-pass edit. Mark L. Van Name diagnosed the problem, my son Jonathan fixed it, and his facility manager, Bill Catchings, allowed Jonathan to borrow a power supply from stores to keep me operating until the new unit came in. This kind of skill and expertise is commercially available (from Mark, Jonathan, and Bill, among others), but I personally don't know enough about computers to have found it on my own.

I dedicated this book to Miss Carter, my first Latin teacher (junior and senior years of high school). I wasn't particularly interested in languages at the time, and I certainly didn't apply myself in her classes. She was nonetheless a good-enough teacher that she instilled a love for Latin which I wasn't aware of until I switched to German when I went off to college. I returned to Latin and haven't been very far from it since that day.

I can scarcely overstate Latin's importance to my life generally and to the Isles series, in particular. Without Miss Carter, I might be without the language and all the benefits it's brought me.

This past summer has been difficult. My wife, Jo, has been enormously supportive throughout.

Every time I create an acknowledgments page I'm reminded of how much my novels are collaborative projects, even though I'm doing all the writing myself. The book wouldn't be nearly as good without my family and friends. Losing a close friend, as I did this summer, drives home how very important my circle of family and friends is to me generally.

Author's Note

I'VE BASED THE religion of the Isles generally on that of Sumer: the sacred triad of Inanna, Dumuzi, and Ereshkigal. The words of power, however, are the *voces mysticae* of the documentary magic common in the Mediterranean Basin during classical times. This was the language spoken to the demiurges who would in turn intercede on behalf of humans with the Gods.

I have no personal religious beliefs, but many very intelligent people believed that these *voces mysticae* were effective in rousing spiritual powers to affect human endeavors. I prefer not to pronounce them aloud. Readers can make their own decisions on the subject.

As usual in the Isles series, the literary allusions in this novel are to classical and medieval writers of our own world. I won't bother to list the correspondences here, but the reader can rest assured that they exist.

I'll mention one further point. I almost always have a photograph or a painting beside me while I work on a scene. That helps me give touches of reality to the fantasy worlds I'm creating. As one example among many, this time I used a copy of *Les Très Riches Heures du Duc de Berry,* an illuminated manuscript from around 1411 A.D.

Readers familiar with horses will know that sidesaddles now put the rider's legs to the left. If those persons will check August of *Les Très Riches Heures,* they'll see that two of the three women riding have their legs to the right.

While I *do* make mistakes, I suggest that this shouldn't be the first assumption readers make when they find something that surprises them.

Dave Drake
david-drake.com

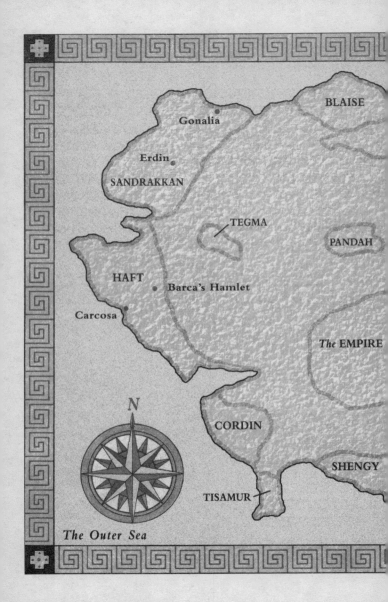

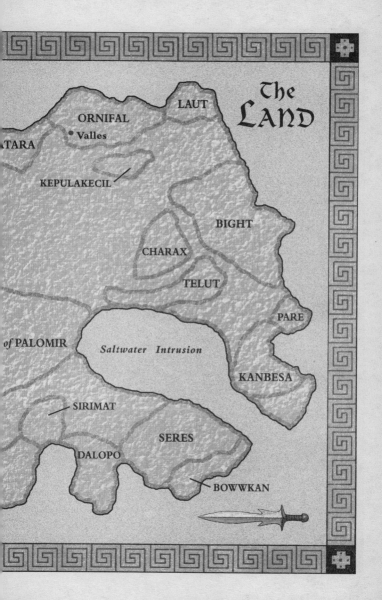

The
LAND

LAUT

ORNIFAL
• Valles

ATARA

KEPULAKECIL

BIGHT

CHARAX

TELUT

PARE

of PALOMIR   *Saltwater Intrusion*

KANBESA

SIRIMAT

SERES

DALOPO

BOWWKAN

The Mirror of Worlds

Chapter

1

ILNA LOOKED DOWN the valley to the gray limestone temple and the slaughtered bodies around it. There were many corpses, though she didn't know precisely how many: when a number was higher than she could count on her fingers, she had to tell it with beans or pebbles . . . if she cared.

Mostly she didn't care. These folk, the humans and the cat men who must've killed them and been killed in turn, were all dead. The dead didn't matter.

Ilna had loved her family, Chalcus and Merota. They didn't matter either because cat men had killed them also.

"It can't've happened long ago," said Asion, the small, dark man who apparently cropped his hair and beard with a knife at long intervals. Ilna'd known the hunter for nearly a month, and she hadn't seen him trim it in that time. "I don't smell them in the breeze."

"There's no breeze," said Karpos, his ginger-haired partner, equally unkempt. He crushed a pellet of dry soil between the thumb and finger of his right hand, letting the dust drift to the ground. It fell straight, so far as Ilna could see. "You're just pretending you feel one."

"There's a breeze," said Asion, crooking his left index finger without taking his eyes off the valley. "The fuzz on my ears feels the wind even when dust won't drift. There's breeze enough that I'd smell them if they'd started to stink."

Karpos' left hand held a short, very stiff wooden bow with an arrow nocked; its point was bronze, thin but with broad wings that'd require only a few heartbeats to bleed out the life of whatever he hit fairly. Asion had a sling with a short staff and linen thongs. For ordinary hunting he shot smooth pebbles, but he carried a few pointed lead bullets in a pouch; one of those was in the pocket of molded leather now.

A word was cast into the metal of the bullets. Asion seemed to think it was a valuable charm, though he wasn't sure because the hunters couldn't read any better than Ilna could.

Ilna didn't believe in charms of that sort. From what she'd seen since the hunters joined her, the strength of Asion's shoulders would be sufficient for most purposes.

Ilna glanced at the strands of yarn in her hands, ready to be woven into a pattern to freeze the mind or stop the heart of anyone who saw it. She could instead knot the yarn into a simple oracle to answer the question "Does an enemy wait for us below?"

She did something similar every morning to choose the direction for the day's travels . . . but such care wasn't required now. She trusted the long, fine fur growing on the top of Asion's ears, and she trusted her own instinct to tell her if something ahead wasn't right, was out of place in a peaceful valley. She didn't feel that here.

Ilna'd lived in a hamlet on the east coast of Haft until she was eighteen. Two years ago a wizard named Tenoctris had washed up on shore and everything had changed. She and her brother, Cashel, had left home forever, accompanied by their childhood friends, Garric and Sharina. And now—

Garric was ruler of the Isles; his sister had become Princess Sharina of Haft; and Cashel had the only thing that'd ever mattered to him, Sharina's love. He could be Lord Cashel if he wanted, but the title meant no more to him than it would've to Ilna.

Ilna's lips looked as hard as knife edges. At one time she'd have said she didn't want anything beyond what her skill at weaving brought her. Then she met Chalcus and Merota, a man and a child who loved her . . . until they were killed.

Ilna smiled. Death was the greatest and perhaps the only peace she could imagine. Until then, she'd kill cat men.

"We'll go down," she said, standing and stepping out of the

brush without waiting to see whether the hunters agreed. That was their business; they'd joined *her,* rather than Ilna os-Kenset clinging to a chance-met pair of strong, confident men for protection. The skills Ilna had learned in Hell were far more lethally effective than the hunters' weapons and muscles. Though—

Ilna knew that meeting Asion and Karpos wasn't really chance. Her oracle had directed her over a ridge and into a valley to the east of the one she'd been following for the first week after she left the royal army and her friends. Her surviving friends. The smell of a fire had led her to the hunters, smoking thin-sliced venison on a rack of green twigs.

Asion and Karpos followed her because they were confused and fearful, while Ilna had purpose. The Change, the mixing of eras by wizardry, had turned the Isles into the single great continent which had existed in its far past. The hunters—Ilna assumed they were from a much earlier time; she and they struggled occasionally with each other's dialect, though they understood one another well enough—had been completely disoriented by what had happened.

Ilna didn't understand the Change any better than the hunters did, but that was simply one more thing that didn't matter to her. She lived to kill the cat men, the Coerli, because they'd killed the man and the child who'd given her life meaning.

The hunters would've been willing to do things they found difficult to be allowed to accompany Ilna. All she asked them to do was to kill, and at that to kill animals rather than men. Asion and Karpos found killing animals as natural as breathing.

Karpos went down with Ilna, angling a little out from her left side and letting his long legs carry him enough ahead that he could be said to be leading. His right thumb and forefinger rested on his bowstring, ready to draw it back to his ear and loose in a single motion. Karpos was a rawboned man with beetling brows. He looked slow and awkward, but he'd shown that he was neither.

Ilna smiled. The oracle of her cords wouldn't have led her

to Karpos and his partner if they hadn't been the sort of men she needed as helpers.

Asion waited on the ridge, watching the back trail as Ilna and Karpos walked down the gentle slope. The men had hunted dangerous game together for a decade, so they were naturally cautious. That was good, though the great scaly herbivores they'd hunted on Ornifal in their own day weren't nearly as deadly as the Coerli they preyed on at Ilna's direction.

The valley'd been planted in barley or oats—the shoots were too young for Ilna to be sure; ancient olives budded in gnarled majesty among the furrows. Ilna gave a tight smile: the trees appeared to be randomly spaced, but they formed a pattern so subtle that she would've said no one but herself or her brother Cashel could see it.

Almost no one, perhaps. Ilna didn't like pride, in herself least of all, and she especially disliked learning that she'd arrogantly assumed she was uniquely skilled. She smiled a little wider: since she disliked herself at most times, having a particular cause didn't make a great deal of difference.

A goat bleated on the far side of the valley. There was a sizable herd, cropping the grass growing among the rocks on that slope. No one had kept goats in the borough around Barca's Hamlet where Ilna grew up. Goats were hard on pastures, though Ilna'd been told they gave better milk than sheep. Sheep's milk and brick-hard whey cheese had been good enough for Ilna and her brother when they were growing up as orphans; good enough when they could afford them, that was.

"They aren't straying into the crops," she remarked, her eyes narrowing as she watched the herd. The goats were aware of her and Karpos, but they didn't appear skittish or even much interested. "Though there's nobody watching them."

The hunter shrugged. "All dead, I reckon," he said. "There's no fires burning and nothing to hear but the birds. And the goats, I mean. Do we have goat meat tonight, mistress?"

"I'll tell you when I decide," Ilna said curtly. The hunters didn't appreciate how well trained the goats must be that they didn't stray into the crops.

There'd been a time when Ilna took certain things for granted. Oh, not in her speech the way most people did, but still in the back of her mind: the sun would rise, the wind would blow, and Chalcus and Merota would go through life with her.

So far the sun continued to rise and the wind to blow, but those might change in a heartbeat; and if they did, that would matter less to Ilna than the loss of her family had. Still, for now there were Coerli to kill.

Three bodies lay just ahead, two middle-aged human males and a cat man. They'd been hacked savagely by swords or axes: one man had been disemboweled and the Corl's head clung to his shoulders by a scrap of skin—its spine was cut through. No weapons were in evidence, but the cat man's muzzle was bloody.

"We don't have to worry about what's behind us, now," Karpos said. "Hold up before we check on what might be waiting inside, right?"

Without taking his eyes off the temple and sprawled bodies, the hunter raised his right arm and waved to his partner. Before returning his fingertips to the nocked arrow, Karpos wiggled his long dagger in its sheath to make sure it was free.

Ilna didn't think they needed to wait for Asion, but she didn't argue the point. If it'd mattered, she'd have done as she pleased—and seen to it that the hunters did as she pleased also. She didn't need to prove her power; that was for weak people.

She considered for a moment, then put the hank of yarn back in the sleeve of her outer tunic. She'd woven the cloth herself, and she'd also woven her cloak of unbleached wool that shed water like a slate roof.

Karpos and his partner wore breeches and vests of untanned deerskin with the flesh side turned out. The packs that they'd left back on the ridgeline included fur robes for cold weather, though the season had advanced so that they were no longer necessary even at night.

Ilna suspected the men continued to carry the robes because the town to which they'd previously hiked every spring to sell packloads of lizard gall didn't exist in the world after the Change. They were unwilling to give up the few aspects of their past life which still remained.

The hunters had decorated their vests by sewing on the scalps of Coerli they'd killed since joining Ilna, a double handful each. Ilna didn't object, but of course she didn't take trophies herself.

All that mattered to Ilna was the killing. When she'd killed all the cat men in this world, she didn't know what she'd do. Die, she hoped, because her life would no longer have purpose.

Asion joined them, holding the staff of his sling in his right hand and cupping the pocket and bullet in his left. "Have you guys noticed the pond?" he said with a frown in his voice. "Why did they do that, d'ye think? Throw the plants in?"

The little temple was set up three steps from the ground. Forsythias grew around both it and the small, round pool in front of the building. Several bushes had been pulled up by the roots and thrown into the water. The men who'd done that had mortal wounds, clearly. One of them lay on the curb with a yellow-flowered branch clutched in a death grip.

"Why do they have a pond there anyway?" said Karpos. "Are they raising fish? It's too small."

"I don't know," Ilna said. She didn't add to the statement, because there was nothing *to* add and she saw no point in wasting her breath. "Let's go on, then."

The pool surprised her as well, though she didn't bother saying so. Ilna hadn't seen a temple till she left Barca's Hamlet some two years—or a lifetime—before, but there'd been plenty of them in the cities she'd passed through since then. Ilna didn't pay particular attention to buildings, but she had an eye for patterns. She'd certainly have made note of a temple facing a pool if she'd seen one. This was the first.

Karpos knelt and placed his right index and middle fingers to the throat of the first corpse, a man lying on his back. The fellow's hair was white, as much of it as was left; his forehead rose to the peak of his scalp. His face was as calm as if he'd been praying, though the wounds that'd killed him—three deep stabs in the lower body and a slash that'd broken the bone of his upper right arm—must've been extremely painful.

"Dead since daybreak," Karpos said, rising and touching the bowstring again. "Maybe a little longer, but not much."

Ilna looked into the pool, her face frozen into a deliberate lack of expression in place of her usual guarded silence. The water was clear and so shallow that she could see the narrow crevices between the stone blocks paving the bottom. Forsythia stems cast jagged shadows, and there were smears where mud'd washed from the roots of the plants.

"He was a tough bastard, I give him that," Asion said, his voice oddly gentle. He nodded to the corpse on the coping of the pool. "He had to crawl most a the way. Look at the trail."

"Yes," said Ilna. "I noticed."

All the corpses were at least middle-aged; this fellow was older yet. To look at, he seemed soft if not precisely fat; the sort of man who did no more work than he had to and was readier to lift a tankard than a hoe.

Perhaps that had been true. The man's last living act, however, had been to pull a full-sized bush out of the ground and drag it ten double paces to the pool while his intestines spilled out in coils behind him. He'd been laid open as if by a cleaver, but he hadn't quit until he was dead.

"Mistress?" Karpos said. He sounded puzzled and therefore worried; people who accept great danger as a fact of life become concerned when faced with things they don't understand; they knew all too well what might be hiding within the unknown. "The cat didn't kill this fellow. It was a blade did this."

"The Coerli had weapons," Ilna said harshly. She turned from the body and the pool. "The survivors took them away. There's nothing amazing about that!"

"Then who was this cat chewing on?" the hunter said, pointing to the dead Corl. "Look at his muzzle, the blood and—"

He saw Ilna's face and swallowed. "Sorry, mistress," he mumbled in a small voice. "I guess it was the cats."

"Mistress, who's this fellow?" said Asion from the steps up the front of the temple. Most of the bodies were there in a ragged pile. "What is he, I mean?"

Asion had stuck his sling beneath his belt to get it out of the way, drawing instead his long steel knife; that was a better weapon for a close-in tangle with anything that pounced on him from the temple. With his free hand he dragged a corpse out by the ankle.

The corpse of a man, Ilna assumed; but its chest was abnormally deep, its belly smaller and flatter than a corseted woman's, and its skin had the smooth black gleam of polished coal. Its genitals were very small.

The corpse was nude except for the round metal shield hanging from a neck strap; its right hand death-gripped the hilt of a sword that looked serviceable for either slashing or stabbing. It could easily have been the weapon which'd killed both the white-robed humans and the Coerli . . . and the fellow's throat had been worried through by what were almost certainly a cat man's long jaws.

"There's more blacks under here," Asion said. "Three or four, I'd guess."

"I don't know who they are," Ilna said coldly. She was angry at the hunter for asking a question that she couldn't answer, and even more angry with herself for not having said so at once instead of forcing her companions to wait.

She walked toward the temple entrance, skirting the corpses. "And it appears that the weapons were in the hands of the blacks, whoever they are," she added, though by this point she did so merely as a public admission of her mistake; the hunters already knew she'd been wrong. "Not the Coerli."

Ilna disliked stone. The rational part of her mind knew she was being silly to think that stone disliked her as well;

but not all of her mind was rational and she *did* think that, feel it deep in her bones. She walked up the leveling courses and onto the porch, smiling at the cool gray slabs beneath her feet.

I'm walking on you, she thought. *And I'm fool enough to think you know that.*

Despite being stone, it was a very attractive building. The porch extended on all four sides, supported on fluted columns. The temple proper had solid sidewalls but only two more columns at the front. Ilna walked between them and into the main room. There were hints of intricate carvings just under the roof, but the only light came through the entrance behind her.

At the far end were two statues on square stone bases: an inhumanly serene woman and a female Corl. The round base between them was empty; the statue, a nude man, had fallen forward onto the floor.

"Hey, why're they praying to a cat man?" said Karpos. His voice startled her; her attention had been so focused on the statues that she hadn't heard the whisper of his deerskin-clad feet entering the temple behind her.

"It's probably the Sister," Ilna said. "The Lady and the Sister, the Queen of Heaven and the Queen of the Dead."

She looked at the image of the Corl again. "Or perhaps a demon. If there're any of these people left alive, we can ask them."

"Not a soul," Karpos said. "Asion's looking around more, but we'd've heard something by now besides the goats if there was anybody."

He didn't sound concerned. The hunters weren't cruel men, but they were hard and even in life the folk of this community had meant nothing to them.

"Why'd they make the Sister a Corl?" Karpos added, scratching his left eyebrow with the tip of his bow. "I never seen that."

"Do I look like a priest?" Ilna snapped. "Anyway, I said it might be a demon."

She knelt, peering at the base supporting the Lady's

statue. Her eyes had adapted to the dimness well enough to see that carved on it was an image of the Shepherd, the Lady's consort. He held his staff ready to repel the hulking, long-armed ogres attacking from both sides. The base beneath the female Corl had a similar scene, a Corl chieftain with a flaring mane who raised his knob-headed cudgel as winged, serpent-bodied creatures threatened him.

The base from which the male statue'd fallen was plain. Ilna rose to her feet, frowning. "There's nothing here," she said. "We'll check the living quarters before we decide what to do next. There's huts on the other slope."

Someone groaned at Ilna's feet. She jumped back.

"Sister take me, mistress!" Karpos said, pointing his drawn bow at the figure on the floor. "That's not a statue! It's a man!"

GARRIC, RULER OF the Isles, faced the largest city of the Coerli. The cat men called it simply the Place, because its ten thousand residents made it unique among a race which generally grouped itself into hunting bands of a dozen or two. When the Change merged eras, it'd wrenched the Place to within twenty miles of Valles, the capital of the Isles.

"Coerli, send out your champion!" Garric shouted. He was the only human who was fluent in the cat men's language, though he'd set scores of clerks and army officers to learning the patterns of clicks and hisses. "Send him to fight me, or send your Council of Elders to surrender!"

"Or we could simply deal with the cat beasts the way I would've in my time, lad," said the ghost sharing Garric's mind: King Carus, his ancestor and advisor. *"Burn the city down and slaughter any of the animals who live through the fire. And go on to the next city and do the same."*

Tenoctris says we need them, Garric thought. *And if she'd said we needed to ally with apes in the trees on Shengy, I'd be down there in the jungle waving bananas and chittering.*

The image of the tall, tanned king in Garric's mind threw back his head and laughed. *"Aye, lad,"* Carus said. *"And you'd be right to, of course. But sooner monkeys than cats who'd eat men if we let them."*

If, Garric repeated with emphasis. His smile and the king's both widened grimly.

Ornifal and the other isles of the kingdom were now a chain of highlands surrounding a great continent. The land hadn't risen in the sense that earthquakes and volcanoes sometimes lifted an island out of the sea—or sank one to the depths with the cities upon it, leaving their doomed, screaming residents to thrash in the boiling waves. The Change had welded the Isles of Garric's day in a ring which clamped together periods in which the Inner Sea was dry land.

A better term would be fragments of periods. Tenoctris, the wizard whose arrival in the surf off Barca's Hamlet had been the first of the events rushing Garric's quiet world toward catastrophe, said she thought at least twenty eras had been thrown together, spanning at least that many thousands of years.

Tenoctris insisted she wasn't a powerful wizard, but her care and impeccable judgment had saved the kingdom repeatedly where someone with greater strength and less wisdom would've added to the looming disaster. Garric had more confidence in a guess by Tenoctris than he did in tomorrow's sunrise. There'd been times in the past two years that the sun *wouldn't* have risen the next day, for Garric or the kingdom or for all mankind, if it hadn't been for the old wizard's skill.

Coerli warriors shrieked from the walls of the Place as the gates shuddered outward. The trumpeters and cornicenes of the royal army brayed a brassy response, and the massed ranks of soldiers shouted and clashed spears against their shields.

"We could cut right through the beasts," Carus mused regretfully. *"Cut and burn and wipe them off the face of the world. But we'll do as Tenoctris says."*

And we'll kill this *Corl,* Garric thought. *So that the rest believe me when I tell them they have no choice but to obey the laws we humans set them.*

Human slaves finished pushing the gate open; they scuttled back within the walls.

The Coerli used men the way men used oxen. Garric's eyes narrowed, but six naked slaves forced to shove on gate leaves wasn't the worst injustice taking place in the world. Worse things were happening a thousand times every day in human cities and on human estates.

But the Coerli *ate* men, just as surely as men ate beef. That would've been sufficient reason to handle the problem in the fashion Carus wanted, if the cat men had balked at Garric's offer of trial by battle.

The Coerli shrieked louder. A Corl chieftain, the biggest cat man Garric had thus far seen, swaggered out of the city. He paused just beyond the open gate leaves and, raising his maned head, bugled a menacing challenge of coughs and screams.

"I am Klagan!" the cat man cried. Garric could hear the Corl even through the brazen cacophony of the royal army. "No one can stand against me!"

"Wait and see, beast," said Carus with murderous relish. *"You and your Council of Elders don't know what you're in for!"*

Carus'd been the ruler of the Old Kingdom when it crashed into anarchy a thousand years before his distant descendant Garric was born. There'd never been a warrior the equal of Carus. If generalship and a strong sword arm could've preserved civilization, then the Old Kingdom would still be standing.

Kingship requires more than military might, though. The anger and furious drive that'd made Carus unstoppable on the battlefield were as much the cause of his kingdom's collapse as the rebels and usurpers springing up whenever the royal army was at a distance. Eventually a wizard had sucked Carus and his fleet to their doom in the depths of the Inner Sea; and because the wizard's trust in his power had been as deceiving as Carus' own, they'd drowned together in the cataclysm.

The wizard's death hadn't saved the kingdom, though.

When death loosed the king's hand, chaos, blood, and burning had followed for all the islands. It'd taken a thousand years for civilization to return—and now the Change threatened to bring chaos in a different form.

The Elders know what's going to happen, Garric said silently as he stretched, feeling his mail shirt ripple like water over the suede jerkin cushioning it. *I offered them an excuse to permit them to surrender, and they snapped it up. Otherwise every Corl in the Place will die, and they know that too.*

He chuckled aloud, then added, *Klagan may not know, of course.*

"He will," said Carus. *"Very soon he will."*

Garric stood ahead of the front ranks of his army by a double pace, the distance from the toe of a marching soldier's right foot to where that toe came down again—five feet by civilian measurement. The timber walls of the Place were only a hundred double paces away, suicidally close if they'd have been defended by humans with bows and catapults.

The Coerli were quick enough to dodge thrown spears and even arrows, so they'd never developed missile weapons for warfare. They didn't use them in hunting either; they ran down their prey, tangled it with weighted lines, and either slaughtered it immediately or drove it back to their keeps to keep it fresh for their females and kits.

The Coerli's preferred prey had been human beings until the Change. That wouldn't be the case for the cat men whom Garric and his government permitted to live in this new world.

"I am Klagan!" the Corl repeated. "Who dares to challenge me?"

"I am Garric, King of Men and Coerli!" Garric shouted. "Bow to me or die, Klagan!"

The chiefs of the Coerli were half again as heavy as the sexually immature warriors who made up the bulk of the male population. Even the chieftains were usually no more than the size of an average human male.

Klagan was an exception; but then, so was Garric. He'd

been the tallest man in Barca's Hamlet by a hand's breadth and, though rangy, would've been the strongest as well were it not for his friend Cashel. Cashel was tall by normal standards, but he was so broad that he looked squat from any distance; and even for as big as he was, Cashel was disproportionately strong.

The Corl champion raised his mace and screamed. He started toward Garric with a springy step, which for a Corl showed unusual caution. Normally a cat man would charge headlong, even though in this case it meant he'd be rushing into ten thousand human soldiers.

"I do not fear your weapons, beast!" Klagan shouted; which meant he did. He had reason to.

The Coerli didn't use fire and therefore didn't have metal. The stone head of Klagan's mace was the size of Garric's fist, and the warrior's leather harness, the only garment he wore, held a pair of poniards. One was hard wood, while the other'd been ground from a human thighbone. They were needle sharp, but they didn't have edges and they'd splinter on armor. In Klagan's left hand was a thirty-foot coil of tough vegetable fiber, weighted with a ball of sun-dried clay in which hooked thorns were set to snatch and tear.

"And his teeth, lad," Carus noted with the calm assurance of a warrior who never underestimated a foe, and who'd never failed to win his fight regardless. *"We'll not forget his teeth."*

"I don't need steel to kill you, Klagan!" Garric said. He lifted off his helmet, a work of art whose gilt wings flared widely to either side. He brandished it in the air, then set it on one of the pair of posts which a squad of his troops had hammered into the soil while the Coerli Elders deliberated on Garric's ultimatum. "You'll surrender or you'll die! Those are the only choices Coerli have in this world that humans rule!"

Garric unbuckled his heavy waist belt. The dagger sheathed on his right side partially balanced the sword on his left, but a thinner strap over his right shoulder supported the rest of the sword's weight. Keeping his eyes on the Corl, Garric pulled the harness over his head and hung it on the crossbar of the post already holding his helmet.

"What are you doing, beast?" Klagan called. "Have you come to fight me or not? I am Klagan! I fear no one!"

"I'll fight you, Klagan," Garric said. He gripped his mail shirt and lifted it off as well. He was tense, knowing he was blind during the moment that the fine links curtained his head. "And when I've killed you with my bare hands—"

He draped his mail over the other post. The links were alternately silvered and parcel gilt. Sunlight danced from them and from the polished highlights of his helmet, drawing the eyes of the watching cat men. Metal fascinated them beyond its practical uses; it cut deeper still into their souls.

"—then the Elders who sent you will see that no Corl can match a human warrior!"

"That'd depend on the warrior, lad," said the ghost in Garric's mind. *"But match you and me together—no, not a one of the beasts!"*

Klagan snarled, now in real anger rather than merely posturing before battle. The big chieftain had paused while Garric stripped off his equipment; now he came on again, grunting deep in his throat. Garric found that sound more menacing than the cutting shrieks of the warriors on the city wall.

Garric undid the fine-meshed net hanging from the sash of his light tunic and picked up the four-foot wand which leaned against the stake holding his helmet. He strode to meet the cat man, grinning in nervousness and anticipation.

Of course he was going to kill the Corl champion; he wouldn't have made this plan if he'd had the least doubt in the matter. But it was a fight, and Garric had been in a lot of fights. Whatever a fighter told himself, the only thing he could be really certain of was that *somebody* would lose. . . .

Garric set the net spinning before him. Its meshes were silk, close enough to tangle minnows and so fine that they looked like a shimmer of gnats in the light rather than a round of fabric. Lead beads weighted the edges. They were just heavy enough to draw them outward when Garric's hand in the center gave the net a circular twitch.

Klagan paused again and hunched, eyeing the net; he'd never seen one being used in a fight before. With another

rasping snarl he came on again, but Garric noticed the Corl
was edging to his left—away from the unfamiliar weapon.
Garric changed his angle slightly to keep Klagan squarely in
front of him.

Garric cut the air in a quick figure eight with his wand. He
was loosening his shoulders and also reminding his muscles
of what the slim cudgel weighed.

He'd chosen wood to make a point to the watching Coerli,
but this staff was cornel—dense and as dead to rebound as
iron. A blow from a cornelwood staff crushed and broke instead of stinging. Garric's wand was little more than thumb
thick, but only a strong man could break it over his knee—
and he'd bruise his knee doing that.

"*He's getting ready, lad . . . ,*" Carus murmured. "*His
cord'll spin around toward your right but he'll come in from
the left.*"

The two champions were within thirty feet of each other,
but Garric could see nothing in Klagan's movements that
seemed in the least different from what they'd been for the
whole length of his approach. He didn't doubt the warning,
though; Carus didn't make mistakes in battle.

Garric crossed his left arm before him, shifting the
dance of silk to his right. For an instant it shone like a slick
of oil in the air. Klagan leaped, not at Garric but toward the
spot of ground at his side; the weighted tip of the Corl's
line was already curving out. Garric jerked his net toward
him while his right hand brought the wand around in an
overarm cut.

Klagan was reacting before he hit the ground. He'd
started a swing that would've crushed Garric's skull if the
cornelwood staff hadn't been in the way; since the staff was,
the big Corl recovered his mace and curved his body to
avoid Garric's blow, moving with a speed no man could've
equaled. His blunt-clawed feet snatched a purchase from the
clay soil and launched him away at an angle more quickly
than the staff swung.

Garric's net belled around the cat man's cord, tangling the

thorns and wrapping the line itself. The weight of the net pulled the cord harmlessly away from Garric.

Klagan landed ten feet away, his mace rising for another attack if his opponent had stumbled or were even off-balance. Garric dropped the net and jerked on the Corl's own line. Klagan bleated in surprise: he'd wrapped the end twice around his left wrist for a surer grip. Instead of trying to jump away like a harpooned fish, he leaped straight at Garric—*Gods but the beast's quick!*—to give himself slack so he could release the line.

Klagan met Garric's wand, still in the middle of the stroke Garric had started before the Corl first charged. The cat man interposed his mace. Its bamboo shaft cracked and flew out of his hand. The cornel staff rapped Klagan's muzzle, breaking out a long canine tooth in a spray of blood.

Klagan slammed to the ground. Even injured and blind with pain he'd spun onto all fours to leap away when Garric landed knee-first on his back. Garric's weight crushed the Corl flat, driving his breath out in a startled blat.

Klagan scrabbled. Garric grabbed the thick mane at the top of the cat man's head left-handed and pulled back. Instead of banging his face onto the dirt—perhaps painful, but pain didn't matter to either party in this fight—Garric punched his opponent's thick neck with his right fist.

Klagan's four limbs shot out convulsively. Garric struck again and heard the cat man's spine crack. Klagan's head came back in his hand, the black tongue lolling from the corner of the jaws.

Garric tried to stand but slipped to his knees again; if he'd gotten up, he'd almost certainly have toppled full length. He was blind and dizzy with fatigue, and he was so weak that his legs couldn't hold him.

People ran to where he knelt, his guards and officers and Liane, the woman he loved. Liane wiped blood and sweat from his forehead with a damp cloth and said, "Darling, darling, are you all right?"

Garric opened his eyes. His stomach had settled; he'd

thought for a moment that he was going to vomit with reaction to the fight.

"Get back," he muttered. Then, loudly and fiercely, "Give me room! By the Shepherd, give me room!"

They moved enough for him to stand. He wobbled, but only slightly; he'd caught himself even before Liane touched his arm in support.

"Elders of the Coerli!" Garric shouted in the cat men's language. "Come out and hear the laws you and your people will keep from now till the last breath you take! Come out before my army kills all Coerli as I killed this warrior!"

He spurned Klagan with his heel. The royal army shouted and cheered, but from the walls of the Place came only wailing.

"PRINCESS SHARINA, WE'RE *so* pleased by your presence!" said the plump man wearing an ermine-trimmed red cloak, three gold chains, and a gold or gilt crown cast in the form of a laurel wreath. Lantern light gleamed from his regalia and the sweat beading his forehead and ruddy cheeks. "No greater honor has ever been done the proud community of West Sesile."

"His title's Chief Burgess," said Mistress Masmon, one of the chancellor's aides, into Sharina's ear. She was trying to speak loudly enough for Sharina to hear but still keep the words private from the chief burgess and the clutch of lesser officials standing just behind him. Bands were playing in three of the four corners of the town square and the whole community had turned out to celebrate. "His name's Clane or Kane; I'm sorry, I can't read my clerk's notes. I'll have his nose cropped for this!"

If Sharina'd thought the threat was serious, she'd have protested. From the chancellor's aide it was merely a form of words indicating that she was frustrated and overtired. Everybody in the government was frustrated and overtired, of course.

Sharina grinned. They'd been frustrated and overtired

dealing with one crisis after another for the past two years. The Change had made the problem only marginally worse when it tore everything apart.

Tenoctris said there'd be no further shifts for at least a thousand years. The future looked bright if the kingdom and mankind could survive the immediate present.

If.

"Thank you, Master K'ane," Sharina said, letting her amusement broaden into a gracious smile. She hoped her slurring would cover the uncertainty over the fellow's name. "Prince Garric regrets he was unable to attend the Founder's Day festival because of his duties with the army, but he begged me to convey his appreciation for West Sesile's demonstrated loyalty to the kingdom."

The burgesses began to chatter volubly. Because of the music and the fact they were all speaking at the same time, Sharina couldn't understand any of them clearly—at best the accents of this region were difficult—but from the words she caught she remained confident she wasn't missing much.

West Sesile had been a prosperous market town during the Old Kingdom, but during the thousand years following the death of King Carus the sea'd risen and covered the site. Because Valles had grown when the Dukes of Ornifal became the Kings of the Isles, the displaced population had moved to the capital instead of rebuilding West Sesile on higher ground. The town hadn't existed in Sharina's day.

Since the Change, West Sesile had reappeared as a suburb of the greatly expanded Valles, now landlocked and well back from the coast of the continent which'd displaced the Inner Sea. In the past, ships had held the scattered islands together. There'd have to be a different system in the future and probably a different capital, but for now the government remained in Valles.

The lives of the citizens of West Sesile had been even more completely overturned than had those of New Kingdom residents, but they'd responded in a remarkably intelligent way. When the first officials of Garric's government had arrived to assess taxes, West Sesile had paid immediately and had added a pledge of hearty loyalty. Clane/Kane and his fellows didn't have the faintest notion of what'd happened, but they knew their only chance to survive was by obeying folks who did.

Sharina—Princess Sharina of Haft—hoped their confidence wasn't misplaced. At least the community was getting a royal visit for its support.

The chief burgess turned to face the crowd. The lugubrious man beside him raised a staff of office. Its finial was a silvered crest of two fish joined at the mouth; Sharina'd initially seen it as a bird with its wings spread.

"Citizens!" Clane/Kane shouted. The man with the staff waved it, and the rest of the burgesses—and their wives, all wearing black and white but in a variety of styles—began screaming. The bands stopped playing; the dancers paused expectantly in their rounds.

"Citizens!" Clane/Kane repeated. "We are blessed by the presence of Princess Sharina, the very sister of our lord and master King Garric. All hail Princess Sharina!"

The cheers that followed were enthusiastic enough for anybody. Even Masmon, worn by the task of extending the government's reach into a land that hadn't existed two months earlier, smiled.

Sharina stepped forward and raised her hands. She was wearing court robes with sleeves of layered silk brocade; the gesture made her feel their weight.

Sharina and Garric's father, Reise, had been landlord of a rural inn on Haft, an island which'd remained a backwater throughout the thousand years since the fall of the Old Kingdom. Sharina went barefoot in the summer and wore an outer tunic over the simple inner one only when cold weather demanded it; she found the court robes she had to wear now both unfamiliar and uncomfortable.

But Reise had taught them to do their jobs. In the past that meant Sharina had washed linen, emptied night soil onto the manure pile, and waited tables when the inn was full of strangers during the Sheep Fair in the fall—many of them drunk and almost all determined to chance their hand at least once in hope of luring the stunning blond inn-servant into their beds.

Sharina smiled brightly. Court robes were a necessary part of her present duties. She didn't like wearing them, but it was better than navigating the bustling common room with her arms laden with trenchers so that she couldn't slap away the gropers.

"Citizens!" she called, wondering if her accent was as hard for the locals to understand as she found theirs to be. "It's my pleasure to join you in celebrating the day your community was founded, because you in turn have joined the kingdom in its new foundation."

They'd have to come up with a name to replace "the Kingdom of the Isles." Of course, even in the past most people hadn't been citizens of the Isles. Sharina'd lived in Barca's Hamlet or perhaps "the borough" around it. Haft was a geographical concept, not her home, and kingdoms were familiar only from the ancient epics which Reise'd taught his children to read.

"In the name of King Garric and of your thousands of fellows who stand firm for peace and unity," Sharina said, "thank you! May you and the kingdom prosper. Now, resume your revels!"

The people crowding the square cheered again. Most of them were in what was apparently formal wear for the community, black-and-white combinations for the women and, for the men, an embroidered woolen apron over a pair of tunics, but a few were masked and in costume. Near Sharina stood a man with a sea wolf's scaly head and a tail of stiffened fabric, and toward the center of the throng was a giant bear animated by a man on stilts.

Sharina grinned. The fur costume must've been even more uncomfortable than her robes.

The bands took up their music again. Each played a different tune. According to Masmon, West Sesile had almost eight hundred citizens—that is, adult males. That was big enough to have neighborhood rivalries, so the three bands playing simultaneously weren't a surprise. Regrettable, perhaps, but not surprising.

"If I may be so bold as to ask, Your Highness?" Kane—probably—said. He paused hopefully; he wasn't in fact bold enough to go on without prompting.

Sharina nodded graciously. She and Masmon were here to encourage people who were willing to consider themselves part of the kingdom. That included the awestruck and tongue-tied people like the burgesses of West Sesile.

"Ah, Your Highness," Kane resumed, his eyes moving in awkward ovals so as never to meet Sharina's. "Is the kingdom united now? That is, in our day there was trouble, you know. Or so we heard."

The sad-faced official banged his staff down in emphasis. "The Earl of Sandrakkan had revolted!" he said in a nasal voice. "That's what *we* heard."

Sharina nodded. "Our day" to him was the end of the Old Kingdom, the collapse of civilization throughout the Isles. These folk had missed the worst of it when the Change mixed eras—though Ornifal hadn't been as badly racked by the cataclysm as the western isles. The Dukes of Ornifal had become Kings of the Isles almost by default.

"The Change has caused great disruption," she said, "but for the most part what you and I think of as the kingdom is as united now as it ever was. We've exchanged couriers with Sandrakkan and Blaise, whose rulers are fully committed to restoring order."

"Which I frankly don't understand," said Masmon, kneading her forehead with both hands. "I'd have expected Sandrakkan at least to claim independence. The Lady knows the earls have done that twice in two generations, and this'd seem a perfect opportunity."

"The Change was too overwhelming for that," Sharina said crisply. The aide, a fifty-year-old spinster, was letting fatigue loosen her tongue. While Sharina couldn't exactly blame her, neither could she permit Masmon's despair to infect this community. "The earl—and all the citizens of

Sandrakkan and the other former islands—are clinging to the best hope they have in such uncertainty."

She smiled. "We're that hope," she said. "We're the only hope mankind has."

The band nearest Sharina's entourage was composed of three slim, mustached men with recorders of different lengths and an ancient woman who played the marimba with demonic enthusiasm. The age-darkened bamboo wands with which she struck the tubes were no harder or more knotted than the fingers which held them.

Two women danced to the penetrating music, striking stylized poses with their arms raised high. One carried a buckler whose convex surface was highly polished, throwing back the lantern gleams and the distorted features of those watching; the other swung a wooden sword.

Though the sword wasn't a real weapon, Sharina's bodyguards—a squad of black-armored Blood Eagles—kept an eye on the dancer. They were men whose philosophy had no room for any gods save Duty and Suspicion.

"It's just that things are so different," said Kane. He nodded to the south. "Even the stars."

"Yes," said Sharina, "but men of goodwill can thrive despite the changes. We just have to stick together. Men and women and Coerli."

She grinned. The constellations were generally the same as what she was used to, but a bright white star stayed just above the southern horizon. It was disconcerting, particularly because it blazed in an otherwise familiar sky.

"We hear things," Kane said apologetically. "From travelers, you know. They say, well, that there's a lot of trouble. That it isn't safe. And there're monsters all about, cat men who're cannibals."

"There're cat men, Coerli," Sharina agreed. "We've brought a number of their keeps, their communities, into the kingdom already. It wasn't hard after they heard how easily we'd wiped out any band which tried to resist."

She didn't bother explaining to the burgess that a cannibal

was an animal that ate its own kind. The Coerli were merely meat-eaters, much like men themselves; and since the Coerli *weren't* men, they made no distinction between men and mutton.

"And King Garric's reducing the cat men's only large city even as we speak," she added with another broad smile. "That's why he's not here."

Sharina knew she was shading the truth considerably; she'd have been here in place of her brother regardless. Princess Sharina's high rank impressed the citizens of West Sesile—or the Grain-Millers Guild, or the Respectful Delegation of the Parishioners of Lanzedac on Cordin. Princess Sharina met and listened to them, then handed them over to the regular officials who'd get to the meat of their business.

In this case and many others, there *was* no meat. People wanted to be told that they were important and that their sacrifices were appreciated by those who demanded those sacrifices. Sharina could do that very well while Garric directed the government.

Both jobs were absolutely necessary if the kingdom was to survive. There were rulers who treated citizens as machines which paid taxes, but they did so only at their peril.

"Praise the Lady to have brought us such a great king as your brother, Princess!" said the man with the staff of office. Even when he spoke with obvious enthusiasm, he managed to make the statement sound like a dirge.

"Praise the Lady," Sharina repeated, dipping slightly in a curtsy to honor the Queen of Heaven. She wasn't just mouthing the words. Sharina hadn't been especially religious as a child, but when fate had catapulted her to her present eminence she'd immediately realized that the task was beyond human capabilities, hers or anybody else's. She could only hope—only pray—that the Great Gods did exist and that They were willing to help the kingdom and its defenders.

The dancer in the bear costume in the center of the square began to rotate slowly as he high-stepped through a figure eight; the crowd gave him room. How long had it been since there were bears on Ornifal? Much longer than the thousand years in Sharina's past when West Sesile had flourished, certainly.

"Your Highness?" said one of the women who'd been standing behind the burgesses. She stepped forward, offering a pottery mug with a hinged metal lid. "Won't you have some of our ale? I brewed it myself, this."

Kane turned with a look of anguished horror and cried, "Deza, you stupid cow! They drink wine in Valles, don't you know? Now the princess'll think we're rubes with no culture!"

"*I* drink beer, Master Kane," said Sharina, taking the mug from the stricken woman. It wasn't her place to interfere with the way couples behaved between themselves, but her tone was significantly cooler than it might've been if the chief burgess hadn't called his wife a cow. "I hope that doesn't make me an uncultured rube in your eyes?"

Sharina sipped as Kane's face slipped into a duplicate of what his wife's had been a moment before. Sharina'd been harsher than she'd intended; but she was tired too, and "cow" *wasn't* a word the burgess should've used.

"Very good, Mistress Deza," she said, though in truth the ale wasn't greatly to her taste. They didn't grow hops on Haft; Reise'd brewed bitters for his taproom with germander his wife, Lora, raised in her kitchen garden.

Sharina glanced at the sky again; the half-moon was well risen, so she'd spent sufficient time here. She made a tiny gesture to Masmon.

As arranged, the aide took out a notebook with four leaves of thin-sliced elm wood. She tilted it to catch the light of the nearest lantern and said, "Your Highness? I fear that we'll be late for your meeting with Chancellor Royhas if we don't start back shortly."

"Oh, goodness, Your Highness!" said Mistress Deza. "You mean you have work yet to do tonight?"

"I'm afraid I do, yes," Sharina said. She smiled, but the sudden rush of fatigue turned the expression into something unexpectedly sad. "Since my brother's with the army, things are . . . busy for those of us who're dealing with the civil side of government."

A third costumed figure had danced far enough into the square for Sharina to get a clear view of it. It was a long-faced, green-skinned giant whose arms would've dragged on the cobblestones if the stilt-walking man inside had let them hang. Instead he was moving the clawed hands with rods so that the creature seemed to snatch at revelers. Even presuming an element of caricature in the costume, Sharina wasn't sure what it was intended to be.

"Master Kane?" she said, gesturing. "Is that dancer a demon?"

"Not exactly, Your Highness," Kane said, clearly glad to answer a question that didn't involve ale. "It's an ogre, though some say ogres are the spawn of women who've lain with demons. The hero Sesir slew an ogre and a bear and a sea wolf to save the colony he led from Kanbesa. According to the *Epic of the Foundings,* that is. Have you read the epic, Your Highness?"

"Parts of it," Sharina said truthfully. But very small parts, because in her day the *Epic of the Foundings* was known only from fragments. None of the surviving portions had mentioned Sesir—or the island of Kanbesa, for that matter.

She handed the mug back to Deza; she'd emptied it. She'd been thirsty, and after the initial unfamiliarity the ale had gone down very smoothly.

"We really have to drive back to the palace now," Sharina said. She smiled at the chief burgess, then swept her gaze left and right to include all the officials and their wives. "It's been a pleasure to meet you and to convey the kingdom's appreciation."

As Sharina turned away to walk back to her coach, flanked by the Blood Eagles, a dancer raised her shield again in a wild sweep. For an instant Sharina thought she glimpsed a pale, languid man in its polished surface.

It must be a distorted reflection, of course.

CASHEL STOOD ON the edge of the mere, listening to the fishermen croon in the near distance as they slid their tiny

canoes through the reeds. The unfamiliar bright star was coming up in the southeast; it'd risen earlier each night since the
Change. A shepherd like Cashel got to know the heavens very
well. When he'd first seen this star it'd been part of the Water
Pitcher, the constellation that signaled the start of the rainy
season, but after a month it was nearing the tail of the Panther.

One man sat in the back of each canoe, poling it forward;
his partner stood in the front with a long spear. Instead of a
single point, the spears had outward-curving springs of
bamboo with bone teeth on the inner sides. When fish rose to
stare at the lantern hanging from the canoe's extended bow,
the spearman struck and caught the flopping victim like a
gar's jaws.

Cashel wasn't a fisherman, and the fishermen he knew in
Barca's Hamlet went out onto the Inner Sea with hooks and
long lines. He could appreciate skill even in people doing
something unfamiliar, however, and these fellows fishing the
reed-choked mere south of Valles obviously knew what they
were doing.

Besides, he liked the way they sang while they worked.
Cashel couldn't carry a tune in a bucket, but it'd always
pleased him to hear his friend Garric playing his shepherd's
pipe the times they watched the sheep together.

"There!" said Tenoctris firmly, straightening from the
squat in which she'd been marking the dirt with a silver
stylus. They were as close to the bank as they could get and
still find the ground firm enough to take her impressions.
Tenoctris took a bamboo wand from her bag, then added
apologetically, "This may be a complete waste of time,
Cashel. I shouldn't have taken you away from Sharina."

Cashel shrugged and smiled. "I don't mind," he said. "And
anyway, you don't waste time that I've seen, Tenoctris."

He cleared his throat and glanced away, a little embarrassed. What he was about to say might sound like bragging,
which Cashel didn't like.

"I'd sooner be here in case, you know, something
happens," he said. "I figure you're better off with me if something does than if you were with somebody else."

Tenoctris smiled warmly. He didn't know how old she was—really old, surely—but she hopped around chirping like a sparrow most of the time. Wizardry wore her down, but wizardry wore down everybody who used it.

It wore down even Cashel, though he wasn't a wizard the way most people meant. He just *did* things when he had to.

Tenoctris was the only wizard Cashel'd met who seemed to him to know what she was doing. And by now, Cashel'd met more wizards than he'd have dreamed in the years he was growing up.

"So," said one of the old men who'd been watching Cashel and Tenoctris, the strangers who'd come from Valles in a gig. There were eight of them; a hand and three fingers by Cashel's calculation. "You folk be wizards, then?"

"She's a wizard," said Cashel, smiling and nodding toward Tenoctris. She was taking books out of her case, both rolls and those cut in pages and bound, codices she called them. "I'm a shepherd most times, but I'm helping her now. She's my friend. She's everybody's friend, everybody who wants the good people to win."

There wasn't enough light to read by. No matter how smart you were—and there weren't many smarter than Tenoctris—you couldn't see the letters without a lamp. She liked to have the words of her spells before her even though she was going to call them out from memory. It was a habit, the way Cashel always flexed his shoulders three times before he picked up a really heavy weight.

"We don't hold much with wizards here in Watertown," the local man who'd been speaking said; the others nodded soberly. "Not saying anything against your friend, mind."

Cashel looked at the group again, wondering for a moment if they were all men. He decided they were, though they were so old and bent down that it didn't matter.

"From what I've seen of most wizards," he said agreeably, "you're right to feel that way. I've watched sheep as had more common sense than most wizards. Tenoctris is good, though."

He paused and added, still calmly, "I'm glad you weren't speaking against her. I wouldn't like that."

Cashel supposed these folk were the elders of the village too far down the bank to see even if it'd been daylight. The younger men were in the canoes, the women were back in the huts cooking the meal that the fishermen would eat on their return. The old men had nothing better to do than be busybodies, which—

Cashel grinned broadly.

—they were doing just fine.

Tenoctris had finished her preparations; she came to join them. Cashel was wondering if he ought to send the locals away, but Tenoctris pointed to the marble pool behind them. To the man who'd been speaking she said, "Can you tell me if there's writing on that fountain, my good man?"

The pool must be spring-fed, because a trickle of water dribbled from a pipe through the curb, then down the side. The flow used to feed into an open channel, also marble, and then down into the mere. Years had eaten the trough away, so only the little difference lime from the stone made in the vegetation showed it'd ever been there.

The pool curb had the crumbly decay—black below but a leprous white above—that marble got in wet ground, but it still seemed solid. There was a raised part on the back like it was meant to hold a plaque or carved words, but Cashel doubted you'd be able to tell if anything was written there even in sunlight.

"Mistress, *I* can't write," said the old man nervously. He backed a step; Cashel's size hadn't scared him, but Tenoctris did—either because she was a wizard or just from the way she spoke that showed she was a lady. "Nobody in Water-town can write, mistress!"

"I think this was built as a monument to a battle, you see," Tenoctris said. "According to Stayton's *Library,* twin brothers named Pard and Pardil fought over the succession to the Kingdom of Ornifal. They and everyone in their armies were killed. A fountain sprang from the rock to wash the stain of blood from the land, and their uncle built a curb and stele—"

She gestured toward the vertical slab at the back of the curb.

"—around it."

She stepped through the group and knelt to peer closely at the pool. Cashel moved with her, not because there was a threat—certainly not from these men—but just on general principle. Sometimes things happened very fast. Although Cashel was quick, he still didn't plan to give trouble a head start.

"So this is the spring, mistress?" Cashel said, squinting to see if that helped him make out any carving on the decayed slab. It didn't.

"There are problems with the story, I'm afraid," Tenoctris said, giving him one of her quick, cheerful smiles. The local men were listening intently; two of them even leaned close to see what they could make from the white-blistered stone. "Pard and Pardil mean Horse and Mare in the language of the day, and the island wasn't called Ornifal until the hero Val arrived from Tegma a thousand years later and founded the city of Valles."

She looked at the pool again, pursing her lips, and added, "But still, this *could* be the battle monument Stayton describes."

An old man who'd been silent till then said, "Mistress, there was swords and a helmet carved on the stone, my gramps told me. And he said more squiggles too. That coulda been writing, couldna it?"

"Your gramps, your gramps!" sneered the original speaker. "Dotty he were, Rebben, and you're dotty too if you think this fine lady's going to take the least note of what you say or your gramps ever said!"

"Dotty am I, Hareth?" said Rebben, his voice rising immediately into something as shrill and harsh as a hawk's scream. "Well, he did say it! And I reckon he said it true, as he always said true. And anyhow, who are you to talk who falls asleep with his face in his porridge most nights if his daughter don't grab him quick, hey?"

"Fellows, don't bump Lady Tenoctris, if you please," Cashel said, moving forward to crowd the old men away without having to touch them. He rotated his quarterstaff, bringing it across at an angle in front of him to make the same point as his words. "If you're going to argue, it'd be good if you went off a ways to do it."

The men scattered like songbirds when a falcon strikes. Hareth and Rebben jumped to the same place, collided, and fell in a tangle with high-pitched cries.

Cashel grimaced and put himself between Tenoctris and the men thrashing nearby. He'd been clumsy and almost caused what he'd been trying to prevent: one of the old fellows bumping Tenoctris into the pool.

That hadn't happened though. Tenoctris walked past with a pert expression, avoiding the men on the ground with the same careless unconcern as she did the muddy patch from the overflow pipe.

"I'm sure this is the place," the old wizard said cheerfully to Cashel, who followed her back to the circle she'd scribed beside the bank. "All I could tell from the spell I worked back in the palace is that the site would become important. I hope I can learn more now that I'm here."

She settled herself cross-legged, facing the figure. She'd written things both inside and outside the circle, but Cashel could no more read the words than Hareth and his friends could've.

Tenoctris raised the bamboo sliver. Before she started calling out the spell she glanced back at Cashel with a wry smile.

"Of course this may not help either," she said. "I'm simply not a powerful wizard, as I've proved many times in the past."

"You've never failed, Tenoctris," Cashel said quietly. "You've always done enough that we're still here. You are and the kingdom is, for all the people who fight evil."

The old wizard's smile changed to something softer, more positive. "Yes," she said. "That's a way to think about it. Thank you, Cashel."

She bent over the circle and began, *"Stokter neoter,"* tapping her wand on the written words of power as she spoke them. *"Men menippa menoda."*

Cashel looked away. Wizardry didn't bother him, especially when Tenoctris was doing it, but his job was to look out for her. Watching Tenoctris chant would be as silly as watching sheep crop grass instead of keeping an eye out for danger.

And there was always a chance of danger when there was wizardry. Tenoctris said she could see the strands of power that sprang from certain places and twined among themselves. Those powers grew from temples and altars, especially old ones, but they came from graveyards and especially battlefields like this one. More men than Cashel could imagine had died here in blood and terror.

Concentrated power attracted those who wanted power more than anything else, and they weren't all human.

The local men had gathered by the side of the pool, standing tightly together and all watching Cashel and Tenoctris. They seemed angry and afraid, though maybe the moonlight exaggerated their expressions. Cashel smiled at them, hoping he seemed friendly, but he couldn't see that that did any good.

Tenoctris droned on. Sometimes Cashel caught a few syllables . . . *morchella barza* . . . but they didn't mean anything to him. The language a wizard spoke was directed at things—demiurges, Tenoctris called them, but that was gobbledygook to Cashel—that controlled the powers that the cosmos turned on.

The bright star in the south continued to rise. The water of the memorial pool was mirror smooth; now it drew the star's reflection into a cold white pathway.

Cashel began to wipe his quarterstaff with the wad of raw wool he carried for the purpose; lanolin in the fibers kept the hickory from cracking and brought out the luster of the polished wood. He'd turned the staff himself from the branch which the farmer who owned the tree had given him as pay for felling it. Cashel'd been little more than a child at the time, but he'd already had a man's strength.

Now that he was a man, he had the strength of Cashel or-Kenset. He smiled at the thought.

Cashel put the wool away and lifted the staff, his hands

spread a little more than the width of his shoulders. He set
the hickory spinning slowly in front of him, loosening his
muscles. When he was ready, he speeded up each time he
crossed his arms till the heavy staff hummed as it cut the air.

Still keeping an eye out—he was on watch, after all—
Cashel raised the whirling staff overhead. He turned his
body under it to face what'd been his back, then forward
again. He moved in quick jumps, using the weight of the
iron-shod hickory to pull him around.

Cashel saw a bluish twinkle in the center of Tenoctris' figure; wizardlight, brought to life by her chanting the way flint
strikes sparks from iron. Cashel felt the hair on the back of
his neck rise, also a sign of approaching wizardry.

The old men watched in amazement, but Cashel wasn't doing this to impress them. He grinned again. He'd impressed
much more important people than these old codgers, and
some of those people'd been trying to kill him at the time.

Ordinarily a little spell of the sort Tenoctris chanted
wouldn't have made him tingle as much as this. Was something else . . . ?

Where the star had shone on the pool, there was now a
man with a shield and drawn sword. The angles were funny;
the fellow wasn't reflected—there wasn't anything but
empty sky to reflect. It was like he was standing straight upright instead of being on his back in the water. His leg
moved forward and he was standing on the stone curb.

The water didn't ripple. A second man was standing on its
surface. Both were naked except for the belt supporting their
scabbards. Their skin was black in the moonlight.

The first man stepped forward, raising his sword. Rebben
noticed him and shouted.

The black man's sword split Rebben's skull like a melon.
As the other old men blatted in terror, the swordsman
jumped into the midst of them hacking left and right.

The second figure was stepping out of the pool.

Chapter

2

CASHEL DIDN'T UNDERSTAND why this was happening, but he knew fights and right now that was the main thing. His hands shifted without him having to think about it.

The first black man was in the midst of the locals, slashing with skill and amazing strength: an old fellow toppled in two parts, his hips and legs one way and his upper body the other. The victim's mouth was open to scream but the sword'd severed his diaphragm; there was nothing to force the air out of his lungs.

Cashel couldn't be sure of a clean stroke in a melee and there wasn't time to chance something that might not work. With his left hand on the shaft and his right on the butt driving it, he rammed his staff toward the chest of the swordsman poised on the curb.

The fellow got his round shield between the blow and his body. It was dull metal and no bigger across than the length of Cashel's hand and forearm.

Sparks flew from the staff's iron cap. The shield gave a tinny bang like an ill-cast bell and slammed back into the swordsman's chest, crunching his breastbone and broad ribs.

The man's mouth and nostrils spewed blood as he toppled into the pool. The sword'd wobbled off to splash in the reeds. Cashel didn't have time to worry about the dead man or his gear, though, because he had his eyes on the surviving swordsman.

At least four of the old men were down, carved apart. Only three were running away gabbling, but Cashel thought he'd seen Hareth duck behind the stone curb. The tangle of body parts where the black man stood could as easily have added to five as four corpses, not that it mattered now.

The fellow shuffled toward Cashel in a wide stance. His sword was waist-high and close to his body, point a little above the hilt and ready to cut or stab. He held the buckler well out in front of him.

Cashel'd hit the other shield hard enough to smash the ribs of the man holding it, but his quarterstaff hadn't made a dent in the round of dull metal. He should've dimpled even a solid ball of iron.

Tenoctris continued to chant her spell like nothing was happening behind her. Maybe she didn't know that anything *was* happening; she was somebody who lost herself completely in what she was doing.

Cashel wasn't like that himself. It was fine for a wizard to concentrate on just one thing, but a shepherd had to know what every one of his flock was doing at the same time. Otherwise the ones you ignored were toppling over cliffs, drowning in bogs, or killing themselves in other ways only a fool sheep could come up with.

Cashel backed a step with his staff slanted crossways before him. His duty was to keep Tenoctris safe, but the best way to do that was to draw the swordsman away. If he put himself between the black man and the wizard, he'd get jointed like a chicken.

The sword must be of the same metal as the other one's buckler. It'd left a bright notch in the curb after slicing through one of the codgers, but the edge was unmarked. The only way to fight a weapon like that was to have plenty of room to dodge.

Fight with a quarterstaff, anyhow. If there'd been a pile of fist-sized rocks handy, Cashel figured he could throw them quick enough that one'd find a spot the fellow hadn't covered in time with his shield. When Cashel threw, a solid hit anywhere from scalp to ankle would put his target down sure as sure.

But there weren't any rocks. And a sword that cut through

a thighbone, even an old man's thigh, would do the same for the quarterstaff.

As Cashel continued his slow dance away, he kept the pool in the corner of his eye so he'd see if another swordsman was coming out of it. He didn't know what he'd do then—probably die, trapped between the pair of them because he *wouldn't* run off and leave Tenoctris—but nothing seemed to be happening there since he'd killed the second man.

The water was dark with swirls of blood, spreading slowly. The corpse floated on its face; its legs and arms hung down, but the broad torso curved above the surface like the back of a whale. The black skin gleamed in the moonlight.

Cashel prodded his staff toward the swordsman with his left hand leading. He meant it for a feint unless the black man stepped in to meet it with his shield. If that'd happened, Cashel would've put his back and shoulders into the stroke, figuring to hit hard enough to upend the fellow before he had a chance to use his sword.

Instead the swordsman crouched low and came on like a crab, the buckler forward but a little out to his left side while the blade in his right remained low and ready. Cashel eased away but the fellow moved *quick,* sword swinging as part of the lunge; he was good and his blade could cut stone and the only way this would go was—

"*Eulamo!*" Tenoctris cried in a cracked squeal.

A sparkling azure filament, thin as spiderweb, twined about the black man's ankles. He pitched forward soundlessly, driving his sword hilt-deep in the turf with the suddenness of his fall.

The glitter bound the swordsman only for an instant before scattering into dust motes, but that was long enough. Cashel punched with his staff instead of swinging it: the leading ferrule drove the top of the bald skull down onto the fellow's back teeth. The arms and legs thrashed, but that was no more than a chicken kicking when you snap its neck. Whoever these black men were, they were too dangerous to take chances with.

Cashel stepped back, breathing hard as he looked around for something else to fight. Nothing moved for a moment; then Hareth poked his head up from the other side of the pool and ducked down again.

Cashel bent to the man he'd just killed, then remembered that the fellow wasn't wearing a tunic that'd serve as a rag. He took out his wool again and wiped blood and brains from the end of his staff. He hadn't expected Tenoctris to throw a loop of wizardlight around the swordsman's ankles, but this wasn't the first fight where being able to react the right way to an unexpected opportunity was the reason Cashel was standing at the end.

That reminded him of Tenoctris. Dropping the bloody wool on the body, he stepped quickly to her. She'd collapsed when she shouted the final word of her incantation but she was trying to get up again.

Cashel knelt and put his left arm under her torso. He wasn't going to lift unless she asked him to, but he'd make sure he was there to give her support for whatever she wanted.

"Cashel, cover the fountain," she said in a raspy voice. "Let me be. Make sure that starlight doesn't fall on the fountain."

Cashel pursed his lips. He withdrew his arm carefully and walked to the pool. He held the quarterstaff slanted in both hands again; excitement had washed the recent fatigue out of his blood.

The pool wasn't very big or deep either one; the body, slowly revolving, didn't leave much room. Peering in, Cashel saw the round outline of the buckler that the dying man'd dropped when his muscles spasmed for the last time.

As for covering the rest of the surface . . .

Cashel looked down at the bodies of the old men. The ground'd been damp from the first; now it was sticky with congealing blood. A shepherd doesn't get picky about what he puts feet in, but Cashel'd tried just out of courtesy to the dead not to step on the bigger pieces.

Courtesy was fine, but sentiment didn't come before need. Rebben was wearing a short cloak; the night wasn't cold, but old men's blood gets thin. Cashel removed it—it'd been pinned with a thorn—and draped it part on the floating body and part on the curb. If he'd laid it on open water, it'd have sunk when it got waterlogged.

There was still a rim of surface gleaming on the other side; moonlight rippled and condensed as the corpse rocked gently. The tunic of the fellow who'd been cut in half was in sections, the jerkin on his torso and the skirt below. Cashel jerked both parts away from the body and covered the rest of the pool.

Rebben's body gave a sudden jerk. Cashel poised the quarterstaff, but that was just a body cooling.

I'm sorry, old man. I'll make an offering to Duzi for you when I get a chance.

Cashel believed in the Great Gods, the Lady and the Shepherd and the Sister, but in the way he'd believed in cities like Carcosa when he was growing up in Barca's Hamlet. They were real, no doubt, and people said they were important—but they didn't touch him. Cashel and other shepherds gave their offerings to Duzi, the figure scratched on a boulder in the pasture south of the hamlet.

He went back to Tenoctris. She was sitting, but she wouldn't be able to walk unaided back to the gig. When the ground got too soft for wheels they'd left the horse, still harnessed, on a feeding peg. It could easily pull up the stake and wander off, but generally it'd just walk in a circle cropping the sedges.

"The pool's covered, Tenoctris," Cashel said, squatting beside the old woman. She looked as gray as last night's corpse; partly that was moonlight, probably. "What should I do next?"

Tenoctris'd scratched a figure with five sides on the ground beside the circle she'd used for the spell she'd come to cast. The new mark was under where she'd fallen so he hadn't seen it before. It made sense that she'd have to do something completely different to tie up the swordsman, but Cashel hadn't thought about it till now. No wonder she looked gray, having worked a second spell!

"We have to get back to the palace at once," Tenoctris

whispered. She closed her eyes, opened them briefly, then squeezed them firmly shut. "Cashel, I'm afraid I won't be able to drive. You'll have to."

"Ma'am, I can't drive a horse," Cashel said simply. "Here, I'll help you to the gig."

Folks brought up with horses—like Tenoctris, who was a lady by birth even though she said her family hadn't had much money—didn't realize that most folk farmed with oxen and got where they were going on their own legs. Horses were for nobles and their servants.

"I can't drive!" Tenoctris said, exhausted and frustrated. "I'm sorry, Cashel, I really can't."

Mind, put a nobleman to plowing behind a yoke of oxen and you'd be lucky if the furrows stayed in the same field as they started. Still, that was neither here nor there. Nobody needed a field plowed or sheep watched or a tree cut so it fell within a hand's breadth of where it was supposed to. Nobody wanted Cashel to do any of the things he'd learned to do in the eighteen years before he left the borough.

"That's all right, ma'am," Cashel said in the calm tone he'd have used to settle sheep for the night. "I'll lead the horse. We'll get there."

He lifted Tenoctris in the crook of his right arm, holding the staff at the balance in the same hand. There were things he'd liked about the life he'd lived in the borough, but he hadn't had Sharina then and he hadn't dreamed he ever would. This was better. And if it meant he kept trouble away from folks like Tenoctris and Sharina who weren't strong enough to handle it themselves—well, that was better than watching sheep, wasn't it?

The gig was only built for two, but that gave Cashel another idea. He'd have called Hareth to help him, but he saw the old man hoofing it away in the direction the other survivors had taken. Well, that was probably as well.

Cashel squatted by the man whose brains he'd battered in, gripped him by the back of the sword belt, and threw him over his left shoulder. The fellow was stiff as a statue; that could happen when you killed a sheep with a hammer, too, though mostly folks in the borough slit its throat with a knife instead.

This time the stiffness was handy because the fellow's hands had frozen on his sword and the double grips of his buckler. People at the palace, especially the soldiers, would want to see those for whatever metal they were made from.

Waddling slightly—the weight wasn't a problem, but it took some juggling to carry two people and make sure the sword in the corpse's hand didn't slice Tenoctris' ear off—Cashel reached the gig. The mare snorted at the smell of blood, but she didn't bolt the way he suddenly realized she might've done.

He tossed the corpse into the far seat, then braced Tenoctris as she climbed off his arm. "It's five miles," she murmured doubtfully. She opened her eyes but couldn't keep them that way.

"That's fine," said Cashel, taking the reins in his left hand and guiding the horse's head back in the direction of the metaled road. "We'll get there fine, ma'am."

He clucked to the animal, wondering what he'd do if it tried to fight him. Pull it till it gave up, he supposed, but the mare didn't make any trouble. Ambling along—he was used to following sheep, and though he mended his pace for this purpose the horse didn't have any trouble in following—Cashel broke into a broad smile.

He'd be seeing Sharina soon.

GARRIC STOOD WITH his arms out at his sides while aides—the son of the Count of Blaise and a great-nephew of Lord Waldron, commander of the royal army—dressed him in helmet, gilded and engraved body armor, and his belted sword. Normally he'd have done that himself, but the fight had left him wobbly with reaction. If the Coerli suddenly attacked, Garric'd be lucky to continue standing while the army fought around him.

King Carus snorted. Garric grinned.

"Sir?" said Lerdain, the count's son and a husky fifteen-year-old. He wore a hook-bladed sword, the traditional weapon of a Blaise armsman, and it wasn't just for show.

"I was just thinking that I've never really been too tired for a fight," Garric said, giving a real answer instead of putting the boy off with "Oh, nothing," or a similarly uninformative response. "Though I've sure felt that way before it started—as I do now."

"You were magnificent, Your Highness!" said Lord Wardaway as he cinched the sword belt into place. He was taller but much slimmer than Lerdain.

"I'll have you back on my brother's estate if you don't learn to hold your tongue till you're a man, Wardaway!" Lord Waldron snapped. "I'd rather have your *sister* here than a babbling boy!"

The army commander was a hawk-faced man in his sixties with an obvious family resemblance to the youth. Age had neither weakened nor mellowed him from the hot-tempered cornet of horse he must've been when he was eighteen, but for all his punctilious concern for his honor, Waldron was a skilled general. His courage went without saying.

The aides stepped back. Garric shrugged to loosen the cuirass over his shoulders.

"All right," he called to Lord Attaper, who'd taken personal command of the detachment of the bodyguard regiment accompanying Garric today. "We'll march to the Gathering Field in the center of town. That's the Council of Elders; they'll guide us. Oh—have four men carry Klagan. That's their champion."

"Their late champion," Carus said reflectively.

The weight of the helmet made Garric's head throb. He'd pulled a neck muscle at some point while fighting Klagan. He wore the armor for show, not because he expected battle. Cowing the cat men with the sheen and hardness of metal was just as important now as it'd been when Garric'd planned the glittering display at leisure.

The ghost in his mind chuckled. *"Pain just means you're alive, lad,"* Carus said. *"I haven't felt pain since the afternoon I drowned."*

In a mental whisper he added, *"It's the one thing I miss, not having a body. The only thing."*

"I'm ready, Your Highness," said Lord Tadai, a plump, perfectly groomed man and one of the richest nobles in the kingdom. He'd become—by being present, willing, and able—the head of the civil bureaucracy accompanying Garric in the field while Chancellor Royhas had charge of the administration in Valles.

Garric grinned at him. "I never doubted it, milord," he said as the Blood Eagles clashed forward on the left foot.

Three aides walked behind Tadai, carrying files that might be required during negotiations with the Coerli. They looked terrified, but the nobleman himself seemed as unconcerned about walking into a city of man-eating cat men as he would've been if the meeting place were an assembly room within the palace. Though he barely knew which end of a sword to hold, Tadai gave the lie to the notion that soldiers had a monopoly on physical courage.

The leading guards reached the Coerli delegation filling the gateway. "Chieftains!" Garric called in the cat men's snarling language. "Lead us to the Gathering Field, where you will receive my commands!"

"We will keep our oath, Chief of Animals," an age-bent Corl replied. "We will accept your commands."

Six human males stood at each gate leaf, ready to push them closed when ordered to. They stared at Garric without comprehension as he tramped through the gate. They were from the Coerli's own period, domestic animals from whom ruthless culling had eliminated all initiative and courage. In all truth they were more like sheep than men . . . but they'd be freed regardless as one of the first acts of the new administration.

Beasts wouldn't rule men while Garric was king. Not even if the men had ceased to be human except in form.

"You realize this could be a trap, Your Highness," Waldron said. The words were respectful enough, but the tone added, "You stupid puppy!"

"Yes, milord," Garric said, "as we've discussed. But I

don't think it is. Nor do I think the sun will rise in the west tomorrow, which I consider equally probable."

He was taking only fifty soldiers into the Corl stronghold, an escort but not a threat. Attaper had of course wanted to bring the whole regiment—though that was under three hundred men: guarding Prince Garric was an extremely dangerous job, and there hadn't been time to induct sufficient volunteer replacements from the line regiments.

Three hundred soldiers wouldn't have made any difference if it came to fighting. Though none of his advisors really believed it, Garric knew that the war had ended when he broke Klagan's neck.

He marched under the gate arch, keeping step with his guards. The walls of the Place were timber. They'd been built with undressed tree boles, but in the ages since then the bark had sloughed away to leave the wood beneath a silky gray with black streaks. It was tinder dry and splashed with shelves of orange fungus.

"Do you think we could fight our way out?" Waldron snapped. "I don't care about myself—I'm a soldier; it's my duty to die for my prince. But what happens to the kingdom if *you're* killed?"

You've changed your tune in the years since we met, Garric thought. He didn't let the words reach his lips, but a smile did. If this stiff-necked old Ornifal nobleman had come to respect him, then Garric had gained something more important than the cheers of city rabble who'd turn out for any spectacle.

Aloud he said, "Milord, how long would it take you to reduce this city? Using the troops assembled outside."

Waldron frowned but glanced about him in assessment. The interior of the Place was a mass of separate wicker compounds; each circular wall enclosed a number of huts belonging to a single clan. There were no streets, just pathways; not infrequently the compounds pushed against one another like lily pads struggling for space on the surface of a pond. Cat men peered through gaps in the walls to watch their human conquerors march past.

"A day to circle the town with earthworks and raise nets on top of them so the beasts can't run," Waldron said. "At first light, pile brushwood on the upwind side of the walls and set fire to it. Go in when the flames burn down and finish off any still alive."

He pursed his lips, then added hopefully, "Though we wouldn't really have to wait for the earthworks—the males don't like to run, and the females won't leave their kits. Is that what you intend to do, Your Highness?"

"It is not," Garric said sharply while the ghost in his mind guffawed. "But can I take it as a given that if you and I were killed, the officers remaining outside the walls would be able to put that plan into effect?"

"You're bloody well told they would!" Waldron snapped. "There isn't a soldier in the army who wouldn't know how to do that. We've burnt half a dozen keeps already when they wouldn't surrender, and this place would burn even better."

"Right," said Garric. "And the Coerli know the same thing. They won't kill me for that reason alone, even if you don't trust their honor. Which I assure you, milord, is just as highly developed as your own."

Garric smiled to make his words friendlier than they otherwise might've been taken. In all truth, there was very little to choose between the ways a Corl chieftain and a nobleman from northern Ornifal viewed the world. Garric had to hope that in the long run that'd make it easier to bring human and Coerli society together, but there'd be many sparks struck before that happened.

"And first survive today, lad," said Carus. His image toyed with the hilt of its imaginary sword.

Garric assumed the Council of Elders was leading the delegation by the broadest way possible, but that became extremely narrow as they neared the center of the town. When Garric paused to let Waldron go ahead of him between compounds whose walls were masses of gray fungus, he heard someone retch violently behind him.

He turned: the youngest of Lord Tadai's aides was on his

knees, vomiting helplessly. Between spasms he whimpered, "Oh Lady, help me, the smell. The smell!"

"Get up, Master Loras," Tadai said harshly. "We have our duty."

He held out his hand to Loras, but the younger man struggled to his feet. "I'm all right," he said hoarsely, but his eyes were closed. He opened them to slits and stumbled forward with the rest of them.

Waldron had paused because Garric did. He went on with a snort.

"I've seen young soldiers do the same on their first battlefield, milord," Garric said mildly when they had room to walk side by side again. "And he didn't drop the document case he was carrying."

"Aye, that's so," said the old soldier. With a half-smile—or at least the closest thing to a smile Garric had seen on his lips since they entered the Corl town—he added, "And the place *has* got a pong, I'll admit. They're cats, that's sure, these beasts."

"Yes," agreed Garric. "They are."

He'd had too many other things on his mind to be conscious of the smell, but the clerk was probably the son of a Valles merchant rather than a rural peasant. Now that Master Loras had called his attention to it, Garric realized that the stink was worse than the occasional summer day in Barca's Hamlet when the breeze blew from the direction of the tanyard.

Lord Attaper at the head of the procession shouted orders to deploy his troops. Three paces on, Garric and Waldron arrived at the Gathering Field, a round of bare clay a furlong in diameter. Coerli crowded the outer edges, but a broad path remained open to the center, where nine undressed rocks waited in a circle.

The Corl Elders sprang onto eight of the rocks and squatted, facing inward. Garric put his left boot on the last, then hopped up to stand on it. His head was well above that of anyone else in the field, able to see and be seen by all.

"Coerli, whom I have conquered!" he said. "Hear my commands and obey!"

As Garric spoke, he turned around slowly so that all the watching cat men had a direct view of him. He towered above them, his face framed by the silvered helm and its flaring, golden wings. His words had drawn a dull growl; as his gaze swept each segment of the crowd, the timbre of the sound shifted higher.

The Blood Eagles were in an outward-facing circle, their shields flush against the chieftains of the cat men, each of whom stood with his chosen warriors at the head of the males of his clan. The human soldiers were a black-armored wall, bulkier than the Coerli and taller even without the horsehair plumes pinned to their helmets.

But the cat men could move the way lightning dances between summer clouds. If it came to a fight, Garric and his whole entourage would be massacred . . . but there wouldn't be a fight.

The ghost in his head was silent; smiling faintly, seeing through Garric's eyes but making different calculations. The cat men were quick, to be sure; there was no defense against their speed. But a man doesn't die the instant he takes a fatal wound. He can keep hacking at his enemies for a minute and more if he's the sort who doesn't mind dying so long as he takes as many of his enemies as possible with him to the Sister. King Carus, the foremost warrior in the history of the Isles, would be directing Garric's sword if—

But that wouldn't happen.

Garric completed his eyes' circuit of the crowd, returning to the Council of Elders. Early in the cat men's history, a chieftain must've held power only so long as he could defeat the strongest of his warriors. If their society had never evolved beyond that, the Coerli would still live in scattered hunting bands and be animals hunting other animals.

Greater numbers and settled communities had required a different sort of organization, leadership based on wisdom and experience instead of merely strength. Even so, the Elders facing Garric now were all former chieftains. They had the heavy bodies and shaggy manes of sexually mature males who'd lived for years on a diet of red meat rather than the fish and legumes of ordinary warriors.

They glared balefully back at Garric; but the eldest, the Corl who'd addressed Garric from the gateway, said, "We are here for you to command, Chief of Animals."

"Then hear me," said Garric. "First, you will send all the men from the Place to my camp. From this day forth, no man will serve a Corl!"

The problems the freed humans would cause for the kingdom were staggering. They hadn't been slaves, they'd been domesticated animals for hundreds of generations. But there wasn't any other choice that Garric was willing to accept.

"I am Barog!" snarled a chief outside the circle of guards. "Shall a Corl chieftain eat fish?"

The Elder who'd been speaking rose to his feet on his rock and pointed to Barog. His mane, silvery but still streaked with pure black, flared out at twice its previous length. "Kill the oathbreaker!" he said.

"How dare—" Barog shouted.

The chieftain to his left grabbed him by the shoulder. Barog spun, baring his fangs in defiance; the chieftain to his right, now behind him, dashed out his brains with a ball-headed wooden mace. The chief already holding Barog sank teeth into his throat. Victim and killers dropped to the ground, the latter worrying the former like dogs with a rabbit.

Warriors whom Barog had led moments before joined in tearing the dead chieftain to bits. At a command from Attaper, the Blood Eagles at that side of the circle dropped to one knee, butting their shields on the ground; otherwise the maddened Coerli would've clawed and bitten the men's ankles as they thrashed.

Garric kept his face set in grim lines, but he smiled in his heart. *Perhaps Waldron'll believe what I've told him about Corl honor now.*

"My government will deal justly with all members of the kingdom, human and Corl," Garric said when the deep-throated growling had subsided enough for him to speak over it. "We'll provide you with hogs to raise for meat, as we've done with keeps who've already accepted my authority."

Something warm was sticking to the back of Garric's wrist; he glanced down, then flicked away a gobbet of skin and hair. In a melee like that, it might not have come from Barog's body. *The Coerli really* are *beasts.*

"I've seen men do the same, lad," King Carus murmured. *"But not all men, not that."*

"From this day . . . ," Garric said. What he'd just seen had brought a new harshness to his voice. "Any Corl who eats human flesh will be killed. Any town or keep or roving band which harbors a man-eater will be destroyed to the last kit. There will be no exceptions and no mercy!"

The lips of several Elders drew back to bare their fangs. There was a fresh chorus of growls from the audience, but this time no Corl protested verbally. An Elder snarled in an angry undertone to the one who'd acted as spokesman. That Corl nodded and fixed Garric with his eyes.

"Chief of Animals," he said, "we have given our oath and we will keep it. But our young warriors—who can control the young, when the blood runs hot and passion rules? Are your young any different?"

"There will be attacks on humans, I know that," Garric said. "And I know also that you Coerli will hunt the attackers down yourselves and slay them, though they be the children of your own blood. You will do this because of your oath, and because the kingdom's vengeance will be absolute and implacable if you do not. Is it not so, Leader of the Coerli?"

The Corl spokesman had settled back on his rock after ordering Barog's slaughter. Now he looked first left, then right, meeting the eyes of his fellows in silence. At last he rose to his feet again.

"I am Elphas, the Chosen of the Elders!" he said. His voice cracked when he raised it to make himself heard over the uncomfortable whine of the crowd. "Does anyone challenge my right to speak?"

The whine grew louder, but no Corl dared put his dissatisfaction into words. Garric felt the hair on his neck and wrists rising instinctively at the sound.

"Then I say this, Leader of the Animals!" Elphas continued. "We do not fear your threats, but we will keep our oath because we are Coerli!"

"Aren't they afraid, do you think?" Carus mused. *"I think I was as brave as most men, but I didn't want to die."*

The chieftains at least would rather die than back down, Garric decided after a moment's consideration. *But they're afraid of their clans and their whole race dying. They know that'll happen if they don't accept my terms.*

"Very well," he said aloud to the Coerli. "Send six of your clerks—"

The Corl word was closer to "counter" than "clerk" but the concept was the same. A city of ten thousand couldn't exist without some sort of administration, though the Coerli version was crude by the standards of a human village.

"—into my camp to meet with Lord Tadai—"

Garric paused. Tadai bowed. He'd heard his name though all the rest of Garric's oration was gibberish to him.

"—and the clerks under his direction. They will explain what the kingdom requires of the Coerli and will arrange delivery of the kingdom's gifts to its new Corl subjects."

He grinned. The cat men were more aware than humans of subtle shifts in expression and body language. By now all the Elders would understand the meaning of a smile. They weren't as good at making verbal connections as humans, however.

"For example," Garric said, making his point explicit, "they will determine how and where we should begin delivering hogs to you."

The sound of the assembled Coerli changed again, this time to a hopeful keening. It was just as unpleasant to a human's ears as the threatening growl.

Tadai already employed Coerli from keeps that'd surrendered earlier. They and the human clerks they worked with were trying desperately to learn each other's languages, but at present only Garric could address and understand the cat men clearly. That was a last gift from a friend, an ageless crystalline Bird, in the instants before the Change; and it had come to Garric alone.

The Shepherd knew that bringing the cat men into the kingdom was going to be hugely difficult even with the best will on both sides. Garric didn't expect exceptional good-will, knowing the Coerli and knowing men even better.

"Aye, lad, but as scouts and skirmishers for the army . . . ," Carus said. The king's image set its fists on its hipbones and laughed openly. *"There've never been humans to match them for that. Maybe your Lady Tenoctris is right."*

"Coerli, you have heard my commands," Garric said. "There will be further decrees in coming days, not because of my whim but because they are necessary. Men and Coerli must stand together against the dangers that will otherwise destroy us all. Remember that!"

Garric poised to step down. He'd told the truth when he said he didn't think the cat men would attack him and his companions . . . but the sound and smell and sight of thousands of angry warriors pressed close would've made a rock uncomfortable.

"Or a dead man . . . ," said the ghost of Carus, smiling in knowledge as well as humor.

"Leader of the Animals!" said the Elder to Garric's immediate left. His fur had originally been beige but age had sloughed much of it away; the skin beneath was the clammy white of a salamander in a deep cave. "I am Keeger. Elphas speaks for me and for all, because he is the Chosen—but may I ask you a question?"

"Speak, Keeger," Garric said, looking down at the Corl. Keeger hadn't risen, perhaps knowing that doing so would've further emphasized the bulk of the tall, armored human.

"You talk of right and the good of all," Keeger said. "But tell me, animal; do you dictate to the Coerli by any right save that which steel and fire give you?"

"In a thousand years they might get enough discipline to

face a human army with sticks and nets," Carus said with a snort. *"Maybe in a thousand years; not less."*

Garric drew his long horseman's sword and held it high; the pattern-welded blade danced in the sun like a snake writhing. "Do you wish to bow to a conqueror rather than work with an ally, Keeger?" he said. "So be it! And Keeger?"

The ancient cat man stared up at him, his lips drawn back.

"Never doubt that if the Coerli break their oath, they *will* have men for conquerors," Garric said. "But those conquerors will have no more mercy than the Coerli themselves would have. There will be nothing left of your keeps but ashes drifting over the bones of your dead!"

"Garric and the kingdom!" Waldron shouted, drawing his own sword and holding it aloft.

"Garric and the kingdom!" cried the Blood Eagles, clashing their spears against the bronze bosses of their shields. "Garric and the kingdom!"

Garric stepped down. "Lord Attaper," he said, putting his lips close to the guard commander's earflap. "March us out!"

The massed Coerli warriors stood in sullen silence, but no one objected as the human delegation stamped and splashed its way through the muck of the cat men's only city. Garric sheathed his sword as he stepped out of the Gathering Field, but the Blood Eagles continued to cheer and rattle their weapons all the way to the gate.

"BIG FELLA, ISN'T he?" Karpos said, straightening and backing against a pilaster. He hadn't drawn his bow, but the broad point of his arrow was pointed at the spine of the man on the floor.

"Yes, he is," Ilna said tartly as she knelt beside the stranger. Though there was nothing overtly threatening in Karpos' tone, Ilna knew that a big man looking at another big man is always thinking about a fight. Her brother Cashel had generally been the biggest man in a gathering. . . .

The stranger groaned again. His face was turned slightly

toward her; his mustache quivered as he breathed, and he had a short black beard as well. She'd guess he was about forty—old enough for a peasant, but this one hadn't been a peasant. His hair and nails were neatly trimmed, and his skin was smooth except for the scars—a cut above the right eye, a trough in the right forearm that could've been made either by a blade or a claw, and a puckering from a sharp point below the left shoulder blade.

A hard smile touched Ilna's mouth: this one was a warrior. She guessed that if she rolled him over, she'd find the mate to the pucker somewhere in his upper chest where the point'd gone in. Why he lay here naked and unconscious while the priests outside had died fighting the cat men was a question to ask as soon as the fellow could speak.

"Karpos, get some water," Ilna said. "I don't see any injury but there's something wrong with him."

"Asion!" Karpos shouted to his partner. "We found somebody! Fetch us water!"

Ilna frowned but didn't object. The hunters were her companions, not servants. Karpos was afraid to leave her alone with the stranger. His concern was misplaced, but it was a harmless mistake.

Ilna only wished that her own mistakes had all been so harmless. If she hadn't made a particularly bad mistake, she'd have a better reason to exist now than the hope of killing every cat man in the world; though killing cat men seemed to be enough.

The floor of this temple was of simple stone flags instead of the designs in tile or mosaic that she'd seen elsewhere. The stranger brushed them with his palms, feeling for a purchase. His eyes remained closed.

"Here!" said Asion, striding swiftly out of the sunlight with a dripping mass in his left hand; the knife in his right pointed toward the ground, not a threat but assuredly ready for any trouble that arose. "I didn't see a gourd around so I soaked some cloth in the fountain."

"Off one of the bodies?" his partner said. "You're no better than a dog sometimes, you know, Asion?"

"Hey, I cut off the skirt," Asion said defensively. "There wasn't any blood on that part. Who's the guy?"

Ilna took the sodden linen from the hunter. She was more than a little inclined to agree with Karpos, but Asion had done what'd been requested. Since she hadn't told him what means to use, she had no right to complain about how he did it.

While she considered whether to daub the corner of the stranger's mouth or perhaps to mop his brow, he lifted his head slightly. His eyes opened, but only a slit. Bracing his arms, he raised his torso and brought his knees up under him.

Asion backed away, wiping his left hand on his rawhide breeches. He raised the knife to his waist with the point forward.

The stranger stood and opened his eyes. He glanced at the two hunters and smiled faintly. Then he looked at Ilna; the smile vanished. He'd risen smoothly, but his body swayed for an instant after he'd found his feet.

Ilna's face tightened in slight irritation. The man couldn't have been as old as she'd thought, not and carry so little fat. She'd mistaken the flaccidity of unconsciousness for softness. Now that he was alert, the flesh was molded tightly over his bones.

She handed him the wet cloth. "What's your name?" she asked.

She sounded peevish. She smiled at a flash of self-awareness: *I spend most of my life in a state of slight irritation, punctuated by moments of extreme anger. It's as well that I don't like being around people, because I wouldn't be very good company.*

The stranger wiped his face, squeezing out runnels of water that splashed onto the floor. When he'd finished with his face, he began to rub his shoulders and chest. The rag was by now merely damp.

He smiled at Ilna. "What is your name?" he said. His words were clear and audible, but his voice had the odd, echoing intonation of a gong speaking.

Ilna glared at him. "I'm Ilna os-Kenset," she said, because

it was quicker to give an answer than to argue that she'd asked him first. "What is *your* name?"

"And what're you doing in this temple?" Karpos said harshly. He'd backed two steps and now had drawn back his arrow enough to spread the bowstring into a flat V. Ilna suspected the hunter wasn't aware of what his fingers were doing. He was dangerously tense.

The stranger looked at Karpos and smiled again. It wasn't an ingratiating smile, simply one of amusement. He dropped the rag on the floor and stretched, raising his arms to their full height. His fingertips came impressively close to the crossbeams of ancient timber supporting the roof trusses.

"Answer me!" Karpos shouted, drawing the bowstring a little farther.

Turning to Ilna again, the stranger said, "My name is Temple?"

She thought she heard a question in the words, but the tone might have deceived her. She glared at Karpos. She'd taken the hank of cords out of her sleeve and was knotting them without paying conscious attention to what her fingers were doing.

"Karpos, put that bow down *now*," she said in a voice that could've broken rocks. "Put it down or I'll leave you here! You'll be no good to me."

Asion stepped between his friend and the stranger, murmuring reassuring words. Karpos let the arrow rotate parallel to the bowstaff, holding both with the fingers of his left hand alone. "What kind of name is Temple?" he shouted to the back wall.

"What is a name?" Temple said; softly, slowly. He still sounded amused, but he looked at the two hunters with a gentleness which Ilna hadn't expected.

Ilna grimaced and began picking out the knots from the pattern in her hands. "What happened here? Why were you spared when the cat men attacked?"

"Was I spared?" Temple said, looking down at his naked body. He was certainly big—as tall as Garric and even more muscular. Temple wasn't a broad plug of a man like Cashel, but he gave the same impression of tree-like solidity. Softly, barely whispering, he went on, "It's been a long time. Very long."

"Answer me!" Ilna said.

He met her angry gaze. "The Coerli didn't attack, Ilna," he said. "Others did. I do not know them, but it was the others."

Then, scarcely audible, "Very long."

"I didn't think it was the cats neither, mistress," Asion said in a tiny voice. He was staring at his right big toe as it drew circles on the stone floor.

Ilna spat out a short, bitter laugh. The cords in her hands gave her the power to kill or compel; she could drive Temple mad or make him say anything she wanted to hear.

And none of that was the least use to her now. She didn't know what it was she wanted, and she needed a better reason to kill than the fact she was—as usual—angry and frustrated.

"All right," Ilna said to the hunters. "There's no point in our staying here. There'll be food in the huts. We can milk the goats before we leave, too. I'd like a drink of milk."

"What about the bodies, mistress?" Karpos said quietly. "Do we leave them, or . . . ?"

The dead were merely meat of a sort that other men didn't eat; they didn't matter. But—

"We'll put them in one of the huts and block the door with stones," she said after a moment to consider. The cold smile touched her lips again. "I suppose that makes it a mausoleum. The sort of thing rich people have . . . when they've become dead meat."

"Ilna, you are leaving?" Temple said.

Ilna looked at him sharply. "Yes," she said. There wasn't much reason for him to remain here at that. "Do you want to come with us?"

Then, in a crisp tone, "You'll have to find clothes if you come."

"I will find clothes," Temple said. He flexed his arms and smiled at her again. "And I will come with you."

"Mistress?" said Karpos. His left hand twitched unconsciously, rotating the arrow back to nock. He caught himself, glowered, and snatched the arrow away with his free hand. "Mistress, do you think that's a good idea?"

"I think it's a humane idea, Master Karpos," Ilna snapped. "I don't insist that being humane is good, but it's how I prefer to act when I can. If Temple doesn't want to remain alone at the place his companions were massacred, then I can't say I blame him. When we arrive at a more suitable place, he can leave us."

She looked at the stranger. He was smiling again, this time very broadly. "Sorry," she muttered. "I shouldn't have talked about you as if you weren't here, Master Temple."

"Just Temple, Ilna," he said. He looked at Karpos and said, "I will not be a burden to you, sir."

"The Sister bloody knows you won't!" Karpos said in an undertone, but it was just words rather than a threat. Ilna knew—and Karpos knew as well—that if she ordered the hunters to carry Temple on a litter, they'd obey.

The chance of that happening, barring accident or serious wounds, was vanishingly small. The man was clearly as fit as the hunters and they'd spent their entire lives in the wilderness.

Asion cleared his throat. "Look, I didn't see weapons out there with the bodies," he said, "but maybe in the houses they have something for Temple. A sickle or a billhook or something. He oughta have a weapon, out where we're going."

"They should've had weapons," Karpos said. "Here in the middle of nowhere without a spear to hand when they needed one!"

"Right," said Ilna, pursing her lips as she considered. Tunics and a cloak for Temple shouldn't be difficult; he was unusually tall, but several of the dead men were fat enough that their garments should cover him adequately if in a rather different manner from the way they did the original owners. Sandals, though, or boots—

"I will have weapons, sir," Temple said. He turned and squatted, then slid his hands to midpoint on opposite sides of the stone barrel between the images of the Gods.

"Are you praying?" Asion said. Then, to his partner, "Is he praying, do you think?"

The muscles of Temple's back and shoulders sprang out in bold relief. For a moment there was silence.

"Look, buddy," Karpos said, "if that's solid, you can forget about moving it by yourself. It weighs more'n all three of us together, aye and the mistress too!"

Stone scraped though nothing seemed to move. Temple's legs straightened with the slow certainty of sunrise. The massive cylinder—it must be at least as heavy as Karpos said—rose with him. He started to turn, balancing the stone above his head.

"Get back!" Ilna cried, but the hunters were already scrambling away. Nobody could balance something that heavy for long. When the barrel tipped one way or another it'd fall to the floor with a crash that'd shatter flagstones into flying splinters.

Temple squatted with the grace of an ox settling, still holding the stone. His smile was as set as that of a bare skull, and his muscles seemed to have been chiseled from wood. He lowered the stone barrel to the floor with no more than a *tock* and a rasping sound.

"By the Sister," Karpos said softly. "By the Sister."

Asion's left hand gripped the amulet bag he wore around his neck. He was mouthing something, probably a prayer. He absently sheathed his long knife, though Ilna guessed he wasn't aware of what he was doing.

Temple shuddered and wheezed, drawing in deep breaths and expelling them with the violence of a surfacing porpoise. He continued to grip the cylinder, now to anchor him so that he didn't topple over backward.

After a moment he turned his head to look at Karpos. Between gasps he said, "I will . . . no-not *burden* . . . you. Sir!"

"I give you best," Karpos said. He sounded awestruck. "By the Sister!"

Ilna sniffed. As a general rule she disapproved of boasting, and the feat Temple had just performed was certainly a boast. Still, it'd settled his place in this community of men without a fight, and it'd opened what turned out to be a cavity beneath the stone by the simplest if not the easiest means available. She walked over to look inside.

"Ilna," Temple said firmly. He bent over the barrel again, squeezing his eyes closed. He opened them and looked at her. "I'll take care of that, if you please."

"Yes," she said, stepping back. She stood as straight as the pillars, her face set. The stranger had rebuked her courteously. She'd often rebuked those who meddled in *her* business, but much less courteously.

Temple stood. She'd expected him to lurch, but the motion when it came was as smooth as all his other movements had been. He nodded to the hunters, bowed slightly to her, and reached down into the cavity.

Ilna laughed; a brief sound and half-suppressed, but even so more humor than normally passed her lips. Both hunters looked at her in surprise. Even Temple, straightening with armor in one hand and a sword in the other, glanced over his shoulder with an eyebrow cocked.

"Temple," she said, honestly saying what she'd thought but not explaining why she'd found it funny, "you and my brother, Cashel, would get along well together. He's a strong man also."

And he, like you, she added within the amused silence of her mind, *doesn't pick fights to prove how strong he is. Though if the two of you did fight, it'd be something to see.*

The hunters were looking at Temple's equipment. Helmet, cuirass, and the round shield were all made of a metal Ilna didn't recognize. It had a copperish tinge, but it was too dark and had a hint almost of purple.

"So what is it, eh?" said Asion. "Is it bronze?"

"A sort of bronze," Temple said. His voice was quickly losing its odd intonation. He set the armor on the ground and, gripping the sheath at the balance with one hand, put his other on the hilt. "It's harder than most bronzes, though."

He drew the sword. The straight blade was of the same dark metal as the armor, but the edge shimmered brightly golden even in the dim light filtering through the door of the building twenty double paces behind them.

"I've never seen anything like that," Asion said, stepping closer. He moved his hand cautiously toward the sword as though he were about to pet a lion. "Where'd you get it?"

Temple lifted the sword slightly, keeping it away from the shorter man. Asion stepped back, and Temple shot the sword home in its sheath.

"I've had it a long time," he said quietly. "A very long time."

"Is there anything more you need here?" Ilna said sharply to break the mood. When Temple shook his head, smiling again, she went on, "All right, then we'll search the houses for food before we—"

She shrugged.

"—bury the dead in one of them. And we'll get you clothes."

"I will bury the Coerli also, Ilna," Temple said. "You need not help."

Ilna glared at him, then shrugged. "If you wish," she snapped as she started for the door. "If you wish, you can walk on your hands all the way to where we're going!"

Temple left the armor where it was for now, but he slung the sword belt around his naked waist as he followed the others into the bright sun.

SHARINA'D MANAGED TO sleep in the carriage during much of her return from West Sesile, but she jerked awake when the iron tires began hammering on the bricks of the Main North Road running along the front of the palace compound. She rubbed her eyes. She hadn't slept well, but any sleep at all was a luxury nowadays.

She smiled. She didn't think she'd had what she'd call a good night's sleep since the Change. There was simply too much for Princess Sharina to do.

And not just Princess Sharina. Mistress Masmon in the opposite corner looked up when she saw Sharina awaken.

Masmon had been annotating a parchment codex by the light of a candle sconce in the side of the compartment. She was using a small brass pen which she refilled by dipping it into the ink horn dangling from the stud of her traveling cloak.

Sometimes when the pressure of work seemed unbearable, it helped Sharina to remember that others were feeling the same pressure and nonetheless continuing to do their jobs. All the people who really understood that the struggle was between Good and Evil and that Good *must* win if mankind were to survive—all of them were working as hard as humans could, and maybe a little harder yet.

Sharina smiled at Masmon in sudden sympathy. The clerk blinked in surprise, then managed a wan smile in reply. She closed her pen, capped and removed the ink horn, and was placing them and the book in a carrying case when the carriage pulled up at the palace gates.

The barred gates squealed open, but a discussion between the guards on the carriage and people in the roadway continued. Sharina couldn't catch the words—partly because she was still logy with sleep and lack of sleep both—so she opened the window shutter and stuck her head out to see what was happening.

Admiral Zettin stood in the gateway, his left hand gripping the headstall of the lead horse while he argued with the under-captain in command of the carriage guards. When Zettin saw Sharina, he let go of the horse and strode back to the box, calling, "Your Highness? May I ride to your quarters with you? There's a problem that I really need to discuss—"

"Yes, yes, of course," Sharina said, her heart sinking into a pit of shadows. She was *so* tired. The only thing on her mind had been having her maid help her undress—you simply couldn't get into or out of court robes by yourself—and getting into bed to sleep. Lord Zettin had been waiting at the palace entrance because he knew she'd have to pass here eventually and he didn't want to leave his problem for the morning.

Zettin opened the carriage door. He lifted himself onto the mounting step but paused with a frown when he saw Mistress Masmon.

"That's all right," said the clerk, snuffing the candle between her thumb and forefinger. "I'm getting out."

Sharina started to protest, then realized that she didn't know where Mistress Masmon's precise destination within the compound wall was; it might well be one of the buildings near the entrance. Regardless, the clerk would feel uncomfortable if the princess forced her to remain: and since Zettin obviously wouldn't discuss his business in front of an underling, the result of the whole exercise would be to keep Sharina awake that much longer.

Sharina leaned out the door by which the clerk had just left. "One of you men help Mistress Masmon with her case!" she called to the guards. "Yes, I mean you! The gate can do with one fewer man for the time it takes."

She sat down again. Zettin settled onto the opposite crossbench as the driver clucked the horses on. Leaning toward her, he said, "It's Pandah, Your Highness. There's a serious problem there, one that I think has to take precedence over integrating the Coerli into the kingdom."

Sharina looked at Zettin in puzzlement. Moonlight through the slatted shutters flicked across his face as the carriage rolled forward, hiding more than it revealed.

"I've stayed on Pandah," she said, trying to make sense of Zettin's words. "Pandah isn't a danger."

It's a sleepy island smelling faintly of spices, and even the breeze is mild.

Pandah was the only major island in the middle of the Inner Sea. Besides providing water and locally raised provisions for vessels crossing the sea, it was a place where regional cargoes could be sorted for shipping to their final destinations by local traders. The people there, from the king on down, were wealthy and focused on living well rather than getting involved in military adventures.

"Yes, Your Highness," Zettin said, probably more harshly than he'd intended. They were all tired and becoming snappish. "That was indeed the case before the Change, but it no longer is. In the years immediately following the collapse of the Old Kingdom, Pandah was a nest of pirates. That seems to be the case now, but the situation is rather worse because the human outlaws are making common cause with cat men who refuse to become part of the kingdom."

Sharina frowned. "How are they doing that?" she asked. "Can they talk to the Coerli? I don't see . . ."

Zettin shrugged. "They manage somehow, I gather," he said with a black scowl. "The cat men're mostly young males, warriors that is, from keeps which surrendered to the army. They and the pirates they're joining aren't very different in attitude."

He turned his head away, though inside the slowly rumbling carriage he wouldn't have been able to see Sharina's face any more clearly than she could see his. "From what those who've fled the area tell us," Zettin said with a careful lack of emotion, "they've taken up eating men. The humans have, that is. If you want to call them human."

Lord Zettin had been an officer of the Blood Eagles and a protégé of Lord Attaper. When Garric had restored the fleet as the only means of enforcing royal authority over the Kingdom of the Isles, Zettin had become its commander— in part because traditional army officers led by Lord Waldron had considered the fleet command beneath them. Now that the fleet had little value to a continental kingdom, Garric had appointed the former admiral as chief military aide to Sharina, who ran the civil administration while he was absent with the army.

"Ah," Sharina said, realizing now why Zettin had been so insistent on bringing the business to her immediately instead of waiting for the morning. "That's something we'll need to deal with promptly, yes. But milord, I'm afraid my brother will make the decision as to precisely how that will happen. This is a strictly military matter, and I keep out of those except in an immediate crisis."

"But Your Highness—"

"Milord!" Sharina said. "Garric—Prince Garric—should return the day after tomorrow at the latest. I'll send the information to him at once, but I will *not* take the decision out of his hands."

"Yes, of course, Your Highness," Zettin said tiredly. "I see that this is . . . a proper way to proceed. But . . ."

He let his voice trail away as the carriage halted. Sharina peered through the slats, then opened her door before one of the guards acting as footmen hopped down to get it. They'd drawn up in front of the bungalow which Sharina used as her private quarters, one of scores of separate structures within the palace compound.

When Garric became regent and the first strong leader the kingdom'd had for over a generation, half the buildings within the walls had been empty and dilapidated. Valles was again the administrative capital of a thriving kingdom, so reconstruction of the palace had necessarily kept pace with the need for office space. What would happen now that Valles was far inland—well, that was a problem for another day if not a distant day.

"Milord . . . ," Sharina said. Zettin's door jerked open, and a Blood Eagle took hers as well. "The situation you describe at Pandah is not only evil but disgusting. Nevertheless it may not be in my brother's opinion the most serious threat the kingdom faces at this moment, nor the best use of the army. You and I and my brother will all put our personal feelings aside and work for the kingdom's greatest good—as we've been doing."

She got down from the carriage. She hadn't told Zettin anything he hadn't already known. He was a smart man, very possibly the cleverest of the high officers in the royal army, but he'd chosen to waste her time in this fashion because he was angry and appalled on a personal basis. There wasn't any time for personal feelings!

Zettin walked around the back of the vehicle—to take his leave formally, she hoped, because the interview *was* closed. The door of her bungalow opened. Sharina looked from the officer to what she assumed would be the maid, her only servant, who'd stayed awake for her—

"Cashel!" she said. He stood solid as an oak in the light of the porch lantern, smiling a greeting. She'd been wrong about there not being time for personal feelings.

Sharina trotted forward as quickly as the robes permitted; they weren't tight, but they were so long and heavy that they were likely to wrap around her ankles and trip her if she weren't careful. Cashel strode down the steps to gather her in. He lifted her soul as well in a sudden flood of safety and contentment.

"Tenoctris is lying down inside," Cashel said. "She had to do some hard things. And there's a thing you need to see."

Raising his head slightly, he said to Zettin, "Sir? You'd better come look at it too. Whatever it is, it's something for soldiers to know about."

"Yes," said Sharina, squeezing Cashel once more before releasing him. She didn't know what the problem was yet, but she knew that neither Cashel nor Tenoctris overstated dangers. Over her shoulder as she mounted the steps she said, "Lord Zettin? Will you call a courier from the duty room in the next building? It sounds like we'll need to summon Prince Garric."

"I've already done that, Sharina," said Tenoctris, standing to the side in the doorway. "The officer in charge there thought Garric should be able to get back by midmorning if all goes well."

"Fine," said Sharina, embracing the older woman lightly as they passed. *It's good to have friends who'll make the right decisions before you need to.* "Then we'll call a council meeting for the tenth hour. Now, let's see what you've got."

It was good to be a person who made the right decisions herself, too. Even when she was really tired.

Chapter

3

ILNA PAUSED AT the head of the valley. She whispered, "Are you going to claim *this* wasn't the cat men's work, Temple?"

She scowled at herself. The pattern in her hand made it clear that the Coerli were well beyond the sound of her voice by now. Perhaps she was speaking quietly in respect for the dead—a thought that made her scowl even blacker.

"No, Ilna," Temple said calmly. "A band of Coerli killed them and did worse, I suspect. There will have been children."

Asion was partway up a tree for a better view of the valley than Ilna and Temple got from the ridgeline. Karpos, crouched several paces behind them watching their back trail, said, "What will we do now, mistress?"

"What?" said Ilna. "We'll go down to the farm and see if we notice anything important from closer up. Then the two of you will track the beasts to their daylight lair—it's a bright day and early enough in the morning that you shouldn't be in danger. And when we know precisely what the situation is, we'll kill them. As usual."

She was surprised to hear the anger in her voice, though she supposed anger was never very far from the surface. The sight of three bodies below had scraped off the cover.

The three *human* bodies, that was. Ilna didn't care about the donkey butchered in the corral to the side of the main house, nor about the milch goat with her kid who'd run nearly a furlong from the kicked-over bucket and stool by the house. At another time she'd have been angry at the way the killers had deliberately torn the nanny's belly open and gripped her intestine so that she pulled it out as she ran, but they'd done the same to the woman who'd been milking her.

She rose to her feet. "I'll wait here," Karpos said. He was out of sight.

Ilna glanced at the cords in her hand, then began picking out the pattern. "There's no need," she said, but she didn't argue with Karpos as she started down the slope. He wasn't doubting her word, just continuing to do the things that'd kept him alive for however many years he'd been hunting dangerous animals. Temple and Asion, who dropped from the tree, joined her.

The farmstead had been neat looking. Oh, not neat by the standards to which Ilna'd kept her quarters and Cashel's in their uncle's millhouse, but with animals and no doubt children as Temple had said, not even Ilna could've guaranteed perfect order.

The walls of the main building were logs trimmed with an adze and chinked with clay; they'd been touched up recently. Several roof shakes were brighter than their neighbors also, showing where rot and wind damage had been repaired.

And none of it mattered now to those who'd lived here, because a band of cat men had killed them all. Ilna's lips moved, though no one watching would've recognized the expression as a smile. She couldn't help what was past, but she was as sure as she was of sunset that this particular gang of beasts wouldn't repeat their slaughter.

"Two days, I'd judge," Asion said, squatting by the corpse of the man who'd had time to snatch a sickle from the outbuilding. It had a wooden blade set with sharp flints, a dangerous-enough weapon if he'd managed to strike anything with it; but of course he hadn't.

From the tear in the corpse's bearded throat and the rope burn on his right wrist, a beast had thrown his line around the fellow's arm and set its hooks in his neck so that his attempt to slash with the sickle only dug them deeper. Either the beast holding the line or one of his fellows had then jabbed a slender point through the man's diaphragm, leaving him to slowly suffocate or bleed out.

Helman, the butcher who slaughtered hogs when his circuit brought him through Barca's Hamlet, did so with equal cruelty, but Ilna herself didn't behave that way. She smiled again, though with no more humor than the expression of a moment before. If the hogs had trapped Helman some dark night on his rounds, she at least would've thought it a rare instance of justice being done.

She entered the house. The door, suspended on leather hinges, was open, but the sturdy crossbar lay just inside, where the cat men had dropped it when they left. There hadn't been time to close the window shutters, so the cat men had entered through a casement, tearing the covering of leather which'd been scraped thin to pass light.

Temple held his bronze sword before him, but his buckler was slung over his back to leave his left hand free. He knelt to touch a spatter on the floor of halved logs, puncheons. The blood was dry enough to flake away, as Ilna would've expected.

"How many do you think it was lived here?" Asion asked. A bed was folded up against the back wall; he prodded the frame with the point of his knife, gouging out a splinter. He seemed tenser than Ilna'd expected.

Ilna realized with a touch of amusement that it made the hunter nervous to be in a house. Had he and Karpos slept outdoors when they'd trekked into town to sell their lizard gall?

She snorted. Most likely they'd stayed drunk the whole time, or at least drunk enough to ignore the roof over them.

"The parents in the bed, with the infant in the cradle at the foot," Ilna said. As she spoke, she climbed to the half-loft above the single room. There was a real ladder nailed to the wall, not merely a young pine with the branches lopped short to form steps. "Up here. . . ."

She looked at the bedding, rolled neatly against the roof slope, and estimated the width of the portion of loft floor which wasn't being used for storage. "Three older children, probably. Though the tallest can't be more than a cloth yard—"

A normal yard and a thumb's-span; she'd heard folk from Cordin call it an ell.

"—unless he sleeps doubled up."

There was no chance, *none,* but Ilna nonetheless crawled to the bedding and pulled it back to make sure that no child had hidden within it when the cat men came. That hadn't happened, but she didn't mind wasting a few moments to be sure she wasn't leaving an infant who'd fallen unconscious after an elder had concealed it. She had enough on her conscience already.

The blankets were goat wool, but they hadn't been loomed here. When Ilna touched the cloth, she got an image of stone-built farm buildings and a pair of old women murmuring as they worked their shuttles.

"And the other man?" Temple asked.

He isn't a peasant, Ilna remembered. Aloud she said, "A hired man; he's wearing the master's cast-off clothes. The tunic's too small for him. He slept in the outbuilding, I suppose."

She came down the ladder deliberately, stepping on every rung and holding the rails. She wanted to get away from the beds the children would never return to, get out of this *house;* but she wouldn't let dislike make her act in haste. Mental discomfort was merely one of those things, like pain and hunger and bleak hopelessness, that you avoided when you could and bore when you couldn't.

Temple gestured toward the fireplace; there was ash on his fingertip. "It's cold," he said. "All the way down to the hearthstone. At least two days."

The cat men didn't like bright light. They must've come at dawn, while the family was starting the morning chores. The pack would be sleeping in the shade of a booth of woven branches at this time of day.

The Coerli showed real talent with wicker and bark cloth, though they didn't grow flax or raise animals for wool. They were beasts. . . .

The wooden chimney had been sealed with a thick coating of clay. Ilna frowned when she saw it, but there wasn't much free stone here; and the family hadn't died from a chimney fire, after all.

The folk who'd built the farm had come from a more settled region. Did it exist now, or had the Change torn this farmstead an unguessable distance in time and space from where it'd sprung?

That probably didn't matter. If it did, then she'd know soon enough.

Asion was tracing the simple carvings on the top of a wooden chest with his fingertip. "My, that's fine," he said. Looking toward Ilna, he went on, "Mistress, where'd the kids go if we didn't find them here? They couldn't've run if the parents couldn't, could they?"

Ilna looked at Temple. The big man said, "The raiding party carried them off, Asion. They'll be more tender than the adults."

There was no expression in his voice. He turned to Ilna and said, "I'd guess there were four or five males, and there may be females and kits in their lair. They'll be hunting again soon."

"Yes," said Ilna. "Asion, take Karpos and locate the beasts. I wouldn't expect them to be very far away. I'll prepare matters here to receive them."

"Yes, mistress," the hunter said, slipping through the door and drawing his sling from beneath his belt where he'd been carrying it. He seemed glad to get away.

Ilna looked around once more, then walked into the farmyard. Temple followed her. She'd hoped there'd be a loom, but that wasn't important; she could knot the necessary patterns by hand. She'd pick out yarn from the dead woman's tunic. The rip would make the task easier, and she could put the blood dyeing the wool to practical advantage.

"Ilna?" said the big man. "Have you a task for me?"

"I'll summon the beasts by lighting a fire on the hearth," she said. "I'll be waiting for them in front of the house, though. You might decide where the three of you should best be to act when they come to me."

Her lips quirked into a smile or a sneer. She said, "After all, you're a soldier, aren't you?"

She didn't like soldiers, men whose life was directed at killing other men.

"Something like that," Temple said equably. He glanced around. "Asion in the goat's byre, under the straw to hide his smell. Karpos in the manure pile for the same reason. I'll wait in the house, because the Coerli won't take time to separate my smell from the previous owners' before they attack."

"Yes, all right," said Ilna, taken aback by the speed with which he'd planned the business. *The hunters would prefer to hide in filth for the hours before the cat men came rather than to be inside a house . . . and Temple noticed that, as I did.* "I'll get to work, then."

"Ilna?" the big man said. "There's tools in the shed. I'd like to bury the dead. Since there's time."

"Yes," said Ilna. "If you wish."

She walked to the woman's corpse. She should've thought of that herself, but it wasn't her real job. Her real job was to kill cat men, and very shortly she'd have a chance to do more of that.

"BUT WE DON'T have a completed survey for the route to Pandah," said a civilian named Baumo. "I'm sure it seems simple to people who don't have to do the work, but most of the residents in that direction are Grass People and don't speak a proper language!"

Cashel didn't know what Baumo's title was or what he did beyond—it seemed—make surveys. Indeed, Cashel didn't know what most of the government officials here at the meeting did; so far as he was concerned, they all sort of blurred together.

It wasn't that he *couldn't* have learned: inside of two days, he'd know the personality of every sheep in a flock of ten tens or more. But he was interested in sheep and not a bit interested in palace officials, no matter how important they were; and officials weren't his job.

"Well, surely there'll be enough food to supply one regiment," said Admiral Zettin. "I don't think we'll need more troops than that. There can't be more than a thousand or so of the pirates and they're disgusting perverts, after all. What we can't afford to do is wait!"

The meeting was in one of the bigger conference rooms and involved far more people than Cashel could count on both hands. Besides the important folk sitting at the table, there were all sorts of clerks and runners standing against the walls waiting for somebody to ask them or tell them something.

A bunch of people started talking, none of them seeming to agree with Zettin but none of them saying the same thing either. Garric hadn't arrived yet and Tenoctris didn't want to get into the business of the black men, the Last as she called them, till he did. Sharina was letting Zettin talk about his notion of attacking Pandah, where Cashel'd been a long time ago. It wasn't the same place since the Change, it seemed.

Sharina sat in the middle of one long side, listening to the argument but not running things the way Cashel knew she could do if she wanted to. She was letting folks talk to keep them occupied while she waited for Garric and the real business.

Cashel let the smile spread across his lips. Sharina was *so* smart, and *so* beautiful; and she loved him, which he'd never dreamed could be when they were growing up together in Barca's Hamlet.

Tenoctris sat to Sharina's left, reading books and scrolls she took out of the satchel which held the things she wanted as a wizard. She didn't even pretend to care about Pandah. Mostly she'd put each book back when she'd looked at it but now and again she'd lay one on the table with a bamboo splint for a place marker.

When it was a scroll Tenoctris wanted to mark, she weighted it open with whatever came to hand, generally a codex. One time, though, she'd whispered to Sharina, who handed over the Pewle knife she wore hidden beneath her outer tunic.

The big knife appearing in Princess Sharina's hand made a lot of eyes bug out. One of Lord Tadai's clerks even started to say something, but the soldier standing next to him clapped a hand to the fellow's mouth and hustled him out of the room. From the look on Tadai's face when he turned to see the disturbance, the clerk was lucky somebody other than his chief had taken care of the business.

Cashel glanced at the gleaming knife. The blade was sharpened on one edge; you could hammer on the wide backstrap if you had to. The seal hunters of Pewle Island used their knives for whatever work came to hand: chopping wood, fixing dinner—or gutting an enemy with a quick upward slash. Pewlemen were often hired as mercenaries, because they weren't afraid of anything. They had no more mercy than the cold seas where they hunted seals in flimsy woodskins.

Sharina'd gotten her knife from an old hermit named Nonnus. He'd died to save her life, and maybe died also to make up for some of the things he'd done when he was a soldier. If Sharina wanted to carry the knife to remember Nonnus . . . well, Cashel figured he'd earned the memory, and there'd been times it was good that Sharina had a big blade.

Cashel looked around the room, his quarterstaff upright beside him. He stood behind Sharina and Tenoctris, not because he really had to worry about somebody bumping them in this gathering but because that was his proper place. Sharina'd told him he could have a seat at the table—that he could be Lord Cashel or Duke Cashel if he wanted . . . but what did a shepherd from Haft know about being a duke?

What Cashel knew was putting himself between trouble and things that couldn't handle trouble themselves. Once that'd meant sheep. Now it was people, especially Sharina and Tenoctris, and there was no work that could better satisfy him.

A couple of soldiers were arguing about whether cavalry could get to Pandah quicker or if the ground was too wet since the Grass People mostly lived in swamps. Baumo was saying something about fodder and horses needing grain. It was all really important to them . . . and it wasn't anything to do with the real business of the kingdom as Sharina and Tenoctris saw it, and therefore as Cashel saw it too. It was just words, till Garric arrived and—

The door of the council chamber opened. "Prince Garric and Lady Liane bos-Benliman!" cried the fellow in command of the guards in the hallway outside, but Garric was already striding into the room. He looked worn but steadfast and really hard—much like the staff in Cashel's hand. He still wore the breeches he'd ridden back in, sopping with foam from the horses' shoulders.

Liane was behind him, quiet and perfectly composed the way she always looked in public. From her expression she could've come straight from the library, but the left half of her traveling skirt was soaked black too. She'd ridden just as hard as Garric—but sidesaddle, of course.

"Milords," Garric said. He nodded across the table to Tenoctris as he drew out an empty chair, handing Liane into it. She sat but then scooted it a little back from the table to show everybody that she was the prince's aide, not his equal.

"Tenoctris?" Garric said as he slid into the remaining chair. "Just who are these Last that you're concerned about?"

"If you please, Your Highness," said Admiral Zettin, sitting at Sharina's left. "Perhaps before we get to that we can conclude—"

"Be silent!" Garric shouted, his chair crashing backward as he shot to his feet again. It was like thunder after the lightning. "Zettin, that you insult me is neither here nor there; but that you insult the woman to whom the kingdom's owed its survival throughout this long crisis, that is unacceptable! Apologize at once to Lady Tenoctris or leave my court."

For an instant Cashel, watching from across the table, could scarcely recognize the friend he'd known all his life. Garric's face had flushed and the skin was tight-stretched over the bone. *He's like an old knife, worn to where there's almost nothing left but sharpness. . . .*

"Your Highness," said Sharina in the stunned silence, "I

apologize for my aide. His enthusiasm on the kingdom's behalf sometimes gets the better of him. Lady Tenoctris, will you please proceed?"

"Right," Garric muttered. He smiled wryly and sat back down. Liane had tipped his chair upright. Zettin hadn't spoken, and none of the flunkies along the wall had dared to move.

"The Last are men of a day not yet come," Tenoctris said, smoothing the margin of an opened scroll for a moment. "They're able to enter the Land on which we live since the Change; and unless they're stopped, the world will surely be lost for all save their kind."

She looked up, beaming at everybody she could see from where she sat. Tenoctris really was a cheerful person, a pleasure to be around; even though quite a lot of what she had to say was stuff nobody wanted to hear.

Zettin was opening and closing his mouth, looking like he'd just been punched in the pit of his stomach. Sharina'd been watching Tenoctris on her right with an expression of consciously polite attention, but she glanced over her shoulder at Zettin on the other side. She tapped two fingers toward him in a signal to be quiet.

Cashel beamed. My! But Sharina was a wonder. The way she'n Garric had taken back control of the meeting was as smooth as if they'd practiced it every day for a year.

It was too bad for Lord Zettin, who seemed to be a decent-enough fellow. But he was pushy, too, and that meant he was going to run into folks who knew how to push back. Here in the palace you didn't get your skull cracked by a quarterstaff, but from the way Zettin looked right now he might've preferred that to the way Garric and Sharina'd hung him out to dry.

"Where are they coming from?" Garric said. "Because if they're going to pop out of any body of water, I'd rather go to their base and choke the raids off at the source."

"I don't think we can go to where the Last are coming from," Tenoctris said, "because I don't believe that's a place on our world. Though I'm guessing."

She grimaced and let her finger waver over the books

she'd spread before her. "There's nothing very clear, you see," she said. "I'd meant to read you the passages I've marked, but only a few of you—"

She looked across the table at Liane and nodded. Liane blushed slightly and lowered her eyes.

"—would understand the way I'm putting references together and coming to where I am. And of course, I may be completely wrong."

"I doubt it," Garric said. "You haven't been in the past. But go on."

Tenoctris hadn't been fishing for a compliment; she really was that modest about the things she did. It was the only subject Cashel could think of where the old woman was likely to be wrong.

Tenoctris gave an embarrassed smile. "They're coming to a place far to the south, on what used to be the island of Shengy," she went on. She pulled a slender roll of vellum from her satchel and undid the ribbon that tied it closed. "I suppose it's still Shengy, even if it's not an island any-more. . . ."

She'd let her voice trail off. Looking up while her fingers spread the fine white parchment on top of the books already covering the table, she resumed forcefully, "I'm going to show you that place. It's not that I doubt you'll believe my de-scription, but perhaps you'll better understand what I feel."

She gave a tiny laugh. "Which isn't panic," she said. "But it'd be fair to call it great concern."

The vellum was already marked with a star having as many points as a hand and two fingers, seven. Tenoctris had drawn the figure in brown cuttlefish ink, but then she'd gone around the edges and written words of power in bright ver-milion with a brush.

"Wizardry?" muttered somebody behind Cashel.

Garric looked up sharply. "Yes, wizardry," he said. "I'll swear on my hope for mankind that all Tenoctris' actions will benefit those opposed to evil, but I won't require anyone to watch a wizard work if he doesn't want to. Anyone who chooses can leave the room now. That includes—"

He looked over his shoulder at the underlings at the wall behind him. His lips smiled but the expression didn't go much deeper than that.

"—the juniors present. On my leave, whether or not the head of your bureau stays."

A clerk, and then another clerk and the boy who was Lord Zettin's aide, slipped out the door as quietly as they could. None of the important people at the table got up, but the plump old soldier who commanded the Valles garrison closed his eyes and leaned his face onto his hands.

"Go on, Tenoctris," Garric said quietly as the door closed behind the boy.

"Yes," said the old wizard. She'd taken books from the table to hold down three corners of the vellum; the Pewle knife weighted the last. She tapped a bamboo splint against the figure and began, *"Bor phor barbo, bar phor baie. . . ."*

Cashel made sure Tenoctris was well set, then resumed looking around the room. He'd never figured watching somebody else work was a good way to get his own job done.

"Mozo cheine alchein . . . ," Tenoctris said. Her wand bobbed from each word written around her figure to the next, though Cashel didn't guess she was reading them off the parchment. Some must be upside down, after all.

There hadn't been so much as a hedge wizard in the borough while Cashel was growing up. Conjurers had come through during the Sheep Fair, but they were just more entertainment like the jugglers and the troupe of mummers who acted out plays on a stage they folded out on top of their wagon.

What Tenoctris did was different but it wasn't scary. Other wizards had tried to kill Cashel or do worse, but he hadn't found them scary either. They were trouble, that was all, and at least so far Cashel'd managed to deal with whatever trouble came looking for him and the folk he watched out for.

". . . kolchoi pertharo . . . ," Tenoctris chanted.

The light in the big room was changing, though Cashel couldn't say exactly how. It wasn't brighter or dimmer, just kinda flat. For a moment he thought the horses and lions carved into the frieze at the top of the walls were moving, but that was probably just the way the shadows twitched.

"*Basaoth!*" Tenoctris cried. People all over the room blurted things. One clerk made a sound like a toad shrieking in the spring rain.

The council room had—well, Cashel didn't know what it'd done. He wasn't in Valles anymore, he was hanging in the air looking down at a crater whose black walls sloped up from an icy wasteland that stretched out of sight in all directions.

The bowl of the crater was covered with ice too, but there was movement in the middle of it. For a moment Cashel didn't understand how big what he was seeing was, but then it seemed—he didn't *feel* that he was moving—that he was rushing downward. From close up he saw that the specks quivering in the center of the ice lens were the Last, a double handful of them, and that they were dancing in a circle. The crater's wall was a distant horizon all around.

"Oh-h-h . . . ," somebody murmured. The sound didn't come from any direction. Maybe it wasn't even a sound, just the frightened thoughts of almost everyone watching.

The Last paced widdershins in a stately form, each gesturing with his shield and drawn sword at exactly the same time. It was like there was only one of them and the rest were mirrors. As they stepped and slowly pirouetted, blurs in the air within their circle congealed into another pair of the Last. The newcomers joined the dance, spreading the circle slightly; and as they danced, more appeared.

Cashel couldn't tell how long it went on. He was conscious of the sky growing brighter and dimmer, but that didn't touch him the way the passage of time should've.

Every time the Last completed the circuit of their dance they paused, faced south, and lifted sword and shield toward the white star blazing on the horizon. It was higher in their sky than it'd been in Valles, but Cashel knew it for the interloper he'd noticed in the south before the Last attacked from the pool.

The dance went on. The circle had spread to the crater walls. Still the Last wheeled, and more of their kind appeared in the center of the lens. A second round of dancers was forming; and another, and more than Cashel could count on both hands.

The Last filled the vast bowl; and still they danced, and still more appeared. There was no end to them, none. They spilled out of the crater in lines marching northward, more and more and no end. . . .

The bamboo wand dropped from Tenoctris' hand. It made a tiny patter on the vellum, no sound at all really, but the council room was back in focus and Cashel bent quickly to catch the wizard as she fell toward the littered table.

It was like holding a bird in his hand. Tenoctris weighed nothing; she was just a nervous fluttering of breath. She'd worn herself out doing this, showing others what she saw herself. Showing what all mankind had to fear.

"When will it end?" said Baumo, the fellow who worried about surveys. Sweat beaded on his forehead now and his cheeks were pasty. "When will they *stop*?"

"When we stop them, Master Baumo," said Garric. His face was tight again, but his voice was normal. "Which we will, on our lives."

He smiled, though most of the people in the room didn't understand that he'd made a joke.

SHARINA RETURNED HER brother's wry smile as she walked back to her chair. One of the problems with being the ruler was that you had to remain calm and sensible while people around you ran in circles and shouted that the sky was falling.

The sky might very well be falling this time, but it might not—and regardless, running in circles wasn't going to improve the situation. You learned that when your family owned an inn, or owned a farm, or for that matter owned nothing at all like Cashel and Ilna. The only people who could afford not to learn it were those who knew somebody else would take care of them and their problems.

"Somebody else" in this case was Prince Garric, helped by the circle of those closest to him. Given that the threat to the kingdom was unquestionably real, Sharina was glad to be one of those helpers instead of another frightened twitterer.

"If you'll all be quiet for a moment, please!" said Garric as Sharina sat down again. He'd learned to call from one hilltop to another while pasturing sheep. In an enclosed room, even a big room like this, he could rattle the roof tiles when he was on his mettle. The present shout wasn't quite that loud, but it got everyone's attention. They rustled to silence.

"Cashel?" Garric went on, now in a normal tone of voice. "You've helped Tenoctris many times. How's she doing now?"

There were stone benches built into the sidewalls. None of the aides had been sitting on them, of course, not in the presence of the prince and princess, but one made a fine bed for Tenoctris while she was recovering. They'd laid a mattress of military cloaks, with Sharina's own half-cape rolled as a pillow. Sharina didn't know how the soldiers felt about it, but in so full a room she was more comfortable without the additional weight of heavy brocade on her shoulders.

"She'll be fine," Cashel said, planted like a pillar in front of the sleeping wizard. His staff was crossways in front of him, not threatening anybody but making sure nobody accidentally backed close enough to disturb his elderly friend. "All she needs is a bit of time, you know. To get over her tired."

"All right, we'll hope that Lady Tenoctris recovers quickly," Garric said. He gave the room a lopsided smile. His fingers were interwoven on the table. From where she sat directly across from her brother, Sharina saw them mottle briefly with strain.

"What we *won't* do," Garric continued with a hint of

grimness, "is to press her beyond her capacity. We need her. Indeed, the kingdom needs Tenoctris more than it needs all the rest of us in this room. Does everyone understand that?"

There were a few mutters, but for the most part people let their silence stand for agreement. Nobody was going to badger Tenoctris when Cashel kept watch, but there was always a chance that somebody with more zeal than judgment would push into her quarters or lie in wait for her when she left there. Tenoctris had better get a full-time detachment of Blood Eagles, a practice that Attaper'd dropped when the regiment's numbers had become straitened and the need for guards had if anything increased.

Sharina smiled, but she didn't let the expression reach her lips. Not long ago she'd have feared Lord Zettin might have a scheme that he'd advance to Tenoctris beyond what others would've considered the bounds of courtesy and protocol. After this morning's rebuke, danger from his quarter had receded considerably.

"Now," Garric went on, "did anybody recognize the place Tenoctris showed us? *Is* it Shengy?"

Liane bent and whispered in his ear. With a rare flash of irritation, Garric said, "Duzi, Lady Liane! Say it to the group, if you please."

"There are volcanoes along the highlands of Shengy," Liane said, her voice cool and firm. She'd opened a book whose narrow pages were slats of bamboo, though she didn't look at it as she spoke. "Before the Change the whole island was covered with heavy jungle, however."

"Your Highness, if that scene was Shengy, then there's nothing we can do anyway, is there?" said Lord Hauk, born a commoner but ennobled by Garric for his ability. "Even if we could find enough horses and oxen to transport an army traveling by land, the draft animals would consume all the fodder they could carry before they'd gone a fraction of the distance."

"Well, the troops can forage for themselves in an emergency like this, surely," said Chancellor Royhas. "I don't mean looting. The treasury can supply silver or if necessary issue scrip for the troops to buy food with."

"Can they, milord?" said Lord Tadai in a bland voice. "We don't have any idea what the terrain between here and Shengy is like. It may well be jungle—or desert."

Tadai and Royhas were rivals if not precisely enemies. Royhas had gained the initial advantage and forced Tadai out of the administration over a year ago, but as a result Tadai had been available to join the army as Garric's chief civilian administrator. He'd spent quite a lot of time in close company with the prince, and it was obvious that he hoped to parlay that association into an advantage over the chancellor.

"We have reports for the region a hundred miles south of Valles," said Master Baumo, a senior clerk in the tax office. "Preliminary reports, that is, and I must admit that these were surveys at three or four points only, not real coverage of the area."

He licked his lips and scowled at the blotched parchment in his hands. It was a palimpsest, a sheet being reused after the original writing had been scraped off with a pumice stone. Apparently it hadn't been erased as well as Baumo now wished.

"Still, the reports suggest smallholdings, scattered villages, and quite a good supply of timber for shipbuilding," he finally continued.

"What bloody use is shipbuilding to us now?" Lord Zettin shouted. "By the Lady, man, use your—"

He caught himself and closed his mouth. Sharina glanced sidelong at the former admiral; his face was pale and his eyes were fixed on the far wall. He must've been aware that she—as well as everybody else in the room—was watching him, but only the jump of a muscle below his right eye proved that he wasn't a statue.

"If what we just saw was a real scene and not a, an allegory . . . ," Garric said quietly. "Which we won't know until Tenoctris is able to discuss the matter, of course. But if it was real and the Last are present in the numbers we saw, then they badly outnumber the whole royal army. Even if we could take the army to where the Last are appearing, in Shengy or wherever."

"Well, they can't get to us either then, can they?" said Lord Holhann, the commander of the Valles garrison, in a harsh voice. He'd been frightened by the wizardry and he was letting out that fear in the form of anger. "Let 'em have Shengy! It was never part of the kingdom except maybe in name. If we can't reach them, then they can't reach us either."

Sharina glanced back to see if Cashel would speak. Seated as she was, she couldn't see him for the lesser functionaries standing in the way; and anyway, she knew Cashel wasn't the person to volunteer that sort of information to a group of educated people.

"What Lady Tenoctris said last night . . . ," Sharina said. There was no point in explaining that Tenoctris had spoken to Cashel and he'd passed the information on to her. "Is that the Last don't need food in the sense we do. They won't be stopped by the lack of supplies along the route from Shengy to the north and western isles, what's now the settled rim of the continent. Though the sheer distance will delay them, of course."

Half a dozen people began speaking, none to any point Sharina could make out. The door at the end of the room opened. Nobody seemed to notice except Sharina, who caught movement at the right corner of her eye and turned to focus on it.

A figure the height of an adolescent boy stepped between the pair of Blood Eagles in the doorway. Sharina blinked. The guards were shoulder-to-shoulder; there wasn't space to walk or even to slide a napkin between them.

At first glimpse the figure seemed to be wearing a shirt and breeches of goatskin, but that was his own hide: he was a brown-furred aegipan, with hooves instead of feet and two tiny black horn buds peaking up from the tousled hair on his head. He carried a sheathed sword.

"Hey!" shouted Lord Attaper, shoving himself between Garric and the creature. "Keep him away from His Highness!"

"I am Shin," said the aegipan in a musical tenor. "I am the emissary of the Yellow King."

One of the Blood Eagles tried to grab Shin from behind. The aegipan moved slightly, and the guard's hands closed on air. The other man drew his sword and cocked it back for a slash that would cut Shin in half.

Sharina had sprung to her feet. Even before her chair could topple to the floor, she seized the guard's sword arm.

"Wait!" she cried. "Didn't you hear? He said he's from the Yellow King!"

"THE YELLOW KING'S a children's story, a myth!" Attaper protested, his sword bare.

Sharina let go of the man she'd grabbed, but she continued to face the guards with her hands on her hips. They'd sooner have charged a phalanx of pikes than defied her.

"Gently, milord," Garric said, touching the back of Attaper's right hand to prevent an accident which the commander would deeply regret afterward. "So are aegipans, you know, but that doesn't prevent this one from seeming to be real."

He stepped past, which Attaper probably wouldn't have allowed if he hadn't been so taken aback by what was happening. There were guards outside the door who should've prevented *any* intrusion, let alone an intruder carrying a sword into the presence of Prince Garric. . . .

"Panchant's *History of All Nature* claims that aegipans inhabit the mountains of the Western Continent," Liane said primly. She was close to Garric, moving so perfectly in step with him that he'd been aware of her only as a blur since his vision was tightly focused on the aegipan. "Of course, there's no reputable evidence *of* a Western Continent and many geographers deny that one exists."

The aegipan—Shin—was grinning. Seen face-on he looked almost human, but when he turned to dart glances around the hall, his long-jawed profile was that of a beast.

"The Yellow King has awakened," he said. His voice

seemed very full to come from so small a chest; but then, a bullfrog was louder still and a great deal smaller. "He's sent me with an offer to save the men of this day—if you have a true champion among you."

"Your Highness," Attaper said, "*please* don't stand so close to the creature, not while he's got the sword." Harshly he added to Shin, "You then, give me the sword. No one but the prince's bodyguards go armed in his presence!"

"Take it and welcome, Lord Attaper," Shin replied, holding the sword hilt-first toward him. His tongue lolled out. Garric couldn't judge from the aegipan's unfamiliar face whether there was as much mockery in his expression as there would've been in a man doing the same thing. "I have no business with arms. I'm only a messenger."

Attaper snatched the sword away. A belt of heavy black leather was wrapped around the scabbard, but there wasn't a dagger or other equipment to balance the blade's weight on the wearer's right side. Though the grip was as rough as shagreen, to Garric's glance it seemed to be of the same dark gray metal as the cross guard and ball hilt.

"What sort of champion?" Sharina asked. Garric was amused at the way his sister's clear tones cut through the babble. *It's as bad as the inn's common room during the Sheep Fair, though the accents here are more cultured.* "Do you mean a soldier?"

The Yellow King whom Rigal and other poets of the Old Kingdom described was certainly a myth. During the Yellow King's blessed reign, men and women ate fruits that sprang from the soil without planting. There was no winter or blistering summer, only balmy days that mixed spring with early fall; all was peaceful and golden.

At the end of ten thousand years the Yellow King had departed, promising to return when mankind needed his help again. Before he left, he taught agriculture and writing that men might continue to exist and to record the Yellow King's great deeds. From then till this day, the lot of mankind has been ever harsher, ever more miserable, and men would not be saved from that decline until the Yellow King returned.

So much was myth; Garric knew that as clearly as Attaper did. But there *had* been a government of men before the first recorded government. There were legends about the Yellow King on every island of the archipelago, even among the Serians and the swarthy folk of Shengy whose languages were nothing like those of the remainder of the Isles.

Perhaps those who'd ruled in the days before the climate changed had all called themselves the Yellow King; the confusion of title might've concealed the details of their succession. The geographer Stane had thought so. As for Garric personally, it seemed to him that Stane or others with other guesses *might* be right. Certainly *some* truth underlay a universal pattern of belief.

Besides, Garric wanted to believe; and if every word of Rigal's myth was true and the Yellow King would return to save mankind in its greatest crisis—so much the better. He'd listen to Shin and hope.

Though the aegipan stood in place, his split-hoofed feet tapped a complex rhythm on the slate flooring. The tiny motions made his body seem to tremble, but there was nothing frightened in his hairy, grinning face.

"It's up to the men of this day to pick the champion they send to the Yellow King," Shin said. "The champion must surmount all the tests facing him, though, so it behooves you to choose well."

He lifted his legs as though he were jumping, but his head didn't move; the hooves clacked down together, hammering a period to his words. *Had he made a visual pun?*

Shin looked from Sharina to Garric. His brown eyes, as solid as chert, changed into caves that sank infinitely far into the earth. Garric felt himself stiffen; the ghost in his mind snatched at the hilt of his ghostly sword with a curse.

"So, Prince Garric?" the aegipan said. "Aren't furry myths from the Western Continent permitted to make puns?"

"What sort of champion?" Garric said, repeating Sharina's question in a tone of command. "What sort of tests will the Yellow King put to him?"

Shin sees my thoughts! And of course he did, but there was

no point in saying that or worrying about it. Garric didn't try
to deceive the people he dealt with, except by the sort of soft-
ening that made human relationships possible. There were
generally ways to refuse requests that didn't involve saying,
"No, you're too stupid for that post," or, "You'd turn the occasion into a disaster, you overbearing shrew."

"The Yellow King will not test the champion, Prince,"
said the aegipan, "but the way to the cave in which the
Yellow King slept will be hard. Perhaps too hard for any human, eh?"

Shin's long black tongue waggled in silent laughter.
Garric felt his face harden, not at the mockery but because
of the evasion.

Before he could speak, Shin continued, "The Yellow King
sent the sword Lord Attaper holds for a test. Its blade is
sharp enough to shave sunlight and so hard it cannot be
dulled or broken. The one who takes it from its sheath is the
champion whom you must send."

"Done, by the Shepherd!" cried Attaper, one hand on the
sword hilt and the other gripping the scabbard. His powerful
forearms bulged. Nothing else moved.

Attaper's face flashed through shock, then anger, and
finally to a grim determination that an enemy would find
more daunting than rage. His hands blotched with strain and
the cords of his neck stood out . . . and still he could not draw
the sword.

Carus threw his head back and laughed with the joy of a
passionate man seeing his dreams answered unexpectedly.
"The Sister take me if he hasn't come for us, lad!" he chor-
tled. *"They'll none of 'em see what you and I see, you know
that!"*

Garric had to keep his face still though he wanted to laugh
along with his ancient ancestor. Attaper would think he was
being mocked—

But it was nothing like that. Garric ruled because it was
his duty, but nothing could make him comfortable as a king.
He relished the times when the safety of the kingdom

required him to be a man, as he'd shown when he defeated the Corl champion in single combat.

And Carus was right: the others in the room wouldn't see it. . . .

Attaper's face was dark red. He swayed, and still the sword remained in its sheath. Suddenly he relaxed, bending slightly forward as he gasped for breath. His lips moved, but he couldn't manage audible words; he continued to hold the sword.

There was a chorus of pointless chatter. Several military officers tried to take the sword from Attaper; he shrugged them off angrily.

"Milord?" said Cashel. "May I try?"

Surprised, Garric glanced toward the back corner of the room and saw what he should've expected: Tenoctris was upright with Liane close by her side holding the quarterstaff. Cashel wouldn't have left his self-appointed post unless he were sure his presence was no longer necessary.

Attaper looked up, but the snarl in his eyes faded when he saw who'd spoken. It was no sign of inadequacy to own that Cashel or-Kenset was stronger than you were. . . .

"Aye, you're the man for it," said Attaper in a ragged voice. He straightened and held the sword out to Cashel. Those closest, all but Garric himself, backed away.

The aegipan didn't move either. He looked at Cashel and said, "Oh, a strong one, a very strong one."

The words were true enough and the tone was respectful, but Garric heard laughter—or thought he did. Shin's tongue waggled again. *Yes, laughter beyond a doubt.*

"Garric?" said Cashel, cocking an eyebrow at his friend.

"You'll pull it out if it can be," Garric said, feeling suddenly awkward. He didn't want to embarrass his friends; but if he'd understood what the emissary meant and the others didn't, then he *was* the right man, wasn't he? The champion? "If there's a trick, though, give it to me and I'll try."

"What sort of trick?" said Lord Holhann peevishly. He was talking toward a corner of the ceiling, apparently speaking simply to hear his own voice. "Is there a catch in the hilt, is that it?"

"All right," said Cashel without concern. He wiped his left hand on his tunic and grasped the scabbard just below the cross guard; then he wiped his right hand the same way and closed it on the hilt. He began to pull.

The room was so nearly still that the guard muttering to his mate, "I seen him lift a whole shipping jar of—" boomed as though he were shouting. The Blood Eagles weren't picked for their social skills, but even so the fellow shocked himself silent before Lord Attaper could deal with the intrusion.

Nothing moved. *Like an ox trying to pull an old oak from the ground,* Garric thought, and for a moment he wondered if Cashel would succeed after all. When they were growing up together he'd known his friend was strong, but how *very* strong Cashel was had become a continuing source of amazement in more recent times.

Still, nobody'd seen Garric the innkeeper's son as a likely candidate for Lord of the Isles either.

Cashel gave up, blowing his breath out like a surfacing whale. He breathed in great sobs.

"My, you *are* a strong one," Shin said, this time with no hint of mockery. "Are there many like you in the world of this time, Master Cashel?"

"There's no one like Cashel," Garric said harshly. Cashel bobbed the hilt toward him, still too wrung out to speak; he took it. "No one, Master Shin!"

Garric examined the sword. The rough metal hilt felt dry and only vaguely warm. The scabbard seemed an ordinary one of stamped tin decorated with a geometric pattern in black enamel. Presumably there were laths of poplar to stiffen the metal sheathing.

"A little room, if you will," Garric said, gesturing the guards away from the door with a flick of his left index finger; they hopped aside with instant obedience. Garric strode forward, swinging the sword from left to right in a hissing upward slash.

The stroke was burdened with the weight of the scabbard as well as the blade, but Garric was a strong man and on his mettle today. The tip crushed through the leather-covered wooden door and the belly of the blade struck the stone pilaster supporting the transom.

Splinters and stone chips flew. A man cried out in surprise and Attaper snarled, "By the Sister!"

Garric drew back his arm. His hand tingled but it wasn't numb, not yet. The ruins of the scabbard dangled from the blade. He'd sheared the tin and stripped much of it away with the wood splints.

The metal of the blade was the soft blue-gray of summer twilight. Its edge was a blackness too thin to have color; it was unmarked, even where it'd gouged deeply into the stone.

Garric looked at the grinning aegipan. The simplest way to remove the smashed scabbard would be to pull it off with his left hand, but sometimes a colorful demonstration is better than quiet practicality. He backhanded the blade against the other pilaster, flinging tin and bits of wood from another crash of powdered stone.

Breathing deeply, Garric turned to face his council. Guards in the outer hall called in alarm through the shattered door, but calming them could wait. Very deliberately he raised the gray-gleaming sword high over his head.

"People of this time!" said Shin, his voice golden and surprisingly loud. "You have found your champion!"

TEMPLE CAME AROUND from the back of the house with his shield slung behind him and, under his left arm, a bundle of poles trimmed from the white shadbush fringing the fields. Ilna turned on the stool where she was working. Before she could speak, the big man tossed the poles aside. With an odd sort of shrug he slipped the shield back into his grip and drew his sword, his eyes on the head of the valley.

By instinct Ilna glanced first at the pattern she was knotting rather than to what Temple had seen. Certain there was no danger she'd missed, she raised her eyes to the distant slope and saw Karpos coming toward them with ground-devouring strides that were just short of a lope.

His apparent haste didn't mean there was a problem: that was the hunters' regular pace when they weren't stalking or adjusting themselves to Ilna's shorter legs. Asion would be watching the back trail.

Temple slipped his sword back into its sheath. "I wasn't expecting them to return by that direction," he said softly. "They'll have doubled back on our trail to mislead the Coerli if they notice that humans have observed them."

"Yes," Ilna said, resuming her work of knotting yarn to the frame of previously gathered poles. "Chances are the beasts won't realize their camp's been found. If they do, though, we don't want to lead them straight here or they might wonder what was going on."

She rolled and set beside her the section she'd completed, so that it wouldn't affect her companions by accident. After a moment's consideration, she chose three of the poles Temple had just brought and resumed her work.

It was a complex task, the more so because the front of the house would be part of the pattern against which she'd lay her skeletal fabric. The gray and russet blotches of un-painted wood allowed subtlety that she couldn't have gotten from the wool alone, but using something other than fabric stretched her skills.

Ilna smiled. She liked learning new techniques. Besides, this was in a good cause, the best cause of all: killing cat men.

Karpos joined them. Before speaking, he braced the belly of his bow against his right knee and bent the upper tip down enough to release the loop of bowstring from the bone notches holding it. Rising, he let the yew staff straighten. Left strung, an all-wood bow would crack before long.

"They're not far," he said to Ilna. Asion was on his way down the track now also. "Maybe an hour ahead. No more than that, anyway. And they didn't try to hide their trail."

"Do they still have prisoners?" Ilna asked as she worked,

judging where each strand must go without bothering to look behind her at the wall. The pattern was set in her mind; all she needed to do was to execute it according to that perfect truth.

"No," Karpos said. "Unless they'd gagged them. We'd have heard people if they'd made any sound. Well, Asion would've."

The two hunters believed that Asion's senses were sharper than those of his partner. Ilna accepted their judgment—because the men said so, and because she herself could discriminate between the shades of two threads which anyone else would've claimed were identical. So far as she was concerned, anything either of them said they saw or smelled or heard was as sure as sunrise.

"All right," Ilna said. "Lay the fire then, please. I've crossed two sticks where I want it. And set out half a dozen billets of lightwood for me to use when they come."

She'd almost said, "Good," when Karpos reported the cat men had already killed their captives. If the prisoners were alive, she and the men would have to attack the beasts in their camp. That could be done, she supposed, but it'd add a further complication to the business.

So . . . Ilna hadn't *hoped* the cat men had slaughtered the children they'd carried off, but since they had—they'd be hungry and looking for further prey. She was going to offer some: herself. And if the beasts managed to kill her, then they'd have earned their meal indeed.

"There's a breeze all the way from here to where the cats're camped, mistress," Asion said as he approached. "We had to swing way wide so we didn't wake 'em up early."

"All right," said Ilna as she wove her three poles together with strands of wool she'd picked from the tunic which the woman had died in. "Help Karpos with the wood, then. I don't want a large fire for now, but I need to have plenty of sticks ready so I can feed it as the night goes on. They may take their time coming."

"Not them, mistress," said the hunter as he passed his partner returning from the woodpile. An extension of the roof overhang sheltered it at the back of the cabin. "But I'll get more wood."

"Have you further directions for me, Ilna?" Temple asked pleasantly. He rested on one knee, polishing his dagger with a swatch of suede he'd brought from the hamlet where they'd found him. He'd used the short blade to cut and trim the lengths of brush; the sap oozing from the layer of inner bark smelled faintly acid.

"No," Ilna said, but she glanced around to be sure of her statement. "I have enough poles."

"Very well," he said, rising and sheathing his dagger. "Then I'll bury the goats and donkey."

Ilna frowned. After providing her with the first bundle of poles, Temple had dug a deep trench and buried the dead family. She'd been amazed at how quickly he worked with only the tools they'd found here at the farm: a dibble of fire-hardened oak, a pick made from goat antler, and a stone adze which he'd used as a mattock.

"We'll be leaving tomorrow morning at the latest," she said. "Probably tonight. If the smell disturbs you . . . ?"

"No, Ilna," Temple said with his familiar slight smile. "The smell does not bother me. Animals deserve courtesy too, though, if we have time to grant it to them."

"*We* didn't kill the goats," Ilna snapped. "They're on the cat men's conscience, or they would be if the beasts had one!"

"All life is the same, Ilna," Temple said. "And we have time. But if you'd rather I not, I will not."

"Do as you please," Ilna said. She was furious with herself for having started an argument over *nothing,* an insane nothing. "As you say, we have time."

Temple gathered his tools and walked toward the dead animals. Ilna wound and knotted, seething inside.

Killing cat men was the only thing that mattered now. And she was about to kill a few more of the beasts.

Chapter

4

GARRIC'D HUNG HIS belt with sword, dagger, and wallet over a finial of his chair back before he sat down. Carus winced every time the descendant whose mind he shared disarmed himself in a public gathering, but Carus wasn't in charge—and he didn't like civilian gatherings to begin with.

"Being in the middle of soldiers is fine, though," the king's ghost said, grinning. *"Even if they're enemy soldiers. I know the rules we're playing by."*

Garric stepped toward the chair. It hadn't fallen over, probably because Liane had put her hand on the back to keep it from tipping when he shoved it back. He held the aegipan's sword high but now he was just trying to avoid shaving pieces off those around him. The blade was as sharp as Shin claimed, even where the edge'd notched the stone.

"Give His Highness room!" shouted Attaper, who seemed to've recovered from his strain. "Back away, I don't care who you are!"

Garric glanced at the guard commander, wondering how he'd taken the fact his prince had figured out a trick he'd missed. Attaper caught his eye and winked, grinning ruefully.

"Careful!" Garric said, drawing his own sword left-handed and setting it on the table. *Duzi, this was no job to be doing in such a crowd, half of whom had no more experience with weapons than they did with Serian philosophy!* Its watermarked blade shimmered in light through the clerestory windows.

Garric had carried that sword into more fights than he could say for certain; it'd served him well. Seeing it alongside the weapon the aegipan had brought was like comparing his father's inn to this palace.

Holding his scabbard in his left hand, Garric slid the new sword home with no more than the usual faint *zing* as the side of the blade rubbed the stamped bronze lip. He shook it slightly to see how loose it was in the new sheath; there was no more play between the blade and wooden battens than there'd been with the sword it'd been made for.

"Are you surprised, Prince Garric?" asked Shin, who was standing as close to Garric's left side as Liane was to his right. Attaper and the guards wouldn't have dared object to Liane's presence, but the aegipan must move like water in a brook. "The Yellow King forged it for the human champion to carry, after all."

"Then . . . I'm meant to use it?" Garric said, trying to keep the desperate eagerness out of his voice. The emotional jolt he'd gotten from the implied offer came more from Carus than from Garric's own soul, though the innkeeper's son had become enough of a warrior himself by now to feel a touch of greedy desire when he looked at the gray perfection.

"If you wish, you can offer it back to the Yellow King when you reach his cave," Shin said. "Until then at least it's yours—though you have to reach his cave, after all."

"Everybody sit down, please!" Cashel said. One of the clerks standing near the wall flung his document case in the air. Even Garric jumped—he wasn't sure he'd ever heard his friend shout in an enclosed room before. "And be quiet."

Tenoctris stood on the bench where she'd been resting. The extra height allowed her to see and be seen by everybody in the hall, but it didn't help her be heard over the confusion. Cashel had done that. He stood on the floor in front of her, looking a trifle embarrassed at the way everybody stared at him.

Garric grinned. For somebody who needed to be heard, the next best thing to having the strongest lungs in the borough was to have a friend with the strongest lungs in the borough.

"Thank you," said Tenoctris. She dipped her head in a tiny nod of satisfaction. "Garric, this isn't the portent I expected—I thought the image I saw in my scrying stone was allegorical. It wasn't. You must go with him."

"Prince Garric has a kingdom to rule," Tadai said. "Lady Tenoctris, I greatly respect your judgment, but in this crisis it'd be irresponsible for the prince to go off to—we don't even know where to!"

"Milord, he must," Tenoctris said. She was a tiny woman who looked now like a bird chirping from its perch, but just now she had a presence that no one else in the room could've equaled. "Or there *won't* be a kingdom for him to rule. The Last will be the only men in this world."

"I'm planning to go, Tenoctris," Garric said quietly. "I planned to from the first."

Carus grinned broadly in Garric's mind, waking Garric's grin as well. *And maybe even a little before I* knew *I was the champion. . . .*

He felt enormous relief. The weight of the crown had been lifted away from him. He was free to be himself again; just a man, a person who made decisions for himself alone.

"I felt that way in battle," Carus said, his face unexpectedly somber. *"That was the only time I was free of being king. But it made me look for battles to fight, lad, and that made me an even worse king than I'd have been if I'd worked harder at the job."*

"How many troops will you be taking with you, Your Highness?" Attaper said in a coolly matter-of-fact tone of voice.

"Ho, and you'd trick the Yellow King into accepting an army when he sent for a man?" said Shin in a trill of golden mockery. "Is that what you think, Lord Attaper? The champion will travel alone, as he knows and as you know also."

"He can fight alone in your tournament or whatever it is," Attaper said harshly. "As he did with the cat men, since he insisted. But he'll have an escort to get there!"

Three voices swelled toward a babble—and cut off sharply when Cashel cracked the butt of his staff twice quickly on the stone floor. "Tenoctris needs to talk!" he said, not quite as loudly as he'd spoken before when he called to get attention, but loudly enough.

The old wizard straightened, using Cashel's shoulder to brace herself. She'd bent forward to speak into his ear so he could hear her. She flashed Garric a smile when their eyes met, but he thought he saw sadness under the bright expression.

"Our own efforts won't save the world for the things *of* this world," Tenoctris said. When she began to speak there were still whispers rustling, but at the first words of her thin voice they stilled. "Lord Tadai—"

Her eyes, momentarily those of a hawk rather than a sparrow, lighted on the commander of the Blood Eagles.

"—and Lord Attaper especially, all of you: we must have help. The Yellow King has offered an alliance at a price we can pay."

The aegipan, quivering in place as his hooves danced, made a half-bow of acknowledgment. The coarse black hairs of his beard seemed to twist more tightly together as though they had minds of their own.

Tenoctris dipped her head in response, smiling wryly. "The world is more important than the kingdom, milords," she said. "If we fail, every man and Corl and sheep in the world will die. There won't even be worms in the ground, because the Last will smooth and bake and *kill* it."

No one spoke for a moment. Garric nodded, stroking the hilt of the new sword with his fingertips. He said, "Lady Tenoctris, have you anything further to add or may we get down to the business of organizing the government during my absence?"

"One more thing, Your Highness," Tenoctris said. The formality wasn't for humor; she was recognizing that the kingdom did still matter even though it couldn't be their first priority. "We'll also need the help of a wizard far more powerful than I."

Garric started to speak. The old wizard waved the words back with a moue of irritation. "This is no time for pretty words. Yes, I've done things and we've all done things, but now we need help!"

"Sorry," Garric muttered, in apology for what he hadn't said. "What do you want from us toward finding a, the, wizard?"

The thought made him shiver inside, but he didn't let that show on his face. Liane recognized it, though; she shifted slightly so that he could feel the warmth of her body so close to his upper arm.

Garric didn't hate or fear wizardry the way many folk— the ghost in his mind among them—did. Nonetheless, with the exception of Tenoctris herself, the wizards he'd met in the past two years were either unpleasant or dangerous or— very often—unpleasantly dangerous. The disaster that ended the Old Kingdom had been caused by a wizard; the cataclysm that shattered Garric's world into its present confusion had been caused by wizards; and the thought of trusting the safety of the world to a powerful wizard was profoundly disturbing.

He grinned. *We've survived this long by accepting Tenoctris' judgment. I'm not going to stop doing that now.*

"All I need at the moment is your permission to leave," Tenoctris said, flashing a brief smile that returned her face to its usual cheerful optimism. "I'd like to go to the Temple of the Mighty Shepherd. When I've done that, perhaps I'll have a better notion of what the next step will be."

"That temple's in ruins, is it not?" Liane said. She stiffened in sudden embarrassment. "That is, it was before the Change. I'm sorry, I shouldn't have spoken."

"It was in ruins in my day too, dear," Tenoctris said. "I intend to meditate or perhaps dream, I suppose, rather than sacrifice. And if I may . . ."

She touched Cashel's shoulder again. He didn't turn to look at her.

"I'd like Cashel to accompany me," she went on. "In part because he *is* a mighty shepherd."

"If Cashel agrees—" Garric said, but it was toward his sister that his eyes shifted. She gave a quick nod of agreement, though her expression had frozen for a moment. "—then yes, of course."

"Sure, Garric," Cashel said quietly. His staff was upright beside him, as usual. "I like to help, and you don't need me here."

Though maybe Sharina does, Garric thought, but that was a matter between her and Cashel; and anyway, she'd agreed.

Tenoctris stepped carefully down from the bench, bracing herself on Cashel's arm. Garric looked around the assembly. "In that case, counselors," he said, "let's rough out the details of the administration during my absence."

A thought struck him; he glanced toward the aegipan at his side. "That is . . . how much time do I have to prepare, Master Shin?"

Shin chuckled, making his beard dance though his feet were still for the moment. "You have all the time you wish to take, Prince Garric," he said. "But I would advise you not to take very long if you wish your world to survive."

"OH, SHEPHERD, HEAR me!" Ilna wailed hoarsely. "Guide my husband to the Realm of Peace. Protect him with Thy staff."

Her voice had a right to crack: she'd been calling in false grief since just before sunset and by now they were well into the fourth watch of the night. The moon had set, and within an hour the light that precedes the dawn would tinge the northeastern sky. Despite Asion's assurance, the cat men had waited.

Ilna glanced at the pattern her fingers were knotting and unknotting, just to keep themselves occupied during the delay. They wouldn't wait much longer, though.

"Oh, Lady, my daughter was a good child," she cried. "Hold her safe beneath the hem of Thy mantle."

To the best of Ilna's knowledge, the cat men couldn't understand human words any better than she could make sense of their yowls and shrieks. Though her present grief was as false as the belief in the Great Gods that she implied, she sang real words because they were part of the pattern she was weaving.

Chalcus would've understood what she was doing, and perhaps Merota would as well. Merota had learned from her and Chalcus to see the patterns that most people didn't, couldn't, see. Patterns in the way a sword blade shimmered, patterns in the way leaves rustled in a forest . . .

Merota was a clever girl, smarter than either her or Chalcus, rich and *educated*. She'd have gone far.

Merota was dead, her skull crushed by a cat man's axe. Chalcus was dead, pierced through by several points; dead on his feet but nonetheless cutting down his slayers and the girl's before he let himself fall. And Ilna os-Kenset had died also, killed by the same strokes that slew her family.

She caught herself. Her eyes were open, but for a few instants she'd seen only the past. The wordless cries which grief had torn from her memory were real.

Ilna tossed three billets of dry, pitchy pine knots on the sunken fire, the lightwood she'd kept ready for this moment. The waiting was over.

"They're coming," she said, speaking to the hidden men. She grasped the hem of the blanket she'd hung across the front of the cabin and waited.

The fire flared, its sudden light winking from the eyes of the four cat men who'd approached the edge of the farmyard. One of the beasts snarled in angry discomfort, rising from his crouch. He carried what looked like a fishing spear, its two springy points spreading from where they were bound to the shaft. The thorn barbs were on the inside so they'd grip instead of killing the victim quickly.

The Corl stalked closer, bending his course to skirt the fire by more than his own height. His three companions rose also, though they were careful not to rush past their leader. The beasts hunted in packs, but from what Ilna'd seen they weren't much more social than cockerels. They fought for dominance frequently, brutally, and to the death . . . which saved Ilna a little trouble, though a kind of trouble she didn't mind.

The Coerli didn't like fire, but they'd followed the haze of smoke back to this farm, which they must've thought was abandoned. The blaze in front of Ilna wouldn't keep them from leaping on her from the sides, of course.

She smiled with anticipation: the fire was to illuminate, not to protect.

The leader growled deep in his throat. His muscles were heavier than those of an ordinary warrior and his mane had begun to sprout, but that was true, though to a lesser degree, of the three Coerli accompanying him. In a fully fledged pack the chieftain limited the amount of meat his warriors ate, since without it the males remained sexually neuter and didn't threaten the chief's dominance. This hunting party probably ate *only* meat, so the members were on terms of dangerous equality.

The beasts weren't going to live long enough to kill one another in dominance battles, however. Ilna jerked the blanket from its pegs, uncovering the pattern she'd laid against the wall.

"Now!" she cried to her companions. Her right hand loosed the silken lasso she wore around her waist in place of a sash.

The leading cat man had started his leap, his arm poised to pin Ilna's throat with his spearhead, before he glimpsed the pattern of threads against the wood in the bright flames. His muscles locked, spilling him onto the ground sideways. The beast directly behind him fell also, as did the one who'd stayed farther out in case Ilna tried to run.

Ilna's lasso looped from her hand, filling a pattern she knew though she didn't yet see it. The cat man farthest to the left shrieked like a hawk as he loped toward her. He leaped, a stone axe raised in his right hand and a dagger carved from rootstock in his left. He moved quicker than a human could respond—

He shrieked again, tangled in the noose that hung in the air through which he'd tried to spring. Ilna jerked hard, turning.

The cat man twisted, but the silk's pull spun him into the

cabin wall. He lost his axe at the impact but still had the poniard when he slammed the ground.

He gathered his legs under himself to spring toward Ilna. Temple's long sword slipped in above his breastbone and out through his spine at mid-back.

The warrior's arms spasmed. He coughed a bubble of blood and, as it burst over his face, went flaccid.

Ilna let out her breath in a gasp. Asion rose, withdrawing the knife he'd thrust through the kidney of a paralyzed beast. The head of the most distant cat man was cocked at right angles to the rest of its spine. As Ilna looked up, Karpos wrung the neck of the pack's leader the same way: one palm on the beast's chin and the other at the top of his skull.

Temple wiped his sword with the edge of the blanket which'd hidden Ilna's trap. "Don't look at this," she snapped as she snatched the sketchy fabric off the wall, bundling the yarn and support poles to break their pattern. She didn't want to take time now to untie the knots and coil the strands into a skein.

"I didn't know how powerful you are, Ilna," Temple said as he continued to polish the hard bronze. "You have a remarkable ability."

Ilna shrugged. She supposed she could toss the snare on the fire; it was of no further use, to her or to others. She chose not to do that, though it'd be the most efficient way to rid the world of something that'd be dangerous until it was destroyed.

The wool and the sticks were nothing in themselves, but they'd helped her kill four cat men. She'd disarm her trap, but if she decided not to destroy the materials that'd served her well—who could tell her she was wrong?

"I wondered when the one kept on coming, mistress," Karpos said. He'd scalped the cat men's leader, using his long dagger with the delicacy of a much smaller knife; now he was walking toward the more distant of his victims to take that trophy also. "I guess you just wanted the kill for yourself, huh?"

"No," said Ilna, walking to the body of the beast Temple had stabbed. "My pattern didn't work on him for some reason."

She lifted the cat man by the scalp lock, the ridge of long hair down the back of his neck. One of his eyes was a normal muddy brown, but the other was as milky and dead as a chip of marble.

"Ah," Ilna said, dropping the beast's face in the dirt again. Nothing to be done about a half-blind attacker who didn't see the same pattern as his fellows. Though if she'd adjusted two threads on the far left end of the fabric, she might've been able to—

Well, she'd keep that in mind the next time. There'd be many more next times, until she was dead or all the cat men were dead.

Ilna dusted her palms together, then slipped free the noose with which she'd caught the beast when her pattern didn't work. She'd been afraid that Temple's thrust had nicked the cord, but on examining it she found the blade had entered the chest above her lasso and exited below the back of the loop. The silk was untouched.

If the thrust had been calculated, it was a very pretty piece of work; and from what Ilna had seen of Temple, it'd probably been calculated. "Thank you," she said. "My noose wouldn't have kept him from jumping straight toward me."

She cleared her throat. "And I appreciate you not cutting my noose, either. Though I could've spliced it if necessary."

"There's very little about fabric that you couldn't do, Ilna," the big man said. His voice was pleasant, but he didn't mean the words as a question. "Yours is a remarkable power, whatever you choose to use it for."

"Right now I choose to kill beasts," Ilna snapped. The hunters had wiped their knives on the pelts of the dead cat men. They stood easily, bow and sling in their hands, waiting for her to tell them what to do next.

"We can go straight to the camp and end the business," she said harshly. "Leave your packs; we'll come back here."

The hunters exchanged glances. Asion started toward the

forested slope to the northeast. "I'll follow," Karpos said to
Ilna, turning to watch the ridge behind them.

It'd be fully light by the time they reached the cat men's
day camp. That'd be helpful if there was more to do there—
as Ilna suspected there would be.

CASHEL SQUATTED WITH his back against one of the two
columns still standing near the southeast corner of the ruin.
There was a stretch of the stone foundation course for a
mud-brick wall, and the bases of other columns that'd fallen
over. Otherwise, the Temple of the Mighty Shepherd was a
lot of loose stones. Cashel'd seen enough temples by now
that he could guess at what it might've looked like, but that
was just guessing.

Tenoctris sat cross-legged way down at the other end,
where the statue would've been in the days there was a
statue. Cashel was uncomfortable about them being so far
apart in case something happened, nearly two tens of double
paces as he judged. She'd said it'd be all right, though, and
that having him close might be a problem because he was so
solid.

Cashel didn't understand what she meant by solid—sure
he was, but she was sitting on a slab of stone. There were
lots of things he didn't understand, though; he'd do what
Tenoctris said. If more of the Last popped out of the ground
the way they'd come from the pond the night before, well,
he'd see how quick he could get to her. When he had to, he
moved faster than people generally expected.

He held the quarterstaff crossways on his thighs as he
polished it, smiling softly. He and the staff had surprised
people, yes they had. They'd surprised people and things
that weren't people at all.

Sparks of wizardlight sizzled blue above Tenoctris, then
vanished. Cashel watched intently for a moment, but it'd
happened before and not meant anything. At each pop and
crackle the tree frogs fell silent, but they were starting up
again as usual.

Cashel listened to the frogs and the night birds, and he eyed the heavens. Once already tonight a shrew had perched on his foot and chittered as it ate a beetle; the wings and then bits of the beetle's shell had tickled his bare skin before the shrew'd scurried off into the night to find something else to kill. Shrews were bloody little fellows, for all that they weren't much longer than a man's finger.

Tenoctris mumbled, or maybe somebody else spoke near where she was. Nobody Cashel could see, anyway. The old wizard's eyes were closed. She wore a calm smile, but Cashel'd seen her smile when she thought Evil was going to overwhelm her and everybody she cared about. Folks who thought courage had something to do with being willing to hit other people needed to spend a little time around Tenoctris.

There were wispy clouds in the high sky, but mostly the stars shone clear. A shepherd spends a lot of time looking at the stars while other people sleep. They're his clock as well as his companion: they keep better time than folk in the palace get from the clepsydra dripping water and a trumpeter blowing the hour when a cup filled and turned over.

The constellations were pretty much what he was used to. The Seven Plow Oxen were strung out a little, and a middling reddish star was in the place of the blue one in the head of the Farrier's Hammer; nothing more major than those things.

Except in the south, where the new white star was so much brighter than anything but the moon. Cashel looked over his shoulder at it, then looked back. He figured that star was part of the problem, but it wasn't for him to worry about till somebody told him it was.

A cardinal started singing merrily, though what it was doing up so late was more than Cashel could guess. It'd been dark for hours; Duzi, it'd been dark by the time Tenoctris stopped the gig here on the eastern outskirts of Valles.

Of what Valles was today, anyhow. Cashel was pretty sure that when he'd been driven through this part of the city before the Change, it'd been solid with many-story tenements.

Cashel didn't miss the buildings—they were dovecotes for people; he couldn't imagine how folks were willing to live like that—but he sort of wondered what'd happened to those who'd been in them. He hoped they were all back in their own time, as happy as anybody could be in tenements.

It was probably good there weren't as many people around as he'd expected, partly because wizardry bothered folks. What Tenoctris was doing now seemed a lot like wizardry, even if she wanted to call it dreaming or meditation or whatever. The sparkles and the sounds showed that.

The other reason—and probably the bigger one—was that this way folks didn't bother *her*. There was no way Cashel could've kept everybody away from Tenoctris if they'd been in the middle of buildings full of people, especially since he had to stay a distance back from her himself. Sure, most folks were scared of a wizard, but there'd always be a few, kids especially, who weren't or were more curious than scared.

A girl stepped into the temple from the front. She looked at Cashel when she passed, though she didn't say anything or even look interested. She was heading toward Tenoctris.

Isn't that just what you get when you tell yourself things are going fine! Cashel thought as he scrambled to his feet. "Ma'am?" he said. "I wish you wouldn't go any closer to my friend. She's busy with, well, a thing that she's got to think about really hard."

The girl stopped in her tracks and turned to stare. She was older than he'd thought, but still not very old; sixteen, maybe, was all. She had flowing dark hair that spread like a cape over the thin shift that seemed to be all she was wearing.

"You can *see* me?" she said. Her voice was as thin and high as the trilling of chorus frogs.

"Yes, ma'am," Cashel said. She had very fine bones; that and the way her legs moved made him think of a bird. "I know I'm not from around here, but I'd really be grateful if you didn't talk to Tenoctris till she's done."

If the girl didn't listen to him when he was being polite, he guessed he'd hold her. It wasn't something he wanted to do, grab a stranger and make her do something because he was stronger, but Tenoctris was depending on him.

The girl just stared. Had he done something wrong? "Ah, my name's Cashel or-Kenset," he said. "I'm just here with my friend Tenoctris, Lady Tenoctris, that is. I carry things for her."

"You see me!" the girl cried. She touched her hands to her face, covering her open mouth. "It's been . . . why, nobody's ever been able to see me! Not since the flood."

"Ah, flood, ma'am?" Cashel said. "I'm not from Ornifal; I mean, I'm from Haft. I hadn't heard about a flood here, I guess."

"No, the *Flood,*" the girl said. "When the waters covered everything and everyone died."

Her tongue touched her lips; Cashel couldn't begin to read her expression. "I died then, but I didn't go away like the rest of them. I've stayed here for ever so long. I don't know why."

"Ma'am, you're a ghost?" Cashel said. She didn't look like a ghost. He wondered if he could touch her if he stretched out his arm, but he didn't try. It'd be impolite, and anyway it didn't matter.

"Am I?" said the girl. "Perhaps I am."

She licked her lips again. "Your name is Cashel," she said wonderingly. "I used to have a name too. I don't remember what it was, though. It was ever so long ago."

"Do you live around here?" Cashel said. "Stay, I mean, if you're not . . ."

"I think I came here after the Flood," the girl said. He couldn't believe that she was a ghost; she seemed just as real as real. "I don't think I lived here before, but I don't really remember."

She shook her head, then gave him a rueful smile. "I don't remember anything from when I was alive," she said, "except that I had a name. I'm sure I had a name."

A thread of ruby sparks trickled out of the sky to vanish again above Tenoctris' head. She didn't move or even notice it as best as Cashel could tell.

From what the old wizard'd said on the drive here, she

wasn't making things happen any more than the flume makes the water that turns the mill. She just put herself where things would happen and maybe pushed them a bit to one side or the other.

The girl was staring at Tenoctris. "Can she see me too, Cashel?" she said suddenly, turning to face him. Her eyes were very dark, but they seemed like real eyes.

"Ma'am," Cashel said, "I don't know. When she's done we can ask her, I guess."

"Oh, it doesn't matter," the girl said, brushing the thought away with a sweep of her hand. "Nothing matters really, not if you take the time to look at it. Do you—"

She raised a hand and traced the line of Cashel's cheek without quite touching him.

"Do you have feelings, Cashel?" she said coquettishly. "Love and hate, things like that?"

"I wouldn't say I hated anybody, ma'am," he said, feeling a little uncomfortable. Still, the girl wasn't bothering Tenoctris and that was all that mattered. "I've fought people and I guess I will again. People and other things. But I don't know about hate."

"I used to feel things," she said, turning away again. Whatever'd possessed her for a moment was gone now, thank Duzi. "I remember that too. When I'm around people I sometimes imagine I can feel again, but mostly I'm alone."

The ground trembled, though the motion was so faint that afterward Cashel wasn't sure he'd felt anything more than a distant wagon with a heavy load. "Now I feel sadness," the girl said, her eyes fixed on Tenoctris. "Everyone in this world is going to be killed the way the Flood killed everyone in my world."

She looked at him abruptly. "That's right, isn't it?" she said. "I *should* feel sad about that? Or should I feel something else?"

Cashel's lips felt dry. "Ma'am," he said, "that'd be sad, but Tenoctris and the rest of us aren't going to let that happen. It'll be all right."

The girl trilled golden laughter. "Yes," she said, "I remember now. There were scholars in my day who were going to stop the Flood, but the Flood came anyway. You'll see that it doesn't really matter, Cashel. When you look back as far as I do, nothing matters. And you feel nothing."

There was a *pop* near Tenoctris, a dull sound. The air was suddenly clearer, though Cashel hadn't noticed a haze beforehand. The old woman slumped, barely managing to catch herself on her arms.

Cashel trotted to her, holding his staff crosswise before him. Tenoctris looked up and smiled when she heard his feet thumping on the turf. She stayed where she was until he was there to help her up.

"Tenoctris?" he said when he was sure she was all right and firm on her feet. "There's somebody who'd like to meet you."

Cashel looked toward where he'd been standing, but the girl wasn't there anymore. For a moment he thought she might've hidden behind one of the pillars, but that probably wasn't it.

"I guess she's gone," he said in embarrassment. "We were talking while you sat here, is all."

Tenoctris nodded and started toward the gig. She touched Cashel's wrist but didn't really lean on him. "The girl was local, then?" she asked.

Cashel grinned. Tenoctris wanted to know more, but she didn't want to make him feel uncomfortable. "I don't know if she was," he said. "She said she drowned in a flood so long ago that she couldn't remember her name. She looked just like a girl, though. A pretty one."

"Indeed?" Tenoctris said in delight. "The Primal Flood, then? My, that's quite interesting, Cashel. And she'd become the spirit of this place, a *genius loci*."

She smiled. "A *genia loci,* I suppose, since you say she was still a girl to look at."

Cashel shrugged; the words didn't mean anything to him. Not even "spirit of this place."

"She couldn't remember much," he said, looking to both sides as they passed between the pair of pillars that were still standing. "She told me—"

He stopped and took a moment to reframe his words. He said, "I told her that you were going to stop the trouble that was coming now. Like her flood."

"I see," said Tenoctris, looking at him sharply. He guessed she really did see what he hadn't said. "Well, while I myself can't stop the Last, I think I've learned how to get the ally we need."

She paused, still watching him as they neared the gig. "I'll need your help again tomorrow, Cashel," she said. "If you're willing."

"Yes, ma'am, I am," Cashel said. "When will you want me?"

He took the horse's reins in his left hand and gripped the frame of the light vehicle in his right so that it wouldn't skitter forward while Tenoctris climbed aboard. She didn't need his help for that, though.

Tenoctris took the reins. "Around midday, I'd judge," she said as he walked around the back of the gig to get in on the other side. "There are a number of things I'll need, and they aren't all in my apartments. We'll be going to the old tombs in the palace grounds."

"I didn't think people were buried inside Valles, ma'am," Cashel said, mounting with the care his weight required. He was a good load for one horse to pull, though the roads back to the palace were smooth enough and flat so he wouldn't have to get out and walk.

"The palace wasn't part of the city when the tombs were built," Tenoctris said. "The family, the bor-Torials, weren't even Dukes of Ornifal at the time."

She clucked to the horse and twitched the reins; he clopped forward immediately. It looked simple. Cashel was pretty sure if *he* tried it, the horse would either look at him or run off in some other direction.

"Well, I'll help however I can, Tenoctris," Cashel said. He'd have said the same thing regardless, but maybe listening to the girl made him put a little more force into the words.

THE CAT MEN had been sheltering from daylight in a ravine between two knobs of limestone that'd been a little harder than the surrounding rock. They'd built a low dome of boughs broken from the neighboring pines.

"There's caves all over here," Asion said in a tone of mild reproach. "Why d'they want to take the trouble to build a hut, d'ye suppose?"

"Maybe they don't like rock," Ilna said, speaking more harshly than the question required. She looked down at the shelter while lying on a slab of cracked, gray stone. Sun and frost had broken the surface into rough pebbles that anybody'd find uncomfortable, but no Corl could *possibly* dislike rock more than Ilna herself did. "How many are inside, do you know?"

Karpos looked at Asion. The smaller man shrugged. "There's one," he said, "but I don't think more than that. And he's got to be hurt or he would've gone after you with the others, right?"

He and Karpos exchanged glances over Ilna's head. "I figure," said Karpos carefully, "that with just one there and laid up, we don't need to be fancy. Besides, it's broad daylight and they don't like that. I'll go down and finish him off, right?"

"No," said Ilna. "I'll stand in front of the entrance. Asion, start a fire and get a torch going. When I'm in place, throw it onto the hut and I'll stop the beast when it tries to get out."

While they waited, Ilna'd knotted a pattern. It seemed right to use yarn from the disemboweled woman's tunic to dispose of the beasts who'd killed her. It shouldn't have mattered, but there are more patterns than those woven in cloth.

She looked past Asion to Temple. "Do you have an opinion?" she demanded.

"It's a good plan, Ilna," the big man said. He stretched. His sword was sheathed, but she'd seen how quickly he could draw it. "I'll stand with you in case the Corl is feverish and doesn't see as he ought to."

Ilna grimaced, but Temple hadn't said anything she could object to. There was no excuse for her mood. The rock bothered her, she supposed, and being awake all night; but there was something irritating in Temple's attitude. He seemed to be judging her as dispassionately as she'd eye a hen while planning dinner.

Ilna stood and walked half a furlong to the right so that she was at the head of the ravine, facing the hut's entrance. The door was merely a juniper bush pulled into the opening, but it was where the cat man would come out.

It was important to stop him in his tracks. If he headed up the far slope instead of attacking directly, there was no certain safety. Even injured, a Corl was dangerous if you let him pick his time.

Temple paced her, keeping to the right so that he didn't block her view of the shelter. His sword was out and he'd released the strap so that the buckler was free in his left hand. His expression was one of mild interest, as though he was contemplating an attractive landscape.

Karpos stood beside Asion with an arrow nocked. Ordinarily that would've been pointless: the cat men reacted so quickly that arrows were no more likely to hit them than a human soldier'd be knocked down by a flung bale of hay. Sick or wounded, the beast might be more vulnerable, though. Besides, it gave the hunter a way to feel useful.

Smoke trailed up between Asion's hands; he rose and whipped his torch to full life. He'd bound branches to a limb wind'd broken from a scrub chestnut a year or more before.

Ilna met the hunter's eyes but started down the ravine instead of giving the signal immediately. She held the knotted pattern before her, where the Corl couldn't avoid seeing it if he looked at her at all. Only when she'd covered half the distance did she call, "All right, now!"

She expected the cat man to charge out of the dome when she spoke. Indeed, it should've been aware of the humans even earlier, from the sounds they'd made if not their scent as well. The beasts' hearing and sense of smell were sharper than those of any human being.

The shelter remained silent. Asion sent his torch spinning end over end into the woven branches. They'd been drying in the sun for several days, long enough to become tinder. The torch bounced off the dome, but the sparks sprayed from the contact. Pitchy needles started burning.

Still nothing from inside. Ilna walked forward, her face set in angry puzzlement. Brush threatened to trip her at every step, but she kept her eyes fixed on the opening. Her feet could take care of themselves.

Had the beast died, or was Asion wrong about one of the pack staying behind? Or—and this was a real concern—had the cat man tricked them? It could've left the bush in place over the entrance but hidden in the hills above, waiting to strike from behind when the humans were concentrating on the empty shelter.

As fire crowned the dome, the bush flew back from the entrance. "It's coming!" Ilna cried, but for the hunters—and Temple as well, she was sure—that was like someone telling her a warp thread was broken.

A cat man came out of the shelter in a crouch, rose with a snarl, and froze in its tracks as Ilna'd intended that it should. It was two double paces away. A part of Ilna's mind that was never completely absent considered the cat's russet fur and rejected it as too coarse for most weaving. As well use the long strands of aloe leaves.

The beast was female. A kit, probably less than a week old, nestled against her chest.

Karpos' arrow entered through the beast's right collarbone; the flared bronze point punched out below the ribs on the left side. The beast sprang wildly into the air. The shock had broken the pattern's effect, but that didn't matter now. It thrashed, spraying blood from its mouth onto the clumps of wormwood and broom, but it'd been dead from the instant the arrow hit.

Karpos came down the side of the ravine with the quick ease of a chamois. He stepped from one outcrop to another his own height below, instead of skidding and scrabbling the way most people would've done. Ilna smiled coldly: *she* certainly would've skidded and scrabbled.

"The kit is still alive," Temple said.

"I see that," Ilna said. She put the yarn she'd picked out of the pattern in her left sleeve.

The female gave a convulsive shudder and now lay as still as a pricked bladder. The infant continued to suckle, its forepaws—its hands, they really were hands—gripping the long hair of its mother's chest.

Ilna bent forward. The burning shelter was too close for comfort, but she wouldn't be here long. She caught the infant by the ankles. It mewled angrily and twisted to bite her. Even so young that its eyes were still closed, it had the instincts of its breed. Ilna couldn't grab it by the head the way she would've done a chicken.

She rose, jerking the infant away from its mother, and dashed its brains out on a rock. She dropped the little body, backed a step, and scrubbed her hands with grit from the floor of the ravine.

Karpos dragged the female's body back from the fire, then knelt to cut from the base of the neck up to the top of the skull, then back down in a single motion. He slid the point of his knife under the strip and trimmed the scalp lock free of the flesh while he pulled up on it.

Temple was looking at Ilna. She glared at him and snarled, "Do you have anything to say?"

Temple sheathed his sword. "No, Ilna," he said. "The kit was too young to live without its mother."

Karpos set the scalp down and began working his arrow out point-first. He'd have to refletch it, Ilna supposed, but that was the easy part of making an arrow. There was no lack of birds to provide feathers. This far from towns a metal point couldn't be replaced and a straight, properly seasoned shaft was the work of more than a year.

"Do you think that mattered to me?" she said. "I'm going to kill all the beasts if I can. I don't care how old or young they are, all of them!"

"It's possible for humans and Coerli to coexist," Temple said, strapping his buckler over his shoulder again. He looked up and met her eyes.

"I don't believe that," Ilna said, "and anyway, I don't care. All of them!"

Temple said nothing. "Aren't you going to lecture me?" she demanded.

"Not now, Ilna," he said with a friendly smile. "Perhaps another time."

"Perhaps never!" she said.

He shrugged. "Perhaps."

Ilna picked up the dead kit by the scruff of its neck and tossed it into the fire. "Karpos," she snapped. "We'll burn the female too when you've gotten your arrow out. Asion!"

"Mistress?" the smaller hunter said. He remained where he'd been, watching while the others were in the ravine.

"Cut some more brush," she called. "We're going to burn the beasts before we leave here."

"I brought the adze along," Temple said quietly. "It'll cut brush."

He started up the side of the ravine, moving almost as easily as he walked on the level. Ilna followed, though with more difficulty. She was angry at the big man, though she was too logical to imagine she had any reason to be.

And she was angrier still at herself.

THE LINKBOY SKIPPED backward, holding out his short staff so that the pool of light from the lamp wobbling from the end of it fell on the ground where Sharina'd next step. The occasional glances he cast over his shoulder couldn't have done any more than make sure nobody was coming from the other direction. He must've memorized all the paths through the palace grounds, or at least all those on which Prince Garric and his close associates were likely to be walking at night.

"Make way for the princess!" the boy cried. He was just showing off. Three men, probably treasury clerks going home after working very late, had already crossed the path on their way to the gate of the compound; there wasn't any chance they'd obstruct Sharina.

The clerks didn't have a lantern, and with the moon as bright as it was tonight Sharina didn't need one either. Protocol demanded it, though, as protocol demanded the squad of Blood Eagles accompanying her. She might not like either thing—and she didn't, any more than she liked the court robes or for that matter her just-completed meeting with Lady Faries, the commissioner of sewers—but they were part of the job of being Princess of Haft.

"All rise for the princess!" the linkboy said as he hopped up the three steps to the porch of Sharina's bungalow. Lamps hung to either side of the door, and the pair of Blood Eagles waiting there were—of course!—already on their feet.

"I guess we can handle it from here, boy," the senior guard said.

"I have my duties!" the boy said.

"Right, and they're going to include getting a clout over the ear if you don't take yourself off, sonny," said the other guard. He wasn't being particularly unkind, but he sounded like he meant it.

Sharina grinned wryly as she climbed the steps. She too found the boy irritating at the end of a long day. It wasn't completely beyond possibility that she'd have clouted him herself if she had to listen to much more of his piercing self-importance.

Diora, her maid, opened the door holding a candle lantern; there were several lamps burning inside as well. A princess didn't have to skimp on lamp oil the way servants in a rural inn did; or at any rate, a princess's servants were of that opinion.

Diora made a deep curtsy. The formality was for the soldiers; she knew Sharina didn't care for it, but they were both actors for so long as there was an audience. "Master Cashel isn't back yet, Your Highness," she said.

Sharina felt her heart fall; she hadn't realized till Diora spoke how much she'd been counting on hugging Cashel and feeling his calm strength. Cashel made people feel safe. It was more than the reality of what his muscles and other powers could accomplish: his very presence seemed to drive back Evil better than walls of stone or any other device could do. He was a good man, good to the core, and around him you couldn't help but believe Good would triumph.

Diora closed the door. Sharina spread her arms to allow the maid to begin undoing the tucks and ties that bound Princess Sharina into her robes. "Would you like something to eat, Your Highness?" she asked as she worked.

Diora'd been Sharina's maid for as long as she'd been princess. They weren't precisely friends, less because of social status than differing interests, but they got along well with each other. Sharina had other people to discuss Old Kingdom literature with, and Diora no doubt knew folks who shared her passion for association horse racing; but the maid didn't mind doing all the jobs for which another noblewoman would expect a whole phalanx of specialists, and Sharina didn't scream curses or slash her maid across the face with a hairpin because she'd tugged a curl a little too hard.

"No, no," Sharina said. "There's a pitcher and mug on the washstand, isn't there? I just want sleep."

I just want Cashel to hold me, but she wouldn't put that in words to anyone but Cashel himself.

"Oh, yes, Your Highness," Diora said, sounding— probably feeling—shocked at the question. That was like asking the maid if she thought Sharina should wear clothing when she went out in the morning.

Sharina chuckled. So that Diora wouldn't think she was being mocked, she said aloud, "The Pool below the city's turning into a large lake now that the Beltis doesn't have the Inner Sea to drain into. That means the sewers will shortly begin to back up every time it rains."

"Really?" the maid said. "I never imagined that!"

Neither had Sharina, but now the government was in her hands. The best solution to the problem was probably to abandon Valles; the site wasn't suitable for a large city since the Change.

They couldn't do that now, however. The Change had already worked too much disruption. To tear up the capital and displace the government on top of it would probably bring the kingdom down. In the short term, Commissioner Faries and a pair of army engineers seconded to her department said that the Beltis River could be diverted upstream of the city, though that would require many men—perhaps the former oarsmen of the fleet?—and also a rerouting of supplies to the city. Lord Hauk, Lord Royhas, and both Waldron and Zettin would have to be involved.

But that was for another day.

"Now, arms straight up, Your Highness," Diora said. Sharina obediently raised her arms; the maid swept the heavy robes up and off her with a single motion. So neat a job took considerable strength as well as skill. Sharina was very well served, and she knew it.

"What now, Your Highness?" Diora asked as she hung the garment on its wicker form. "Shall I wait till Master Cashel arrives?"

"No, no," said Sharina. "Just go home, Diora. You can take a lamp with you."

The maid laughed. "You think I can't find my way to the barracks with the moon so near full?" she said. "Well, have a good night, Your Highness. I'll be back in the morning."

Ordinarily at least one servant would sleep in the anteroom of a bungalow occupied by members of the royal entourage. Sharina didn't need or want that, and Diora had an arrangement with a pleasant young under-captain of the Blood Eagles. The guard officers slept with their men, but they had separate apartments in the barracks blocks. The situation benefited both mistress and maid.

Sharina left the lamp burning in the anteroom but she snuffed the lantern's wick between her thumb and forefinger before walking through the drawing room to the bedroom beyond. She didn't know when Cashel would be coming in; clouds might've covered the moon by then.

She'd have liked to go with him and Tenoctris, both because they were her friends and because she would *so* much rather be helping the wizard than making decisions about sewers—which she knew nothing about, but which would affect the health and comfort of tens of thousands of people.

What Tenoctris did affected all mankind, today and forever, but it was Tenoctris rather than Sharina who made *those* decisions. No matter how much the older woman denigrated her abilities, Sharina and everyone else trusted her completely.

A set of hair implements was neatly arranged on the dressing table against the outside wall. Sharina took a coarse comb and worked it slowly through her hair. There was a silver mirror, its back embossed in the same pattern as the brushes and other combs, but she left it where it was. Combing her hair was just a way to settle her mind; she wasn't tired after all, now that she was truly alone for the first time all day.

She stepped to the side and looked up at the huge moon. Diora had slid the upper halves of the casements down, leaving the windows open down to the height of Sharina's chin.

She pulled at the comb, working it back and forth on snarls, as she thought about the life she was living now. Wealth and power hadn't made her happier; but Cashel made her happy. If they'd all stayed in Barca's Hamlet, the innkeeper's daughter wouldn't have been allowed to wed the poor orphan boy. Cashel wouldn't have asked her! Sometimes the things you gain from your choices aren't the obvious ones.

The panes of the casement were diamonds the size of Sharina's palm, set in lead. The glass had been blown and rolled out flat before being cut. It was as clear as expert craftsmen could make it, so in daylight she could've looked out with only slight distortion on the boxwood hedge separating this bungalow from the nearest building.

At night and doubled, the casements were at best translucent. When Sharina glanced down, she saw her blurred reflection. Except—

She stepped back and stared at the image. The *images*. She could see herself, but there was someone else with her.

Sharina glanced over her shoulder, raising the comb to strike. She was alone in the room. She peered again at the reflection, wondering if she saw herself in both casements simultaneously. But though she moved, the hazy other seemed to remain steady. She squinted, trying to make out the face of the second figure—

And she was hanging in space. She shouted, dropping the comb as she tried to fling herself back.

Her shoulders hit a wall that wasn't in her bedroom. She was in an apartment with high, peacock-patterned walls and swags of gold cloth. Smiling at her was an androgynous-looking man in a long crimson robe; behind him were two man-seeming creatures of featureless, silvery metal.

"Greetings, darling Sharina," the man said in a voice as smoothly pleasant as his face. "I've brought you here to save you."

Chapter

5

Fine," SAID SHARINA, twisting for a quick glance behind her. She was in a rotunda and had backed into one of the eight fluted gold pillars supporting a dome of crystal and gold above her. From the smooth coolness to the touch of her hand, the pillar might've been real gold. "Then take me back. I don't need to be saved, by you or by anyone else."

"Please, Sharina," the stranger said, spreading his hands palm-upward at waist level. "You're free to go back any time you wish, but I hope you'll first listen to what I have to say."

Sharina considered. She didn't have even the comb for a weapon because she'd dropped it when she began toppling *here*. She often wore the Pewle knife as a talisman under her outer robe, but a meeting with the commissioner of sewers was tiresome rather than being stressful. She'd have taken off the knife and its heavy sealskin belt as soon as she entered the safety of her bungalow anyway.

"Quickly, then," Sharina said, darting glances to either side without seeing anything that seemed to offer a better solution than taking the fellow at his word.

"Of course," the man said. "And I *do* apologize for my presumption, but I had no choice. I'm Prince Vorsan, by the way."

"Quickly, I said!" Sharina repeated. The shrillness of her voice warned her that she was nearing the limits of her control. Vorsan was her height and a bit heavier, but he didn't look muscular. She wasn't sure she could throttle him with her bare hands, but she'd try if she had to.

"I built this asylum because I saw that my world was going to be destroyed," he said, gesturing with his left hand. "Your world in turn is about to be destroyed, so I'm offering you safety and immortality. I've never granted this to anyone else in all the ages in which I've lived here, dear Sharina. Won't you sit down while I explain?"

The outer wall of the rotunda was four double paces beyond the ring of pillars. There were eight doors in the gorgeously painted wall and two impossibly perfect mirrors. Beneath each mirror was a low couch, seemingly upholstered with peacocks' tail feathers to match the walls. The floor was a translucent blue-green. It shone and shifted, suggesting onyx chips or possibly real ocean beneath a smooth, invisible barrier.

"I don't care to sit," Sharina said. She spoke harshly because otherwise her voice might've trembled. It was as much fatigue as fear working on her; in fact, she wondered if this might all be a dream or a hallucination. "Send me back to where I belong, if you will!"

"Please, a moment only, Sharina," Vorsan said, frowning in frustration. "The Last will wash over your world as the seas did mine. There's no way to stop them. Your only hope is to save yourself, and I offer you that safety. You will have food, wine, books."

At each word, he pointed to a different door. The valves had the same golden sheen as the pillars and were molded in high relief. The figures on them were delicate and so perfect they seemed to move.

"And we'll have all eternity to enjoy them," Vorsan continued. "There's no age or sickness or infirmity in this sanctuary which my genius has created."

He smiled. "Try a glass of wine, why don't you?" he said. "I have a thousand vintages, all bottled at the perfect moment."

A faceless silver statue stepped solemnly toward Sharina. On a salver that appeared to grow from its hand rested a squat bottle of green-glazed earthenware.

"No!" Sharina said, reaching behind her for the Pewle knife which *of course* she wasn't carrying. With careful calm she continued, "Prince Vorsan, you've convinced me that you're a great wizard, but I don't want your wine or food. I want to go home."

On the salver which the other metal figure—they weren't statues, clearly—was holding were a round loaf and a slab of cheese the color of old ivory. That figure hadn't moved, and Sharina'd be just as happy if it didn't.

"As you wish, Sharina," Vorsan said. He didn't give a noticeable signal, but the figure with the wine stepped back and froze again into metallic stasis. "Please don't call me a wizard, though; wizardry is mummery or madness. *I* am a philosopher of natural science, achieving my triumphs by knowledge and application rather than whimsical thrusts with powers I don't understand and can't really control."

"Oh," said Sharina, startled and not fully able to comprehend what she'd just heard. Her opinion of most wizards—all wizards except Tenoctris—was in complete agreement with Vorsan's, but she didn't see the difference between wizardry and making statues walk.

After clearing her throat and still not coming up with a useful way to continue that discussion, she said, "Well, I thank you for your concern, Your Highness, but as you noticed, my kingdom—my world, if you prefer—is being threatened by invaders. I have duties, especially in such a crisis, and I need to get back to them."

"Sharina, there's nothing to be done," Vorsan said forcefully. "Will you watch my projections of the end of your world? I've calculated all the factors, just as I did with the Flood. Others tried to stem the waters, but I knew the only hope was to create a cyst in the fabric of the cosmos. I can show you!"

"I'm not interested in seeing your fancies!" Sharina said. "I have duties and I have friends, and I'm away from both of them so long as I'm here! I want to go home, Prince Vorsan."

"Sharina, please try to understand," Vorsan said, opening his hands toward her. "My studies have generally been enough for me, but I've occasionally sought other companions. Never, though, never have I offered what I'm offering you. I want you to be my eternal consort, immortal and immaculately safe."

His crimson robes moved easily as though they were tissue thin, but bronze plates couldn't have concealed his body more completely. She wondered if he was heavier than she'd thought at first.

"Prince Vorsan, I'm asking for the last time," Sharina said, stepping toward her host. The stoneware wine bottle would make a satisfactory weapon, though striking Vorsan down wouldn't in itself get her home. And would the living statues take a hand if she attacked their master?

"Wait!" Vorsan said, holding his left palm up in bar. "Go back, then; I've never wished to keep you against your will."

"How—"

"Stand where you were when you came," he said sharply. The anger furrowing Vorsan's high forehead was the first emotion to break through the mask of waxen good humor he'd been wearing. "Yes, that's right."

She glanced behind her to make sure all was as she remembered it being, then stepped almost against the pillar.

"Now look into the mirror."

"Which—" Sharina said.

"Either mirror!" said Vorsan. "It doesn't matter. Just concentrate. As you did when I brought you here."

The mirror on the far wall of the rotunda was so clear that Sharina had half-believed it was really an opening. She saw herself against the gleaming pillar, her face composed and regal. *What am I supposed to concentrate on?* she thought, glaring at her own fierce eyes—

And she was back in her bedroom, its moon-cast shadows muted after the bright rotunda. The silver comb she'd dropped when she fell toward Vorsan rang on the floor like a bell.

THE CROWD INSIDE the gate must be half the palace clerks and servants besides all the high officials, and judging from the noise coming over the high brick walls there were more people than that in the street outside. Cashel felt a trifle itchy, though the line of Blood Eagles between the spectators and Garric's immediate friends meant he didn't have to use his weight and quarterstaff to keep folks from squeezing against Sharina. It *felt* like he might have to, though.

He had on a pair of tunics which his sister'd woven. They were simpler than the clothes that just about everybody else present wore to see Garric off, but Ilna's work always impressed the people who saw it.

Sometimes Cashel wondered what he'd do when he ran out of her tunics, but the other thing about Ilna's cloth was that it wore like iron. He'd make do. Mainly he hoped that Ilna was all right. She'd had a hard time, what with Chalcus being killed and just the problem of being Ilna. There wasn't much anybody could do about either one.

"Garric didn't want anything like this," said Sharina. She sounded worn and looked worn too, though the first thing anybody thought when they saw Sharina was that she was beautiful. "Word must've gotten out, and people are so afraid of the prince leaving now when everything's happening."

Sharina hugged Cashel's arm and gave him a wan smile. "And they're right," she added. "*I* dread to think what'll happen to the kingdom if he doesn't come back."

She'd still been awake when Cashel returned with Tenoctris from the Temple of the Mighty Shepherd. That wasn't uncommon—they liked to wait up for each other when they'd had to spend the day apart—but Cashel didn't think Sharina slept during the rest of the night either.

He didn't know what was wrong since she hadn't told him. He hadn't asked, of course. Sharina'd let him know when she was ready to. He was sorry to see her looking so tired, though.

"I guess Garric'll come back fine from this trip to see the Yellow King," Cashel said. "He's done harder things. And you'll run things till he comes back just the same as you've done before, with Liane helping and all the other people. There won't be any difference this time."

What he was saying was the simple truth. Somebody as smart as Sharina ought to be able to see it: everybody else, Garric especially, did. But Cashel'd learned that Sharina needed him to say that sort of thing, which was easy enough to do.

They'd kept back from the crush right around Garric, but now a servant came out of the circle of high officials, nodded politely to Cashel, and said to Sharina, "Your Highness, Lady Liane would appreciate you joining her and the prince, if you would."

"Right," said Cashel, smiling. Making a passage for Sharina through folks who were too excited to be polite was something he could do better than most.

Though the servant leading back into the mass of gorgeous tunics and gleaming breastplates didn't do a bad job either. Liane employed two sorts of people for her work as spy master: bookish ones and tough ones. This fellow was as courteous as could be and wore a tunic appliquéd in the latest fashion with a scarlet phoenix, but he wasn't a scholar.

Lord Waldron and two other soldiers were talking to Garric—or talking at him, anyway, because he seemed to be paying more attention to Liane and the small man in leather breeches holding a sabretache—sort of a saddlebag but for him, not the horse—in both hands. Cashel would've expected Attaper to be there too, just because his rival Waldron was if he didn't have a better reason. He was nowhere to be seen, though.

Cashel grinned. He wasn't sure Attaper or Waldron either one thought there *was* a better reason to do something than because the other of them was doing it. Anybody who'd watched two rams in the same meadow knew what was going on, but Cashel didn't have to look any farther than his own heart to understand it.

Garric had people around him on one side and on the other the horse he'd be riding: a rangy brown gelding. It looked strong, which Cashel supposed was the main thing. He wasn't wearing armor for the journey, just the new sword and a wicker shield, but he was a big man regardless and there was a packed bag hanging on either side from the crupper.

The horse made a nasty wheezing sound when it saw Cashel. That probably didn't mean anything, but Cashel didn't like horses in general and there wasn't anything about this one to change his opinion of the breed.

Sure, they moved faster than oxen so you could plow a longer furrow in a day; but they were skittish, you had to feed them grain, and they were apt to take sick for no better reason than the wind changed. Cashel'd take an ox to a horse any day.

He realized his face'd gotten hard; that made him smile all by itself. Imagine letting something as puny as a horse make you angry! And it wasn't as though anybody was asking *him* to ride.

Garric saw Sharina and Cashel coming toward him. "Excuse me, milords," he said, and pushed between Lord Waldron and a younger fellow also dressed in cavalry boots and a short cape.

Putting his arms around his sister, Garric looked over his shoulder and said, "Lord Waldron, would you and your men please give me a moment with the princess and Master Cashel before I take up my new duties as ambassador to the Yellow King?"

He grinned. In that expression Cashel saw the happy young fellow he'd been friends with all his life.

Lord Waldron backed up because he had to and bumped

somebody, which also he didn't have much choice over with things being so tight. He clapped his hand to his sword hilt and shouted, "By the Lady, sir!"

The other fellow was a civilian who Cashel thought had something to do with the roads. "Move aside and give His Highness some room!" Waldron said. "Move or I'll make the room myself!"

The aegipan, Shin, came around from the other side of the horse. Because he was so short, the people crowding didn't pay much attention till his hairy shoulders brushed their bare forearms; then they jerked back, some of them mouthing curses. The little fellow cleared space about as well as Waldron did, and he did it without shouting.

Shin saw Cashel watching and lolled his tongue out. "So, Master Cashel," he said. "Do I remind you of your former charges, then?"

"Sir," said Cashel, "I tended sheep, not goats. There's folks who think they're the same, but they never tended either. And anyway, you're not a goat."

Nor was he. Besides not really looking like one, the aegipan didn't smell any more like a goat than he did a man. Cashel's nose wrinkled as he considered. What his smell most resembled was a chicken, which wasn't anything he'd have guessed before getting this close to Shin.

"Sharina," said Liane, touching the courier's pouch. "You've been busy too, and I haven't kept you informed as I should've done. The Last have appeared at seven other places that we know about, all cities. At Lady Tenoctris' suggestion, Prince Garric has sent urgent warnings to all the cities of the kingdom—"

"I've signed my name to warnings that my able secretary composed," Garric said, putting his hand on Liane's shoulder. She reached up and pressed it firmly.

Liane'd been crying, though she seemed composed now. The powder and rouge on her cheeks—usually she didn't wear makeup—couldn't hide the puffiness around her eyes.

"I simply transcribe what His Highness requests," she said firmly, looking at Sharina. "In any case, we've sent warnings that these appearances have to be crushed immediately and the reflecting pools which the Last are using must be blocked off from the sky. From the star—"

She nodded toward the south. The new white star wasn't bright enough to see in daylight, but everybody knew what she meant.

"—that is. In some cases our messengers have crossed with reports from the localities which've been attacked, as with these dispatches from Erdin."

The courier thrust forward the sabretache, but Liane gestured it away with a flash of irritation. That wasn't any more usual for her than the makeup was.

"Thus far, there've been no reports of attacks in places which we haven't warned, however. We can hope that will continue, but His Highness—"

She broke off and looked at Garric. The silliness of talking about Garric as "His Highness" while she stood there with his hand on her shoulder had choked her.

"Right," said Garric easily. "Sharina, you'll be handling this while I'm gone, but there may not be anything more to do. Still, I thought I'd tell you myself before I left."

"Yes," said Sharina in a funny sort of voice. "I suppose I'll have to delegate my usual duties. I wonder what will happen about the Valles sewers?"

"I can loan you two trustworthy clerks," Liane said, her head close to Sharina's. "They can meet with petitioners and précis requests, though you'll still have to make the decisions."

"Yes, I'd appreciate that," Sharina said in the same low murmur. She looked at Garric again and said in a normal voice, "We've warned the cities, you say; but what if the Last appear somewhere else? There're ponds and pools everywhere, lots of them in places which nobody but a herdsman or a hunter would ever see."

"We're doing what Tenoctris told us to," Garric said with a shrug. He looked worried, though.

"Ah, Garric?" Cashel said. He wasn't comfortable butting into other people's conversations, but this time he knew something that the others didn't from chatting with Tenoctris in the gig. "Ah, what Tenoctris told me was that it isn't just the ponds, it's the ponds in a place with a lot of, you know, power. Wizard power. And those places always draw people or else it's all the people that draws the power. Regardless, if you warn the cities, then you get all the places the Last are likely to come at."

"Lady Tenoctris is very wise," Shin said in his pretty voice. "If you follow her instructions, you will buy enough time for your champion to reach the cave of the Yellow King. Though she knows and you must know that this is only a temporary help. If they must, the Last will march to the northern coast of your continent from the glacier where they arrive. They're on the way now, and they will not stop unless the Yellow King helps you stop them."

"Sir?" said Cashel. "I hope you and Garric have a safe journey; we'll be glad here for any help you can bring us from the Yellow King. But we've fixed other things without his help, and I guess we'll do our best to fix the Last too."

He thumped his staff down on the bricks harder than he meant. A spray of blue wizardlight shot from the top ferrule and made the clouds seem to dance.

Garric laughed and clasped Cashel forearm to forearm—using their left rather than the normal right because of the quarterstaff in that hand. "Watch yourself, Cashel," he said.

"And you watch yourself too, Garric," Cashel said, feeling embarrassed again. "We'll be glad to see you riding back, all of us."

Garric kissed Liane hard but quickly, then put his left foot in his stirrup. The horse whickered. It might've tried to lurch forward if Cashel hadn't seen the look in its nasty brown eye and grabbed the cheekpiece of the bridle. He'd held oxen; holding a horse was no work at all.

Garric walked his mount through the palace gate with a wedge of Blood Eagles clearing a path for him. The crowd outside gave a great cheer.

Cashel put his left arm around Sharina, just holding her. As Shin ambled out at the horse's side, he turned and stared at Cashel. His laughing tongue dangled, and then he too was gone.

ILNA FROWNED. ALL the men working in the barley fields of the valley below were armed. No hearth smoke rose from the village of considerable size nestled beneath the shrine on the western slope. The villagers had moved to a camp of huts made from hides, blankets, and brush on the other side of the valley—but why?

"Mistress?" Karpos said. He knelt nearby while his partner stood a distance back with a bullet in his sling.

Ilna disliked being prodded, but she didn't let the irritation touch her lips. She'd made it clear to the hunters that she'd make all the major decisions and that they could leave if they objected. She couldn't therefore complain if they wanted her to get on with her job.

"We'll go to the village," she said. "The new one. Karpos, leave your bow strung but don't nock an arrow."

She thought for a moment, then added, "And I'll lead. I'm not as threatening as the rest of you."

Temple chuckled. When Ilna looked at him sharply, he said, "People see what they expect to see, Ilna. But often that means that they see very little."

Ilna sniffed and started off, picking a route among the outcrops. The slope wasn't bad, but there wasn't even a track to the new camp. A path leveled with terraces and cuts led to the shrine and the original village.

Her fingers knotted complex patterns as she walked. Mostly she was keeping them—and the part of her mind that most disliked rock—occupied, but the skeletal fabrics she created were a weapon if she needed one.

She thought about Temple's comment and grimaced. *She* wasn't a threat to anybody, so long as they behaved properly.

Most people, much of the time, didn't behave properly. If they became a problem to her, then Temple was right in what he'd suggested. Ilna grimaced again, certain that if she turned she'd see the big man smiling. She didn't turn.

The folk in the fields noticed the newcomers, but for the most part they continued with their work. Whatever had them carrying spears and long knives, it wasn't fear of four strangers arriving in their valley. Two men who'd been pruning olive trees started up the slope; they'd reach the new village a little before Ilna's group did.

"Hello, friends!" Temple called in a carrying voice. This time Ilna did glance at him. He was waving toward the men who hastened up from the field. After a moment one of them waved back.

"Do you know this village?" Ilna said. The crops and the way the people dressed were like those of the community where they'd found Temple.

"Not this particular one, Ilna," Temple said. "Though I saw many like it once."

She nodded curt understanding. The Change had wildly jumbled times, but people in the borough had raised sheep and grown the same crops for as long back as the books Garric and Sharina read told about. The same was probably true here.

Ilna'd gotten past the worst of the broken rock. The remainder of the way to the hut village was clear enough that she could eye the shrine across the valley while she walked.

It was round and, though not large, nonetheless more impressive than she'd have expected here. Most villages made do with a sacred grove or a wooden statue under a thatched roof. Barca's Hamlet didn't even have that, though the shepherds made offerings to the face of Duzi scratched on a hilltop boulder in the South Pasture.

This shrine and the altar in front of it were dressed stone, though the chest-high wall around the sacred enclosure was of fieldstone slabs laid in rough courses. The houses in the abandoned village were also built of fieldstone, but with mud chinking; the roofs were thatched.

The priest's house inside the enclosure was like the rest, though bigger than some. Ilna thought she saw movement behind one of the small windows, but it was too far away to be sure.

For *her* to be sure. "Mistress," said Asion from behind her. "There's somebody in the house by the temple there, and there's somebody in the temple too. Except I don't know that what's in the temple is people."

"What do you mean?" Ilna said, hearing the edge in her voice. "If they're not people, what are they?"

"Mistress, I don't know," Asion replied humbly. "It was just movement I saw, but it didn't seem right."

"Welcome, travelers!" called the eldest of the four men who'd come from the huts to meet them. The pair who'd been in the fields joined them, puffing a little from their scramble. "Have you traveled far?"

All the men had spears, though they were just knife blades bound onto poles with sinews. Each point had a little wicker cover so that nobody'd get poked by accident. The villagers were prepared for trouble, but they made it clear they weren't going to start it.

"We've been traveling for more than a moon," Ilna said. "May we shelter here for the night, or would you rather that we go on?"

If they turned her and her companions away, Ilna would think they were a sullen and miserly lot. She supposed people had a right to be sullen and miserly, because if she started punishing that sort of behavior, it'd be very hard to know where to stop. Besides, it wouldn't help her with her real business in life, killing cat men.

There were women behind the group of men, the village elders, she supposed. There were children, too, some of them watching from trees and rocks higher up the slope where they got a better view.

"We notice that you're traveling with soldiers, mistress," the village spokesman said. He was bent and had a wrinkled face, but there were still streaks of black in his hair.

"They're armed," Ilna said. "We mean no harm to you or any other human, though."

She halted two double paces from the villagers. Her hands were clasped over the pattern she'd woven, but she could spread it in an eyeblink if she needed to.

"Breccon, you're an old fool!" said an old woman who pushed herself through the line of men. Her red and blue striped linen sash was obviously expensive and well made, for all that Ilna sniffed at the garish color choices. "Lady, what my husband means is we're hoping we can hire your soldiers to kill the demons troubling us. They're your body-guards, are they?"

"They're my companions," Ilna replied, more sharply than she needed to have spoken. It embarrassed her to have assumed hostility when none was meant. "We have nothing to do with demons—"

She paused, remembering that she'd just misjudged these people harshly.

"—but what demons do you have, then?"

"Come, bring them in where we can sit like decent folk and explain things," said Breccon, obviously hoping to take charge again. "Ah, we don't have a proper village hall to put you up in, but we can find you room in our shanties if you're not particular."

"We choose to stay together," Ilna said. She was sure by now that the villagers weren't hostile, but if something happened during the night—a fire could sweep through these crowded-together hovels in no time at all—she didn't want to have to search for her companions in the confusion.

"That's all right, Breccon, we'll put them in ours," said the old woman. "I'll sleep with Mirra and Doan, and you can find a place for yourself, I guess."

"Now, Graia—" Breccon said.

Ilna couldn't see the look Breccon's wife directed at him, but he and his fellow elders saw it. His mouth shut and his head jerked back as if he'd been slapped. The fellow next to him, missing two fingers on his left hand, grunted and said, "You can doss with me'n Weesie, I guess, Breccon. For the one night, I mean."

"Well, let's sit down and talk it over," Breccon said, working at being cheery as he led the way between the straggling huts to where broken rock stuck out of the hillside. He paused, looking at the site, then growled, "For the Lady's sake! Some of you bring straw and blankets for our guests to sit, won't you?"

Ilna glanced at her companions. Karpos had his knee in the belly of his bow and was unstringing it; Asion had put the lead bullet back in his pouch and slid his sling staff under his belt. Temple—

That was odd. Temple didn't look dangerous at the moment, though he was a big man even without the very serviceable sword and dagger on his belt. When he'd struck the Corl through, however, he'd been as surely Death on two legs as any man she'd seen besides Chalcus.

A village boy sidled up to him and whispered a request. Obediently Temple stretched out his left arm and let the boy swing from it. An even smaller girl, probably the boy's sister, ran from her mother's side and grabbed on also. The children squealed and laughed as Temple jiggled them with his arm straight out as if they weighed nothing.

Ilna's mind filled with buzzing whiteness.

When she could see again, she was seated on a rock with a folded cape beneath her for a pad. When Temple was sure she was alert, he let go of her shoulders and stepped back. His expression was neutral, but he was watching very carefully.

"Oh, mistress!" said Graia, who'd come back with a bowl of fresh milk. "A touch of sun, was it? Breccon, you fool, why'd you put them here in the open?"

"Nothing of the sort!" Ilna said, embarrassed and therefore even more angry at herself than she usually was. This notch in the slope was indeed sunny, but the day had never been warm enough for that to be a problem. "I was simply dizzy, that's all."

And because it *wasn't* all, and because she preferred embarrassment to lying, Ilna added, "I thought of something. Now, tell me about your demons."

She'd thought about Chalcus and Merota. She could usually avoid that, but seeing children swinging on the arm of a very strong man had brought the past back with unexpected vividness.

Temple went down on one knee beside her; the hunters knelt just beyond him. Personally she'd rather have stood than kneel on broken rock, but the men seemed to be used to it.

The villagers squatted or sat on mattresses they'd brought from their huts. They'd had enough time to gather their household goods when they left the village across the valley. The bowl from which Ilna sipped goat's milk was glazed with interwoven green and white zigzags. She didn't know pottery, but it looked like the sort of piece she'd expect only the richer households in Barca's Hamlet to own.

"The demons," Ilna repeated. She was less forceful than she'd have been if the delay hadn't been caused by her own weakness.

"Well, it's because of a woman named Bistona," Breccon began. The elders were closest to Ilna and her companions, but everybody in the village crowded around. More people were coming up from the fields as the sun dropped lower. "She was a wizard, but she'd never done any real harm before."

"Be fair, Breccon," said the man who'd offered to take the spokesman in for the night. "We were all glad to have Bistona in the valley, and you were too. I recall her finding that necklace of Graia's you were so sure somebody'd stole, down in the big stewpot you don't use but once a year for the Lady's Feast."

Breccon gave his wife a black look. "I still don't see how it got there," he growled.

"Regardless, it was," said the man with missing fingers. "And she's done that for everybody, a scissors or a lost lamb or Pauli, Pauli's son, when he didn't come home. Isn't that so?"

"My boy was still dead!" cried a woman shrilly from the fringe of the crowd.

"Aye, he was dead, Arma," said the man, glancing back and pointing his damaged hand at her. "But you had him to bury, which you never would've done otherwise, him being down in that crevice which even the buzzards couldn't get at. And you were thankful, as you should've been."

"And she was a good mother herself," said the woman who now held the girl and boy who'd been swinging on Temple's arm.

"That's so," and, "None better," came from the villagers without seeming to involve particular mouths. It was as though the breeze had found a voice.

"That was the trouble, I shouldn't wonder," said Breccon. "She was witching warts off her two boys last moon when everything around here went funny. Do you know what I mean?"

His latest attempt to take control had the advantage of returning the discussion to its proper subject. Ilna'd learned over the years that prodding rambling speakers didn't bring information out any quicker, but there'd been times—and this was one of them—when she'd willingly have hung some fool up by the toes if she'd thought it'd help him get to the point.

"Yes," she said aloud. "I've heard it called the Change, but I don't suppose the name matters. It happened everywhere."

"Well, I happened to be walking up to see Bistona then," Breccon went on.

"Right, old man!" said a younger man. "A love spell, was it?"

"You shut your turnip trap, Treelin!" said Graia fiercely. "Unless you want the whole village to learn what I know about you'n your sister. D'ye hear?"

Nobody actually spoke, though Ilna heard several snickers.

"Go on, Breccon," Graia said. "Tell the lady your story."

"Bistona lived just the other side of the hill, you see," Breccon said, gesturing vaguely across the valley. "Not that she wasn't welcome in the village, but she liked a bit of privacy. I was just starting down the path when it all happened. I thought my head was tearing apart, I swear I did!"

"We all remember the Change," Ilna said. "Go on with your story, if you please."

"Well," said Breccon, "around where Bistona sat it got misty on both sides. I heard one of the boys shout something but I didn't think anything about that, with what was happening to me. But then there were two demons! And they ate the boys, they tore them both to pieces and ate them right there."

He made a face like he was swallowing something sour. "Well, I guess they did," he admitted, "but I turned around and ran back to warn people, you see."

"You ran to save your neck, Breccon," said the friend with missing fingers. "*That's* what you did."

"Well, wouldn't you've?" Breccon demanded in a rising voice. He looked at the faces of his gathered neighbors. "Is it any of you who wouldn't have run when he saw two demons?"

Nobody spoke. There were even a few nods of agreement.

"Well, I figured they'd put paid to Bistona too," Breccon continued. "And I did call folks to get out with their spears, though I didn't figure we could do much. They were big as houses, each one, and there was two of them. But then she come over the hill with them beside her like they was puppies."

"Like they was her boys," said a woman who hadn't spoken before. "Seller on one side and Ballon on the other, each holding her hand. Only these didn't have hands."

"Describe the demons, please," Ilna said. She wasn't sure what "big as houses" meant, but she'd get to that next.

"They're snakes on legs," said a man.

"They've got wings too, Chillin," said Breccon, "only they don't fly."

He frowned. "Can't, I guess," he said. "The wings aren't near big enough."

"The bodies're too fat for any snake, Breccon!" another elder objected peevishly. "They're as big around as a horse and not so very much longer than that—in the body, I mean, they got all that tail and neck."

"A moment, good people!" Temple said. Ilna suspected the lungs in that big chest of his could've bellowed much louder, but he certainly made himself heard over the rising chatter. In the stunned silence he went on, "Breccon, are the demons two-legged with beaks like an eagle's?"

"What?" said the old man, just a word to give his mind

time to catch up with the question. His eyes scrunched together for a moment; then he continued, "Why yes, that's them. And they're blue, smooth and shiny and *blue*."

"Aw, that's not really blue, it's gray!" a woman said.

"The one of 'em's blue!" said Breccon. "The other, all right, you could say it was gray, but—"

"Silence!" Ilna said. Her voice was more of a whiplash than Temple's thunder, but she was pleased to note that the villagers quieted down. That was good, and good for them as well; her fingers had already begun knotting a pattern to use if the word alone hadn't been sufficient.

"Temple," she said in the calm. "You recognize these demons?"

"They're wyverns, Ilna," he replied with a nod. "Creatures from the far past of the Coerli. They aren't demons, just dangerous predators; though indeed the Coerli remember them as demons."

Ilna'd never had much concern with the natural world: all manner of things hopping and chirping in hedgerows were to her "little gray birds" and of no more interest than so many clods of earth. Images, though, even images carved in stone, were another matter.

"The base of the statue where we found you," she said. "There were that kind of monsters on it, wasn't there?"

Temple nodded with pleased agreement. "That's right," he said. "Demons attacking the sky-god Huill. But really wyverns. If they're full-grown, they're probably three double paces long and as high at the hips as I can reach stretching my arm up."

"They do as Bistona says," Breccon said softly, looking into his hands. The old man was beyond posturing. He seemed to have sunk into the past, grasping feebly at thoughts that floated past him. "She marched up to the shrine with them. Redmin was the priest of the Lady's Oracle there. The two boys who helped him, they skinned over the back wall and kept running, I guess. Anyhow they've not come back. Redmin stood in the gateway and told Bistona she couldn't enter the sacred enclosure because she was unclean."

"I never gave Redmin credit for guts," a man said.

Graia sniffed. "*I* figure he was blind drunk," she said, "seeings as he generally was."

"Regardless," muttered Breccon, "the demons kilt him, tore him to bits and ate him. It was like two terriers on a vole. And they've lived in the shrine since then, a moon and more."

Ilna frowned. "What do they eat?" she said. If they weren't really demons then they had to eat, didn't they?

"They hunt at night," said Breccon. "Not people, I'll say that for Bistona, not if we stay on this side of the valley. But we can't keep goats anymore, and the people who used to come for the oracle, well, all that money's gone, you can guess that."

"She let us get our goods out of our houses the first day," the man with missing fingers said. "If anybody goes up there now, the demons come out. They don't chase you if you run, and nobody tried it who didn't run."

"The Lady knows I ran," muttered a young fellow whose legs were nearly as long as Karpos'. "I must've been crazy t' think of going back for a stupid bracelet!"

He glared at the girl beside him. Her face sharpened; for a moment it looked as though she was about to say something, but she noticed Ilna's eyes on her and subsided.

"We kept hoping Bistona'd take the demons away," said Breccon, "or anyway, that they'd wander off themselves. But all this time and they stay in the Lady's shrine."

He cleared his throat and said with the cracked brightness of a certain lie, "I don't guess it'd be hard for three soldiers to drive the demons out, would it? And we'd pay!"

"We'd all help you, you know," said the man with missing fingers. "All the men of an age to help. But we don't have swords or strong bows like you real soldiers do."

"Mistress, we need help," said Graia. "There's more coined money here than you might guess, from the shrine being an oracle, you see. But if you won't help us, then we'll have to move, sure as sure. One of these days the demons won't find a goat or a deer, and then they'll come for who-ever's nearest. We'll *have* to move."

"Be silent for a moment," Ilna said. Her tone was sharp, not because of anything the villagers *were* doing but because they might do something. She'd learned over the years that if she didn't tell people to shut up, they'd yammer at her while she was thinking. Given that as best she could tell most people didn't spend any time at all thinking them-selves, she supposed the mistake was a natural one.

Ilna didn't have any interest in killing demons—or wyverns, or men, or anything else except cat men. The ora-cle she wove each morning to give them direction had brought them here, though. That didn't mean they couldn't go on tomorrow, traveling to the southwest as she'd been do-ing since she left First Atara immediately after the Change, but perhaps.

And besides, walking away from a problem had never been her way.

She looked at her three companions. "I won't order you to get involved in this," she said. "If they're as big as you say, Temple, it may be more than we can manage even with the villagers' help."

"Keep that lot out of the way," Asion said, looking over his shoulder in obvious disgust. "Farmers aren't good for squat on a hunt. They just stir up trouble and leave you in the bag onct they stirred it."

"I don't mind taking care of this, mistress," Karpos said quietly. "It'll be a little different, I guess. But closer to what me'n Asion did before we met you."

"Temple?" Ilna said. He was smiling at her again!

"I don't need to be ordered to rid the world of monsters, Ilna," he said. "I can occupy one of the wyverns while you and our companions kill the other. Then you can give me such help as I require."

"Alone?" Ilna said, feeling the start of a frown. "If they're as big as you say?"

"I have some experience with the work," Temple said, as

calm as if he'd said something about the clouds overhead. "And you'll be free to help me shortly."

Movement across the valley drew Ilna's attention. From the shrine's entrance stalked a wyvern, then the second. On the shadowed eastern slope the colors were indistinct, but Ilna had an eye for such things: the creatures were a light blue-gray and darker gray with brighter blue mottlings. They were so tall that they'd have scraped the building's transom if they'd stretched their legs to full height.

A woman came out of the priest's dwelling and stood between the monsters. They were staring toward the new village of shanties. Their stubby wings were scaly instead of being feathered.

"Are they looking at us, d'ye think?" said Karpos carefully.

One wyvern, then both, raised their beaked jaws and shrieked. They were as raucous and shrill as marsh hawks, but very much louder.

"They will be in the morning," said Ilna, rising to her feet. "When we go across the valley and kill them."

THE TWO TRACKS in the road might look like wheel ruts to city folk, but Garric was a peasant: they were the cuts made by packhorses passing in opposite directions. If it'd been raining today as it would be in fall, his gelding would've sunk in to its belly; now it just clopped up dust to coat his breeches to mid-thigh.

"Before the Change, this all was swamp," Garric said. Since there wasn't much traffic, Shin walked alongside, easily matching the horse's measured pace. "The folk in these farms—"

The hedges to either side of the road and between the long, narrow fields were boxwood, so ancient that the lower stems were the size of a woman's calf. On horseback Garric could look over them to stone houses in the distance; the roofs were turf, speckled white with daisies.

"—lived at the very beginning of the Old Kingdom, Liane says. Before Ornifal was part of the kingdom, in fact."

"How do they take to you becoming their ruler, Prince?" the aegipan asked. "They're prosperous folk and you'll probably expect them to pay taxes."

"The Coerli helped with that," Garric said with a wry smile. These *were* prosperous farms, growing wheat on rich black soil, but he wondered how Shin came to know that. The hedges were opaque, and they had solid wickets instead of barred stiles between them and the road. "They raided several times after the Change; that stopped when we burned the keeps the raiders came from, with the raiders inside."

In his mind, King Carus laughed. He said, *"I never met anybody who liked to pay taxes. Given the choice, though, they'd rather fund the royal army than feed the cat beasts."*

An old woman came toward them, holding a little girl by the hand. When the pair got close enough to see what the aegipan was—or at any rate to see that it wasn't any of the normal things it might've been, a pony or a bent old man in brown homespun—they froze and flattened against the hedge. From the look on their faces, they were about to run back down the road till they dropped from exhaustion.

Garric swept off his broad-brimmed leather hat and bowed low in the saddle. "Greetings, good ladies," he called. "You brighten our journey early on a long day."

Shin hopped in front of the horse and began walking on his hands, waggling his hooves in the air as he did so. The little girl stared with fascination, while the expression of the older woman—her grandmother?—at least faded from panic to neutral interest. They didn't speak, but when Garric was well past he glanced over his shoulder and saw they were still watching.

Shin backflipped onto his feet again and grinned sardonically at Garric; he'd had no difficulty keeping up with the horse while walking on his hands. Apparently to underscore his abilities, the aegipan did a series of handsprings before settling back to walk beside Garric again.

"I practice arts of meditation which require perfect mastery of my body," he said. "Fortunately, I've found that people will accept me as a mountebank when they wouldn't as a philosopher."

Is he serious? Garric thought. He burst out laughing.

"It doesn't matter whether you're serious or not," he said aloud, though he knew he could've saved his breath: Shin and Carus, his only companions, could hear his thoughts. "I'm glad you're so agile, Master Shin. I needn't worry about you if something comes up on the way."

"Don't think I'll fight for you, champion," Shin said. It was hard to judge the aegipan's expression, but Garric thought it was more serious than perhaps it'd been a moment before. "You'll survive or fail on your own abilities. You'll live or die, that is."

"I don't recall ever asking someone to do my fighting for me, sir," Garric said quietly. "But I'm armed, so I have a responsibility for your safety as long as you're guiding me."

His fingers toyed with the hilt of his sword. He'd picked up the habit from the ghost of the warrior in his mind, but by now it was natural to him as well. He *was* a warrior, after all . . . though he'd been seventeen before he'd ever touched a sword. Indeed, he'd seen such weapons only during the Sheep Fairs. They hung from the belts of guards some of the wealthy drovers brought with them when they came to Barca's Hamlet to chaffer for wool and sheep.

Shin gave his gobbling laugh. "Oh, don't worry about my safety, Prince," he said. "Though the concern does you credit. No doubt you're a paragon among rulers, but you'd best put that aside for the present time."

"I *have* put it aside," Garric said. "There's things I'll miss about leaving the kingdom this way—"

Carus grinned broadly, but he knew that the emptiness his descendant felt was for the company of his friends—certainly including Liane, but not Liane alone.

"—but I don't miss being ruler. Because I'm not such a paragon as I'd like to be."

Clearing his throat and staring until the aegipan cocked his head up to meet his eyes, Garric continued, "And inasmuch as I'm not a prince anymore, Master Shin, and that I like to be friends with whoever I'm around, I'd prefer that you call me Garric. And I'll call you Shin, if that's agreeable."

Shin laughed again. "As you wish, Garric," he said. "Though I don't see what you expect to gain from friendship."

"A more pleasant journey, Shin," Garric said. "Even if things turn out badly, I'd regret it if my last days alive were awkward ones."

The road had been rising gently for the past several miles. Garric couldn't be sure, but he thought they were probably beyond what'd been the coast of Ornifal in his own day. Ahead to the south, wooded hills stretched into the far distance. The path continued, but it shrank to a trail not unlike the one leading west from Barca's Hamlet.

When he was a boy Garric had occasionally dreamed of going to Carcosa, the ancient capital on the far coast of Haft; he'd dreamed, but he'd never really expected it to happen. He'd been to Carcosa after all, and then he'd gone much farther before returning to Carcosa as ruler of the whole kingdom, the Lord of the Isles.

But now the Isles themselves were as much in the past as Garric or-Reise, the innkeeper's son, was. Garric was riding into the heart of a continent that should've been the sea, in order to pass a test that hadn't been described to him and thereby to save mankind from a doom that wasn't rightly part of the world.

He was lost and alone and afraid, all those things to a degree that he couldn't have imagined when he was a boy. But he was going on. That was all he understood: that it was his duty to go on.

Laughing, Garric turned to look at the world he was leaving. The road wound back between the hedgerows and the bright green of sprouted wheat.

His eyes narrowed at the other thing he noticed. "Whoa," he muttered to the gelding, lifting back on the reins to pause before riding down into the forest.

On the northern horizon, probably a good ten miles behind them, was a cloud with a faint golden brightness. Early in the morning he'd have guessed it was mist rising from a pond, but the sun was too high in the sky for that to be the case.

"Shin?" he said. "Do you know what the fog back there is? I don't recall ever seeing something like it before."

"Do you know the story of King Kalendar, Garric?" the aegipan said. He was standing on one leg with the other crossed on it; his hands were on his jutting hips.

"The myth?" Garric said. "Well, I've read Pendill's *Books of Changes*. King Kalendar swore he'd wed Merui, the virgin priestess of the Lady, even though the goddess forbade the match. He marched on Merui's temple with his whole army, but the goddess trapped them in a maze of fog in which they marched until they all became spruce trees."

He frowned, trying to get the details right. He liked Pendill, but an *awful* lot of people seemed to have become trees or birds or springs when they got on the wrong side of the Great Gods.

"After it was too late, Merui regretted refusing Kalendar and searched the forest for him," he continued. "Eventually she became an owl and now flies among the trees, calling out in mourning."

"Merui was indeed a myth," said Shin, "and King Kalendar was actually a mercenary leader named Lorun who swore he'd sack the palace of a wizard."

He gobbled laughter.

"A great wizard, I will say. But the fog was completely true. Captain Lorun and his men walk in it to this day."

Garric stared at the aegipan, trying to make sense of what he'd just been told. "Do you mean," he said, "that the cloud I'm seeing behind us is Lorun and his soldiers?"

"No, Garric," Shin said calmly. "Lord Attaper decided to follow you with a troop of Blood Eagles, ignoring my direction and your command. They now march in a maze which will hold them until they're released or the world ends."

Garric went cold. His knuckles were mottled on the hilt of

his sword, and his face was as tight as that of the ghost in his mind.

"Release them, Shin," he said. His voice was so thick and harsh that he wasn't sure he could've recognized the words himself.

"In good time, Garric," the aegipan said.

"Now, by the Shepherd!"

"No, Garric," the aegipan said, "but when we're another day or two days gone and beyond any chance of them following us. Then they will be released, perhaps wiser."

Garric lifted his hand from the sword hilt and massaged it with the other. It'd been on the verge of cramping. He didn't speak, and he continued to look toward the glowing cloud.

"It's that, or you may return to Valles now and preside over the doom of your world," Shin said. "The test is for the champion alone."

Garric cleared his throat. "We'd best be riding on," he said. By the end of the sentence, he'd gotten his voice back to where it should've been. He faced around and clucked the gelding into motion.

When they were below the brow of the hill and could no longer see the glowing cloud, Garric said, "Shin? If I hadn't noticed the fog and made a point of it, when would you have released Attaper and his men?"

"You did notice, Garric," the aegipan said. "I cannot predict the future based on a past that did not happen."

"That's the sort of question you don't want to ask, lad," said King Carus. *"You might've gotten the wrong answer. It'd be bloody difficult to reach the Yellow King if you'd just chopped your guide in half the way you'd need to then."*

The ghost paused, then added judiciously, *"Mind, it'd feel good at the time."*

Chapter

6

IT SURPRISED GARRIC that the group of buildings in the clearing was an inn, because for over an hour he'd been smelling bacon curing. He'd been right about the bacon, of course—it wasn't the sort of thing you could mistake. Gray smoke blurred out of the last ground-floor window of the right wing and spread slowly through the forest.

There were outbuildings of notched logs, but the timbers of the main structure had been squared with a saw. It bothered Garric to see such a waste of wood when clapboards would've sealed the interior as well, but he'd grown up in Barca's Hamlet, which had been settled for thousands of years. There was no need to be miserly with wood in this dark wasteland of trees.

The central part of the main building had a second story with a gallery. Three men sat on a puncheon bench there, looking down at Garric and Shin approaching; they didn't speak. The skull of a great-tusked boar was nailed over the door transom.

A boy squatted on an upended section of tree trunk in front, cleaning a pair of knee boots with a brush of twigs. He watched them for a moment, then slipped inside through the open door taking the boots with him.

Garric dismounted, feeling a mixture of pleasure and pain as the blood returned to pinched muscles. Carus grinned at him.

Because of his ancestor's long practice, Garric could ride as well as any noble from northern Ornifal, but his muscles were still those of a boy whose personal experience with horses had been limited to walking the beasts to water on a rope halter when a rider arrived. A day spent in the saddle left him feeling as though two of the Sister's demons were chewing the insides of his thighs.

A heavyset man came out of the inn, wearing a bloody leather apron. He'd dunked his hands in a bucket and was wiping them on the dried pulp of a bottle gourd.

"Good day, sir," he said in a friendly tone. His eyes flicked over Shin, but they didn't linger and his voice didn't change. "I've just been butchering a hog. Will you be staying with us tonight?"

The boy slipped out behind the host and sat on the section of tree bole. He picked up his brush again, but though he made halfhearted cleaning motions, his whole delighted attention was on the aegipan.

"Yes, and glad not to be sleeping rough," Garric said. "You've a stable for my horse?"

"An excellent one, sir," said the innkeeper, pointing to the passage between the left wing and the central portion of the inn. "Around the back. There'll be an extra charge for oats, or will hay be enough?"

"Oats, if you please," said Garric. It was odd to be on this side of a transaction that'd been one of his earliest memories. "And a private room, if you have one."

"Indeed, indeed," repeated the innkeeper. "Will your, ah—"

He made a two-finger gesture toward Shin but didn't look squarely at him.

"This one, that is, be foraging for himself or are we to feed him as well?"

"Porridge for me, Master Hann," the aegipan said. His drawl perfectly mimicked that of a Sandrakkan noble; Garric suspected that it would read as an upper-class accent to the innkeeper. "And turnip greens, raw, as well."

He looked at Garric and added in feigned boredom, "The worst thing about travel is the shifts one's put to for food, wouldn't you say, master? Though I suppose we must be thankful for what the Lady offers."

The innkeeper—who Garric had just learned was named

Hann—stared at Shin for a moment with his mouth half open. Then he bowed low and said, "Please come in to my house, Your Lordships. And, ah . . . ?"

"You may call me Shin, my good man," said the aegipan. "Just Shin."

"Lord Shin," the innkeeper resumed, "there are still a few apples from last year's crop. Would you like them in your porridge?"

"I would indeed, Master Hann," said the aegipan with what struck Garric as real enthusiasm. "Dried apples would be an unexpected pleasure."

Garric slung his saddlebags across his left shoulder and untied the heavy cloak bound to the crupper. In his mind Carus grinned and said, *"Our friend Shin can take care of himself, right enough. Watching him move, I wouldn't be surprised if he could teach a cat beast something too."*

More soberly the ghost added, *"Don't underestimate that one, lad."*

I don't, thought Garric.

Hann's eyes lit on the boy. "Megrin, stable His Lordship's horse in the first stall," he snapped. "And see to it he has oats when he's cooled down. Tell the mistress a full pannier, mind."

"I've got Master Orra's boots," the boy said shrilly. "Have Mirri do the horse, why don't you?"

Hann leaned forward with surprising speed and slapped Megrin over the ear. The boy sprawled in the dirt, then hopped up and took the gelding's reins. "Pardon, Your Lordship," he muttered as he trudged through the passage to the stables.

Garric kept his face still as he preceded Shin and Hann inside, but he was professionally offended by what he'd just seen. Reise's lessons had fitted Garric and Sharina to rule the Isles. Shouts, insubordination, and violence would've been very bad training, for kingship or for life.

"Aye, lad," Carus agreed, *"as I know to my cost. But this is a harder world than your father's was."*

The hearth was on the right end of the common room. A girl

younger than Megrin tended three pots, two on cranes and the third among the ashes at the corner farthest from the low fire.

The men from the gallery had come down by the straight staircase to look over the newcomers. Two wore dressed skins, though their breeches from knee down were home-spun. They must be trappers who expected to stand in water frequently. Cloth will dry but leather—particularly rawhide—shrinks and cracks.

They didn't speak, but the barefoot third man—presumably Orra, whose boots lay outside where the boy had dropped them—said, "If I may ask, Your Lordship, where is it you're traveling from?"

"How do they guess you're a noble?" Carus said. *"You're wearing plain wool and your tack is no better than any common trooper's."*

Garric would've smiled dryly if he hadn't been concerned that Orra would misinterpret it. His ancestor had no doubt seen his share of peasants, but he'd always been riding past them at the head of an army.

Because I'm wearing a very good sword, Your Highness, he said silently. *Which would cost more in ready cash than any of these people, Hann included, will see in a year.*

"I'm Garric or-Reise, sir," he said politely as he settled onto the bench built into the front wall. He was taller than any of these fellows; by sitting down, he made himself less threatening even though that meant he had to tug on his sword belt so that the scabbard could stand upright between his legs. "I'm traveling to see new lands."

He gestured with his left hand. "All this was sea in my day, sirs," he said. "Before the Change, as folk call it in Valles, where I come from."

The innkeeper had stepped behind the bar on the wall opposite the hearth. He returned with a tankard of tarred leather and walked to Garric. "Here you are, milord," he said. "We brew our own cider here at the Boar's Skull Inn. I think you'll say we have a right to be proud of it."

Garric drank deeply and smacked his lips with false enthusiasm. "An excellent pressing, my good host!" he said. That wasn't exactly a lie: it may well have been good, though Garric didn't care either for cider or for the taste of tar. Some did, he knew; his father kept several jacks for travelers who asked for their beer in leather. Folk in the borough, Garric included, generally drank from elmwood masars.

"Ah, and your companion, Your Lordship?" the innkeeper said, eyeing Shin sidelong. Garric's insistence that he was a commoner obviously hadn't done much good.

"I'll drink water from your rain barrel, Master Hann," the aegipan said. "Were I to become drunk on your strong cider, who knows what might result?"

Garric looked at his companion sharply. Shin certainly had a sense of humor, but that didn't mean his deadpan warning wasn't a warning in fact.

"My name's Orra," said the barefoot guest as he sat down on the bench facing Garric. His breeches and short tunic were of good cloth, but his vest had been cut from the pelt of some spotted cat. "I wonder since you come from Valles—can you tell us anything about the new government?"

"They sent a pair of fellows by on horses like you, Your Lordship," said the innkeeper. "They told us we were in a kingdom, now. They were just doing a survey, they said, but there'd be other folks coming later. We're concerned about what this new king has in mind."

Carus laughed. Garric smiled wryly and wiped his lips with the back of his hand.

"I can't tell you much," he said truthfully. "I believe the government in Valles tries to be a good one. Human beings, even the ones who try to be just and fair, fail part of the time, though. And there'll be taxes, I'm sure, but I couldn't tell you what they'll be."

I couldn't even say what this region would use to pay taxes, he thought. *Apples? Muskrat pelts?*

"There's a great danger facing the world," Garric went on aloud. "Creatures that'll destroy all life but themselves. They call themselves the Last. It may be that you as well as others will be called to join the army to face them."

One of the trappers said, "I come out here so I'd not serve

nobody. If other folks want to fight, then they can do it without me."

"Your only chance of survival is that men stop the Last," Garric said without raising his voice. "Others will do it for you if you're unwilling to save yourself."

The trappers looked at one another. The one who hadn't spoken said, "Suits me," in a gravelly voice. They turned and went up the stairs again; the treads squealed beneath their weight.

Hann watched them go. "There's so much going on," he said, lacing his fingers. "I've built this place up over the past fifteen years, fifteen! That's what I've invested here. And everything's changing. I'm worried, Your Lordship, and I don't mind telling you so."

"I'm worried too, Master Hann," Garric said, rising to massage his thighs. "But if everybody does his part, we'll come out of it all right."

"If enough of you do, you mean," said the aegipan sardonically. "And if you're lucky besides. Don't forget being lucky."

"AND THIS IS the warrant setting up the Fourth Regional Assembly," said Liane as she slid a perfectly indicted document on a piece of fine vellum before Sharina. "It'll meet in Carcosa. We have more information on Region Four than on most of the new lands, since the Viceroy of Haft was already beginning to explore the district before he got back in contact with Valles after the Change. It's mostly settled by Grass People."

Sharina was very tired, but she made a point of signing these warrants carefully. They were too pretty to deface with a blotted or hen-scratched signature, and by the time they'd been decorated with seals and ribbons, they'd be works of art to be hung beneath the rostrum every time the assembly met.

"I suspect Lord Reise, the viceroy's chief of administration, was responsible for the patrols," she said dryly. "My father isn't a dynamic leader, but he was certainly two or three steps ahead of anyone else in Barca's Hamlet at seeing what was going to be necessary."

It seemed even more strange to call her father Lord Reise than it was to think of herself as Princess Sharina—in part of course because she *didn't* think of herself as a princess, though people called her princess and she did the sort of work a princess did.

She looked across the table at which she and Liane were working. Cashel, sitting on the bench beside the door into the chamber, smiled back at her. The frieze just beneath the ceiling showed cherubs doing all manner of adult jobs from bottling the year's wine vintage to a fuller's shop where they trod woolens in troughs of urine to clean them.

Cashel had been examining the paintings while he waited. Most of the cherubs' tasks were things Cashel wouldn't have seen in real life: every housewife in Barca's Hamlet baked her family's bread on her hearth, so the commercial bakery with big brick ovens was as alien as the cosmetics factory next door to it. Despite his ignorance, Sharina recognized in Cashel's expression the delight he took in all things whether or not they were familiar.

"And here's the last warrant," said Liane, offering a fifth sheet of vellum. "We haven't had as much contact with Donelle as I'd like, though that's possibly because of the distance. Pandah's in the middle of the direct route, of course, so couriers have to swing widely around it."

Sharina chuckled as she signed. When she passed the warrant back, she noticed Liane's lifted eyebrow.

"If I'd been asked what a princess did when I was a girl in Barca's Hamlet," Sharina said, getting to the core of the implied question, "I'd have said she ate dainties and chose between suitors for her hand. That's what they did in all the stories I read, anyway. I don't think I'd have guessed she signed her name over and over again, setting up councils for tracts that haven't been properly surveyed, let alone brought in the kingdom."

Liane blushed slightly. "I'm sorry," she said. "Garric, that is, the prince, liked—"

"He's been my brother Garric all my life, Liane," Sharina

interrupted. She *was* tired or she wouldn't have misworded her comment that way. "He'll stay Garric among the three of us, please. And I wasn't objecting to what we're doing: this is the best way for me to learn what's really going on with the kingdom that I'm suddenly ruling."

"Yes," said Liane with a grateful smile. She wiped her eyes quickly with a handkerchief; tears had started at the corners. *We're* all *very tired.* "That's what Garric says too. And really, the regional councils seemed the best way *to* incorporate folk from other periods. By offering the local leaders medallions of office—Lord Tadai's come up with some suitably gaudy ones—and scrolls of office signed by Princess Sharina—"

Liane smiled, looking younger and happier than Sharina'd seen her in some time. Certainly since Garric rode off, anyway.

"—then they'll *want* to become part of the kingdom."

"I certainly can't imagine a better plan," Sharina said. She rested her head in her hands. She was sure it was a good plan, but for the moment *she* couldn't imagine tomorrow's sunrise. She felt completely overwhelmed.

Liane had asked to stay behind after the council meeting. Sharina had agreed gladly. They'd sent away even the clerks who were normally as much a part of the business of governance as the polished cherrywood table at which they were working.

Cashel had stayed too, of course. He had no business here except to be Cashel, imperturbably solid; and the way Sharina felt at the moment, there was nothing in the world more valuable.

"It's the army that's worst," Sharina said softly, her palms covering her eyes. Time with Liane in Cashel's silent presence was actually better than solitude. She desperately needed friends: completely trustworthy, sympathetic friends. "I don't know anything about soldiers. These appearances of the Last . . ."

"All the incursions have been stopped and the pools have

been covered over," Liane said when she realized Sharina's voice had trailed off. "No one could've done a better job than you did, dear."

"But there were almost eight hundred dead and wounded on Tisamur, Liane," Sharina said, raising her head and putting her hands flat on the table before her. "That's what the messenger himself says, anyway, and since Lord Lomar, the resident advisor, doesn't give a figure in his formal report I'm inclined to believe the messenger. That's terrible, isn't it? Someone must've blundered badly. Should I replace the military commander?"

Liane put her right hand over Sharina's left. "We don't know," she said. "We can't know. And we don't have to worry about it now."

She squeezed Sharina's hand and grinned. "Because we have *far* more important things to worry about," she added.

Sharina smiled back. She felt relieved, though nothing had changed. "Garric would know what to do," she said, without the bitter despair that would've been in the words a moment before.

"I really don't think he would," Liane said musingly. "But King Carus would, I'll agree. He had an instinct for that sort of thing. His technique for dealing with foreign envoys lacked subtlety, however."

Sharina burst out laughing; an instant later Liane was laughing also. They'd both watched Carus behead the ambassador from Laut as part of the same motion in which he drew his sword. At the time, of course, it hadn't been funny; and perhaps they wouldn't find it funny now if they weren't on the verge of hysteria.

There were voices in the hallway; the rhythms though not the words were audible through the chamber's thick door. Cashel got up silently, nodded to the women, and opened the door just enough to slip out. Sharina found watching him move to be a continuing wonder and delight. Cashel didn't seem to do anything quickly, but he never made a false step and he never slowed because he'd run into something solid or heavy.

A moment later, he reappeared with Tenoctris. "I told the

guards it was all right," he said. "You didn't mean her not to come in when you said they shouldn't let in anybody."

"Of course!" said Sharina. The trouble with the way Attaper trained the Blood Eagles was that they tended to interpret orders very strictly. Thinking about it, she wasn't sure they'd have passed even Garric without discussion.

Tenoctris always seemed alert, but this evening her expression had a febrile brightness that Sharina found disconcerting. Though she smiled toward Liane, it was to Sharina that she said, "Dear, I believe I'm as prepared as I can be. With your permission, I'll put my research to the test in the Old East Burying Ground now."

Sharina nodded calmly, though her heart had gone to ice again. Aloud she said, "I told Lord Waldron to give you any assistance you wished. I trust he's done that?"

"He offered me a regiment of soldiers," Tenoctris said with a twinkling smile. "Actually, he offered me my *choice* of regiments, as if I'd know one from another. I believe he was pleased that I'd gone to him rather than Lord Attaper. I asked him for ten men who were willing to dig if necessary, which he assured me they would be."

She cleared her throat. "And I would also like Cashel to accompany me, Sharina," she continued. "I believe I'll need his company for some time."

"Of course," Sharina repeated. "We'd all assumed that, I think."

She got up and waited for the dizziness to pass, then walked briskly around the table and threw her arms around Cashel. She hadn't expected Tenoctris to say "need," though. She didn't know what that meant, but she didn't see any advantage to pressing the old wizard for a detailed explanation.

Cashel was as solid as a great oak. While Sharina was with Cashel, nothing could go wrong. And she was about to lose Cashel's presence.

"Excuse me, Tenoctris?" Liane said from the world outside Cashel's arms. "I'm not familiar with the Old East Burying Ground."

Sharina squeezed Cashel and stepped out of his embrace, though she continued to hold his hand. She looked between the women.

"The name is from my age, not yours," Tenoctris said. "It was quite old even a thousand years in your past, however, and it'd vanished into the sprawl of shanties beyond Valles proper before the Change. I believe that in a tomb there I'll find the ally which mankind needs."

Is it safe to drag an ancient wizard from his grave? Sharina thought, and of course it wasn't—but if Tenoctris was doing it, there wasn't a better solution available. The realization made her stomach churn.

"We depend on you, Tenoctris," Sharina said aloud, gripping Cashel's hand hard. "Well, on you and Garric, but the Yellow King was a myth to me from before I could read. I'm afraid I still feel that way."

"We'll both hope you're wrong, dear," the old woman said, smiling wistfully. "When I was very young, I read Hohmann's *Grammar of the Powers* in what was left of the family library. I found that I could make a feather lift in the air. I certainly never thought I'd be at a pivot of history, though."

She shook herself or perhaps shivered. "Well," she said. "Cashel, if you're ready, shall we—?"

"Excuse me, Tenoctris," Sharina said. She blurted the words without consciously meaning to, though they'd been on the tip of her tongue since the wizard entered the room. "I—something happened last night. Could I talk to you and Liane? It's sort of . . . a woman problem."

She glanced at her companions. Tenoctris was brightly quizzical, Liane was carefully neutral.

Cashel was Cashel, smiling softly and as firm as the bedrock. "I'll go chat with the guards," he said. "Besok was a shepherd on Cordin."

He closed the door softly behind him. Sharina took a deep breath. She *couldn't* have talked about Vorsan in front of Cashel.

"Last night when I returned to my room I saw a reflection

in the window," she said in a firm voice. "I fell into it, I don't know how; I was concentrating on the reflection and then I was in a room with a man who called himself Prince Vorsan. He said he'd made a place to preserve himself from the Flood. He wanted me to join him."

Her mouth was dry. She licked her lips and went on, "He said the Last would destroy us as the Flood did his world."

"How did you escape, dear?" asked Tenoctris quietly.

"He didn't try to hold me," Sharina said. It sounded impossible when she tried to explain it. "He told me to look into one of his mirrors, and when I did I was back in my room."

She paused, trying to focus on important details. "The mirrors seemed to be glass, not metal," she said. "I've never seen anything like them."

Tenoctris shrugged. "Your Vorsan sounds very interesting," she said. "I wish I had leisure to learn more. Perhaps I could even meet him, but—"

Her smile was perfunctory; a polite dismissal.

"—I'm afraid I don't. He doesn't appear to be a serious threat, or indeed a threat at all. And other matters certainly are, I'm afraid."

"I'm just to forget him, then?" Sharina said. She managed to keep her voice calm, but she was more angry than she'd have expected.

"Yes, dear, if you can," Tenoctris said. "Or perhaps . . ."

She looked appraisingly from Sharina toward the door, then back. "If matters go as I hope they will tonight," she resumed, "Cashel and I will be doing a great deal of traveling until the Last have been defeated. You and the kingdom will need a wizard to advise you in day-to-day matters while I'm gone, though. That person, my replacement, may feel otherwise about Prince Vorsan. I won't be offended if you take his or her advice over mine."

"You're leaving us!" Sharina said.

"Yes, dear," said the old wizard. "We'll come back frequently, but I can't promise to be available to answer your questions in a timely manner."

She gave Sharina a lopsided smile and added, "Unless I fail tonight, that is. If that happens, it won't really matter what else I do. I don't see any hope for mankind if I fail tonight."

"I see," said Sharina, though she didn't see. Her head was filled with buzzing whiteness; she wondered if she were about to faint. "I'll pray for you."

I'll pray for all of us.

Tenoctris went to the door and opened it. "I think we'd best leave now, Cashel," she said. "I'd like to have everything prepared at the tomb before sunset."

"Yes, ma'am," Cashel said, walking back into the room.

Sharina threw her arms about Cashel again and kissed him hard. He was too shy to've taken the initiative, but he held her firmly and kissed her back.

For what may be the last time.

TENOCTRIS LOOKED DOWN the hillside with a satisfied expression, then took three brisk steps to the right. Cashel followed, carrying the satchel with the books and powders she used in her wizardry. Instead of taking something out of it, however, Tenoctris pointed at the ground.

"Here," she said to the officer commanding the soldiers. "There should be a sloping trench leading southwest for about fifteen feet. Lay it open, please, and remove what I expect will be a stone blocking the doorway at the far end."

"You heard the lady, lads!" the officer bellowed. "Make me proud of you or you'll *never* get off latrine duty!"

The double handful of soldiers were already at work with mattocks and shovels. They *had* heard Tenoctris, after all; they were close enough to touch her and she'd spoken in a normal voice. Cashel didn't understand why soldiers—and sailors—seemed to shout whatever they were saying, but it was one of the things that made him glad he'd been a shepherd instead.

He'd followed Tenoctris back so they weren't in the way of the digging. The men were good at it, no question; it was a treat to watch how one fellow broke ground with his mattock and the next shoveled the dirt into a wicker basket, all without getting in each other's way.

They had nice tools, too, with metal blades. In Barca's Hamlet, most shovels were shaped from wood with only a shoe of iron over the cutting edge. Lots of folks used digging sticks, even.

Cashel looked at Tenoctris. She'd taken a gold locket from under her silk robe and held it as she watched the soldiers. She looked, well, not as cheerful as usual, so he said, "I thought you might have to do a spell to find what you wanted."

"Not here, I'm afraid," Tenoctris said, smiling though she didn't look around. "It's rather like saying, 'What sort of device do you need to discover a forest fire?' Graveyards often hold a great deal of power, but here it's not just death and reverence. The man buried there—"

She nodded to the trench. The soldiers had cleared the layer of dirt and were now digging out the slot cut in the rock beneath. It was porous volcanic tuff, as easy to carve as the chalky limestone of the hills around Barca's Hamlet.

"—was a very powerful wizard. I don't ordinarily care to work in a place where power is so concentrated."

"What was the wizard's name, Tenoctris?" Cashel asked. It only seemed polite to know a fellow's name when you were digging up his grave.

She smiled again and this time met Cashel's eyes. "I don't know, I'm afraid," she said. "I don't even know how long ago he lived. Though I'm sure he was male; that I can tell from what remains."

Her eyes drifted across the slope spotted with small cedars and outcrops of tuff. It wasn't much to look at, it seemed to Cashel. There were potsherds in the coarse grass; he turned one over with his toe and found it'd been painted on the underside.

"That was a grave marker," Tenoctris said. "On Ornifal in my day, people were buried standing. An urn with a hole in the bottom put over the grave. On the anniversary of the death, relatives and friends dropped wine and food into the mouth of the jar."

Cashel frowned, looking harder at the bit of pottery. He couldn't guess what the painting might've shown when it was whole: all he had left to judge by were the parallel strokes of blue and blue-green against the earthenware background. "If they were dead, it didn't matter, did it?" he said.

"It mattered to the relatives and friends, Cashel," the old woman said. "And they were the ones doing it."

"Ah," Cashel said, smiling at himself for not thinking of that. He was pretty good at figuring out what people'd do once he'd been around them awhile, but not always about why they did it. Ilna was worse, of course: she got mad when folks didn't do things the way she thought they should.

Ilna was smart, no mistake. Sometimes Cashel thought that he and his sister had about two people's amount of brains between them, but they'd mostly gone to her. He loved Ilna, but he was glad most people in the world didn't think the way she did. He was pretty sure Ilna was glad of that too, whatever she might say aloud about how most people behaved.

"Here, we got a stone!" called the soldier at the far end of the trench. He and his partner were down over their heads; other soldiers from where the cut was shallower had been carrying away baskets of dirt and emptying them for some while now.

The man who'd spoken dragged the pick on the other end of his tool into the crevice between the block and a doorway cut in the tuff bedrock. "Hey, it's two stones," he said. His partner shoved the handle of his shovel—not the blade, which would've bent—into the opposite crack. They levered the stone out alternately, working like a perfect team and all without needing a word between them.

The officer looked up. Cashel smiled at him, then nodded toward the soldiers now lifting the top block up for two more men waiting at the lip of the cut to take it. The officer beamed, pleased that somebody who understood the work was watching his men do it.

The lower block was twice the size of the upper stone that'd wedged it in place. "Hey, Top?" the man with the mattock called. "I think we're going to need ropes for this one."

"Let me try it," said Cashel. "Tenoctris, will you hold this?"

He gave her his quarterstaff. He could've laid it on the ground, but he'd rather give it to a friend when he couldn't hold it himself. It was just a length of straight-grained hickory, but he'd had it a long time. It'd been a friend when he needed a friend.

"Let me try," Cashel repeated as he strode over to the cut. The soldiers had ignored him the first time. That didn't bother him; it was the sort of thing you got when somebody new tried to join a group that'd been together for a while. It happened just the same with sheep.

The trench was three double paces long and sloped down to the depth of a man's head at the doorway end. Cashel squatted, looming over the men there. "I can maybe lift that without ropes and people pulling from up here," he said.

"He might at that," one of the soldiers muttered. "What d'ye think?"

Instead of answering, his partner called, "Top, is that all right?"

"Yes, of course it's all right," said Tenoctris testily. "I'll tell Lord Waldron that haste was important, if you like. Or I'll ask Princess Sharina to tell him. I'd like there still to be natural light when I enter the chamber!"

"Right!" said the officer. The men beneath Cashel were already moving away to give him room. "If you want to try, sir, go ahead. But it looks like a load even for somebody as big as you."

"Well, I'll try," Cashel said. He dropped into the trench with his left hand on the lip so that he didn't come down with his full weight on his toes. He touched the block. It'd been chipped from the same soft stone as the trench was cut out of. Cashel wasn't one to brag, but this wasn't even going to be hard.

He rocked the block forward a little to make sure it was

loose; it was. He squatted, placed his hands, and then straightened up from the knees. Everything was smooth as you please till the block was at the top of the trench and Cashel started to fling it down the slope.

"Get out of his way!" Tenoctris shouted. Cashel didn't understand what she was talking about till he realized four soldiers had stepped into what'd been an empty space. They had their arms out, ready to take the block from him the way they'd've done if their friends had been lifting it.

The soldiers moved fast when they saw what was happening, but it was still close. Even Cashel couldn't hold that much weight with his fingertips alone when he'd started it flying, but he was able to brake it enough that the men all scrambled clear before it thumped the ground and tumbled away.

"Sorry," Cashel said. His breath was coming hard, as much from almost crippling a couple of people accidentally as the weight of the stone. "I didn't expect anybody to be there."

"By the blessed Lady," said one of the soldiers who'd almost been in the wrong place. He didn't sound mad. "If you throw stones like that, maybe we can carry you along with us instead of a catapult, hey?"

"Sorry," Cashel said in embarrassment. "I wouldn't make a good soldier."

The men laughed. Cashel realized it'd been a joke, but that was all right since they thought he was joking too.

Tenoctris came down the opened trench, bringing her bag of gear and the quarterstaff both. Usually Cashel or somebody carried the satchel for her, but she was really a lot stronger than you might think to look at her.

"Please go inside, Cashel," she said as she held out the staff to him. Though she smiled, she was also reminding him that he was in the way. "I'm quite sure I'd be more able to move the stone door than I would you."

"Yes, ma'am," Cashel said. He took the satchel, holding it in front of him as he hunched through the doorway. "Careful, there's a step down here."

Though the air inside was cool, it was dry and musty rather than dank as Cashel'd sort of expected. The covered passage was a double pace long, leading to a doorway with posts and a lintel. It was all cut from the living rock. Beyond was a step down into the tomb chamber. Cashel could stand upright there.

Tenoctris followed him in. There was a low bench on either side. Each had legs and a frame, but it was all rock. One was empty; the other had a stone coffin whose lid had been slid off. It'd broken when it hit the floor.

Cashel peered inside. The box was empty.

There was plenty of light in the tomb to see by for the moment. The doors and trench beyond lined up due west, so the low sun came right in.

Tenoctris looked around with the perky cheerfulness of a wren. She peered at the ceiling, then touched the carvings on the coffin with her fingertips.

"Where'd you like me to put the bag, Tenoctris?" Cashel asked. He hefted the satchel to call attention to it.

"Oh, just set it on the other bench, if you would," she said with another quick nod. "I won't need tools to summon the former resident, I'm now sure. I hadn't fully appreciated just how powerful he was, Cashel."

She smiled in a way that made her for just that moment look more like a puppy than a bird. She added, "How powerful he *is*, I should say, though for the moment he's not present in this world."

"Is that a problem?" Cashel said. He spread his feet a little out of reflex. This'd be tight quarters to fight with a staff, but a straight thrust with the butt could finish things quick even if there wasn't room for tricks and spinning.

"No, quite the contrary," Tenoctris said, but her smile seemed almost forced. "We came here to gain a powerful ally, after all."

She cleared her throat and said, "I think I want something from the satchel after all; a lamp."

As Tenoctris searched in the bag, Cashel eyed the coffin. It was made from alabaster carved so thin that you must've been able to see light through it when it was freshly polished. Even protected underground it had the frosty look marble gets when it's open to the air for a while.

The long side toward Cashel was decorated with people in a city. When he looked closely at the carvings, he saw they were all dead or dying; from a plague, it looked like. Some were sprawled at the altars in front of temples, some lay in bed or in the streets. A family held hands on a flat rooftop, all dead.

Cashel generally liked sculptures as much as he did paintings. He didn't like this one, though, and he guessed he wouldn't have liked the fellow who wanted it on his coffin.

He stepped around to look at the end toward the doorway. The carvings showed dead people again, this time being torn to bits by weasels. There didn't seem much point in looking at the other end, let alone worrying about the side against the wall.

Tenoctris' lamp was flat earthenware, the same as any house in Barca's Hamlet—or anywhere—had, except words in the curvy Old Script were molded around the oil hole in the middle. She'd filled it from a stoppered bottle, also in her bag. Now she pointed her finger at the wick, which lighted with a *pop* of blue wizardlight.

"There," she said, turning to Cashel with a pleased smile. "Before I get into the sarcophagus, Cashel, I have a favor to ask you."

Tenoctris brought out the locket again from under her robe. She looked at it for a moment in the palm of her hand, then lifted it on its thin gold chain over her head.

"Please keep this, my dear," she said. She pursed her lips, then touched a catch on the bottom and spread the two leaves of the gold case. In each side was a face painted on a disk of ivory. They were small and the sun was setting fast, but Cashel thought they were a man and a woman.

"My parents," Tenoctris said. She closed the locket and placed it in his left palm. "I didn't know them very well. I'm afraid I must've been a trial to them."

She smiled with the touch of soft sadness Cashel'd seen

before. "Not because I was bad, of course," she explained, "but because I was very different from them and the children of all their friends. I embarrassed them."

"Tenoctris?" Cashel said. "How long do I keep it for you? Just tonight?"

"Keep it until you feel it's the right time to give it back to me, Cashel," the old woman said. "And if ever I cease to be myself, destroy it immediately. Promise me this. There's no one else I could trust with this duty."

"Yes, Tenoctris," Cashel said. He thought for a moment, then hung the chain around his neck.

Tenoctris hopped to the bench, then stepped into the coffin—the sarcophagus—by herself. She seemed brighter, stronger than she had been.

"Now, Cashel," she said as she laid herself flat in the stone box, "all you have to do is wait and watch while I sleep."

With her head on the stone bolster carved in the bottom of the coffin, Tenoctris began to chant softly. The words had the rhythm of words of power, though Cashel couldn't make out the separate sounds.

He walked to the door to the chamber and stood there, watching the sky turn darker. He rubbed the shaft of his quarterstaff, but the familiar touch of the hickory didn't settle him.

Cashel didn't mind not understanding what was going on around him; he was used to that. But this time he was pretty sure he *did* understand, and that worried him a lot.

"YES, I'M SURE I'd rather deal with a wyvern alone, Master Asion," Temple said. He gave "sure" just a hint of emphasis. "None of you are equipped to fight the beasts at close quarters, and I'm unable to fight them any other way."

He bowed slightly to Ilna and added, "This is your first experience with wyverns. You'll find the three of you have enough to do with the beast which doesn't go after me, I believe."

"We'll know soon enough," Ilna said. To the hunters she added, "Come along."

Dew congealing out of the clear air made the morning dank. There wasn't a cloud in the sky, however. The day'd shortly be hot enough and dry, for those who survived the next few hours.

The villagers were up but silent save for whispers as they watched the strangers prepare to fight the monsters. They stood on the slope above their shanties as if to make clear that they weren't part of the business in case it went wrong. Occasionally a child wailed.

Ilna didn't think about whether Temple and the hunters were accompanying her. They were, of course; but once she'd set out to do this thing, the choices other people made no longer mattered.

If she attacked two wyverns by herself, they'd kill her as surely as sunrise. She could freeze one in its tracks, but the other'd snap her up like a caterpillar in a wren's beak. That would end the problem to which Ilna saw no solution: how she could kill all Coerli, wipe out the beasts to the last kit and gray-maned ancient?

The hunters began to angle out in front of her, one to either side. "No," Ilna said firmly; she wouldn't get angry if they obeyed immediately. "I have to lead. It's necessary that the brute comes straight at me."

Temple was well to the right, heading toward the abandoned village. His long strides gave the impression of being languid until you noticed how much distance each one covered. The wyverns had torn the thatch roofs off several houses and the front wall of another had collapsed inward, so it didn't seem to Ilna that the buildings brought much safety.

She shrugged mentally. The big soldier had the confidence of a man who knew his business. Often enough that meant very little, but Temple had proved to be an exception in the past.

The wyverns lounged beside the altar in front of the temple. They'd made a kill during the night and brought it back to eat; by now they'd torn the carcass to a scattering of bloody bones. The mottled wyvern was lying on its right side. It lifted the stripped remains of a thigh to its jaws with the talons of its left leg, then bit; the bone cracked in half.

"I guess that's a goat?" Karpos said.

"I guess," said his sharper-eyed partner. "It's past caring, whatever it was."

The pale wyvern had been following Ilna and the hunters with its eyes. It got to its feet without haste. Its claws folded up against its ankles so that the points stuck out forward; that was how they stayed sharp when the creature walked.

Ilna had knotted her pattern of yarn before she started into the valley. That was the sensible thing to do, of course, but she'd have preferred to have the task yet before her to keep her fingers busy. The thought irritated her because it showed weakness.

She smiled minusculely. She wasn't weak enough to allow discomfort to affect her reactions, of course.

The pale wyvern raised its head to the sky and shrieked, vibrating its black tongue. Its mottled partner sprang to its feet in a single motion and started downhill. The knob of the bone it'd been eating sailed high in the air, flung away unnoticed. The beast was striding toward Temple, who'd just started up the north slope toward the village.

The pale wyvern crouched, vibrating like a plucked lute string. Ilna continued forward at the deliberate pace she'd set herself to begin with. She kept her eyes on the creature she intended to kill, ignoring the stones and sharp leaves her bare feet touched as she walked. There'd be time enough for lotions and poultices after the job was done; if she missed some foreshadowing of the beast's intentions, however, it might be her thigh that it cracked tomorrow.

A woman came out of the shrine. She stood on the porch to watch what was happening. Her hair was dark blond and tangled, and her only tunic had a stiff, russet stain down the right side.

Temple began to run uphill, moving easily. He hadn't drawn his sword, and he held the buckler close to his body.

The sky was bright enough to show color, but the sun hadn't risen to wink highlights from the polished metal.

The pale wyvern launched itself toward Ilna like a stooping hawk. Its wings stuck out from its shoulders, tilting like the pole of a rope-walker as they and the tail balanced the creature's downward career.

This early in the year, the creek at the bottom of the valley was still running. Ilna walked through the water, grimacing at the feel of pebbles washed smooth and slimed with cress. She started up the north slope, holding the pattern folded between her clenched hands. She heard the whirr of Asion's staff sling, and the corner of her eye told her Karpos had raised and half-drawn his bow.

The wyvern shrieked as it kicked off from an outcrop of grayish limestone. Each leap took the beast twice its own length toward Ilna and her companions. One more and it would be on them.

Ilna opened the pattern between her hands and raised it overhead.

The oncoming wyvern stiffened in the air. Instead of skimming toward Ilna and the hunters, it tripped and crashed to the ground. After skidding nose-first for a moment in a spray of coarse dirt, it rolled over on its left side. Its frozen muscles couldn't correct for the angle it'd been leaning at when Ilna's pattern struck through its eyes like a thunderbolt.

The wyvern had small ears. The right one vanished in a splash of blood, shot away by a sling bolt that'd just missed crushing the skull. Karpos' broadhead buried itself to the fletching at the base of the creature's right wing.

The wyvern continued to slide, its powerful hindquarters slewing ahead of its half-open jaws. A pall of yellow-gray dust rolled downhill ahead of it. Ilna turned to keep her pattern toward the beast. Its eyes were a brilliant blue and had vertical slits for pupils.

Karpos shot the wyvern in the throat; Asion's second bullet punched a dimple in the fine gray scales of the creature's chest. Blood splashed, but the impact didn't shatter the wyvern's breast keel as Ilna'd hoped it would.

She continued to turn as the beast slid past. Asion straightened to shoot again, putting his torso between Ilna's pattern and the wyvern's eyes. It sprang uphill toward the hunter as though it hadn't been wounded at all.

Asion threw himself aside. As the wyvern snatched at him, an arrow snapped between its open jaws and banged out the base of its skull.

The beast bent double, its head almost touching its long, tendon-stiffened tail. The legs kicked violently, the right one clawing a divot the size of a bushel basket from the soil; Ilna closed her eyes reflexively as the grit sprayed her. The wyvern thudded downslope, then rolled till its head lay in the stream. Blood trickled from its mouth. The right leg continued to twitch, but its eyes didn't react to the fine dust that was drifting over them.

Ilna knelt and breathed deeply. The dust was still settling; she sneezed and covered her face with the sleeve of her inner tunic. It was just luck the wyvern's momentum hadn't carried it straight ahead, plowing through her and the hunters. Even if the impact didn't finish them, she'd seen how quickly the beast had reacted when her pattern no longer held it. She'd made a mistake. . . .

"That was too bloody close," Asion said quietly. He wiped the palm of his right hand on his tunic, then gripped the sling-staff again.

Karpos looked down at the wyvern; it spasmed violently. "I'll never get those arrows back," he said. There was a red patch on his left wrist where the bowstring had stung it. "It'd take all day to cut 'em out, and long odds the shafts're split anyhow."

"I'll help you turn new ones," Asion said. "That was *too* close."

Ilna got up and dusted her tunic where she'd been kneeling. She held the pattern bunched in her left hand; she wouldn't pick out the knots until she knew what'd happened to the other monster.

"Come," she said, angling now toward the abandoned village. "I'll lead. We'll find Temple."

The houses mostly trailed along either side of the track leading into the valley, but at the upper end they spread in a skewed checkerboard below the wall around the shrine. Dust was settling there, but nothing else moved.

Karpos had an arrow nocked. He glowered at the drystone hut on his side of the narrow street and muttered, "This is too tight for comfort. It's bad as going after a tiger in brush."

"I don't hear the brute," Asion said. "It called a couple times when it took after Temple, I heard that. I wasn't paying much attention, though. They could run down deer, it seemed like, the way the gray one was coming at us."

The street kinked around a house bigger than most of those in the village. It was built on three sides of a courtyard. There was a brushwood fence across the front to pen goats at night. Asion's staff whirred, and Karpos drew the string back to his ear.

Ilna raised the pattern before her and stepped around the corner.

The blue-mottled wyvern lay in the ruins of another courtyard house, its head buried in fallen stone. The beast must've lunged forward when it got its deathblow, demolishing the thick wall. Temple's sword had pierced the wyvern's chest just below the right wing, leaving a gash as wide as Ilna's palm. The wound had stopped bleeding, but judging from the blood covering the street and neighboring buildings it must've spurted like a millrace.

Temple sat on a feed trough in the courtyard, polishing his sword with a tunic the householders had left behind when they fled. His back was to Ilna and the others, but he watched them in the mirrored face of the buckler which leaned against the wall.

"Greetings, Ilna," Temple said, sheathing his sword. He draped the cloth over the trough. "I'm glad you three are all right."

Ilna bunched her pattern and started immediately to pick it back to strands of yarn. It would've worked on Temple also, if he'd been facing her directly.

"By the *Lady,* friend!" Karpos said in amazement as he

relaxed his bow. "How did you do that? How did you kill the brute by yourself?"

Temple turned and slung his buckler again by its strap. "They're quick, as you saw for yourself," he said calmly, "but they don't think more than one step ahead. I dodged around walls until I was in a place where the step it took was past where I was hiding."

Asion lifted one of the wyvern's claws with the butt of his sling-staff, then let it drop flaccidly. The middle claw on each foot was as long as a man's hand, thick, and as sharp as one of Karpos' arrows.

The little hunter looked at Temple. "That was a good job," he said, but his tone sounded harsh to Ilna. "Putting the blade between two ribs the way you did. If you'd hit bone, you'd have had a problem, wouldn't you?"

Temple shrugged as he stood up. "I told you I had experience," he said.

He looked across the valley. Ilna followed his eyes and saw villagers streaming toward the homes they'd abandoned when the wyverns came.

Ilna looked at the yarn in her left hand. "There's still the woman, Bistona," she said. Sharply she added, "I don't intend to kill her."

Asion grimaced; Karpos gave an unconcerned nod. Temple smiled and said, "Of course, but we'd best be with her when her neighbors arrive. They may be less charitable than we are."

Karpos looked puzzled and said, "She's crazy, isn't she? And the Lady protects crazy people. They wouldn't hurt her."

Ilna sniffed. "It's possible Master Breccon and his fellows are less religious than you are, Karpos," she said. "Yes, let's see to Bistona now."

The main street led directly to the archway into the temple enclosure. There was no gate and the posts were stuccoed wood with a wicker trellis to form the arch. The grapevines planted at the base of each column were only beginning to leaf out. In summer when the foliage had spread, broad leaves would hide the wicker.

Ilna smiled faintly. That'd be a pity, because whoever'd woven the willow shoots into an arch had been quite skillful. Her craftsmanship—Ilna touched the wicker for a fleeting image of the maker, a woman well into her sixties with gnarled fingers—was of more interest to Ilna than the artless twistings of vines.

Bistona stood between the two pillars of the shrine's porch. They were wood also and had been carved as statues, though the paint and details had weathered off. Ilna couldn't tell if they were meant to be men or women.

Or both, she supposed. She'd seen statues in Erdin that were women from the waist up and men below; Liane had called them hermaphrodites. Ilna had better reasons to dislike Erdin than a few statues, but the statues had disgusted her.

The compound was littered with the stinking remnants of the wyverns' meals. Their jaws were strong enough to shear the largest bones, but they were messy eaters. For a month, bone splinters and bits of flesh, now rotted to pools of liquid, had been flung in all directions.

There was no clear path to the steps of the shrine, so Ilna tramped through the filth. Initially her face was set with distaste, but it suddenly struck her that only a few minutes ago it'd seemed likely that her own corpse would be contributing to the mess.

"You're smiling, mistress?" said Asion in surprise. The little hunter was walking almost beside Ilna. She'd intended to lead.

But she was in a good humor, so she merely said, "I prided myself on neatness when I kept house for my brother and me. It'd have been very unpleasant to become part of this garbage midden."

Asion blinked but didn't speak further. Temple, walking behind them with Karpos, chuckled.

Bistona stood like a third statue across the front of the porch. Close up she looked much younger than Ilna had thought from across the valley; her wild hair was blond, not white. She was probably only a few years older than Ilna herself.

Bistona's staring eyes looked generations' old. Well, so did Ilna's own, she supposed.

Ilna walked up the first of three steps to the porch, then paused on the second. She held a pattern, this time a gentler one, knotted in her hand, but instead of opening it, she said, "Mistress Bistona? We've come to help you."

Is that a lie? Well, we've come to save her from being burned alive by her neighbors, at least.

Bistona shuddered; her eyes focused on Ilna. The irises were bright blue, disconcertingly similar to those of the wyverns.

"My sons are dead," she said. Her voice cracked; perhaps she hadn't spoken since the Change. "I thought they were still alive, but I was wrong."

Bistona was filthier than the wyverns because unlike them, she didn't lick herself clean. Ilna kept from sneering only because she had a great deal of experience in holding her tongue. That would've surprised many of those who knew her, but they couldn't see what was going on in her head.

"I'm sorry about your sons," Ilna said. "We've killed the animals responsible."

After thinking for a moment—the priest's house was close by, but it was probably as squalid as the shrine's compound—she added, "Mistress, let's go to your home. You need to lie down, I'm sure."

The villagers had returned. Most of them were going first to their own houses, but Breccon, Graia, and the elder with the mutilated hand had entered the compound. The men were muttering bitterly about the disorder.

Bistona turned and reentered the shrine. Something inside croaked harshly.

Ilna frowned but walked in behind the woman. She was mad, just as Asion had said, and it was possible that her seeming normalcy would vanish into murderous rage at any instant. Still, they'd determined to help her, so Ilna didn't have any choice.

The interior of the shrine was lighted only through the front doors, but that was enough for the small room. A mosaic of the Lady spreading her hands was set into the back wall; it was made with bits of colored glass, not stone, and She wore the broad smile of a simpleton.

There wasn't a statue, however. Where it should've been was a couch. It looked real, but even the bolster and the tucks in the mattress were carved from marble. Bistona lay on it as though it was stuffed with goose down.

Open trusses supported the roof. The raven perching on the end beam croaked again, startling Ilna. She hadn't noticed the bird in the shadows.

"No!" she said sharply to Karpos, but he was already relaxing the bow he'd drawn in surprise. She smiled: it hadn't been just her.

The shrine's interior smelled like a snake den in winter, though the wyverns hadn't fouled it with their droppings. The plastered walls had been painted deep red, but the beasts had worn much of that off. Scratching themselves, Ilna supposed. Sheep did the same.

"Have you found the demonspawn Bistona?" Breccon demanded.

Ilna turned. Breccon stood on the porch with his wife and the other elder. They might've tried to follow her and the hunters in, but Temple had drawn his sword and slanted it across the doorway.

"There's no need for that," Ilna said tartly to Temple.

"Perhaps," said the big man with a smile. He sheathed his purplish blade with the smooth ease of water poured from a ewer, but the villagers remained where they were. As he'd intended, obviously; and perhaps he was right after all.

"Bistona's lying on the couch," Ilna said to Breccon. "She's not responsible for the monsters, and from what she said a moment ago she may be coming back to her right mind."

She paused, feeling her face harden. "You're to treat her as one of your own," she continued. "I may never return to your village, but if I do and Bistona's been mistreated, I'll consider you no better than the monsters we rid you of this morning."

Bistona called, *"Lamo eararacharraei anachaza!"*

"What did she say?" Asion demanded, looking from the reclining woman to Ilna. "I didn't understand it."

"Richar basumaiaoiakinthou anaxarnaxa!" Bistona said. Her eyes were open but unfocused; her hands were crossed over her chest like a corpse's.

"It's wizardry," Ilna said. The words meant nothing to her, but she'd heard Tenoctris and others speak words of power often enough that by now she recognized the tone and rhythms.

And a very inconvenient time for it, she thought, though she didn't add that opinion out loud. Bistona's chanting was bound to make the villagers uncomfortable, and they obviously blamed her for their misfortunes already.

"Breccon, she's speaking for the Lady!" Graia said excitedly. "Redmin's dead, but the Lady's made Bistona Her oracle in his place!"

"How's that an oracle?" Asion said. "Can you understand it?"

"Phameta mathamaxanrana echontocheritha!" said Bistona.

"No one understands it, not even wizards," Ilna said contemptuously. She'd seen this sort of fakery before. No doubt Bistona would shortly "awaken" and announce to the village that she was now their priest and they should honor her. Well, that was the sort of result Ilna'd wanted, but it still irritated her to see it done through a lie.

"Ilna os-Kenset!" croaked the raven. "The straight path is crooked, the crooked path is straight."

Its voice was harsh but completely understandable. There was no chance Ilna was misinterpreting the sort of sounds birds ordinarily made.

Graia gave a shout of delight and clutched her husband. The other elder knelt and touched his forehead to the floor of the porch. He crossed his hands, whole and maimed, over his head.

"You must turn aside," said the raven, "or you will not reach your goal."

Bistona stirred on the couch. She blinked twice and rubbed her eyes with the back of her hand.

"I'd never heard a bird talk before," said Karpos, not frightened but wondering.

"Yes, yes," said Graia, "the Lady always speaks through the Servant, good sir. Well, when she does."

"A lot of times Redmin says the Servant told him the answer and the suppliant has to leave his gift for the Lady," Breccon explained. "But sometimes it's like this."

"Graia?" said Bistona, sitting up on the stone couch. "How did I get here?"

Then, with a hint of shrillness as she touched her filthy garment, "What's happened to me?"

Temple gestured the old woman inside. Graia hesitated a moment, then scurried to Bistona and grasped her hands. She began speaking, quickly but in a low voice.

The raven croaked and spread a wing to preen its feathers. The bird had the mangy look of extreme age.

The elders whispered to each other, but Temple and the hunters were looking at Ilna. "Do you expect me to say something?" she said angrily. "There's nothing to say. I don't have a goal!"

Her companions didn't speak. Ilna brushed past Temple and went quickly down the temple steps. She knew that she was leaving the shrine lest the bird say something more to her. That showed weakness and made her even angrier.

Ilna faced around. Temple and the hunters had come out onto the porch.

"I've never turned aside," Ilna said. "I'm not going to start now!"

But as she spoke, she remembered that once long ago she'd given herself over to evil, to Evil. She *had* turned aside from that.

If she hadn't, if she'd continued on the path she'd set for herself, this world would be an icy desolation . . . as she had seen.

THE SCREAMING HORSE awakened Garric, but his sword was in his hand before his own senses were alert. King Carus had the instincts of a cat and the reflexes of a spring trap; he never forgot where his sword was, and anything untoward sent his hand to it.

That complicated Garric's life, because it generally wasn't appropriate for a prince to snatch out his sword. There'd been times it'd kept him alive, though, and this might be one of those times.

The horse screamed again. The sound cut off with a snap of bone, though other animals continued kicking and braying in the stables below Garric's window.

The shutters of Garric's room were barred, but the right-hand one sagged and let in moonlight. He laid the sword across the mattress stuffed with corn shucks and pulled his boots on quickly. Stepping on a pitchfork in the dark could be the last mistake he ever made.

"Do you know what you'll be getting into if you go down there?" Shin asked.

"No," said Garric. His belt was still hung from the peg at the head of the bed; he buckled it on. Not only might he need his dagger, he was likely to want to free his hands while keeping the sword available in its scabbard.

"You could wait here," Shin said. "The room's sturdy. You have no idea what creatures roam this region."

The private rooms of the Boar's Skull Inn were at the back of the second floor. They were built for merchants who wanted to lock themselves, their guards, and their baggage in for the night. There was plenty of space for Garric and the aegipan, though the latter'd chosen to curl up on the floor rather than share the mattress with its coverlet of sewn sheepskins.

Garric threw open the shutters and looked out over the slanting stable roof. He didn't reply. He wouldn't like himself if he'd been a person who thought in Shin's terms; and anyway, Shin hadn't asked a question.

The boy, Megrin, stood at the edge of the forest bawling something. Garric couldn't make out the words; perhaps they weren't words at all, just terror given voice. The next window over opened. Master Orra looked out, met Garric's eyes, and ducked in again. His shutters banged.

The ghost in Garric's mind laughed. *"There's no lack of folk wanting someone else to do their fighting,"* Carus said. *"I never minded being that someone."*

Garric's shield leaned against the wall below where his sword had hung; he picked it up by its twin handles. It was wicker waterproofed with a covering of waxed linen, meant for skirmishers. It felt uncomfortably light compared to the line infantryman's brassbound round of birch plywood that Garric had worn in battle, on his arm and far more often in Carus' memory, but even so it was more than most travelers would have.

"It'll do, lad," said Carus in a husky whisper. *"It's what we have, so it'll do."*

Garric stepped onto the roof, the shield in his left hand and the shimmering gray sword in his right. His smile mirrored that of the ghost in his mind.

The stable roof was of arm-thick poles laid side by side. They hadn't been dressed, let alone squared, but enough bark had sloughed away that if there'd been light in the stables Garric would've been able to look through them and see what was going on.

And if I had a hundred Blood Eagles with me, I could let them take care of the problem, he thought, grinning. This would do.

The stable doors had been opened outward. Garric judged the ground below—it was clear—and jumped with his knees flexed to land in the shelter of a door valve.

The doors were built on the same massive scale as everything else about the inn. If he'd dropped in front of the opening, something could've leapt on him before he turned to face it. Judging from the way the horse'd screamed before its neck broke, that would've been the end—and a nasty end.

Garric made sure of his footing, got his breath, and swung into the doorway with his shield raised. He stood there, letting his eyes pick out forms in the dappled shadows instead of rushing straight in. The pause would've been suicide if he'd faced human foes who'd have him as a silhouetted target for an arrow or even a thrown knife, but the grunts and slobbering gulps from the gelding's stall weren't human.

The creature which'd been crouching over the dead horse turned toward Garric. It was a distorted image of a man, very broad and too tall to stand at full height though the ceiling was ten feet high at the rear of the stables. Its face was long and flat; when its jaws opened, they dropped straight down instead of hinging at the back.

"Ho!" it bawled. "This horse was stringy, but here's a morsel come to offer itself as a tastier dinner!"

A lantern from behind threw its light over Garric, then past him into the stables. The creature's hide was faintly green where it hadn't been bathed in the gelding's blood, and it was female.

"May the Shepherd help us, it's an ogre!" squealed Hann. "Milord, run! No man can fight an ogre!"

King Carus laughed. It was only when Garric heard the sound echoing from the stable rafters that he realized he was laughing too.

"Milord!" the innkeeper repeated, this time in a scandalized tone.

Garric backed a step. Carus was plotting the next move and all the moves to follow, a chess master who gamed with real humans and himself at their head.

"I'll lick the flesh off your thighbones, little man!" the ogre said. Her four breasts, flaccid but pendulous, wobbled as she bent forward slightly. "And you'll still be alive when I do it!"

"The ogre reads minds, Master Garric," said Shin from somewhere behind him. Garric wondered if the aegipan had jumped from the roof as he had or had come out a door on the ground floor with the innkeeper. "Not my mind, of course."

"Then she knows exactly how I'm going to kill her," Garric said. The words came out in a growl; his mouth was dry. "She'll have to hunch to get through this doorway, and when she does I'll put my sword through her. It'll cut stone, you know, Shin; it'll slice that ugly skull of hers like a cantaloupe."

The ogre roared and rushed forward—but *toward* the

door, not through it. Garric stayed in his waiting crouch. He laughed, at the trick and at the way he and Carus had anticipated it.

The ogre's arms were long, even for a creature so big. If Garric'd lunged to meet her, she'd have snatched him while he was off balance and dragged him inside, probably slamming him a time or two against the doorposts along the way. By standing his ground a little way back from the opening, Garric had time to meet a clutching hand and lop it off. *This* sword's edge would make nothing of the ogre's big bones, and if she read his mind she was sure of that.

The ogre backed and bellowed again, flexing her arms at her sides. It was like watching a crab threaten a rival. The arms were amazingly long, eight feet or so; her knuckles'd scrape the ground if she hunched over.

"Bring a bow and arrows!" Garric shouted into the night. He turned his head slightly, but he could still see the ogre with both eyes. Hann had left his lantern on the ground and vanished, but Garric was sure everybody in the Boar's Skull was listening to him. "Javelins, any missiles! I'll keep her from coming out while you shoot her full of arrows!"

"So you think you can stop me, my little morsel?" the ogre said loudly. "Do you doubt that I'll pull your head off even if you manage to find my heart with your sword?"

Carus barked a laugh. Garric said, "No, I don't doubt that. But I *will* find your heart."

He tossed his shield down and drew the dagger with his left hand. The wicker wouldn't be any use if the ogre rushed, but he might drive the dagger home even if she tore the sword from him after his first stroke. It wouldn't matter to him, of course, but the quicker the ogre bled out, the less chance there was of her killing anybody else.

Somebody has to do it. This time that somebody is me. That was the decision you made when you became a shepherd, or a soldier, or a prince.

The ogre reached up and tore at the roof; the poles crackled in her grip. Garric poised. She could break out of the stables, but the roof and walls were too sturdy for her to do so easily. *When she gets her head and shoulders through the hole, I'll lunge. I'll put the point in through her diaphragm and rip down to spill her guts on the stable floor. It's not as quick as a stroke to the heart, but it'll kill—and I might even survive the encounter, unexpectedly.*

The ogre suddenly backed and leaned against the side-wall, making a sound like rocks grating. After a moment, Garric realized she was laughing.

"Well, you're a brave one," she said affably. "And a clever one besides. I've never met a man like you before, I'll tell you that."

She cocked her head to the side and let her jaw drop; her front teeth looked like a wolf's, but behind them were great molars that could crush a horse's thigh.

"She's smiling, if you wondered," Shin said. "She doesn't have lips like a man's, so she's trying to make an expression that suggests a smile. Personally I don't think it's a very good copy, but I suppose she deserves something for making the effort."

"I'll give her something," Garric said in a thick voice, mouthing the words Carus spoke in his mind. If he rushed, he was almost certain to get home with the dagger as the ogre concentrated on the longer blade. . . .

"Here!" said the ogre sharply, straightening. "You're a king, you have a whole nation depending on you. There's no point in the two of us killing each other. I made a mistake coming here, I freely own it. You go your way and let me go mine, and I'll never trouble you again."

"No," said Garric hoarsely. "You're right, I'm a king. I'm not going to loose you on people who trust me. Tomorrow it might be a child, it might be Liane. . . ."

His mouth was dry as ashes, as dry as hot sand. He trembled with the need to act, to move. He'd thought he could wait for someone to bring a bow and arrows, but he couldn't; he was going to rush very soon now and kill this monster as it'd killed his horse, as it'd killed who-knew-what in the past.

"Prince Garric, I wronged you!" the ogre said. She knelt on one knee—her legs were in normal human proportions to her body—dipped her head slightly, and touched her fingertips to her forehead. That was a sign of obeisance among the Serians. "I killed your horse."

"You've killed more than my horse," said Garric, as startled as if the monster had begun to sing a hymn of praise to the Lady.

"You know nothing of my past," the ogre said. "Besides, the world before the Change was a different place—for you, for me, for everyone. What happened in *this* world is that I killed the horse which you needed to reach the Yellow King. I will be your horse, Prince Garric. I will carry you as surely and safely as that stupid quadruped could ever do."

The absurdity of the situation made Garric dizzy. He would've laughed, but his mouth was too dry. "Do you have a sea wolf friend that I could sail across seas on too?" he croaked. "Why in Duzi's name do you think I'd trust you?"

"Oh, her oath is binding, Garric," Shin said cheerfully. "Though far be it from me to dissuade you from being torn limb from limb. I'm sure that's what a proper hero like your ancestor would insist on doing, isn't it?"

"How can that be?" Garric said in amazement. "Trust that monster?"

He almost turned his head to look at the aegipan but caught himself. Big as the ogre was, he'd seen how quickly she moved.

"You're surprised?" said Shin. "I don't know why. *Your* oath is binding, isn't it? Even if you gave it to an ogre?"

Shin walked in front of Garric, eyeing the kneeling ogre with the cool judgment of a drover pricing sheep. "You couldn't use your saddle, of course, but I'm sure you could improvise harness from hides. There's no lack of hides in this place, is there? After all, we have a longer way to go than I'd care to walk in those clumsy boots of yours."

He gave his gobbling laugh. "Though of course that won't matter," he added cheerfully. "She'll certainly tear you apart if you fight. It will be a very heroic death, no doubt."

Garric coughed, started to laugh, and coughed again. His sword was trembling. He was going to have to do something.

"Ogre!" he said. "Do you swear . . . what do you swear by? Do you have Gods?"

The ogre mimed a distorted smile again. "What do the Gods care about the affairs of humans like me or creatures like you either one?" she said. "I give you my word, Garric or-Reise, that I will bear you like a horse, that I will not harm you, and that I will not harm others whom you wish me not to harm."

Garric shot his sword home in its scabbard. "And I swear to you, ogre," he said, "that I'll treat you as well as I would a horse or a good servant for so long as you keep your word to me."

"Her name is Koray," said the aegipan, out of the doorway. "Spelled K-O-R-E. Though I suppose you can continue to call her ogre. You didn't have a name for the horse, did you?"

"Come out, Kore," Garric said, "and let me look at you in better light. Besides, you must be cramped in there and I promised I'd treat you properly."

He still had the long dagger in his left hand; he must've forgotten it. He sheathed it as the ogre ducked low to pass under the door transom and then rose to her full height, easily twelve feet.

Kore stretched, then said, "While I realize this may be an indelicate question, master, I broke into these stables because I was very hungry. If you don't have a better use for the corpse of your former steed, may I resume my meal?"

Garric began to laugh, but the ghost of Carus laughed even harder.

Chapter

7

CASHEL WOULD RATHER'VE been outside under the stars, but he didn't mind waiting in the tomb with Tenoctris. He had his back to the threshold with the quarterstaff across his knees. There was enough oil to keep the lamp at the other end of the chamber burning all night, and it'd be all right even if it went out.

When the breeze was right he caught snatches of the soldiers talking. Instead of standing around the trench, they'd moved onto the top of the hill. From there they could see anybody coming toward the tomb but still keep a little ways away from the wizardry.

The chant Tenoctris had started when she lay in the stone coffin continued as a rhythm well below the level Cashel could hear it as words. It wasn't Tenoctris speaking now, or anyway her lips didn't move: he'd leaned close to make sure.

Cashel smiled. Probably as well the soldiers had kept their distance. It'd been a treat to watch them dig the tomb open, but likely the sound would bother them if they'd been close enough to hear.

The lamp dimmed to the blue glow of the wick. Cashel leaned forward as he stood. If he'd hopped straight to his feet he'd have cracked his head on the stone transom. He could stand upright in the tomb proper, though.

It wasn't quite high enough for the quarterstaff, so he held it crossways. He didn't know what was coming, but he was as ready as he could be.

The lamp brightened again. Cashel frowned; he was glad of the light, but it wasn't what he'd expected. The oil Tenoctris'd poured from her stoppered bottle ran thinner than any Cashel'd seen before. Maybe that was why it acted this way?

A man stepped from the air toward the other end of the tomb. He didn't come out of a wall, Cashel was sure of that; there was an oval mistiness, then this fellow walking through it and standing at the foot of the coffin. He was young to look at, scarcely sixteen. His silk robes were so thin you could see the lamp through them; the cloth was bright blue with words embroidered on it in gold. Cashel recognized the curvy Old Script.

"My but you're a big one, aren't you?" the stranger said, smiling in a way Cashel didn't like. "What's your name, pretty boy?"

"I'm Cashel or-Kenset, sir," Cashel said, shuffling his feet slightly to be sure they were set right. "Are you the fellow who was buried here?"

The lamp was burning brighter than ever, but the stranger's features were sharp even where they ought to have been in shadow. And speaking of shadows—

Cashel glanced at the wall of the tomb on the other side of the stranger from the lamp. Instead of the shadow of a young man, it showed a spindly, lizard-headed demon. Lamplight shone through the wing membranes, casting lighter shadows than the body itself; they flicked open and closed as the stranger talked.

"Buried?" said the stranger. "Dear me, what a thought. But your friend came here to find me, if that's what you mean."

He looked down at Tenoctris and smirked. "I can certainly see why she wanted me to take charge of the business," he said. "My, if I'd been such a pitiable weakling, I'd just have hanged myself."

He smiled at Cashel, obviously waiting for a reaction that didn't come. Cashel didn't let words get him mad, especially when that was what the other guy was trying to do—like here.

Of course not being mad didn't mean he wouldn't take a quick swipe with the quarterstaff, slamming the fellow into the wall hard enough to break bones. Cashel wouldn't do *that* this time either, because Tenoctris really had come here to meet him. Thinking about it made Cashel smile, though.

The stranger tittered, turned, and walked toward the back of the chamber before turning again. His shadow rippled over the rough-hewn wall with him.

"I wanted the First Stone," he said musingly. "Well, of course I did—anyone would. But I knew where to find it and how to get it . . . almost."

He laughed again but there was no humor at all in the sound, not even the joy of a torturer. "That 'almost' was expensive, pretty one," he said. "It cost me time, more time than you can possibly imagine. I was beginning to think that it'd cost me eternity; all the time there ever will be."

Briskly, cheerfully, he walked toward Cashel with his left hand out. "But now your friend has come," he said. "I paid and paid well for my information, and at last I'm able at last to use it to get the First Stone. Give me the locket you're holding for me, my little flower, and we'll get on with the business I've waited so very long to complete."

"No," said Cashel. He didn't raise his voice, but he heard it thicken. "Tenoctris gave me the locket. I'll keep it."

"Do you think you can threaten me, you worm!" the stranger said. "Threaten *me*?"

He was—he didn't become, he *was*—a lion bigger than any real lion, a beast whose open jaws could swallow Cashel whole. Its gape reeked with the flesh rotting between its fangs.

Cashel hunched. He'd strike with his right arm leading in a horizontal arc, then bring the other ferrule around from the left in a blow that started at knee height. But not *yet*.

The lion was too big for the tomb chamber to hold. Cashel faced it on a flat, featureless plain—but the plain might not be real; and if it wasn't, neither was the lion. A stroke at something that didn't exist would pull him off balance, and that could be the end of the fight. The stranger might not be a lion, but he was something—and something very dangerous.

"Give me the locket, worm-thing!" the lion shouted.

Cashel twitched the quarterstaff just a hair, widdershins

and then sunwise. He'd said all he had to say, so he didn't speak again. There were folks who thought blustering before a fight scared the other fellow, but Cashel didn't believe that. It didn't scare him; and besides, he generally didn't need help.

The lion tittered and was the slender young man again. "Oh, the fun I used to have when I was alive!" he said in the arch tones Cashel heard around the palace when courtiers were each trying to be snootier than the other. "Happy days, happy days."

He smiled at Cashel; and as he smiled, his body *flowed* through the side of the stone coffin and merged with Tenoctris. It was like watching honey soak into a slice of coarse bread.

The lamp had sunk back to its usual flicker. There was no sign of the stranger. Tenoctris groaned.

"Tenoctris?" Cashel said. Should he have stopped the thing from touching her? But she hadn't said so, and he wasn't sure what he could've done anyway.

The old woman sat up carefully. Cashel offered his left arm; she gladly took it.

"Are you all right?" he asked, lifting her down to the tomb floor. She felt no heavier than a pigeon on his arm.

"I've gotten what I came here for," she said softly. "Tomorrow we must go with Sharina to the Place; we have dealings with the Coerli. But tonight—"

She gestured to her satchel.

"—please bring that, my dear. Tonight I must sleep, because I'm as tired as I've ever been in a long life."

GARRIC SAT ON the stump of a great tree in the clearing behind the stables, working a rawhide thong through awl holes to sew pieces of pigskin. He'd expected to cut the new harness alone, but Winces and Pendill, the trappers staying at the Boar's Skull, were delighted to do most of the work for him.

"You could live to twice your age, boy . . . ," said Winces. He held a pigskin up in his left hand and stepped on the lower end, then sliced a strap freehand with a butcher knife. Garric had worked enough with leather to understand how strong the trapper's wrists must be to do that in a single stroke. "And not do as much've this as Pendill'n me have."

The other trapper—the men were cousins—chatted affably with Kore as he fitted her with the chest band and shoulder straps that they'd already cut and sewn. Garric glanced at them. "Ah," he said, though he knew it was a silly question, "you and your cousin aren't related to any poets, are you?"

"Poet?" said Winces, frowning. "What's a poet?"

"Someone who puts words together so they have rhythm and maybe rhyme," Garric said in embarrassment. Carus was laughing in his mind, and Shin turned to laugh as well. "There was a famous poet of the same name as your cousin, but I realize he must've lived a long time after, well, you do."

"I could've done a little better than friend Winces," the ghost of Carus said. *"But I won't pretend I'd have cared any more about poetry than he does. It's one of those things I never saw much point in, like learning to rule without keeping my hand on my sword all of the time."*

Orra came through the passageway carrying two saddle-bags over his left shoulder; his tunic bulged with the bulk of the money belt concealed beneath it. He was trying to be unobtrusive about the fact he held a small crossbow. It was cocked.

"Master Orra!" Garric called. He waved but deliberately didn't stand and walk the five or six double paces over to the other traveler. Orra was obviously nervous about seeing him; he'd kept his face turned, watching Garric only out of the corner of his eyes.

"Tsk!" Carus snorted. *"Watching the ogre, more likely. And I don't know that I'd blame him."*

"Ah, yes, Lord Garric," Orra said, staying close to the wall of the inn. His posture hinted that he'd have liked to rush into the stables without speaking, but he knew that he couldn't saddle his mount and ride out before Garric reached the entrance. "Congratulations! I saw you rush into the middle of things last night, and I'll admit I didn't expect a good result."

Winces looked at Orra and snorted, then went back to his leatherwork. Shin, Pendill, and Kore hadn't paid him any attention to begin with.

Garric rose slowly to his feet and stretched. "I didn't expect this particular good result myself," he said. "Assuming it's a good one, of course. Be that as it may, I've a favor to ask you. Master Hann told me that you're riding south?"

Orra looked even warier than before. "I've no taste for company, milord!" he said sharply. "These are hard times, and I hope you'll not feel insulted if I say that a man's better off by himself than at close quarters with a stranger. I've a crossbow here—"

He lifted it slightly.

"—that I loose off at anything that comes up on me. Anything or anyone."

"It's nothing like that, sir," said Garric. He kept his friendly smile, but he couldn't help thinking of how useful an ally with a crossbow would've been while he faced the ogre. "I'd like you to give notice that I'm on my way when you reach the next inn. I trust you can see your way clear to doing that?"

Orra frowned. He was a merchant of some sort, or at least said so. Neither Master Hann—who might have lied out of policy—nor Megrin—who'd have told the truth if only to spite his father—had been sure what Orra's precise business was.

"What do you mean, notice?" he said warily. "Hostelries here in the Great Forest don't have royal suites, you know."

"I didn't imagine they did," Garric said, finding his smile increasingly hard to maintain. "But I'd like them to know that the man who'll be arriving soon on an ogre is friendly and pays in good coin despite the strangeness of his mount."

He reached into his purse and spilled coins from one hand to the other—copper and silver only, of course. Gold would be as difficult to change in this wilderness as it was in Barca's

Hamlet; a traveler might as well try to barter lodging with rubies.

"I don't want to cause needless concern," Garric said. Silently he added, *Nor do I want to learn there are folk more willing to fight an ogre than you were last night*.

"Yes, all right, I can do that," Orra said. He paused a few heartbeats, then said, "Now, if you'll forgive me, I must be off. Good luck to you on your journey, sir."

"And to you, Master Orra," Garric said, but the other man had already vanished into the stables.

"All right, let's try this on," said Winces, patting the strap he'd completed. His hand was scarcely less tough than the tanned pigskin. "If we've got the length right, then it's only left to sew them together and you've a saddle."

"Yes, dear master," said Kore, standing at her full height. One leg strap with its stirrup hung from her chest band; the sling that Garric was to sit in was ready though not yet tied in place. "I'm so looking forward to displaying my talents as a beast of burden."

"I didn't ask you to kill my horse," Garric said sharply. "I didn't particularly care for the animal, but I didn't have to worry about it being sarcastic."

"You didn't know what it was thinking," the ogre said. "It would be dishonest of me to dissemble my feelings the way that brute beast did."

Master Orra trotted out of the stables on his white horse. He turned through the passage to the main track without speaking further or even looking back.

Garric sighed. "Kore," he said, "I've promised you I'd be a good master. I would appreciate it if you didn't goad me into using the flat of my sword on you, all right? Because at some later point I'd probably regret having done so."

The ogre laughed; Shin laughed with her. And after a moment, Garric laughed also.

"THIS IS FAR enough for today," Ilna said, though the sun was scarcely midway from zenith to the western horizon.

They'd been marching through evergreen scrub since day-break, and this mound of grass and flowers under a holly oak attracted her. They weren't in a hurry, after all.

Asion brought up the rear. He nodded, put two fingers to his lips, and blew a piercing summons. Karpos was out of sight ahead of the rest of the party today. The hunters said the whistle was a marmot's warning call. Ilna didn't doubt that, but she couldn't see that the form of signal provided any concealment here where there weren't any marmots.

"I'll set some rabbit snares," Asion said. "Maybe a dead-fall too. There's plenty of wild pigs, judging by the drop-pings."

Ilna nodded. She was suddenly very tired. Asion vanished into the brush.

"What is our goal, Ilna?" asked Temple. He was laying a fireset around a dry hemlock twig which he'd furred with his dagger. He didn't look up from his work when he spoke.

"*My* goal is to kill all cat men," she said sharply. "You're welcome to leave if you don't approve of that."

"I've joined you, Ilna," Temple replied, smiling down at his neat workmanship. "It's my destiny, I believe. But I was curious as to where we're going."

She snorted. "In the longer term, we're going to die," she said harshly. "Until that happens, I'm going to act as if life had meaning and kill cat men."

Ilna turned and walked up the mound. She didn't know what it was about the big man that irritated her. Perhaps it was that she got the feeling he was judging her, though he never said anything of the sort.

Temple glanced up at her. "You've earned your rest, Ilna," he said. "We'll rouse you when dinner's ready."

"I'm just sitting down," Ilna snapped. "I'm not planning to go to sleep."

When she sat and leaned her back against the oak, she felt a rush of weariness. She frowned; there wasn't any reason for it that she could see. Every morning she knotted a small pattern to give them a direction of march. That took more ef-fort than might be expected by someone who didn't wizardry—for she was forcing herself now to admit that her talent *was* wizardry rather than simply an unusual skill at weaving. Still, a trivial prediction wasn't enough to explain her present longing for sleep.

Wildflowers brightened the mound like embroidery on a coverlet of grass. There were buttercups and pink and blue primroses. She thought she saw gentians as well, but she'd have had to get up to make sure. She didn't care to find the energy to do that.

Merota had loved flowers. Chalcus would've woven the girl a chaplet if they were here now. Perhaps that's why Ilna'd wanted to stop.

The mound was probably man-made. There were a number of rock outcrops scattered across the plain, but this was earthen and too regular an oval for nature to have raised it.

There were no signs of a city on the plain they were crossing, no tumbles of weathered rock that had carvings on the protected undersides. Perhaps nomads had buried a chief and passed on in ancient times. The holly oak was very old, and there was no telling how long after the mound was raised that it'd sprouted.

Ilna could hear the crackle of Temple's fire and smelled meat grilling. The hunters must've returned with rabbits, though she hadn't noticed them.

Berries weren't out at this time of year, but ordinarily Ilna would've plucked young plantains and dandelion leaves to go with the meat. She didn't feel like getting up now, however.

I'm going to sleep after all, she thought; and presently she did.

SHARINA WORE BREECHES and knee boots. Her garb scandalized the wardrobe servants, but Lord Attaper would've insisted on it for safety even if she hadn't made the decision herself on the basis of what Garric'd told her about the Corli city.

She didn't mind filth the way a delicately brought-up girl

might've. The things that hid in the filth were dangerous, though. Sharina stepped carefully over a human rib bone that'd been cracked for the marrow. If there was a better way to get blood poisoning than by stabbing a sliver of rotten bone into your flesh, it'd thankfully escaped Sharina's imagination.

Even Cashel wore wooden clogs as he tramped along like an ox on a muddy track. He looked about him at everything, as placid as a man could be.

If there were cause for alarm, Cashel'd see it before the soldiers did, and Sharina trusted his response farther than she did that of the soldiers. Not that trouble was likely. The cat men seemed fascinated by their human visitors, but there was no hint of hostility.

She brushed closer, though she didn't try to hug Cashel while they were walking between the Coerli dwellings. She wasn't afraid of an attack, but the close presence of this many Coerli was making her dizzy.

"The smell's *awful,*" Sharina said. "I think it's worse than the tanyard back home. Though I don't see that it can be; maybe I've just gotten spoiled by living in a palace."

"They're cats," Cashel murmured as they strode through the muck. "They eat meat. I'd never smelled so much piss from meat-eaters as there is here."

"Oh!" said Sharina, and of course he was right. People in Barca's Hamlet had thought Cashel was slow because he didn't know a lot of the things they did; but many of the things other people knew were false.

Tenoctris rode ahead of them in a litter carried by two of the twenty Blood Eagles. Attaper led the escort personally. He wasn't happy with the situation, but he'd accepted that Sharina was regent in Garric's place.

Sharina smiled slightly. Attaper'd also learned that she was the prince's sister in more ways than one: she'd listen to advice, but when she turned her decision into an order, she meant it to be obeyed. It was also possible that the day and a half Attaper had spent wandering in a mist with a company of his men had made him more willing to take direction than he'd been before he disobeyed Garric's direct order. . . .

The eight Coerli chieftains who'd been guiding them through the warren turned. The leading squad of Blood Eagles spread out in the open space that Garric had described, the Gathering Field.

The Elders hopped onto the rocks; Tenoctris got out of the litter carefully. The Blood Eagles' spears were blunted with gilt balls. They held them crosswise to form a barrier against the Coerli spectators.

The crowd pressed close, but the adult Coerli didn't try to push past the guards. There were females and kits among the spectators this morning, though, and one of the latter kept reaching toward Sharina. The mewling kit's mother gripped the scruff of her neck to keep her from squirming through the guards' legs.

Sharina looked around. Tenoctris had made the arrangements, so this was the first time Sharina had seen the complete human contingent.

"Tenoctris?" she said, hoping her voice didn't convey the frustrated amazement she felt. "You haven't brought any interpreters."

Perhaps some of the cat men present had learned human speech, but Tenoctris still should have one or more clerks from Lord Royhas' bureau to check the Coerli. Of course, now that Garric was gone, *no* one could communicate well between the two races of the new kingdom. . . .

Tenoctris glanced at Sharina in mild irritation. "Ah, I'd forgotten," she said. "I'll take care of it now. You'll need to talk to your new wizard, of course."

Tenoctris spoke in the cat men's own tongue. One of the Elders replied. Another, probably the youngest of the eight, rose on his rock with a low growl.

Sharina realized she was clutching Cashel's forearm hard, though of course he didn't react. She opened her grip but continued to rest her fingertips on his solid muscles.

A canal curved around the rear of the Gathering Field. Water flowed in it—bits of debris on the surface moved downstream, if not quickly—so it was the community's sewer rather than a cesspool. Tenoctris walked between the seated Elders and pointed her right index finger toward the fluid which gleamed like fresh tar. *"Pikran dechochoctha!"* she cried in a voice that didn't sound like hers.

A bolt of wizardlight crackled from the wizard's finger. For an instant the canal was a curve of crimson; then the water geysered upward, sizzling and still mounting. When it'd risen into a pillar that pierced the scattered clouds, it exploded outward in silver splendor. Sharina felt a faint dampness.

"Golden-furred lady!" a tiny voice called through the clamor. "Golden-furred lady!"

The Corl kit is calling to me, Sharina realized. *And I understand her.*

Tenoctris walked back to them, smiling in satisfaction. "There," she said. "That'll take care of the communication problem, I think. For everyone who breathes the spray, that is, but the wind's carrying it in the direction of Valles."

Tenoctris' curt incantation had lifted only the water, leaving on the bottom the trash and foulness which'd been suspended in it. Oily sewage slowly began to refill the channel.

"How . . . ," Sharina said, but she caught herself. She looked at Cashel. He didn't say anything, but the hand that didn't hold his quarterstaff touched the locket he'd taken to wearing.

Tenoctris *couldn't* explain how she'd ripped the water skyward and apparently done far more important things in the same action. That was wizardry, and Sharina wasn't a wizard. She might as well ask a Serian philosopher to describe his doctrine to her in his own language.

What Sharina'd really meant was "How did you gain such power, Tenoctris?" Cashel had already told her the answer to that, the being which'd met and merged with Tenoctris in the ancient tomb.

Sharina looked at Tenoctris, then back to Cashel. She squeezed his arm.

"What do we do next, Tenoctris?" Sharina asked calmly. If Cashel was satisfied, then she'd assume that the old woman beside her continued to be the friend who'd helped save mankind so many times in the past.

"Now I find you a wizard to provide counsel while I'm busy elsewhere," Tenoctris said. She gave Sharina a slight smile that wasn't a familiar expression on her face, then turned to the Elders.

"Chiefs of the True People!" she said, speaking in harsh glottals and sibilants which sounded in Sharina's mind—though not her ears—like the old noblewoman's usual cultured accents. "Take me to your Council of Wise Ones. The kingdom has business with one of them."

The shaggy Elders muttered among themselves. Sharina could hear some of the words, but they were too cryptic for her to understand what was being said without a context.

The oldest Corl got down from his boulder. "I will take you to the house of the council, beast," he said. "But I can tell you, none of our wise ones have the power you do."

Tenoctris laughed triumphantly. "That's all right," she said. "Until very recently, I didn't have such power either."

She went along after the Elder on her own feet instead of getting back in the litter. "No," said Sharina with a quick gesture to Attaper as he and his men tried to surround Tenoctris. "Follow us, but you and your men wait outside the building."

She'd seen how Tenoctris' enchantment of the canal water had left several Blood Eagles trembling. They were brave men beyond question, but wizardry had the same subconscious effect on many people that snakes or spiders did. Sometimes that overwhelming fear came out as violent rage. The last thing the kingdom needed now was for a berserk soldier to begin slaughtering the cat men's chiefs and wizards.

With Cashel behind her, Sharina entered the shingle-roofed longhouse to which their guide led. She had to duck to go under a transom meant for the Coerli.

The last thing she glimpsed over her shoulder as she entered was the canal. It was full again, and as black as the heart of Evil.

Chapter

8

"THAT'S A STRANGE thing to find in the middle of a bog,"
Garric said, eyeing the tower half a furlong to the left as they
passed. After a moment's further thought he added, "And
rather an unpleasant one."

Kore looked as she jogged along. Her gait wasn't uncomfortable once Garric'd gotten used to it. Riding her was
more or less equivalent to standing in a horse's stirrups
while holding on to the reins, though he had to lean back
rather than forward. The "reins" were a leather harness over
the ogre's shoulders, supporting her burden like a knapsack.

"I would say that perhaps they have trouble with ogres
here," Kore said, "though I don't scent my kind."

The ghost of Carus laughed. *"It's a peel tower, lad,"* he
said. *"There's more sorts of raiders than ogres, and when
such ride up, here's where the local folk hide. Or if you prefer, here's where the raiders come to divide the loot when
they return."*

The tower could have three stories, though the only windows were narrow ones around the top level; the lower portion might've been a single room with a vaulted ceiling. The
door facing the road was massive and had two iron-strapped
leaves.

"Just what you'd need to drive the cattle in quickly, lad,"
Carus commented. *"Though I'd have said the ground hereabouts is too soft for cattle."*

"The tower was not part of this region before the Change,"
said Shin. The aegipan trotted alongside Kore without difficulty, though his hooves twinkled through three strides for
every one of the ogre's. "There are other anomalies of the

sort. Generally they involve a concentration of powers which wrench the site from its previous period. That was certainly what happened in this case."

"Wizardry, you mean," said Garric.

"Perhaps wizards," Shin said.

The tower disappeared behind them as the track curved down a slight hill. Garric took his hand away from his sword hilt.

He had no reason to feel relieved: there hadn't been signs of life in the tower, let alone hostility. Besides, few bullies or bandits would bother a swordsman riding on an ogre.

Nonetheless, it *was* an unpleasant place.

CASHEL PAUSED TO let his eyes adapt when he stepped inside the door at the end of the longhouse. Triangular windows under the peaks of the saddle-backed thatch roof were the only openings except for the door. The wicker walls hadn't been caulked with mud, though, so they let in air if not much light.

The wicker wasn't woven any old way, any more than his sister's woolens were. The withies of split willow were twisted around the vertical posts in patterns that Cashel could sense but not really follow. It'd have meant something to Ilna, though.

It was a shame Ilna'd gotten it into her head that she needed to kill all the cat men. Cashel didn't think that way about things. He didn't mind killing when he needed to, but once an enemy gave up, Cashel was willing to let the business end. He didn't like to fight, for all that he'd done plenty of it, and he *sure* didn't like to kill.

Ilna was smarter than him, no doubt about that. But Tenoctris and Garric and Sharina were smart as they came, and they felt the same about it as Cashel did. Still, there'd never been any point in arguing with Ilna; and if it'd been Sharina instead of Chalcus and Merota that the cat men'd killed . . .

Cashel didn't let his thoughts stay there very long. He

moved closer to Sharina, though, as Tenoctris said to the cat men squatting at the other end of the longhouse, "Wise ones of the True People, I've come to pick one of you to advise the golden-furred female beast during the time I must be absent from her. She rules the kingdom of which you are now part."

Sharina leaned toward Cashel and whispered, "I've never seen Coerli in a mixed group before, have you?"

Cashel thought about it. "No," he said.

He hadn't noticed it because he'd been thinking of the cat men as people. There was nothing funny about a group of people—human people—having old men and boys, old women and young mothers. That was what these cat men were. One of the females cradled a kit in each arm. They suckled as she listened to Tenoctris still-faced with her fellows.

But Sharina was right: cat men didn't mix the same ways as humans. The young males, the warriors, kept to themselves, and females with kits didn't mix with other females. The crowd outside in the Gathering Field was split into wedges like a pie.

These cat men were together because they were wizards. That was more important than age or sex or anything else, just like with humans.

"A female cannot rule a kingdom," said an older male with the bulk and mane of a clan chief. "A woman cannot rule the True People!"

The chiefs ate a diet of red meat, which they allowed only sparingly to anybody else. Cashel didn't know what extras the cat men gave their wizards, but the handful of other males in this group were ordinary warriors, even the one with gray streaks in his fur who looked pretty old.

"And yet she rules you, vassal!" Tenoctris said. "The golden-furred one is Sharina, littermate of Garric, the warlord and chief of chiefs. As surely as Garric killed your champion with his bare hands, so will his littermate give you all to fire and the sword if you foreswear your oaths."

Her voice was richer than Cashel had heard before, but it was still Tenoctris speaking. Thing is, somebody powerful isn't the same as they were when they were weak, even though they're the same person. The Tenoctris haranguing the cat men now wasn't the bent old woman Cashel had waited in the tomb with the day before.

The chief who'd spoken rose to his feet and looked at his squatting fellows. There were more of them than Cashel could count on both hands and maybe twice that many.

"I am Komarg!" he said, glowering at Tenoctris. He waggled his wooden mace overhead; it was carved with all manner of designs, but the dried bloodstains on it showed that it hadn't stopped being a weapon. "I am a great chief and also chief of the wise ones. I will go with the blond-furred one and advise her."

Komarg was taller than Tenoctris, as tall as a good-sized man, in fact. Not as tall or *near* as strong as Cashel himself, of course.

"I'm not interested in braggarts or fools, Komarg," Tenoctris said contemptuously. She took a cast snakeskin out of her sleeve and waggled it. It was pale brown and crinkly.

Cashel had met his share of people like Komarg, and in this he guessed cat men were *just* the same as humans. Oath or no oath, Komarg was going to swipe at Tenoctris. The quarterstaff was already swinging down to stop him when Tenoctris shouted, *"Saboset!"* and flicked the snakeskin like a whip.

Blue wizardlight blazed through the longhouse. Cashel saw the bones of his hands gripping the staff. His ears wanted to flinch at the crash of thunder, but this lightning was silent.

In the place of Tenoctris stood a two-legged snake with a body the size of an ox. Cashel backed with the staff crossways in front of him. He didn't look behind, trusting Sharina to keep out of the way. They could retreat to the doorway; then he'd figure out what to do next. A beast this size wouldn't make anything of going through even the best-woven wattling.

"Demon!" the cat men were screaming as they scrambled backward. "Demon! Demon!"

Komarg half-turned but the snake darted its head at him. He knew he was too close to get away, so he swung his mace at it with both hands.

The snake took the blow with its flaring wing and grabbed Komarg around the waist. He screamed as it flung him in the air. Blood splattered from his belly; it looked like somebody'd laid him open with a saw that cut in and then back at a different angle.

Komarg bounced off the ridgepole, losing his mace. As he dropped, the snake caught him again, this time by the head, and shook him like a dog with a rat. When it tossed him over its back into a corner, he was limp as a rag. Blood oozed from his wounds; his heart had stopped.

What Cashel'd thought was a solid wall behind the pack of cat men turned out to be a curtain of woven straw covering a door. All of them had run out that way except a scraggly old female. She'd spilled dust on the board floor and drawn a curving zigzag design in it. The pattern didn't close, but when Cashel followed the ends of it with his eyes he *felt* a broad oval.

The Corl wizard squatted where she'd been from the start, snarling words. Cashel recognized the rhythms as those of a wizard chanting spells.

He'd reached the door they'd entered by, but he didn't back into the open air yet. Tenoctris had either raised the demon or was the demon, and it hadn't gone after anybody but the cat men. He knew Garric said that humans and cat men were all part of the same kingdom now. That was fine, but Cashel was still going to wait till he knew more before he mixed into what didn't seem to be a fight for human beings.

The snake—the snake-demon, he guessed, because it sure wasn't just a snake—bent close to the old female and shrieked like a hawk. Well, a really big hawk. She blinked but kept on chanting.

The snake-demon reached its right leg out with the long middle claw extended; its wings quivered to balance the big body. When the sickle-curved claw crossed the line on the floor, there was a blast of crimson wizardlight. It was nigh as bright as the blue when the creature had appeared. Dust flew in all directions like a whirlwind'd swept it up.

The Corl leaped to her feet and swiped at the demon's muzzle with the slate wand she'd used to scribe her line. Old as she was, the motion was still quicker than that of any but a handful of men Cashel'd met—and maybe quicker'n them too.

The wand didn't strike anything because the snake-demon wasn't there—wasn't anywhere, in fact. Tenoctris stood back where she'd been to begin with, tucking the scrap of snakeskin away in her sleeve and smiling faintly.

"So, my fellow wizard," she said. "My name is Tenoctris. What's yours?"

The Corl drew her lips back in a snarl. Cashel was beside Tenoctris again, though after what he'd just seen he didn't doubt she could take care of herself. Still, he raised the quarterstaff slightly to stick it in the way if he needed to.

The cat man looked at the wand in her hand, then threw it onto the floor. It clacked, rolled against the wall, and rolled back.

"I am Rasile!" she said. "But why would *you* care, Tenoctris?"

"You just demonstrated why I care," Tenoctris said. "I knew there was a powerful wizard among the True People. I came to meet you, Rasile."

She eyed the Corl critically; Cashel did the same. Rasile wasn't much to look at, that was sure: her fur was worn thin on the joints, and the flesh sucked in between the bones of her forearms. You didn't often see an animal that old in Barca's Hamlet; they aren't good for much, and peasants are too close to the edge even in a good year to feed useless mouths. Of course Rasile wasn't an animal, exactly.

"You could make yourself young again," Tenoctris said. "Why haven't you?"

Rasile growled with disgust. "Why would I want to extend my life in this misery of a world?" she said. "I'll live the years the fates have given me, but I don't like pain so much that I'll willingly extend them."

Tenoctris laughed. "It's not such a bad world when you look at it in the right way," she said, "but I'm not here to argue with you."

She picked up the wand and handed it to the cat man. "You'll be needing this," she said.

Turning, she went on, "Sharina, allow me to present your new wizard and advisor, Rasile of the True People. I think you'll find her very satisfactory. And now, Cashel, you and I must go back immediately to the tomb where we spent last night."

Tenoctris smiled in a funny way and said, "I have nothing further to do with the one who was interred there, but it's a concentration of the power that will be useful for the next stage of our business."

"YOU'VE COME, ILNA, you've come at last!" cried Merota. "Chalcus, look, Ilna's here!"

Ilna opened her eyes. Her mind was blank. Merota threw herself into Ilna's arms. "Oh, Ilna!" she said. "We're all together again and I'm so happy!"

Merota was a warm, solid weight that squirmed against Ilna as she always did when they'd been apart for a longer time than usual. And though Ilna might've been imagining something she wanted as much as to be with her family again, the holly oak's coarse bark against her shoulders felt completely real.

My family. . . .

Ilna stood, holding the girl close. Chalcus was striding toward her, coming from the round temple that faced them across a pool.

"I never doubted you'd come, dear heart," he called. "Though I don't mind saying that the wait was the hardest thing I've known in a life that's—"

Chalcus grinned with the hint of wolfishness under the pleasure that Ilna remembered so well.

"—had its share of hard things, and not all of them things that I did to others."

Ilna ran to him, holding Merota's hands, and they embraced. Chalcus' hard muscles were as rippling and tender as they always had been. "It's been a long time," he whispered, but perhaps Ilna was hearing her own whisper instead.

When she blinked the tears out of her eyes, she stepped back slightly and looked around. She didn't see any building save the temple, but smoke rose from hearths hidden in the trees beyond. There was a handful—more than a handful—of other people in sight. One was a shepherd on the nearby hilltop, watching the sheep on the slope below him.

The curb and the temple were well made but very simple. Both were built of yellowish-gray limestone, and the temple's pillars weren't fluted.

A halved log lay as a bridge across the brook in the near distance. On it knelt a small boy drawing with a stick of charcoal, while a woman in white robes kept her eye on him. She felt Ilna's stare and looked up, then waved.

Ilna looked at Chalcus again, this time taking in the details instead of letting herself be swept away by a fierce tide of love. He wore a loose shirt of crimson silk, the sleeves pinned back by gold armlets; a brocade sash, silk again but dyed a fierce blue that made Ilna squint when her eye tried to follow the line where it met the shirt; and black leather breeches decorated with suede appliqués of dancing girls.

Ilna'd never seen any of the garments, but they added up to Chalcus in his dress finest. He'd been a sailor, after all, not a delicate aesthete from Valles—and most certainly not a prim girl from Barca's Hamlet with a loathing for self-advertisement.

In that respect and many, Chalcus was the other half of Ilna os-Kenset; far more than half of her soul had died when the cat beasts killed him. And here he and Merota were, complete to every stitch and placket except—

"Chalcus, where's your sword?" Ilna said, speaking quietly. There was nothing in her expression that might suggest to anyone watching that she was concerned. "And the dagger?"

"Oh, you dear silly heart!" the sailor said. He raised her

hand and made as if to twirl her, but she stayed where she was and met his eyes with fixed determination.

"Dearest Ilna," he said, "nobody's taken them away from me, but the sword isn't needed here. Come, I'll show you. I hung them in the temple as an offering to the Youth. I'll wear them if you'd like. Come!"

"You don't need to prove to me that you're telling the truth!" Ilna said. "Of course I believe you."

"Oh, do come," Merota said, tugging Ilna's sleeve. "The statue's lovely, you'll see. And it's real gold!"

Chalcus laughed and tousled the girl's hair. "When you've had as much gold drip through your fingers as I have, child," he said, "in taverns and mayhap less suitable places, then you'll better understand how slight a thing it is. But yes, dear heart, let's look at the statue, for it's very beautiful."

Ilna walked widdershins between them around the pool, Merota holding her left hand and Chalcus' fingers lying warm on her waist. He said, "The Youth—the man himself, I mean—is buried in the mound where you came back. I shouldn't wonder if that's how you were able to join us without . . ."

He smiled apologetically and made a quick circle in the air with his right hand, spinning the rest of the thought away.

"You shouldn't say 'buried,' Chalcus," Merota said in a tone like a schoolmaster's. "She'll think the Youth is dead."

She looked solemnly at Ilna and explained, "He isn't, you see. He's sleeping in the mound in a crystal case. He'll arise when the time is ripe to lead all mankind into Paradise."

"Aye, so you say, child," said Chalcus. His tone wasn't quite as dismissive as the words—but almost. "And you're learned and I'm no more than a sailor, so I have no doubt you're right. But—"

He paused and embraced Ilna again.

"—I can't imagine another Paradise than being together again with the heart of my heart. As I am now."

Ilna detached her hand from Merota's to put both arms around Chalcus. She hugged him; she'd never thought she'd feel those rippling muscles again. Yes, Paradise indeed.

She stepped back. "Chalcus?" she said. "How *did* you come here?"

The sailor shrugged. "I'm not a priest, beloved," he said. "There aren't any priests here, though I don't put any special meaning on that. We're here because the Youth willed it, I suppose. Me and Merota and you, all three."

They'd reached the entrance to the temple. The columns supported a thatched roof. The solid-walled enclosure behind the columns had a door of pale beechwood planks joined by a walnut Tree of Life overlay. Like the rest of the building, the carpentry was simple but of excellent craftsmanship.

Ilna smiled faintly. Much like one of her own fabrics, in fact.

Chalcus opened the door. The walls were a hand's breadth short of meeting the conical roof but still higher than the eaves, so the only light was what came through the doorway. The statue in the middle of the small room nonetheless blazed, smooth and warm and comforting. It was of a nude young man, holding his hands out as though offering bounty to those who approached.

Hanging on twists of twine from a peg beside the door were Chalcus' sword and dagger, as he'd never worn a sword belt that Ilna recalled. He took down the sword and slid the sharkskin scabbard through his sash; his fingers caressed the eared horn hilt.

"You shouldn't draw it here, Chalcus," said Merota in a tone of disapproval.

"Of course not, child," he said reprovingly. He stepped out of the enclosure, then walked beyond the porch as well. Ilna stood in the doorway, watching.

"Looking back, I'd agree that I've drawn it many places that I ought not to've," Chalcus said. "But I was never so ill-bred as to distress the Youth in His temple."

As he spoke, the slim, incurved sword came out in his hand and danced a complex figure in the sunlight. He tossed it in the air, turned to face Ilna, and caught the hilt in his left hand. Smiling, he made another complex gesture and sheathed the sword before pulling it, scabbard and all, from under his sash.

"You see, love," Chalcus said gently with the sword in the flat of his hand. "Nothing but courtesy prevents me from wearing this. Or from using it to slit the throats of any number of people, hundreds, I expect. I doubt there's anyone in this place who could so much as give me a fight, eh?"

"You wouldn't do that!" Merota said.

Chalcus hugged her close. "I've done it, child," he said. "I've done that and worse. But no, I wouldn't do it again. The man I am now would rather die."

He pecked Ilna on the cheek, then stepped past her to hang the sword back on the wall. "I haven't wanted the blade since I came here," he said, putting his arm around Ilna's waist in the doorway. "And now that the heart of my heart has come back forever, I want it all the less."

"Chalcus, I can't stay here," Ilna said. She felt as though she'd stepped into a pit filled with rose petals, lovely and sweet-scented and smothering her softly. "I'm not *dead*."

"Indeed you are not, dearest one," he said with a smile. "Nor do you ever need die, now that you've joined us again."

"Until He leads us to Paradise," Merota said, faintly disapproving as children can be when an elder doesn't show the sense of propriety which the child thinks is warranted. She softened into her usual brightness and added, "But until then, yes. And we'll still be together or it wouldn't be Paradise!"

"But I can't," Ilna said. *I'm sinking into roses.* . . . "I have duties in the world. The other world."

Chalcus laughed and kissed her. "To take revenge on the Coerli for killing me and Merota?" he said. "But we're not dead, dearest. We're here and you're here. Whatever could be better than that?"

The child sketching on the bridge had gotten up; his mother brushed his tunic with her hands while he prattled to her. *I wonder what looms they use here?* Ilna thought. Even from this distance she could see that the mother's white garment, too long and flowing to be called a tunic, was of a very delicate weave.

"Yes, Ilna," Merota said, hugging her tightly about the waist. "You have to stay. Otherwise you won't be happy."

"That doesn't matter!" Ilna said, her voice as sharp as if she'd just been slapped. She straightened, instinctively drawing away from the man and child. "That's never mattered."

"But it matters now, dear heart," Chalcus said, touching her shoulder, his solemn eyes on her. "And nothing else matters."

"Yes, Ilna," Merota said. "You *deserve* to be happy with us."

Ilna looked into the pool. Instead of showing a reflection of the tomb across from her, the water rippled with an image of the world where she'd fallen asleep. Temple and the two hunters stood on the mound with desperate expressions. Asion was calling with one hand cupped to his lips; the other held his dagger.

"Your happiness is all that matters," Chalcus said.

Ilna jumped feet first toward the pool. She was fully clothed and didn't know how to swim, though the water might not be deep enough to drown in.

"Ilna!" Merota cried.

Ilna landed on the plain, almost stepping into Temple's fire. Three rabbits were grilling flesh-side down on a frame of green twigs. They'd already been on too long, forgotten in the men's worry. Ilna snatched up the grate by two corners as the quickest way to remedy a problem she was responsible for.

"Mistress!" cried Karpos. He'd strung his bow and held it with an arrow nocked. "Where have you been?"

"I'm back now," Ilna said harshly. "I have duties, you know."

She touched her dry lips with her tongue. "Get out your digging tools," she said. "There's something in this mound."

"WILL THESE QUARTERS be satisfactory, Rasile?" Sharina said, gesturing through the open door. She'd have preferred to say, "Mistress Rasile," but there was no provision for that in the Coerli tongue. She could've said, "Female Rasile," but the implications would be just as insulting to a Corl as they were to Sharina herself.

"If they were not," said Rasile, looking past Sharina's shoulder while a squad of Blood Eagles watched uncomfortably, "I suppose I could carry in muck to make the rooms more similar to the hut in which I live in the Place."

She growled. Sharina's new sense of the Coerli tongue couldn't translate the sound but she did realize it was amused rather than threatening: the wizard was laughing.

"And perhaps," Rasile added, "you could find me garbage to eat as well. That was good enough for an old female, you see. Had I not been a wizard—"

She gave a hunch to her narrow shoulders; a shrug in human terms as well.

Sharina'd asked that the bungalow nearest to hers be left empty. Many of the buildings in the palace compound had become run-down before Garric replaced Valence III, but this one had been in excellent shape—perhaps because it stood in a beech grove and the trees broke the force of storms that might otherwise have lifted roof tiles or torn off shutters.

Nobody'd argued with her request, though. She was, after all, Princess Sharina of Haft. If she wanted her privacy, she would have it.

She'd sent a messenger back to Valles ahead of them, directing the chamberlain to have the place cleaned. The lamp burning in a wall niche showed that had happened, but there hadn't been time to clear the mustiness even with the door and windows open. Still, Rasile didn't seem concerned as she walked in and looked around.

The servants preparing the bungalow had brought in a few pieces of furniture: a couch whose bolster was slightly too large, a pair of bronze-framed chairs, and a table which'd probably been retired to storage when the ivory inlays began lifting away from the wood. Sharina couldn't complain given how short a time they'd had, but the part of her that was still an innkeeper's daughter winced to see what she was offering a guest.

She made a quick decision. To the under-captain commanding her escort she said, "Stay outside, if you will. I have private business to transact with Rasile."

"Your Highness, I'm afraid I can't allow that," said the Blood Eagle in an upper-class Cordin accent. She didn't recall having seen the man before. He was relatively young to be an officer in a regiment chosen from veterans. "It's not safe for a woman like you to be alone with a cat beast."

Sharina's mind went blank for an instant. Over the years, she'd had many men tell her what she must or couldn't do because she was a woman. She'd never liked it, and tonight she was very tired.

She smiled. "You can't allow it, you say?" she said. "Well, then you can sit in the corner and chat with the spirits of all the people you've killed in your life. You do realize that Rasile is a wizard, don't you? Or instead of the spirits, maybe we'll bring back the bodies."

Sharina felt her smile widen, though the expression was no deeper than her lips. She said, "Have you ever talked to a man who's been dead for six years, Under-Captain? I have. It's not an experience *I'd* want to repeat, but if you really have to come inside with us while we perform an incantation . . . ?"

The officer had begun backing away the instant Sharina said "wizard." His troops were studiously looking in other directions, pretending not to hear the confrontation.

Sharina took a deep breath. She was trembling. She'd been cruel to the man, behavior which she disliked as much in herself as when she saw it in others, but—

She shut the door between her and the soldiers before she started to giggle. The look of horror on the under-captain's face had been *so* funny! And he *was* a pompous twit. Though he doubtless had her best interests at heart, he was too stupid—too narrow, at least, which could be the same thing—for her to trust his discretion.

Sharina turned to face the room. Rasile was watching her intently. "So, Sharina," she said. "You are a wizard too?"

"No," Sharina said. She shrugged. "I suggested a possibility to make the guards leave us alone. I was confident that the under-captain wouldn't call my bluff."

Rather than take the couch or one of the chairs, Rasile squatted on the mosaic floor. It was laid in a garden pattern with caged birds at the corners. The Corl positioned herself carefully so that she appeared to be sitting under the pear tree in the center of the room.

She gave a growl of humor again and said, "I was wondering, you see. I could make that warrior see the faces of his victims, but to bring the actual bodies would be difficult. I would be impressed if you could do that, Sharina. And I think even your friend Tenoctris would be impressed."

Sharina sat on one of the chairs; its bronze feet clicked against the stone. "Tenoctris said I should ask you about a . . ."

She gripped her lower lip with her teeth while she wondered how to phrase the request.

"A problem," she decided at last. "A man named Vorsan, Prince Vorsan, watches me from mirrors. I've seen his face several times, generally only for a moment. He drew me in with him once, though. He says he's a wizard, well, a scientist, from before the Great Flood. He wants me to join him in his world because the Last are going to destroy this one."

Rasile's pupils were vertical slits like those of a real cat; they made her fixed stare even more disquieting than it'd otherwise have been. "So, Sharina . . . ," she said. "How did you escape from this Vorsan?"

Sharina grimaced. "He didn't try to hold me," she admitted. "But I'm not comfortable knowing that at any time he could take me back with him. Can you drive him away?"

Rasile shrugged again. "Perhaps," she said. "But tell me, Sharina—can you see into the future?"

"No, of course not!" Sharina said. "Why do you ask?"

"I cannot either," the Corl said, "at least not clearly. But I believe you would be better off letting Vorsan be."

"All right," Sharina said. She felt a wash of regret, though she knew that Vorsan was at most an irritation. Perhaps she'd been focusing on him because so many of the greater problems facing her seemed completely intractable.

She stood. "Is there anything more you need?" she asked. "There should be food in the larder, but it may not be to your taste."

She grinned and added, "For example, I'm pretty sure that the steward didn't include garbage. If there's a problem, tell a guard—there'll be two of them outside—and he'll find someone to correct the situation."

Normally a servant would sleep in the alcove off the bungalow's pantry. Sharina was fairly sure that there'd be a mutiny among the palace servants if she ordered one of them to enclose herself for the night with a man-eating Corl. The Blood Eagles—whom Attaper had insisted on to control Rasile rather than to protect her—would do.

"Aren't you going to argue with me about ignoring Vorsan?" Rasile said.

"What?" said Sharina, wondering what she'd missed in her tiredness to have brought such a question. "No. Tenoctris told me I could trust you."

"And you trust Tenoctris?" the Corl said. She got to her feet with a degree of controlled grace which was more impressive to watch than mere quickness would've been.

"Yes, of course," said Sharina. "Rasile, my duties are hard enough without me doubting my friends."

"I see," said the Corl. She stepped to the couch and tossed the bolster on the floor, then prodded it with her foot.

She looked at Sharina and chuckled, adding, "This will do, I believe. It's softer than I'm used to, but my bones are old enough without sucking cold into them from the stones."

"I'll see you in the morning, then," Sharina said, putting her hand on the door latch.

"Yes, in the morning," said the Corl. "It will be best if you come with me while I talk to those who can tell us where the greatest danger from the Last may be."

"All right," Sharina repeated. She had various duties, but it appeared to her that Rasile's request was indeed the most important business she had in hand. "Who are the people we'll be talking with?"

"Who *were* they, rather, Sharina," Rasile said. Her lips drew back from teeth which were impressive despite being worn and discolored. "I will call up the humans whom the Last killed three nights ago when they attacked Tenoctris."

She laughed again. Perhaps the idea was more humorous to a Corl than it was to Sharina.

THE INN WAS half a mile down the valley in a grove of trees. Garric probably wouldn't have noticed it immediately if the whitewashed walls hadn't gleamed in the late sun.

"This one's built of sawn boards," he said to Shin and Kore. "I wonder if they'll have straw mattresses rather than corn shucks?"

"I could pull apart a stable built with boards," said the ogre musingly. "It's my own bad judgment that's reduced me to being a beast of burden. Had I but controlled my hunger and traveled south for a day, I'd be the free-living creature that the Fates intended me to be."

"Or you could've caught a wild pig," said Shin, "and saved yourself the effort of pulling down a stable as well."

"I had a whim for horsemeat," Kore said in a tone of dignified rebuke. "A splendid being like me has a right to her whims."

"Which in this case means the right to carry the human champion as an alternative to having your heart cut out," Shin commented. "I'd expect a true philosopher to be considering whether the taste of pork was really so bad."

The track was wider here along the river bottom than it'd been on the granite slope they'd just come down. Tree stumps sprang from the undergrowth. They'd been saw-cut, Garric noted with interest, rather than axed or simply ringed and left to fall over in a windstorm after years of decay.

Weather—perhaps flooding, but a bad frost could've done it—had blasted two oaks just above on the ridge. Their branches stood out, seeming to writhe in silent horror.

A woman wearing a red jumper strolled from the inn, holding a child by the hand. Garric lifted off his broad hat and waved it. "Halloo!" he cried.

"Can she hear you, do you think?" Kore wondered aloud.

The woman screamed, snatched up the child, and rushed back into the building. Garric didn't have any trouble hearing *her,* at least.

"Did Orra not tell them I was coming?" Garric puzzled aloud. "Well, *we* were coming. I don't think . . ."

He glanced at Shin and found the aegipan looking up at him. "No," Shin said, "I *don't* think that folk who were warned that you were arriving on an ogre would be terrified to learn that an aegipan was part of the group also. Though I'm flattered that you'd consider such a possibility."

He vaulted onto his hands, then backflipped onto his hooves again. He grinned sardonically up every time he was facing in Garric's direction.

"I've never noticed that humans were notably trustworthy," said Kore. "Do you consider it unlikely that this Orra would have forgotten to tell or chosen not to tell the innkeeper that you were arriving on so marvelous a mount as me? Were you friends with Orra?"

"No, I wasn't," Garric admitted. "Though I wouldn't have said we were enemies either. Though . . ."

"Aye," said King Carus. *"We don't know what Orra's business is. If he thought you were a rival, that'd be reason to make your path a little harder."*

"He might even have told folk that a great and terrible ogre was coming to eat all their horses," Kore said. Garric couldn't be sure from her tone whether or not she was being serious. "Indeed, I wonder what *is* in the stable tonight?"

Three men tumbled out the front door of the inn. Two of them wore leather clothing and carried short, powerful bows; the third was older and held a double-bitted axe. It was a woodsman's tool rather than a weapon, but the man's arms and shoulders looked impressive even if the belly bulging his apron was heavier than it'd probably been in his prime.

As Kore continued to jog forward, another man ran from the stables with a wooden pitchfork, closely followed by a little boy who'd been sent to fetch him. One of the archers raised his bow and sighted past the arrowhead, though the range was still too great to chance a shot with a hunting weapon.

"Hold up!" Garric said to the ogre, pulling back on the reins. Well, the straps. "I'll go talk to them."

Kore stopped by spreading both clawed feet in the rutted track. Garric swayed forward and banged his breastbone against the back of her head.

Carus smiled ruefully. His trained reflexes ordinarily made Garric as sure a rider as any cavalryman from northern Ornifal, but Carus didn't have any more experience riding an ogre than his descendant did.

"Now here's an ethical question, Shin," Kore said. "If my master is shot full of arrows by yokels he walks up to, am I bound to pine over his corpse till I starve as a noble steed in the ballads would, or am I permitted to wander off looking for fillies?"

Garric stepped down. "You're replacing a gelding," he said. "Fillies are out."

He unbuckled his belt and handed it with both sword and dagger to the ogre. "But you can hold this, if you will," he added. "In hopes that if I look peaceful enough, the sturdy yeomen hereabouts *won't* fill me with arrows."

Garric strode forward, waving his hat in his right hand. "Hello the house!" he cried. "I'm a friend!"

He'd come within half a furlong, a clout shot even with a short bow if the archer knew his business. Which these fellows might not: people tended to think of hunters as dead shots, but it wasn't true. Often enough they made their kills by waiting in patient silence till the target was close enough to spit on.

"But you'd sooner not learn," said Carus. *"I've had three arrows cut out of me, and the cane one some savage on Dalopo put through my left calf almost finished me when it started to fester. This pair is using cane too."*

"Pardon me my steed," Garric called. "He's strange, I know, but just as harmless as a pony. It's a long story, and I'll willingly recite it when I buy the house a round of ale."

The older man rubbed the axehead on his apron. "We drink cider in these parts," he said argumentatively. "Bloody good cider, if I do say so myself."

"Then won't you all join me in a cider?" said Garric, walking up to the group, by now all four men and the boy. The woman and child were peering down from a second-floor window.

Garric brought out a silver piece, a grapeleaf from Ornifal with the worn face of Valence II on the other side. He spun it up from his thumb to sparkle in the light, caught it, and handed it to the tapster. The latter frowned, rang the coin on his axehead to judge the silver content, and said, "All right, then."

"Are them two coming in?" said one of the hunters, bobbing his bowstaff in the direction of Kore and the aegipan. A patch of his scalp was pink scar tissue; he'd tried to grease the remainder of his black hair over the injury to hide it.

Garric turned, partly to give himself time to decide on an answer to the question, and waved to Kore and Shin. "You can come forward, now!" he called. "The gentlemen know that we're friendly travelers with money for lodgings."

The men staring at him *weren't* convinced yet, but phrasing things that way could help disarm their suspicions. Garric smiled at the innkeeper, the least hostile of the group, and said, "I'm not surprised at your concern, of course. An earlier traveler had promised to bring word of my coming and my companions, a Master Orra. Did he not mention that?"

The innkeeper frowned. "Orra?" he said. "We've seen no one of that name. When was he to arrive?"

"He should've been here earlier today," Garric said. Shin and Kore were approaching, the aegipan walking on his hands ahead of the ambling ogre. "Riding a flea-bitten gray. Ah— we traveled at a good pace, but we didn't pass him on the way."

"No white horse been by here since a year ago my birthday," growled the stablehand in a scarcely intelligible accent. "And that was afore the Sister dragged everything down t'Hell and spit it back up again."

"Not a bad description of the Change," Carus remarked. His image wore an engaging smile, but Garric felt a cool undercurrent as his ancestor's mind judged how best to move if everything went wrong: snatch the axe, punch the helve into the temple of the hunter on the right, bring the blade back around to eliminate the tapster and the other hunter in the same stroke. . . .

The ancient warrior's reflexes weren't needed now; they were almost never needed. But they *were* available, and sometimes that'd saved Garric's life and perhaps the kingdom.

Shin hopped upright; the ogre knelt, dipped her head, and offered Garric's sword back to him on her upturned palms. Garric nonchalantly buckled his weapons on, silently amused by Carus' background calculations of how best to kill everyone around them now that he had the sword. Just in case, of course.

"Thank you, Kore," Garric said. "You may rise."

Looking at the local men again, he went on, "My jester, Shin, will—"

The aegipan bowed low.

"—share the room with me. You do have private rooms, do you not?"

"Here?" the innkeeper said. The silver piece had wiped away his initial truculence. "Why, no sir, there's no call for that here at the Notch House."

"You got the lean-to out back for a pantry, Noddy," the scalp-scarred hunter said. "You could put 'em in there."

"That won't be necessary," Garric said quickly. "The common room will do very well. As for my mount—"

Kore curtsied, cleverly throwing her left foot back rather than her right foot forward—which might've given the impression she was lunging at the locals.

"If you have a dry outbuilding, I think that would be better than the stables. Kore's quite harmless—"

If Carus'd had a physical body, his laughter would've been ringing from the steep sides of the valley.

"—but her presence might spook the other animals."

"No *way* it's going to be spending the night with me!" the stablehand said. He hopped backward, bringing the pitchfork down tines-foremost in a posture of defense.

"There's the grain shed, I guess," the innkeeper said, rubbing his chin with his knuckles. "He, ah . . . Does he eat grain?"

"I assure you your grain is safe from me, Master Noddy," Kore said. "Though I trust you won't object if I rid the building of some of its rats?"

One of the hunters looked at the other and said quizzically, "What is he, then?"

"Why do you suppose he's asking his partner, Kore?" the aegipan said in an arch tone. "Surely it's obvious that any of the three of us would be the proper party."

"To begin with, I'm not 'he,' gentle sir," Kore said. She gestured to her upper, then her lower, set of dugs. "And appearances are deceiving. On the face of it, I'm a perfectly proportioned female ogre in the prime of life, scarcely three hundred years old. In reality, however, I am a beast of burden, bearing Master Garric with a modest deportment rarely to be met with in a horse—no matter how good that horse might taste."

"Gentlemen," Garric said, "I'm very thirsty, and I could use supper as well."

"As could your jester, dear master," said Shin. To Noddy, he added, "I don't suppose you have asparagus at Notch House, do you?"

The innkeeper stared at the aegipan, then raised his eyes to Garric's. "What might asparagus be, sir?" he asked.

"Shin will settle for porridge and some fruit," Garric said. Seeing Noddy frown he added quickly, "Or vegetables. At least some onions?"

"We might run to onions," the innkeeper allowed. "Leest, run back quick and tell your mistress to throw some porridge on to warm. Now!"

The boy sprinted for the frame building. He wouldn't have raced off like that to carry out a task, but he was excited at the chance to tell his mother what he'd learned—little though that was in fact.

"And a lamb, perhaps?" said Kore. The men walking toward the house stopped and turned, wide-eyed. "No? Well, a haunch of mutton?"

"We've ham," said the innkeeper. "And sidemeat."

The ogre gave a theatrical sigh. "It's fitting," she said to the sky, "quite fitting. I will gnaw my hog femur and think deeply philosophical thoughts about the advantages of a diet of pork."

Garric cleared his throat and started the procession on into the house again. The scarred hunter unstrung his bow, though his partner still kept an arrow nocked.

"Is there a side trail Master Orra could've taken between the Boar's Skull Inn and here?" Garric asked.

"There's game tracks," said one hunter. "Hogs and deer. I guess he could've gone off down one a those if he wanted."

"Why'd he want to?" the other hunter said. "If he could afford a horse, he wasn't hunting for meat and hides."

"We passed a peel tower, I believe the name is," Shin said as he trotted up the three steps to the front door. His hooves clacked on the boards. "Who is it that lives there, if I may ask?"

"Well, I can't rightly tell you, ah, Master Jester," said the innkeeper, opening the door for his guests. "It wasn't here before the Bad Time, you see."

"I wish they wasn't there now, *I* do," said the stablehand, frowning as he picked bits of horse manure from the tines of his fork. He glared at the innkeeper with a fierceness that surprised Garric. "It's all right for you, you get the profit. But it's me drives the hogs there and I don't half like it!"

"Now, Cayler, you needn't act so put upon," Noddy said, bowing Garric ahead of him into the common room of the inn. "Don't I give you all the cider you can drink each time you come back? And don't you drink it?"

"Excuse me, Master Noddy," Garric said, wondering as he spoke whether that was the innkeeper's birth name or merely a nickname. "Does your stablehand go to the tower regularly, then?"

Noddy cleared his throat. "Rabanda!" he called up the stairs in the corner. "Come down here and help me with our guests!"

He set the axe on the bar in some embarrassment, then turned to face Garric again. "Well, a servant comes from the castle every ten days or so—"

"Oftener!" the stablehand said.

"Well, it's been oftener recently, that could be," Noddy admitted. "And maybe there's two different servants, but if it is they're as like as two peas. They don't talk, but the first time he brought a potsherd with PIGS written on it—"

"Can you read, Noddy?" said the scarred hunter in surprise.

"I most certainly can," the innkeeper said, tilting his head so that he looked down his nose at the hunter. "Regardless, he brought the note with silver shaved off a block, nineteen parts out of twenty pure. So I sent Cayler back with him to lead six hogs. Since then they've been back—or the one has, I can't say, as I told you. They don't bother with a note now, just bring more silver."

"There's no pigs in the tower now," said Kore.

Everybody turned quickly. The ogre squatted on her haunches outside. She could probably have gotten through the open doorway, but she wouldn't have been able to stand or even squat without tearing a hole in the ceiling.

"Which she could easily do, of course," said Shin, replying to the unvoiced observation.

Garric grinned. "I smelled hogs," he said, thinking back to when they'd jogged past the tower. At the time he'd ignored it, because the fact hadn't concerned him; the information was still in his mind when required, though.

"The freshest pig droppings in the road were seven days old," the ogre said, her long face exaggerating the solemn precision of her speech. "The smell from the tower itself was somewhat more recent, I grant—but I would've heard pigs if they'd been present."

A woman—the one Garric'd seen when he rode into the valley—crept down the stairs; she'd left the child on the upper floor. She slipped through the back door to the outside oven, casting nervous glances over her shoulder. By contrast, the men in the common room seemed to have relaxed.

"I did, however, hear a horse," Kore added. "Though muffled, as if it'd been snaffled."

Garric looked hard at the innkeeper. Noddy grimaced in discomfort. "I don't know anything about who lives in the castle!" he insisted.

"Except that their silver assays nineteen parts pure," Garric said without inflection.

"Look, I don't know how it's like where you come from!" Noddy said. "Around here, though, we keep ourselves to ourselves. That's why we came out here, often enough."

He looked at the hunters for confirmation, but they turned their faces away. The one who still had an arrow nocked rotated it parallel to the bowstaff. He glanced apologetically toward Garric, then unstrung the bow.

"Never figured how a stone castle could set there," the other hunter said, watching his partner intently instead of looking toward either Garric or the innkeeper. "It's next to being a swamp even in front of where it stands, and in back it *is* swamp. I saw a hart mire hisself there. Before the castle come, I mean."

"Well, what am I supposed to do?" Noddy demanded. "Go on, tell me! What?"

"Well, Master Garric," said the aegipan. His tongue waggled in visual laughter. "We're safely past the tower, so we don't need to worry about it either."

"We'll eat and sleep here tonight," Garric said. "We'll start back just before dawn so there's light when we arrive. I'm not willing to chance the business at night."

Carus was visualizing the climb up the tower's rough stone wall. It'd be possible if he went barefoot and used both hands. He could carry the dagger in his teeth, but it wouldn't help if the mute servants tipped a vat of boiling oil over the parapet when he was halfway up. Though if the ogre lifted him as high as she could reach and then tossed him the few remaining feet—

"What is it that you expect your horse to do tomorrow, master?" Kore asked. "For that's what my oath requires me to be, you'll recall."

Garric looked out at the squatting monster. He flushed with anger that came from the ghost in his mind—but the gust of laughter that followed it a moment later was Carus' reaction as well.

"I expect you to carry me to the castle or wherever else I decide, Kore," he said, "and then to wait quietly while I determine my next step. If you think you're likely to stray then I'll tether you, but the gelding you replace would stand drop-reined."

"Look, fellow," said the scarred hunter, still looking at his partner. "I'm not afraid of trouble, but I don't borrow it. I've kept clear of that castle ever since I got an eyeful of it the first time. I don't see you've got call to do otherwise."

"I disagree," said Garric. "But I accept that you don't feel the same duty to act that I do."

The duty didn't have anything to do with having become a prince, of course; he'd be doing the same thing if he were an innkeeper. He was doing what he thought a man should do.

He gave Noddy a wry smile. "Now, good host," he said, "I would *very* much like a meal."

"And I," said Kore, "will practice standing drop-reined. I hope that by morning I'll have learned that skill to my brave master's satisfaction."

Garric joined in his ancestor's unheard laughter, while the three local men watched in puzzlement.

Chapter

9

TENOCTRIS DREW BACK on the reins, halting the gig on the crest above the opened tomb. Cashel hopped out and tied the mare to the base of a bush—probably forsythia, but it was past blooming and he wasn't sure. He used the lead rope rather than the reins to give the horse more room to browse. She'd probably tangle the line in the brush, but at least he'd tried to make her a little more comfortable.

Cashel drew the satchel with her gear from behind the seat as Tenoctris dismounted. She moved carefully, but she didn't need his help like she used to for doing common things like, well, getting up and down from a gig.

"I thought there'd be guards still here," he said, looking down at the excavation. In truth he'd been surprised that they'd been able to leave the Coerli city without having an escort of soldiers. Things were different with Garric gone. It wasn't that Sharina didn't care about him and Tenoctris, it was just that she didn't believe Cashel or anybody Cashel was looking after needed other help.

Cashel smiled, standing with the staff in one hand and the satchel made from a rug in the other. He wasn't as strong as Sharina seemed to think; but he doubted a soldier—or an army—could handle any likely trouble better than him alone.

"I'm going to lie in the sarcophagus again," Tenoctris said, taking short steps down the slope. "I don't need it the way I did the other night, but it's such a powerful focus that it'll reduce the process to a few minutes."

She chuckled. "That concentration of powers is the only thing of value here," she explained. "And it's of no more use to ordinary thieves than a vat of molten steel would be."

Cashel scrambled to get in front, just in case the old wizard slipped. There was next to no chance of his own bare feet going out from under him, but he slanted the quarterstaff out for a brace anyway.

He paused at the top of the trench to judge the sun. It'd be down soon, but the twilight would last long enough to see by for another hour.

"I'm going to make myself younger," Tenoctris said.

Cashel stepped into the tomb and turned to make sure Tenoctris didn't have trouble in the doorway. She maybe thought he was surprised to hear what she'd said, because she went on, "Oh, not for vanity, I assure you. It's just a practical response to the difficulties of what we'll be doing. I need a more supple body, you see."

Cashel helped her onto the bench and held her hand as she got into the coffin. He looked again at the carvings and wondered about the man who'd wanted to be buried in such a thing.

Tenoctris opened her satchel and took out a simple stylus of lead. With it she marked a triangle on the bottom of the stone box down at the end where her head'd lain when they came here before, then wrote words on each of the three sides. She looked at Cashel with a little grin and said, "Well, maybe a little from vanity too. Just a little."

Cashel smiled again, but he didn't say anything. She was joking; she wasn't any more vain than he was. Sure, Cashel was a good judge of what he could do, so he knew he could do a lot. He didn't go around bragging to other folk, though, and all the same things were true for Tenoctris.

She lay in the coffin and started murmuring her words of power. Cashel turned toward the entrance. His job was to make sure nobody came in while she was in a trance.

Cashel thought about the man who'd been buried here, if he was a man and not the demon his shadow made him. He took his left hand from his quarterstaff and touched the locket from Tenoctris. He wasn't sure why he was keeping it, but there was bound to be a good reason. Tenoctris always had good reasons.

The hair on his arms and the back of his neck lifted. Bright wizardlight lit the tomb with a crackle like lightning ripping down an oak tree. The iron ferrules of his quarter-staff spun off whirling blue whiplashes.

Cashel turned, his hands spread on the shaft so he could strike right or left as need required. Tenoctris lay in a tube of pure blue light, her hands crossed peacefully on her chest. Her lips moved, but Cashel couldn't hear her words over the tearing sound of wizardry.

He backed slightly; the cocoon of light made his chest prickle, like being too close to a blacksmith's fire. He could stand it if he had to, but he didn't see any need.

The coffin glowed with the wizardlight that leaked from Tenoctris. As Cashel watched, the figures on the side got fuzzy and began to flake, the way marble does when it's left in the weather a long time. Patches of rotten stone shelved out like fungus, then dropped away.

The light cut off, again lightning-quick. Cashel blinked and rubbed his eyes with the back of his hand. If something came at him now while he couldn't see—

His brief blindness gave way to shadows, then real shapes in the twilight. For a moment Cashel wondered if he should've lit a lamp after all, but then he could see Tenoctris sitting up with a smile on her face.

Then things really fell into focus. "Wow!" Cashel said.

He knew he was looking at Tenoctris because the lines of her face were the same, but this Tenoctris was his age. She *couldn't*'ve been more than twenty years old. "Tenoctris, it worked!"

The young Tenoctris got to her feet. She bumped the coffin and the whole front of it crumbled like a wall of sand in the tide. Laughing merrily, she stepped down from the bench.

"So . . . ," she said. "Do you like me, Cashel?"

Raising her arms overhead, palms out so the fingernails touched, Tenoctris pirouetted. She was so small that she didn't touch the ceiling, even on tiptoe.

Cashel blinked. This was really amazing. Tenoctris still

had fine bones, but her face was rounder than it'd been when age wrinkled her cheeks. He couldn't tell the color of her hair, but it fell in long curls instead of being in a tight bun on top of her head.

"That's really good, Tenoctris," he said. "That's really you, then? I mean, it's not just changing how you look?"

"A glamour, you mean?" she said. "No, no—this is how I looked when I was twenty-one. If you'd like a glamour, though . . ."

She turned her palm toward her face and murmured. Part of it was *". . . brimo maast,"* or something like it.

Scarlet wizardlight twinkled. When Tenoctris lowered her hand, she had lustrous black hair, full lips, and a bosom that noticeably bulged her silk brocade robes.

"Do you like this better?" she said. The voice was still Tenoctris, but nothing of the woman Cashel'd known so well for two years was there in the features. Smiling, she lifted her hand again. "Or this?"

The dusting of wizardlight was blue again this time, mild compared to the glare that'd dissolved the stone coffin but still bright enough to leave afterimages on Cashel's eyes. Tenoctris lowered her hand.

Cashel's mouth opened in amazement. Sharina, tall and blond and as perfect as she'd been when he saw her a few hours before, smiled back at him.

"You're really something to do that!" he said. "I think we'd best get back to the gig, though. We're losing the light, and there's some bad potholes till we get back to the main road."

"So . . . ," said Tenoctris. "You don't find me attractive, Cashel?"

He couldn't have said how the change happened, but what hadn't been Tenoctris slumped away or soaked in or something. She was back to being herself, only young.

"What?" said Cashel. "Sure I do. You're really pretty, as yourself or any of the other ways. But I don't want us to break a wheel on the way out."

He smiled. "Though I guess we could walk back if we had to now," he said. "Since you're young again."

Tenoctris gave a funny little laugh. "Yes," she said. "That was the point, after all, wasn't it? And you're right, we need to get started. We have a great deal to do, my friend."

She picked up the satchel herself and walked out of the tomb. Her strides were quick and birdlike, and her back was very straight.

THE THREE MEN would've been more than happy to open the mound themselves, but Ilna insisted on joining in with the digging stick which Karpos had cut for her from a cedar as thick as his wrist. The fresh cedar oozed sap so her hands were now sticky, but that just gave her a better grip. She stamped the wedge tip into the dirt and levered upward.

Asion's mattock clinked on rock; he worked it sideways. "I've got something here," he said. "It's not pebbles; it's fitted stones!"

"Here," ordered Ilna. "Let me."

They'd carved down to the depth of her forearm through the turf at one end of the mound. It was certainly artificial, made of topsoil instead of changing quickly to the yellowish clay that underlay the surrounding meadow. That didn't prove the truth of what Merota'd said, that the Youth who'd sucked Ilna into that dream world was buried here, but it made that more likely.

Had it really been Merota? And Chalcus, his arms as strong and supple as they'd been before the cat beasts'd swarmed over him slashing and stabbing . . . ?

"What is it you expect to find, Ilna?" asked Temple. They'd been piling loosened earth onto Ilna's outer tunic. The big man had lifted each bundle out of the excavation and dumped it well from the mound where it wouldn't get in the way later.

Ilna chopped fiercely at the dirt, opening a crevice between two large rocks. She didn't have to spare her implement the way Asion did the mattock: if she broke the end off the stick, Karpos would simply sharpen it again.

"I don't know," she said. She didn't look around, concentrating instead on the task she had in hand. As usual, of course; as she'd done all her life. "Perhaps bones, perhaps nothing."

The chest-sized stones under the layer of turf hadn't been shaped by tools, but they'd been laid with a good deal of care. She drove the digging stick into a crack she'd cleared, then put her weight against it.

The cedar was too supple to make a good crowbar, but she lifted the upper stone enough to notice those around it crunch and grate. This wasn't simply a heap: the individual rocks were wedged together into a dome of sorts.

"What will you do when you find what you're looking for, Ilna?" Temple said.

Ilna jerked out the digging stick and turned. "I don't know that either!" she said. The sun shone from directly behind Temple's head, turning his blond hair into a cloud of blazing light.

The hunters stood back slightly. Their expressions showed they were afraid that no matter what they did or didn't do, Ilna was going to flay the skin off them. Ilna glared and opened her mouth; they cringed.

She closed her mouth again. She'd been about to snarl at them simply for existing, which was precisely what they'd been afraid she was going to do.

Ilna barked a laugh. It wasn't a very good laugh, but she didn't have much experience with the process.

"We're going to have to lift the rocks off carefully before I can see what's inside," she said in a calm voice. "Otherwise the dome will collapse into a worse mess."

"I can lift this stone, Ilna," Temple said. He leaned forward and tapped the block whose edge she'd cleaned with her stick. "Then you can look inside."

Ilna felt her anger returning. There was something so *assured* in the man's tone that it made her want to snap at him—or worse.

She placed the yarn back in her sleeve. She'd started to knot a pattern that would've doubled the big man over retching; nobody could sound self-assured while vomiting his guts up.

"All right," Ilna said. "Since you believe you can."

She didn't believe he could do it; neither did the hunters, judging from the sidelong glances they offered each other. Temple smiled faintly and bent to the stone block, easing his fingers into the cracks on either side.

"You're going to have the weight of the ones it's touching to lift too, you know," Karpos warned, frowning. He'd locked his hands together and was flexing the fingers hard against one another.

"Yes," said Temple calmly. "It's going to be difficult."

His shoulders bunched; the tendons stood out on his arms. Ilna stepped farther off to the side. Temple had the same calm assurance as her brother Cashel. Though she couldn't believe he was really strong enough to pull the block out by himself. . . .

Temple stood like a sun-drenched statue, bent and motionless save for drops of sweat dribbling from his hair. They ran down his back and massive arms.

Stone ground on stones. Temple began to straighten, his arms withdrawing toward his body by a hair's breadth at a time.

"It's coming!" said Asion. "By the Lady, it's coming!"

The hunters scrambled up opposite sides of the mound, obviously expecting Temple to let the stone bounce away wherever its angles and gravity took it. Instead he dropped to one knee, rotated his palms upward, and tilted the block onto them. Straightening his legs cautiously, he set the block on the turf to the side of where they'd cut into the mound.

"May the Lady shelter me," Karpos said softly. "I didn't think anybody . . . I just didn't think anybody could lift . . ."

Karpos, who was more than ordinarily strong himself, was even more amazed at what Temple had been able to do than Ilna was. Ilna didn't know what the stone weighed; more than three men certainly, and perhaps a great deal more.

Temple turned, flexing his hands. His fingertips were

bright red with the fierceness of his grip. He smiled and said, "You may look inside now, Ilna. And make up your mind."

She stepped past him without speaking. Though irregular, the block had come out as neatly as a cork from a bottle; the stones around it remained as firm as a window casement. Those who'd built the mound were quite skilled despite their crude materials.

Ilna smiled tightly. She'd always give craftsmanship its due, even when the craftsmen had used stone.

She looked down into the chamber. The sun shone past her, and the crystal coffin within spread its light throughout the interior.

It was indeed a tomb. Despite the dust of ages and the scattering of dirt that'd fallen in while they prized at the stones, the coffin was clear enough for her to see the body of the man within. His skin was the hue of ivory, and there were no signs of decay.

Ilna looked at her companions. "Chalcus was right," she said. "It's the man who took me . . ."

She shrugged angrily, trying to find the right word. "To wherever it was," she snapped at last. "To a dream world. It's the Youth."

"Did the Youth harm you, Ilna?" Temple said.

It was just a question; there was nothing more in the words or tone than Ilna'd have expected if he was asking for a water bottle. Despite that it took conscious effort to keep her voice level as she said, "I told you: he snatched me away."

"Yes, and you returned," Temple said. The hunters were watching the discussion warily. "I assume you were allowed to return. That's not surprising, since He appears to be a God of peace. You lost a few minutes of your time with us, then?"

"He . . . !" Ilna said. She stopped and felt a wry smile lift one corner of her mouth.

"He gave me a chance to forget my duty," she said. "That's what you mean, isn't it?"

"I don't mean anything, Ilna," Temple said, but he smiled also. "I was just asking a question."

"And if an opportunity was all I needed to forget my

duty," Ilna continued, "then I'd be a poor excuse for a human being."

She sniffed. "Well, there's enough of that sort in the world already," she said. "So no, I wasn't hurt."

"Mistress?" Asion asked. "What do we do now?"

"Do?" said Ilna. "Cover up the tomb again, I suppose. Temple, do you want help in replacing the stone?"

"I don't think that will be necessary, Ilna," the big man said, flexing his hands again with his palms out at arm's length. His smile was very broad now, and as warm as that of a mother looking at her newborn.

Ilna turned and walked a few steps away from the men as they started undoing the work of the afternoon.

"Goodbye, Chalcus," she whispered to the setting sun. "Goodbye, Merota. I hope you understand."

But in all truth, Ilna wasn't sure that even she really understood.

SHARINA STOOD NEAR the marsh, watching Rasile take knuckle-sized chips of quartz from a leather bag and space them in a circle on the wet soil. The Corl wizard glanced at her and said, "I'm marking the points of a twelve-sided star around us."

"Ah," said Sharina, nodding; a polite response to a polite explanation. Then she said, "Is this better than drawing the lines out the way, ah, others do?"

She'd started to say, "the way Tenoctris does," but she'd caught herself. She didn't know Rasile—or the Coerli more generally—well enough to know what might be read as an insult.

Sharina smiled. It was bad enough dealing with human beings whom you didn't know very well; and often enough you could say the wrong thing with people you *did* know.

Rasile smiled also, though her pointed teeth made the expression a trifle equivocal. "The figure in this world doesn't matter, Sharina," she said, "except for what it evokes in the wizard's mind."

The Corl gave her growling laugh. "For someone as powerful as your friend Tenoctris," she said, "I doubt any material symbol would be necessary to perform a task as simple as this."

"Ah," Sharina repeated. She almost said that Tenoctris hadn't always been so powerful, but on consideration she let the thought rest unspoken.

Sharina knew she didn't begin to understand wizardry, despite having been close to Tenoctris for years and having been *too* close to other wizards during that period. She decided she was better off not offering opinions to Rasile, who quite obviously understood a great deal.

The sun was fully down; stars would've been visible in the west if the mist hadn't already risen so thickly from the surface of the marsh. The fishermen Cashel had mentioned weren't out tonight; the only lanterns were those of the soldiers escorting Sharina and the wizard.

Sharina smiled faintly again. Attaper hadn't wanted her to accompany Rasile. When she'd insisted, he'd asked Lord Waldron to send a company of skirmishers from the regular army along with his Blood Eagles. He wanted to be prepared for threats that heavy infantry couldn't fight hand-to-hand.

The black-armored bodyguards waited in near silence, but the skirmishers—javelin-throwers from northern Cordin, shepherds in civilian life—squatted around small fires and chattered cheerfully. They'd melted cheese in a glazed pot and were dipping chunks of barley bread into it for supper.

Water dribbled from the pool from which the Last had attacked Cashel, though it'd been piled high with brush to prevent the white star from reflecting on its surface. Lord Waldron had been ready to tear the curb down and block the spring with boulders, but Tenoctris had said not to; it might be useful.

Sharina tugged her short cloak tighter around her; it was a cold night. She grinned at herself: anyway, it was a cold business.

She looked toward the southern sky but didn't see the white star. Hadn't it risen yet, or was the mist just too thick to see it?

The mist was *very* thick.

"Are you ready, Sharina?"

Sharina jumped; Rasile was standing at her side. "Yes," she said, smiling in embarrassment. "I'm sorry, I was wool-gathering."

Rasile chuckled deep in her throat. She nodded toward Sharina's hand, which'd reached for the Pewle knife hidden beneath a placket of her outer tunic.

"You are a female," the wizard said. "I feared that the fe-males of your species were trembling breeders like those of the True People. I see you are not."

Sharina's smile widened a little. "Not all of us," she said. "Of either of our races, I'd judge. I watched Tenoctris pick you."

Rasile laughed again. "I am not female," she said. "I am merely old, and soon I will be done with this world. How-ever, before that—"

She walked to the center of the figure; it was about ten feet in diameter as best Sharina could judge in the rank grass.

"Come stand with me, Sharina," the Corl directed. "We'll go to a place that will test your courage in the fashion Tenoc-tris tested mine. I do not doubt that you'll pass."

She grinned as Sharina stepped to her side. "It may well be that we both will die, but your courage won't be wanting."

Rasile began to chant. The syllables weren't words as a human would understand them, even words of power, but the rhythm was that of every wizard Sharina had seen working.

The soldiers grew silent; the Blood Eagles fell into tighter ranks. The skirmishers' cook fire flared as they added fuel and stirred it to quick life, but the mist rising from the black water seemed to thicken also.

The chips of quartz lit with sparks of wizardlight, blue and then red; the air grew charged. Incandescence too pale to have color quivered from the brush-covered spring. For a moment Sharina thought the nearby pond cypress and the oaks at a greater distance were waving; then she realized that the air was distorting them as it did on a hot day.

She and the Corl wizard dropped into a glowing gray haze. She didn't feel motion or vertigo: the world, including the muddy grass under her feet, was gone. She hung in a palpable *nowhere*.

Rasile continued to chant. Sharina *almost* found meaning in the wizard's wail, and the realization frightened her at a visceral level.

I'm not meant to hear that! No one is meant to hear that! For the first time she realized that the difference between wizards and laymen like herself might be the ability to understand certain things without going mad.

Shapes formed in the grayness. At first Sharina thought her eyes were tricking her into believing there was something more than endless fog around her; then she decided that she was seeing the moss-draped cypresses on the other side of the marsh, their shadows cast onto the mist as sometimes happens on mountain passes.

A shadow swept closer. For an instant she saw fangs as gray as the blotched visage they were set in. The horror gave a despairing shriek and was gone.

Rasile stopped chanting. She squatted, panting harshly. When she glanced toward Sharina, she lost her balance. She snarled and dabbed a hand down to avoid toppling sideways.

Sharina dropped to one knee and put her left arm around the Corl. She'd seen many times how exhausting major wizardry was, and whatever Rasile'd done to bring them here was major.

And how difficult will it be to get us back? But that was a question for later, after they'd accomplished their business.

Another of the shapes approached but darted away— silently, though Sharina could hear a distant chorus of wails. The creatures were shaped as uncertainly as icicles. She was sure she could've seen through the diaphanous forms if there'd been any light.

Rasile looked at the Pewle knife and chuckled. "Sharina,"

the Corl said, "you are as brave as the mightiest chief of the True People, I do not doubt; but put your knife away, if you please. You could as well cut moonbeams. And besides, you may need both hands to hold me."

"Yes, all right," said Sharina. She sheathed the big knife with much more difficulty than she'd slid it out reflexively. She cleared her throat and said, "Rasile, what are they?"

Rasile stood; Sharina rose with her. She was ready to grasp the Corl by the arm or shoulders if she started to fall, but that wasn't necessary.

Three more figures swelled out of the emptiness. Their mouths opened like those of carp gulping air in the summer, but these gapes were jagged with teeth longer than a sea wolf's.

The one in the center screamed like a stooping hawk; the others joined a half-tone to either side of it. They drifted to the side and vanished.

"They were men," Rasile said. "Now . . . now, they're what you see. These were your folk, but they are very old. When spirits've been here for as long as these have, there isn't much difference between man beasts and True Men."

Something approached slowly, walking rather than sliding through the fog. It was still too distant for Sharina to make out its details.

"Are they ghosts?" she asked. Her voice was higher-pitched than she'd intended. She cleared her throat. "Rasile, what good are they to us?"

"Those were only hunger," the Corl said. "But there are others, and they will come."

The walking shape approached, becoming a man who carried a long spear and a tall, curved shield made from the hide of a brindled bull. He stared at Sharina with vacant eyes.

"Sir?" Sharina called. She desperately wanted to hear a voice other than hers or the wizard's. "Who are you? I'm Sharina os-Reise."

The soldier walked past silently, though his head turned to watch her. He continued to look back until he was out of sight.

The wizard resumed her chanting, though this time the rhythm was subtly different. The fog coalesced into a blob which in turn slowly split into three figures which became increasingly distinct. They were old men, staring sullenly at the Corl.

"Why do you summon me?" one asked in a querulous voice.

"They are alive," said another. "They have no business with us, nor we with them."

"I command you to tell me of the creatures who killed you, the Last," said Rasile. "Your own kind and all life in the world depend on your help. Where is the most immediate danger from the Last to your race and mine?"

"We have no business with the living," a spirit wailed.

"I *command* you!" said Rasile. She began to chant, but the spirits screamed before she'd called out the third syllable.

"Speak!" Rasile said.

"Pandah!" said the middle figure.

"The Last will destroy Pandah," said the one on the right, "and from Pandah they will spread to conquer the world."

"The Last will conquer the world!" cried the third. "If not from Pandah, then from the great ice lens on Shengy. The Last cannot be halted!"

All three began to howl horribly. Their shapes blurred and became elongated; their mouths swelled into fanged caverns.

"Begone!" Rasile shouted. "I release you!"

As the three old men dissipated into the fog, the wizard began chanting again. Her harsh voice started weak but seemed to grow stronger.

Sharina squeezed her hands together, her lips moving in a silent prayer: "Lady, protect me if it is Your will. Lady, do not let me perish in this place far from those I love."

Lights glowed in the fog. With a rush of thankful delight, Sharina realized that the mist around them had risen from the marsh and that the lights were the soldiers' lanterns and campfire.

Rasile slumped, but Sharina caught her before she hit the ground. The Corl was very light, as light as Tenoctris.

"All praise the Lady!" Sharina shouted. "Praise the Lady Who brings us from darkness!"

THE SUN WAS still beneath the eastern horizon, but the sky was light enough to show that the peel tower's great double doors were open. Garric didn't see anyone nearby.

"*Go!*" Carus shouted in Garric's mind. "*Don't waste the chance! Go! Go!*"

"Go on!" Garric said, restraining his impulse to kick his mount in the ribs. That wasn't necessary with Kore. Besides, he wasn't sure the ogre's willingness to act like a horse extended to being *treated* like a horse. "Up to the door!"

He spoke urgently but he didn't shout. He had no desire to warn the people living in the tower until they'd noticed him on their own.

"I have it on good authority that there are horses who buck, master," Kore muttered, but she lengthened her stride from a jog to a jolting gallop. "Though most of those I've seen had an ogre rushing them."

The footing was uncertain. Kore slipped, spurning a flake of rock hard against an outcrop behind them; it cracked like a ball from a catapult. Her left arm went out while she tucked her right into her ribs, keeping her balance without slowing.

Garric had wondered whether to draw his sword—Carus' reflex and firm belief—or to leave it sheathed in case there was no need for it after all. He'd been reaching for the hilt as he spoke, figuring that a charging ogre would be viewed as an attack whether or not the man on her back waved a sword.

The first slamming impact of Kore's foot against the path changed his mind; he grabbed the flailing straps. Even Carus could see that they were *certainly* coming off their mount if Garric didn't concentrate on riding rather than what might happen after they reached the tower.

Where the track was narrow, Shin followed them; he paced just to the ogre's left in the wider stretches. The aegipan's twelve-foot leaps easily matched Kore's strides.

"The tower's empty!" he called. "They're behind it, all of them!"

Garric heard the muffled whinny of a horse. He wouldn't have been able to tell for sure over the crash of the ogre's clawed feet, but it certainly could have come from the bog beyond the tower.

"Go around the building!" he ordered.

Kore left the main track, leaning to the side as she angled toward the peel tower. On the second stride her foot splashed ankle deep in wet soil. She staggered and Garric threw his left arm around her neck. The aegipan had dropped behind.

"The ground's soft!" the ogre said. Her feet splashed geysers of mud at every step. "It'll be softer yet behind the tower!"

"They got a horse back there, didn't they?" Garric shouted. Carus was a flaming presence in his mind, silent but pulsing with eagerness for battle. "Go around!"

Beyond the doorway, the tower's interior was a dark void smelling of blood and fear. The air oozing from it was noticeably warmer than the dawn breeze following Garric down from the ridge.

Kore swung to the right, the direction Garric was leaning. Her right leg plunged to the knee in muck; she threw her arms back to keep from overbalancing. Her left leg, kicked far forward to brace her, sank to the crotch. She belly flopped, lifting sedges in a ripple of mud.

Garric flew clear and landed at the base of the tower. He'd tightened his rib muscles when he realized what was happening, so though hitting the soft ground was a shock it didn't knock his breath out.

He got up, drawing his sword as he started around the tower. At each step he sloshed to mid-calf. He couldn't imagine how the inhabitants'd gotten a horse over soil like this; it should've sunk to its belly.

"There are three men," said Shin, clicking along at his left side. The base of the tower flared outward in a skirt to deter battering rams. The aegipan's hooves sparkled as he ran on the stone, his inner leg tucked high to keep his slight body upright. "And the horse they are leading."

Garric came around the curve of the building. Two men in drab clothing drove a white horse like the one on which Orra had left the Boar's Skull. One hauled on the reins while the other followed behind, cracking a quirt viciously into the beast's hindquarters. The white horse pitched and whinnied, but the band tightly around its muzzle smothered the sound into a desperate whimper.

The third figure was taller and thin; his garments shimmered in the first light of dawn. He stood at the edge of the sinkhole Garric had noticed when they'd passed the tower on the previous afternoon.

When the tall figure saw Garric, he shouted to his servants in a language that sounded like birds calling. They turned, drawing curved swords from under their robes.

Freed, the horse bolted to its left and immediately mired itself. There was a firm path beneath the surface, though only mud with a sheen of algae showed to a stranger's eye.

Garric found the path, a causeway of stone barely below the mud. It was as slick as wet ice, but he still felt a jolt of triumph. He drew his dagger with his left hand and started forward.

He'd have rushed the trio just the same if he'd had to swim. After all, the servants didn't have any better footing than he did.

"You've decided they're enemies without parley, Garric?" Shin said judiciously. "Well, I think you are right in that."

The figure in gleaming robes held a silver athame in his left hand. He pointed it at Garric and chanted, *"Churbu bureth baroch!"*

The hair on the back of Garric's neck tingled, but to survive he had to concentrate on one thing at a time. . . .

The servant who'd been behind the horse made a series of wide, curling cuts in the air. *"A farmer with a sickle could do better!"* Carus sneered as Garric stepped in.

Garric held his sword low and the dagger advanced in his left hand. He had to finish the first servant before the other joined the fight. The hidden causeway was narrow, but the other fellow might be smart enough to splash through the muck and trap him between them. Don't underestimate your oppo—

The servant slashed. Garric blocked the cut with his dagger, his muscles poised to thrust the fellow through the body, topple him dying into the mire, and rush the remaining man before he was prepared for the attack.

Blade met blade with a squealing crash. Garric felt the shock to his shoulder and his left hand went numb. His body twisted with the blow, fouling the neat training-ground thrust he'd been ready to make.

He'd underestimated his opponent. Whatever the thing was, it wasn't human—or anyway was inhumanly strong.

Garric stumbled forward with the blades locked, shouldering the servant in the chest. He thought there was something harder than bone beneath the robes, but he didn't have time or need to worry about it. He punched the sword upward, in through the belly and out through the spine between the servant's shoulder blades.

The fellow spasmed but didn't let go of his curved sword. His tongue protruded from his pale lips and he began to grunt like a farrowing sow.

Garric pushed hard with his left hand—the feeling was beginning to come back—and jerked down on his hilt to clear the sword. His cross guard was against the servant's ribs. If the blade hadn't been uniquely sharp, he might not have been able to withdraw it from so deep a thrust. As it was, it cut bone as easily coming out as it had going in.

The dead servant flopped on the causeway. The living one recoiled slightly to avoid tripping.

Garric lunged, thrusting. His driving foot slipped on wet stone and he dropped to his left knee. His point didn't go home, but neither did the servant's roundhouse slash.

Carus—it was his reflex, not Garric's—flicked his blade up instead of recovering the way a swordmaster would've directed after a failed thrust. The sword's tip touched the servant's wrist and sheared muscle, sinew, and bone.

The servant's curved blade spun into the sedges and sank.

His hand dangled at right angles to his forearm. He turned to run, his robes flapping, but his foot skidded just as Garric's had a moment before. He fell off the causeway with another hoglike grunt.

Carus would've stabbed the floundering servant just in case, but Garric didn't have his ancestor's ruthlessness. He stepped past the man, his eyes on the wizard who stood chanting and pointing the athame at him.

"Artaie thaimam thar!" the wizard called. Garric froze where he stood.

The mare had been trying to regain the causeway since bolting off it the moment she'd been released. She put her forehooves in the middle of the servant's chest and tried to lift herself upward; instead she drove the man into the bog with a final despairing grunt. Slime bubbled.

"Arbitha rathrathax!" said Shin in a musical voice.

Shards of red wizardlight, invisible till that moment, flaked away from Garric. They splashed on the wet earth and vanished hissing. He was free again. The aegipan stood on the causeway, grinning his goat's grin.

The wizard beside the sinkhole shouted in disbelief. Garric started forward. Though momentary, the pause had robbed him of his momentum. His muscles ached from the ride and the fight.

But he could still kill a wizard. There was no question about that.

The wizard must've realized that too. He pointed his athame at the bog and mumbled words that Garric couldn't hear over the roar of blood in his ears. Garric took another step, a careful one because he didn't need to hurry: the wizard had nowhere to go but into the bog or the sinkhole.

The wizard stepped off the causeway and strode through the sedges. He wore slippers of gilt leather. They sparkled with scarlet wizardlight every time they touched the surface, but they didn't sink into the mud.

The wizard had a thin, imperious face. He glared with contempt as he passed safely beyond the reach of Garric's arm and sword, but he watched the aegipan with a combination of hatred and fear; he raised the silver athame as if to bar an attack. Shin merely laughed and lolled his tongue.

Garric started back down the causeway. "Don't bother," said Shin.

Garric stopped. He couldn't get past the aegipan without stepping into the bog. He didn't trust Shin's judgment, but he was too tired to argue about it.

The wizard reached the base of his tower and started around it, keeping his face toward Garric and Shin the whole time. When the curving stone wall half-shielded him, he pointed the athame again and said, *"Thora amaim—"*

Kore reached down with a long arm and gripped the wizard's ankles.

"Urk!" the wizard shrieked as Kore jerked him into the air. She dashed his brains out against the side of the tower. His athame clinked from the stone, then splashed into the bog.

Kore continued to hold the corpse upside down. With his robes hanging from his shoulders, the wizard looked like a chicken plucked for boiling. His skin was hairless and a waxen white.

"I did this on my own, master," she said. The stone causeway must continue around the tower on this side, because she was standing in only a thin layer of mud. "Since I'm not satisfied with the quality of the food you offer me, I thought I'd kill a man to eat. You can't object, since he was clearly your enemy."

"I do object," Garric said. At first he thought the ogre was joking, but the realization dawned that she very well might be serious. "I certainly object! You're not to, ah, to eat men!"

He'd started to say, "You're not to kill men." Under the circumstances that would've been not only foolish but churlishly ungrateful.

"Would you stop your horse from eating oats from a dead enemy's storehouse?" Kore demanded.

"I wouldn't let my horse eat men," Garric said, "and I won't let you either!"

A sucking roar came from the sinkhole. Garric turned, wondering if the edges were collapsing and about to pull him in with them.

A pincer with blades as long as Garric was tall reached up from the sinkhole. It groped, then squelched down in the muck like a paddle. A thing with one eye in the middle of its headplate and a nest of tentacles around its gaping mouth lurched into sight, followed by another pincer.

The creature's body was the diameter of the peel tower. Duzi—or the Sister—knew how deep its body reached back into the sinkhole.

Shin laughed. "I don't think it's what your mount wants to eat that should be concerning you at the moment, Garric," the aegipan said.

Chapter

10

GARRIC FELT CARUS place a cold overlay on the image of the monster before them. He was a warrior, a man of war first and foremost. Dangers—the huge pincers, the tentacles that writhed five or six feet out from the lamprey-like mouth—and weaknesses—joints and the great central eye—were highlighted, while the rest of the creature remained a shadowed bulk.

Garric knelt and wiped his sword on the tunic of the corpse lying across the causeway. He looked at his dagger. The servant's blow had notched the steel a finger's breadth deep; it'd been sheer luck that the blade hadn't snapped instead of blocking an otherwise fatal stroke.

He threw the dagger down and wrenched the curved sword from the dead man's grip. The servant's hand was slender but ridged with sinew; the skin had a grayish cast.

There was a nick just below the fat part of the blade, but nothing that seriously impaired its usefulness.

"Or you could run," Shin said. "Many people would think that was the only sane course, Prince Garric."

"I don't think I will," Garric said, turning to face the monster. That was the choice with evil, after all: you faced it, or you fed other people to it in hopes that it'd eat you last. Running away was just a way of feeding others to it.

King Carus laughed with harsh good nature. *"Run, lad?"* he cried. *"There's one of him and one of us. Easy odds!"*

The monster had a dome-shaped body that moved on four broad paddles. The causeway supported it as it splashed forward, but Garric suspected it'd do well in the mire or even the open sea.

The creature probably wouldn't move as well on the rocky hills in the direction of the Notch House, but there wouldn't be any way for Garric to learn that. It'd get to Notch House over his dead body.

"Or more likely after swallowing you, I think," Shin said in a conversational tone. He'd retreated to where he could lean against the tower; his right leg was cocked back against the flared base. "I suppose that would be entertaining to watch."

The monster swam closer. Though its carapace didn't flex as it moved, neither did it give the impression of being either slow or clumsy the way a tortoise would.

Carus judged the strength of the peel tower, then said, *"The stonework might hold but I wouldn't count on it. Regardless, we couldn't fight a thing like this through a few arrow slits. Go for the eye, lad, and we'll hope for the best."*

"Shin, can you help?" Garric called without looking over his shoulder again.

"A champion can't be expected to defeat wizards, Garric," the aegipan said. "This isn't a wizard, though; and it remains to be seen whether you're the champion the Yellow King requires."

Garric laughed. Nobody'd ordered him to do this thing, so he didn't have any right to complain if nobody volunteered to help him either.

The mare, her white coat slick with mud and algae, managed to get one, then both of her forelegs onto the causeway. Garric wondered whether she'd consciously swum toward the hidden surface or whether chance had led her to the nearest solid support. Nothing he'd seen of horses made him think they were any smarter than sheep, and sheep were on the intellectual level of rabbits.

The mare's shoulders bunched. The monster lunged forward like a snake striking, sending up a huge gout of mud and sedges. One pincer closed on the horse's neck and jerked the beast out of the mire. Blood spouted and the muzzle band finally tore loose. The horse managed a blat of terror before the pincers crushed her windpipe.

The other pincer gripped the mare's left ham and pulled, stretching her out. The monster slammed her down on the causeway, shattering her spine and ribs, and started to tear her apart.

Garric rushed while the monster was occupied. Before, he'd slipped and skidded all over the slimy stones, but now his balance was perfect.

He jumped onto the dead horse. The monster had turned its prey sideways and continued to pull until her hide split; its tentacles were at work in the body cavity, scooping the organs and ropes of intestine into its pulsing mouth.

A tentacle wrapped around Garric's right thigh. Instead of suckers for gripping, these arms had tiny teeth covering the paler inner surface. Stabbing through Garric's breeches, they began to shred cloth and skin as they twisted.

Garric slashed with his straight sword, severing the tentacle holding him and cutting off the tip of his boot. He missed his big toe by little enough that he felt the chill touch of the metal. There wasn't time to be cautious.

He jumped to the monster's face, his right foot on the muscular lip from which the tentacles sprouted. He couldn't quite reach the eye, but if he raised his left foot onto one of the bony bosses protruding from the carapace he could—

Tentacles gripped both his ankles and tugged. He struck with the curved sword, cutting deep into the muscular tentacle but not severing it. The monster's grip tightened instead of releasing.

Garric hacked with the straight sword. Though the edge was impossibly keen, he couldn't free his right leg either. The angle was too awkward.

Both pincers were bending toward him. Because of the creature's thick armor, the arms weren't quite flexible enough to reach even with three joints. When Garric fell backward, though, they'd pick him to pieces—if the monster didn't instead stuff him whole into its mouth. The stench from its gullet was worse than that of a week-dead mule.

Garric dropped the curved sword and grabbed the boss he'd hoped to stand on. His fingers slipped: the chitin was waxy and still covered with muck. He was going over.

The tentacle on his left ankle stopped pulling, though it didn't release. Garric turned to his right and hacked again at the tentacle on that side, this time cutting it through. The severed end flopped and quivered, then fell away.

Kore had waded up behind Garric. She'd braced her feet to either side of the monster's maw and was chewing on the tentacle holding his left leg. Her long arms were spread, gripping the lower blades of both huge pincers so that they couldn't close. The chitin edges weren't as sharp as metal and apparently couldn't cut without the upper blades for an anvil. Some of the monster's tentacles writhed on the ogre's legs, trying to pull her loose. She was holding for the moment, but it wouldn't be long.

Garric was free. He stepped onto the boss, sprang upward, and thrust the full straight length of his sword into the great eye.

The creature lurched backward with all four paddles. Garric's legs flew up in the air, but he didn't lose his grip on the sword. His torso slammed into the headshield, but he continued to hang on while his blade twisted in the creature's skull.

The pincers clashed beneath him; Kore'd lost her grip. He hoped she'd been thrown clear instead of being crushed or engulfed, but everyone dies and *he* might die in the next heartbeat.

The paddles on one side lashed forward again, but the other pair flailed the surface like women washing clothes. The creature's right side lifted, then slammed down. Garric swung like a pendulum.

The blade pulled out. He slid down the creature's head-plate and bounced from its lip. A tentacle lashed him but couldn't hold; he hit on his back in a spray of mud. His right arm and chest were slick with clear humors that'd leaked from the monster's eye, and the feeling that was beginning to return to his body was solely pain.

If I'd fallen on stone instead of into the bog, Garric thought, *I'd probably have been killed.*

He started to laugh. It was agony, and that made him laugh even harder. He still held the sword, but he had to let go of it because he was afraid he'd slash himself as the pain drew his arms close to his chest.

The ogre lifted him in the crook of her left arm. Holding him as gently as a mother, she paced toward the peel tower where Shin waited.

"My sword," Garric whispered. Had it sunk out of sight already? But he *couldn't* have kept holding it.

"I have it," said Kore. She kicked the dead servant into the bog instead of stepping over him again. "You'll want to wipe it, I'm sure, but Shin has rags."

"And fresh clothing," said the aegipan, holding up a drab tunic. "No doubt you can sew one of these into breeches as well."

"I can walk," Garric said. He sounded like rattling death even to himself, but he knew what'd happen to his bruised muscles if he let them stiffen. "I think I'd better walk."

Kore handed the slimy sword hilt-first to the aegipan, then lowered Garric's feet to the pavement at the base of the tower. She held his shoulder till they both were sure he could stand unaided, then released him.

The monster's hindquarters were slewed into the bog, sinking slowly, but the sunken causeway supported its head. The lower blade of the nearer pincer had been wrenched from its socket; it hung by a strand of pale muscle. Kore splashed toward the huge corpse.

"Kore?" Garric said. "Where are you going?"

The ogre turned. "To get my dinner, master," she said. "I only helped you because I didn't fancy another meal of pork. Are you going to tell me that seafood such as this—"

She gestured toward the monster. Her arm was incredibly long when she stretched it out at full length.

"—is forbidden your faithful mount also?"

"The last time I told you what you could eat," Garric said, "that thing came out of the sinkhole. I'm not in any shape right now to deal with another one, so you go right ahead and eat your fill."

He started laughing again. Though he tried to hold himself upright on the side of the tower, he still sank to his knees. Pain proved that he was alive.

That thought made Garric and the ghost in his mind both laugh even harder and more painfully.

THE HUGE BRICKWORK cylinder was several miles west of Valles. Cashel didn't know why Tenoctris had brought them to it.

He entered ahead of her. He'd expected it to be full of vagrants or at least choked with their trash, but instead there was only echoing emptiness and the smell of bird droppings. Pigeons cooed nervously; two lifted off with the familiar rattle of flight feathers.

The building was windowless, so the only light was what the moon cast through the doorway. By it, Cashel could tell that the interior was domed instead of being straight-sided like the outside, though even so it was very large.

Tenoctris walked in, carrying her satchel. Cashel'd asked her to wait with the gig till he looked the place over, but he hadn't really expected her to listen to him. Even before Tenoctris called up the demon, she'd been a lot less cautious about danger than he'd liked.

Cashel was used to it, of course. Sheep were the same way.

"I'll get the rest, Tenoctris," he said as he walked out to the gig. Tenoctris had tied the reins to a piece of iron no bigger than a clenched fist. The bay horse could've run off easily, but instead it just backed as far as it could get without moving the weight. It rolled its eyes at Cashel as he lifted the sword and bronze tripod from the back of the vehicle, but it seemed afraid even to whinny.

Cashel frowned slightly. They didn't want the horse to wander away, but there wasn't a good place to tie it. Still, the fear in the animal's eyes bothered him a bit.

Tenoctris was always polite and kindly, but under the surface . . . The horse made Cashel realize that he'd never seen the wizard hesitate to do anything or use anything she had to get her job done.

He grinned. Tenoctris was on their side. He guessed that was all that really mattered.

"Set the tripod here," Tenoctris said, gesturing to the center of the floor. She'd swept away leaves that'd blown in and placed a handful of twigs with rough, scaly bark on the cleared space. "Over the fireset."

It didn't look like a fireset to Cashel, not to heat a tripod with a bowl big enough for Ilna to do the wash in. He obeyed without arguing, though: there were lots of things he didn't understand but other people did. He trusted Tenoctris.

She waited while he positioned the tripod, then nodded approval. She'd unstoppered a tiny bottle—it wasn't but the size of Cashel's thumb—and now poured its contents into the bowl. It was way too dark to be able to tell the color of what she'd poured out, but he'd have been willing to swear that it had a violet tinge.

"What kind of place is this, Tenoctris?" Cashel asked, looking around him. There were niches in the ceiling, but they seemed just to lighten the structure. The pigeons liked them, that was true.

Tenoctris gave him a quick smile. "Another tomb," she said. "This one belongs to the wife of a rich man of the Old Kingdom. Tombs concentrate the powers better than anything except a battlefield, and there are problems with battlefields."

Her grin widened. "They attract other things as well, you

see," she said. "That's also why I chose not to return where we'd been before. A mouse that uses the same hole too often will one day find a cat waiting."

Tenoctris touched the rim of the tripod, then stretched her hand out toward him. "Now the sword, if you please, Cashel," she said.

He gave her the sword he'd brought back to the palace after the fight with the Last. She drew it and tossed the scabbard toward the distant wall. The gray metal gave back the moonlight as a distant shimmer.

"Stand close to the tripod," Tenoctris said, looking down the blade with a critical eye. As Cashel obediently moved, she pointed the sword toward the gritty floor and said, *"Siskibir kebibir."*

A spark snapped from the sword point, touched the floor, and lit the point blue. Tenoctris swung the sword sunwise in an arc.

"Knebibir sadami samomir."

Wizardlight as pale as sulfur flames quivered and continued burning. Tenoctris walked around the tripod, chanting as she went. Cashel moved to keep out of the way, though she was far enough out that it'd probably have been all right.

"Merych rechar—"

The clamps holding the tripod's legs to the bowl were shaped like lions. As the blue light reflected from them, their manes rippled and Cashel thought he saw their forelegs move.

"Paspar!" Tenoctris said, then stood breathing deeply. The circle of light was complete.

She looked at Cashel and smiled with satisfaction. Despite her young face, Tenoctris *seemed* a lot older than she had before the demon.

"I'm not used to being able to command such powers," she said. "I find that I like the experience."

Tenoctris held up the oddly shaped sword and examined it in the flickering light of the circle. Cashel cleared his throat and said, "You didn't used to use metal wands, Tenoctris. Just the bamboo slivers that you threw away."

She chuckled, stroking the flat of the blade with her fingertips. "Yes," she agreed. "I worried that I wouldn't be able to control the forces I was working with if I let them build on previous spells. I needn't worry about that, now."

Still smiling, Tenoctris pointed the sword toward the stook beneath the tripod. Again a spark popped, briefly coating the twigs like a blue corposant. They began to burn much brighter than such little bits of wood should've been able to. They had a sweet, pungent odor; Cashel sneezed.

"It's cassia," Tenoctris said without taking her eyes from the bowl. "From Tisamur."

Pointing the sword at the bowl, she began to chant. At first it was so soft that Cashel couldn't hear the words.

He smiled at the thought. He wouldn't have understood them anyway, of course.

Feathers slapped, blowing dust from the floor over his feet; he turned. It wasn't a pigeon but a raven, big as a cat even with its black wings folded. It sat just outside the circle and cocked its head, staring at Tenoctris with an eye which reflected the blue flames.

A second raven flew in the door and lighted an arm's length from the first. It hopped a double pace sideways around the circle.

Cashel darted a glance to see what Tenoctris was doing. The cassia blazed like dry honeysuckle, but it didn't burn itself up. The liquid started to steam. There was only a thimbleful of liquid in the bowl, but the cloud curling up started to fill the great vault. It was faintly violet.

A third raven flapped in, opened its chisel-shaped beak, and croaked. Cashel heard only a faint whisper of sound before the circle of flame roared into a solid wall of light. He felt like he was falling, but he and Tenoctris stood on the solid stone floor where the fire burned under the bubbling bowl.

The wizardlight grew paler, finer; it had the texture of moonlight on a pond. The ravens had vanished, but things moved in the shadows.

The smoke curving from Tenoctris' tripod swelled into the face of a man. He looked upward and screamed, "Time, just a day more of life!"

He was gone, vanishing like the splash of a raindrop. The smoke shrank into another face and another and then a thing that wasn't human, could never have been human: a lizard's head with fangs the length of a finger and an eye as cold as the ravens'. Then that was gone too.

"Nakyar sisbe," Tenoctris said, pointing the sword at but not into the curling smoke. *"Kayam!"*

The face of a man, as still and perfect as a statue of the Shepherd, rippled. It seemed to suck all the vapor into it and grow solid.

"Why do you call me?" it thundered. The words echoed from much farther away than the brick dome.

"I must have the key for which the Telchines have searched these many ages," Tenoctris said. The voice was certainly hers, but it had an unfamiliar harsh certainty.

"That is not permitted!" said the face of smoke. "Trouble me no more!"

Tenoctris drew a symbol in the air with the point of her sword. The face bellowed in pain and rage.

"Where is the key?" Tenoctris said. "Speak!"

"It is not yours to grant!" the face shouted. "Only He Who took the key from the Telchines can—"

"Speak!" and the sword twisted again. Cashel felt his eyes squeeze together with a stabbing pain even though he saw the motion only from the side.

The face cried out wordlessly, then said, "On the Tomb of the Messengers! And may you never know release from agony for what you have done!"

Tenoctris dropped the sword with a clang. Bending, she seized the tripod by one clawed leg and picked it up. Cashel frowned, but he remembered she was no longer a frail old woman.

Tenoctris upended the tripod over the fire, smothering it instantly. The ring of wizardlight blazed up, then vanished to leave only darkness.

Cashel faced outward, holding his staff crosswise. He couldn't tell where danger might come from.

Moonlight streamed through the doorway. Tenoctris

swayed. Cashel reached out to steady her, but she caught herself without help.

"You'll have to bring my bag, I'm afraid, Cashel," she whispered.

"Yes, Tenoctris," Cashel said. "What are we going to do?"

"We'll go back to the palace and sleep," Tenoctris said. "Tomorrow we have to go even farther, and I must be prepared."

She laughed triumphantly. The sound echoed from the brick vault of the tomb.

SHARINA'D SET TONIGHT'S council meeting in the large gazebo overlooking the water garden. The plash of water—routed from the River Beltis through an aqueduct which'd been restored by Garric after being out of order for a generation—reminded her of waves rustling against the seawall beneath her father's inn. It'd rained earlier in the afternoon, though, and the frogs screaming among the lilies weren't of the same varieties as those she'd heard in Barca's Hamlet.

She smiled and found that the expression felt good. It'd been too long since she'd last done it, she realized.

"Councillors," she said, looking around the table of seated magnates. Their aides stood among the pillars supporting the gazebo's roof, more hidden than illuminated by the hanging lanterns. Most of the military men were eyeing Rasile unhappily. Some even fingered the lips of their empty scabbards—they weren't permitted to be armed in the presence of the regent.

"Lady Tenoctris is carrying out other duties on behalf of the kingdom," Sharina said. "In her absence she's deputized Rasile here—"

She gestured to the Corl wizard.

"—to advise us in her place. Through the use of her art, and in my presence, Rasile has received information indicating that the army must move at once to relieve Pandah, which is being besieged by the Last."

"I say let them kill each other!" said Admiral Zettin, and his was only the first voice in the chorus of protest. At least six of the fourteen councillors were objecting, and several of the others glared at Rasile while they whispered to aides.

Sharina smiled again. In the epics, kings gave orders and everyone obeyed, unless perhaps a boorish villain was set up to be humiliated for questioning the king's wisdom. The reality that she'd seen, under Garric as surely as now, was that people who were fit to manage the chief bureaus of the kingdom were also more than willing to give the monarch the benefit of their opinions when they disagreed.

"A moment, please," Sharina said in a normal tone. None of those speaking paid attention. She didn't try to shout over the tumult: First, because she wouldn't have succeeded and at best would've added one more voice to the babble. Second and more important, though, she didn't shout because that would've reduced her status. If she didn't project herself as Princess Sharina, these powerful soldiers would mentally relegate her to the status of a barmaid.

She and Liane had known this would happen if neither Garric nor Cashel was present, so they'd made preparations. Sharina nodded, and Liane struck the eight-inch brass gong in front of her. Though her mallet was wood rather than metal, the gong's plangent note nonetheless silenced all the voices at the table.

When those arguing had all closed their mouths—the more perceptive in embarrassment, the others with looks of puzzled irritation—Liane stilled the gong between the thumb and forefinger of her left hand. Sharina smiled faintly and said, "Lord Waldron, would you state your objections first, please."

"Your Highness, we don't know what the supply situation on the route to Pandah is," the army commander said. "Before the Change we could load supplies on merchant ships and sail them to where they'd meet us. Now, we either forage on route or we pack them along—which means the draft animals eat up more than they leave."

"I see the practical problems," said Sharina. "Admiral Zettin, would you state your objections now?"

"I don't mean my men can't do it," Waldron added hastily. "But it's not going to be easy."

"I'll return to you shortly, milord," Sharina said, trying to put steel in her tone the way she'd heard Garric—or anyway, King Carus—do in the past. She wasn't sure she'd succeeded, but at least Waldron subsided. "Admiral, succinctly, if you will."

"Pandah's a nest of pirates and cannibals," Zettin said with a nod. He was pushy, and young in more ways than being thirty years Waldron's junior, but he was also very clever. "The Last aren't human. The longer they fight each other, the stronger the kingdom is. We shouldn't interfere."

"Very good," Sharina said. "Rasile, please respond to the admiral's point."

Chancellor Royhas looked up from his close conversation with Lord Hauk, presumably discussing payment and procurement for supplies if the army marched on Pandah. "Your Highness," he said, "I don't think it's appropriate for an animal to address us. Even if it does speak like a human now."

"As you please, milord," Sharina said, trying to stay calm. It seemed to her that the chancellor'd spoken more sharply than he would've to Garric. "Lord Tadai?"

The plump, perfectly groomed nobleman sat across the table from Royhas; he'd been whispering urgently with two clerks, scratching notes on a sheet of sycamore bark. He met Sharina's gaze and lifted an eyebrow in question. "Your Highness?"

"Lord Royhas is giving up his portfolio," Sharina said. "Are you willing to accept the duties of chancellor?"

"Your Highness, wait!" Royhas said, rising from his chair abruptly and catching his knees under a table that was lower than he was used to. He flopped back down. "Please!"

"I've willingly served the kingdom in whatever position you or your royal brother appointed me to, Your Highness," Tadai said unctuously. He carefully avoided letting his eyes drift toward the discomfited man across the table. "I would be honored if you chose to use me in the capacity of chancellor."

"Your Highness," Royhas said, calm once more. He stood and bowed low, then straightened to meet her eyes. "I apologize. I misspoke because I'm tired. But Your Highness, if I cannot claim to be tireless in carrying out my duties, I've certainly been honest and efficient. I believe even—"

He turned to glance at his rival, then faced Sharina again.

"—Lord Tadai would grant that. I made an error of speech. It will not recur."

He bowed and sat down again.

Sharina nodded. "Well said, Chancellor," she said. "Lord Tadai, I'm fortunate to be able to retain you as head of my civil affairs section when I march with the army."

She gave Waldron a hard smile and added, "As I expect to do shortly. Rasile, please explain why you believe we must go to Pandah."

She hadn't threatened Royhas about what would happen if he—not to put too fine a point on it—insulted her again. He knew, everyone at the table knew, what would happen. So did the guards and so did the clerks and the servants and the courtiers watching events through the open sides of the gazebo.

Sharina smiled with her lips pressed tight together. She didn't like being regent, but she hadn't liked emptying chamber pots at the inn either. Garric depended on her, and she supposed the kingdom did too—though it made her very uncomfortable to think in those terms. Therefore she *would* be regent.

"The Last are without number," Rasile said. "They do not grow weaker, warrior, any more than the sea is weakened by striking against a cliff. But it wears the cliff down as the Last will wear down Pandah; and while they are doing so, they're fortifying the pool by which they enter this region. If you do not stop them while you can, you will speed their conquest of this world by two years—or perhaps three."

The Corl spoke in a mix of clicks and labials, but owing to Tenoctris' remarkable feat of wizardry, the listening humans understood her perfectly. The thought jerked Sharina's mind to wonder about Tenoctris as she now was—and to concern over what Cashel might be facing to protect the wizard.

"I don't see how these Last get into the water," said Lord Hauk, looking at the mass of documents spread on the table before him. "Do they swim here, is that it?"

"Rasile?" Sharina said. "Please explain the matter."

She'd asked the wizard the same question, but rather than retail the information she thought she'd let it come from the original source. Among other things, that might raise Rasile's status in the eyes of the councillors. Royhas certainly wasn't alone in distrusting and disdaining their Coerli allies.

"The Last do not touch the water," Rasile said. "They cross from reflection to reflection. If you distort the surface of the site they choose, you block them."

She coughed and paused. *How old is she? How old do Coerli get?*

"They cannot use every body of water as their mirror," Rasile resumed. "There must be a focus for their art, a dense braiding of power. Save Pandah, you've blocked every such focus already in your portion of this world."

The Corl laughed, a bestial sound that probably wasn't meant to be threatening. "Your Tenoctris is a very great wizard. I am not fit to be her lowliest slave . . . and yet she chooses to serve your kingdom instead of gaining hegemony over this universe."

Her shrug was identical to that of a puzzled human. She laughed again and added, "It is almost as if Tenoctris were me, only vastly more powerful."

"I don't understand what the cat means," said the minister of the post plaintively to her neighbor, the burly commandant of the Valles Night Watch. The latter's deep frown didn't suggest to Sharina that he was going to be much help with the question.

The minister of the post felt eyes on her and looked up in horror, then clapped both hands over her mouth. It was a charmingly innocent gesture, but one which reminded Sharina that the lady was a political ally of Chancellor Royhas.

Sharina rose to her feet. "What it means," she said, though she knew the minister'd been asking a much more basic question than the one she chose to answer, "is that however difficult it may be to root out the incursion of the Last at Pandah, we must do so in order to buy time till others can deal with the creatures in a permanent fashion. Is there anyone at the table who disagrees with that assessment?"

There was silence. They were intelligent people—well, most of them were—and pragmatists. Given the facts, they'd come to the same conclusion she had.

"Lord Waldron?" she prodded, looking down at the old soldier.

"My men are talking to Master Baumo's men now," Waldron said, nodding toward the tax office clerk. "We'll have an operational plan ready before morning."

He smiled grimly and added, "If I'd been looking for an easy life, I wouldn't have been a soldier. And if any of my men had thought it was going to be easy, I'd have run them out or ground them under."

Sharina felt a sudden wash of contentment. It was late at night, but the guests' bed linen was clean, the common room had been swept, porridge for the morning was simmering on the kitchen fire—

And the chamber pots had been emptied.

"Very good, Councillors," Sharina said. "We will do our jobs here so that Prince Garric and Lady Tenoctris can save us by doing theirs."

And Cashel can save us, she thought. *Before he comes back to save me from lonely darkness.*

ILNA AND TEMPLE joined Asion on the limestone ridge, looking down at the land spreading below. The valley behind them was a waste of blowing dust and woody plants sheltering in the lee of outcrops; ahead was tussock grass, not the lushest of vegetation but proof of *some* water. Stretching toward them up the gentle slope were broad fields irrigated from the creek lying at the base of steeper hills across the valley; cottonwoods grew on the banks.

Asion turned and signaled to his partner. Karpos was less than a furlong behind, much closer than usual because the landscape they'd just crossed was too barren and dusty to conceal a stalking enemy.

"That's odd," said Temple. He pointed toward the southern end of the valley, where the creek spilled down from a notch in the rock wall. "Impressive, at least. That's a dam. If the watercourse on the other side of it flowed naturally, the whole valley would flood."

"How do you—" Ilna said, then scowled at her stupidity. She disliked stone so much that it was apparently robbing her of intelligence. "Yes, I see that the dam's high, and that the water spills over the top."

She returned her attention to the village on the other side of the creek. The walls were drystone, blocks laid without mortar, and the buildings were thatched with tussock grass. There were more houses than she could count on both hands; but not, she thought, twice that number. The line of shadow from the sun behind her was beginning to darken the tawny roofs as well.

"Seventeen huts," said Temple. "I'd judge they were of a size to hold six or eight family members each, wouldn't you guess?"

"Where's the people?" Karpos said as he joined them. "And where's the goats too? I don't see any."

Asion pointed. "There's a door," he said. "In the rock there."

It took Ilna a moment to realize that he wasn't pointing at a rock among the houses but rather to the side of the hill beyond. There *was* a door, braced like a city gate though not nearly as big. The man standing in it was far enough back in the shadow that she hadn't noticed him till he moved, but the hunter had.

She smiled slightly. There were many people in the world who had special skills. Asion and Karpos wouldn't have remained in her company had they not been among those people.

She glanced to her side. And Temple had skills as well. Temple very definitely had skills.

A different man came out of the door and waved toward them. He cupped his hands into a megaphone and shouted.

"He's saying, 'Quickly,'" said Asion, frowning. He looked at Ilna.

"Yes," she said. "There's no point in our staying here."

"I'll lead," said Karpos, moving down the slope at a swinging jog. He kept both hands on his bow with the nocked arrow slanting to his left. He didn't seem to hurry, but he covered the ground very quickly.

"And we'll move quickly," Ilna said, breaking into a trot. "Since the fellow calling us knows more about this valley than we do."

She wondered if she'd embarrass herself; running wasn't a skill she'd cultivated. On the other hand, there were worse things than falling on her face in front of not only her companions but also the locals. More of the latter had come out of the cave, a handful and one—six.

"Run!" they cried. They were shouting all together now. She could hear the words even over the pounding of her feet on the loose soil. "Run!"

Those worse things might be about to happen.

Ilna smiled. That would be all right. She wasn't good at running, but she knew how to stand and fight.

She took a handful of yarn out of her sleeve and knotted it as she jogged. It wasn't for a weapon against the unnamed *Something* that the locals were concerned about, it was just to occupy her with something she did well and found relaxing.

Ilna's stride fell into a pattern. She no longer worried about tripping or the way the bindle pounded her back. She should've tightened the straps before she started down, but it didn't really matter.

The wheat in the fields was flourishing; the soil here must be very good. She supposed that was why the villagers had gone to all the effort of damming the river: the silt that'd settled out of slow water over the years would be far richer than that of valleys that'd been sunbaked and wind-scoured for centuries.

She glanced over her shoulder. Temple smiled faintly when he caught her glance. He ran on his toes, holding his shield and scabbard to keep them from swinging. He could obviously keep up this pace—or a quicker one—for a very long time. Well, so could Ilna if she had to, but they'd reached the cottonwoods and Karpos had already crossed the creek.

She was glad of the wooden bridge. It wasn't necessary, but fist-sized stones in the streambed might've turned or slipped beneath her if she'd tried to splash across at a run. She didn't *like* stone.

The sun was below the horizon. The sky was still bright, but there'd been a change. Ilna didn't look back again. There'd be time for that when she reached the cave. She could see the door now, even more massive than she'd thought at a distance. The staples on the inside would hold a bar as thick as her thigh.

Karpos had joined the locals. They seemed ordinary farmers, much like the people Ilna'd grown up with on Haft. Their tunics were goat's wool rather than sheep's wool, but someone less familiar with fabric wouldn't have noticed the difference.

"Inside, quick!" cried a burly man with a ginger beard. He held a simple spear. His fellows were armed with similar spears, save for the pair with clubs.

Ilna reached the villagers standing outside. Beyond them were women and children watching nervously from well within the cave. Karpos grimaced a question to her.

"Quick, before the demons get here!" cried Ginger-beard. Instead of obeying, Ilna turned to see what was pursuing them.

Nothing was. The wheat moved only to wisps of breeze that even the hairs on the backs of Ilna's arms couldn't have felt.

But another sun was in the sky, a dim, red orb midway toward the western horizon. The air had an unfamiliar texture that wasn't quite a smell. A gray gauze began to curtain the ridge from which Ilna and her companions had first seen the valley, and on it was the outline of a door.

A Corl warrior, then two more, slipped through that outline like light glancing from polished metal. They raced down the slope, spreading out as the Coerli always did while hunting. They carried the usual weapons: small axes, throwing lines with weighted hooks, and spears with springy double points.

Another trio of cat men, then another, raced from the outlined doorway. The red sun was too dim to cast their shadows, but their rippling fur shone as they moved. They were agile as well as quick, sometimes making leaps downslope that no man could've equaled.

"We must shut the door!" the ginger-bearded local man said desperately. "Come in or we must close you out!"

"Not yet," said Ilna as her fingers told the knots in the pattern they'd woven. "I have to see more."

A clot of cat men came from the distant outline, more than the total of the groups who'd come through before.

"I'm closing—" the local said, his voice rising.

"No," said Temple. He didn't speak loudly, but the syllable could've been chipped out of quartz.

"We have to—"

"*No,*" Temple repeated.

The cat men were coming very swiftly. They were all warriors without the chieftain who'd normally have been leading a band so large.

Ilna's fingers worked, searching for the answer her conscious mind wouldn't have been able to arrive at. There *was* an answer, she was sure. . . .

"Ilna," said Temple softly. "We will do as you choose we should do. But for myself, I would rather fight the Coerli at a later time."

She had it!

Ilna stepped inside the doorway. Temple himself slammed the panel closed behind her; it was as massive as the gate of a border fortress.

Ginger-beard and his fellows slid the bar into place; Ilna

heard the pattering of the cat men's light axes on the outer door. It was no more dangerous than hail tapping the slate roof of the mill Ilna had grown up in. The cat men shrieked in frustration.

"I've found the way to what I'm searching for," Ilna said, speaking to the blurred figures around her. There were lamps farther back in the cave, but it was taking a moment for her eyes to adapt to them. "Finally."

"Mistress?" said Karpos. "Which direction is that?"

"Through the door that the cat beasts opened to come here," said Ilna. "Of course, we'll have to kill all of them first."

She felt her lips tighten like the blade of a curved knife.

"But we'd want to do that anyway," she added.

Chapter

11

$\mathcal{F}$ROM THE OGRE'S back, Garric could see through the tops of thorn hedges on either side of the rutted red dirt track, but for the most part Kore herself wasn't visible to the peasants working in the fields. They were startled to see a man looking down at them from fourteen feet in the air, but they didn't drop their tools and run screaming.

The pair of chattering women who saw Kore as they stepped through a gap in the hedge *did* run screaming, tossing away the leaf-wrapped bundles they'd been carrying on their heads. Their bright cotton robes fluttered like parrot wings behind them.

Shin sniffed appreciatively. "A paste of chickpeas, potatoes, and tomatoes in a wrapper of flatbread," he said. "*Very* nicely seasoned, including a touch of saffron. But—"

He grinned at Garric—or possibly at Kore.

"—it would be wrong to deprive hardworking farmers of their dinner."

"I suspect you'd be depriving stray dogs of unexpected bounty," said Garric as the ogre trotted on, "but yes, it'd be wrong. We'll purchase dinner in normal fashion when we stop for the night."

"And may I hope for a nice haunch of beef, dear master?" said Kore. "This is cattle country, I scent."

Calling this "cattle country" was stretching the point. A few of the farmers were plowing behind a single bullock, obviously adult but no bigger than a young bull of the breed folk in Barca's Hamlet gelded into oxen. Even those were rare: most of the folk Garric saw in the fields were breaking ground for seed with a hoe or a dibble.

Kore's comment made him wonder how much of what she said was joking and how much was true. He suspected both were the case: that the ogre whimsically stated things which were in fact true—including that she'd eaten humans in the past and was looking forward to doing so again when she ceased to be under Garric's control.

Which in turn made Garric wonder about the morality of *his* position. Could he in good conscience release a ravening monster on the world after he'd completed his embassy to the Yellow King?

The king in his mind chuckled grimly. *"If you're worried about that, lad,"* he said, *"there's some troops in your army you'd better be worrying about too. And not the worst troops either, when there's hard fighting to do."*

Shin trotted beside the ogre, occasionally leaping into a somersault to vary his routine. Now he laughed and said, "A more cautious person might've said, '*If* I completed my embassy.' But you're obviously a sanguine young man as well as a great champion."

"Tsk, Shin, he's merely a logician," Kore protested. "If he's torn to bits or devoured or any of the other likely fatal results of this journey, then his moral quandary vanishes. You should rather worry about how his faithful mount will fare after the probable disaster."

"Ah, but *I* am not a philosopher," Shin said. "In such an event, my first concern must be to avoid becoming your next meal."

"A good point!" Kore said. "Now that you call my mind to the matter, I don't believe I *have* as yet tasted aegipan. Indeed, I'll keep that in mind for the future."

Surely they're joking. . . .

Garric cleared his throat and said aloud, "There's forest not far ahead. Hardwoods, and some of them pretty tall."

"There are men waiting for us where the road enters that forest," the ogre said, snuffling deeply. Her nose was flat, little more than a ridge with two vertical slits, but it was obviously very sensitive. "I think twelve. . . . Yes, twelve men, one of them wearing what I believe is patchouli. The others smell mostly of muck and their own sweat."

"A squad of soldiers under an officer," Carus said. *"I don't imagine they'll be much in the way of troops, but twelve's still a good number. And I'd guess they have bows."*

"We'll hope for the best," said Garric equably.

"And we'll keep our sword loose in the scabbard, I trust," Carus said, but his image was grinning. It'd take more courage—and bloody-mindedness—than Garric or his ancestor either one expected from local militiamen to start a fight with a swordsman on an ogre.

They passed beyond the last field. With no hedges to block the view, Garric saw a belt of scrub a furlong wide and then the trees themselves. Some rose nearly two hundred feet in the air.

"Teak," said Carus with the satisfaction of a man sure of an identification. *"I ran into it on Sirimat. A bloody hard wood for a stockade, and it didn't burn the way I'd expected. We had to go over the walls."*

A soldier wearing the same clothing as the farmers in the fields—a straw hat, a loincloth, and a loose cotton vest— stood at the base of one of the nearer trees. He shouted with excitement and grabbed what Garric thought was a crooked bamboo spear leaning against the bole of the tree. It was a bow taller than he was, and the stone-pointed arrow he nocked was five feet long.

More men, as like the first as so many peas, jumped up from where they'd been sitting or sleeping in the shade. Some did have spears, but there were several more bows. The weapons were crude, but as Carus had noted—there were a lot of them.

"Greetings, friends!" Garric called, waving cheerfully with his left hand. His right wasn't *on* the sword hilt, but he could get it there in a hurry if he needed to. "Please pardon my mount. She's harmless! We're merely travelers passing through your country and ready to pay for food and lodging."

"Harmless!" the ogre sniffed, but she kept her voice down. She even slowed to an amble, though even that pace wasn't enough to quell the soldiers' nervousness. One half-drew his bow, then slacked it. Garric wondered what the range of the long arrows might be.

The officer stood. He must've been putting on his breast-plate, an arrangement of shiny disks on chains. It struck even Garric as useless; Carus burst out laughing. It was sparkly, though, and that was obviously all the fellow had in mind.

"Stop!" the officer cried in a high-pitched voice. He had a mustache so thin it might've been drawn with a brush; the ends stuck straight up in the air like the horns of the local bullocks. "You must not come closer or my men will assuredly destroy you!"

To demonstrate his determination, he drew his curved sword—on the second try, and then only after gripping the scabbard with his left hand. When it came out, Garric saw that the blade had rusted to the mouth of the scabbard. "Do not come closer!"

Garric pulled back lightly on the straps; if Kore'd been a horse he'd have been sawing on the reins, but all the ogre required was a hint. Assuming she was willing to obey, of course; which fortunately she was in this instance.

Garric wondered if he ought to dismount. He said, "Your Worship, we're peaceful travelers."

"That's rather a stretch to believe from a man on ogre-back, wouldn't you say?" Shin commented cheerfully.

"If they weren't afraid, they'd be dangerous," Carus said, looking out through his descendant's eyes with cold contempt. *"If you were a trader leading a pack mule, they'd rob you. And if you were traveling with your wife, so much the worse for her. Oh, I know this sort."*

"You must not come closer!" the officer shouted, spraying spittle. He was terrified. "You must not!"

"Hold up," Garric murmured to Kore, fifty feet from the squad. If he continued to approach, it was a toss-up whether the soldiers'd scatter like sparrows or if they'd blindly attack. Maybe the choice really was to draw his sword and charge, hoping to push them toward flight. . . .

"Let's see what a little mummery can do, shall we?" the aegipan said. He picked up a handful of the red dust and minced toward the men calling, "Who wishes to see marvels? I'm a great wizard! I'll open to you secrets undreamt by mortal men!"

He tossed the dust into the still air. Instead of settling back, it formed into the image of a big-hipped, buxom woman. He continued forward while the image danced above him, gyrating violently and sometimes bending backward so that her head was at the level of her ankles.

That can't be possible! Garric thought. But though a figure of dust needn't be any more realistic than what an ordinary sculptor carved, he got the feeling that Shin had created not only *a* dancer but a *particular* dancer.

"Walk up slowly," Garric said to the ogre in a quiet voice. "Stop behind Shin and I'll dismount."

"Do you find her pretty?" Shin said, pausing a double pace from the edge of the forest, into which the soldiers had retreated at his approach. The officer was the only one who hadn't moved, perhaps because his back was to a young tree already. He didn't have the concentration to spare to slip around one side or the other of the thigh-thick trunk.

"Would you like me to walk on my hands, master?" asked Kore as she started forward.

"No," said Garric. He frowned and asked, "Could you?"

"That's Laila," the officer said in a choking voice, staring at the dancing image. His mouth opened and he looked at the aegipan again. "That's *Laila*!"

"Is it indeed?" Shin said. His voice was always melodious, always cheerful. He picked up more dust.

"It might be an unexplored talent of mine," Kore replied archly. "But of course if you prefer that I conceal my creative spirit beneath a mask of dull conformity, I will."

Garric laughed out loud, which startled the soldiers but also relaxed them. One had been poising his flint-pointed spear to throw, then easing it forward again. He lowered its butt to the ground.

Which maybe was just what the ogre had intended, Garric thought as she knelt for him to step out of the straps. It wasn't the kind of help he'd have gotten from the gelding.

"Tasty though the gelding was, I should in fairness remark," Kore said.

Shin tossed up the second handful of dust. It too swirled and shimmered into a full-sized figure. The small amount of material shouldn't have more than hinted at the outline, but she looked as solid as the dancer: heavy-bodied, heavy-featured; waddling rather than spinning.

The officer cried in horror and closed his eyes. He slashed twice across nothingness, then dropped his sword and ran off at an angle to the woodline. He was sobbing.

Shin moved out from under the images. They collapsed as quickly as they'd formed, settling onto the plants on the floor of the open forest.

The aegipan laughed and said, "I shouldn't wonder if he imagined he saw his wife in that second figure. Perhaps he was afraid that she'd notice his mistress, do you think?"

Most of the common soldiers had melted away, hunching through the scrub to gain the fields rather than retreating into the teak forest. A few had remained, however, watching the strangers with dumb resignation.

Garric took a few bronze pieces from his belt purse. He displayed them in his left palm as he walked toward the nearest soldier, a bowman.

"As I said, my good sir, we're peaceful travelers," Garric

said. "Can you tell me if we'll find an inn as we follow this road?"

The local stared at the money, seemingly oblivious of all else. He didn't reach out to take it, though.

"Here, fellow, it's yours," Garric said, jingling the coins in his palm.

He didn't want to drop the money on the ground—it'd be demeaning, though he doubted the local man would care—so he took the fellow's right hand in his, opened it, and poured the coins into it. "Is there an inn on this road?" Garric said.

A second soldier had been watching the whole event silently. Now he burst out, "There's nothing on this road but Lord Holm's domains."

He spat on the ground and added, "Much good may you do each other!"

CASHEL PUT HIS hand on the trunk of the nearest tree in the grove, just to feel the familiar springiness in the plates of bark. Even city folk could identify a shagbark hickory, at least if they'd ever seen one before. Which they wouldn't have if they'd spent all their lives on Ornifal, Cashel would've said—until just now when Tenoctris halted the gig beside this grove on the west side of the palace compound.

"Tenoctris," he said, "did these trees come here because of the Change? Because I'd never seen hickories on Ornifal before, and these are old ones."

"They were planted by a young woman," Tenoctris said, continuing to mark a five-sided figure as she spoke. "She was a bor-Torial—a princess, in fact. Her lover was the emissary of the Count of Haft. He was lost at sea on his return to Carcosa."

Her scriber was the sword he'd taken from the Last. Cashel guessed she knew what she was doing.

She paused and looked at him. "That was the story, at least," she said. "I think I might learn something else if I looked into the matter, but it was three generations ago, and it wouldn't help defeat the Last. In any case, she planted this grove."

Cashel pursed his lips in thought. "Is she buried here?" he asked.

Tenoctris was writing words around the edges of her completed figure. Besides the leaf litter, a mixture of ivy and honeysuckle snaked across the ground. It'd be hard even for the person who wrote the words on a surface like that to read them, but from what Cashel'd seen, wizards thought it was important just that the words be *there*. They didn't have to be visible, at least to the eyes.

She looked toward Cashel again with a soft expression that he wasn't used to seeing on her face. "No, Cashel," she said. "She asked to be, but propriety wouldn't permit it. She's buried with the rest of her family in the great bor-Torial tomb west of the city walls. But her . . . heart, if you will, her hopes are buried here. Her longing created a concentration which will help what you and I are going to do now."

She patted her thigh. "Come closer," she said; and with Cashel standing beside her, she began to chant.

Instead of listening to the words, which were only nonsense syllables anyway, Cashel looked at the trees. The leaves had unfurled, though they hadn't reached their full size.

Cashel didn't miss Barca's Hamlet, exactly, but he'd been pretty much content with his life there. He smiled: other people might've thought it was hard, but it'd suited *him*. That was what mattered.

Smiling wider, he let his palms slide on the hickory quarterstaff just to feel the polished wood. It was good to think about Barca's Hamlet.

And as he smiled, the tall gray trunks began to spin about him. They started swiftly, but they slowed till they stood frozen without even the normal tremble of a breeze ruffling leaves or an insect drifting past.

The grove vanished. Cashel and Tenoctris stood at the base of a flat-topped hill. Around them stretched a plain of rust-colored oat grass, spotted here and there with acacia trees and low but equally thorny bushes. The vegetation moved in the dry breeze; in the high sky a single vulture wheeled on tipping wings.

Tenoctris looked up the steep-sided mound, then turned to Cashel. The wind fluttered her hair into her eyes. She didn't wear it in a bun since she got young again. She swept it back with a look of irritation, then laughed like the girl she appeared to be.

"That's what I get for vanity, I suppose," she said. "Well, I think I'll simply accept the punishment."

She nodded to the hill and went on, "This is the Tomb of the Messengers. Supposedly two messengers were sent to guide Mankind out of darkness, but instead they became corrupted and were imprisoned beneath this escarpment."

Cashel's lips pursed again. "Who sent them, Tenoctris?" he asked. "And who buried them here?"

Tenoctris shrugged with a mocking smile. "Every religion has an answer to that question," she said, "but no two answers are the same. Your priests in Barca's Hamlet would say that the Lady sent the Messengers and that the Shepherd imprisoned them when they turned to sin. I'm not sure anybody really sent them, and I'm not certain that they're imprisoned; but they're here, and they teach arts of great power to wizards who can wrest the knowledge from them."

There weren't priests in Barca's Hamlet, except in the fall when they came from Carcosa for the Tithe Procession. They pulled the images of the Lady and the Shepherd through town and collected the money due the Great Gods for the year.

Cashel didn't correct Tenoctris, though, since the mistake didn't matter; instead he looked at the long hill. It was layered sandstone without many plants growing on it. Where there were bushes, they grew in dirt the wind blew into crevices, he was pretty sure. Some sandstones weren't too hard; but even so it was going to be a job if they had to dig any distance into it.

"Is there a tunnel already?" he asked. "Or do we make one?"

Cashel wasn't worried. He guessed that if they needed tools beyond what they usually carried, Tenoctris'd have told him to bring them. And if for some reason she expected him to bash a hole in rock with other rocks that'd weathered off already, well, that's what he'd do.

The wizard had been looking for something within her satchel. She looked up with a hint of humor, then let her face soften before she said, "We won't be entering the tomb, Cashel, though there is a way. Everything the Messengers teach is evil, whether or not it seems that way on the surface."

She paused, looked into the satchel again, and raised what was either a scriber or a thin wand; it was no longer than Cashel's hand. It glittered the way only a diamond can. She set it back with a funny expression.

"Cashel," she said, "I was never tempted to visit the Messengers. I knew my capacities, and therefore knew I couldn't possibly force them to give me the knowledge I might seek. Now, though—I actually could do that. It's odd, isn't it, that power itself leads to temptation?"

Cashel thought about the question. "No, ma'am," he said. "It's always that way, any kind of power. Of course if you're a decent sort of person, it's not a problem. You just know that you don't go around starting fights, and if the other fellow's too drunk to have sense, you try to keep out of his way."

Tenoctris looked like she might be going to laugh; instead she stepped close and patted his wrist. She hopped back again before he could do anything—he wasn't sure what he'd have done if he'd had time to think, to tell the truth— and said, "I believe I'm going to have you work the oracle yourself instead of me doing it."

She gestured to the oat grass in which they stood. "Strip one of the seed heads into your hand, if you would," she said with the sort of courtesy people use when they don't expect any answer except, "Yes, ma'am."

"Yes, ma'am," Cashel said. Shifting the quarterstaff to his left hand alone, he pulled his right thumb and forefinger up the nearest stem and collected the seeds in his palm. The grass head was sharp and hairy, but it wasn't going to harm his calluses.

"Yes, ma'am?" he repeated, this time to tell Tenoctris he was ready for whatever she had in mind for next. The ground here was rocky, so even the hardy oat grass was sparse. It looked like a solid field when you looked across the tops, though, because the plain rolled so far into the distance.

"Throw the seeds up in the air," she said. She tented her fingertips together, a gesture Cashel remembered from when she'd been old. "They'll fall pointing to the object I've come for."

"Just throw them up?" Cashel said, thinking he'd heard wrong. In a breeze this stiff, they were going to scatter to the south at an angle away from the hill.

"Yes, up," Tenoctris said. "*Now,* if you please."

Cashel obeyed. After the way she'd snapped at him, he wasn't surprised that the seeds formed a triangle in the air like geese before settling to the ground. He was willing to bet that they'd stayed in order, despite the stems of other grass plants hiding the pattern.

"Can you follow the direction that pointed, up the hill?" Tenoctris said. "Follow it exactly, I mean?"

"Yes, ma'am," Cashel said. "That's what I'd mean too."

He held out his staff at arm's length to sight along, not so much because he needed to but to show Tenoctris that he understood. Now that she was young, she didn't seem to trust people quite the way she had when she was older.

A wormwood bush grew from the rock maybe a furlong up the slope at the angle they'd want to travel. Above that, on the horizon along the way the arrow pointed, was a spike of rock like a nose.

Both markers were like any number of other places on the hill, but they weren't the *same.* Cashel wouldn't have any trouble keeping his bearings.

"Then lead me, please, Cashel," Tenoctris said. She smiled apologetically. "Because *I* certainly couldn't do that."

Cashel smiled. He didn't say anything as he started along the slope, but he felt better that Tenoctris was sorry for the way she'd spoken. Everybody got snappish now and again— well, almost everybody did. But when you knew you'd done it, you at least could try not to do it again.

"We aren't interested in the Messengers," Tenoctris said from behind him as he picked their way over the rock. "But their presence has drawn other things here. It's one of those things I need, a key of sorts."

"Does it really look like a key?" Cashel asked. He paused.

There was an acacia in front of him, no bigger than a sapling. Knowing how slow things grew in this dry climate, though, it was probably as old as he was.

"I don't know what it will look like or what it'll be made of," Tenoctris said. "Though it might be quartz."

Cashel decided to mark his line and go around instead of trampling straight on. Breaking the tree flat for Tenoctris to follow wouldn't be hard, but—well, it'd put in a lot of effort to get this old. It wouldn't hurt them to walk around.

On the other side, a nub of quartz poked out of the red soil among the acacia's roots. Cashel drew his knife, a peasant's tool with an iron blade and horn scales, and scraped around the quartz. He took his time about it, careful not to nick the roots any more than he had to. If he'd flattened the little tree, chances were he wouldn't have noticed the glint of white stone.

Tenoctris moved around to where she could watch. She didn't interfere, though, not even to ask why he thought this was what they were looking for. He didn't know; it'd just caught his eye.

When he had the end of the milky stone dug clear, he wiped his knife and put it back into its wooden sheath. He squatted over the scraped-out cone, gripped the quartz between thumb and forefinger—just like he'd stripped the oat grass, he thought with a smile—and used his knees to pull straight up. It was only about the length of his little finger. When he pulled, it came out in a spray of red soil.

He rubbed the dirt off the quartz with his tunic, then held it out to Tenoctris. "Is this what you were looking for, ma'am?" he said.

"Yes, Cashel," she said with a broad smile. "I believe it is. Now, let's return to our own world."

Tenoctris turned and started down the hill to where they'd appeared in this sunbaked landscape. "We're going back to the grove, then?" Cashel said as he followed her carefully.

"No," said Tenoctris. She glanced over her shoulder at him with another of the odd looks she'd been giving him ever since she got young again. "I think we'll join the army on the march for Pandah. Sharina is with the army, you see."

SHARINA'S FOOT SLIPPED in wet clay the leading regiments had trampled to slick mud. Trooper Lires, the bodyguard to her left, swore and grabbed her arm. She hadn't been likely to fall, though, and even that would've meant nothing worse than a wetting.

The scouts had charted the best route for the army's march to the southwest, but that didn't mean it was an entirely good one. Here rocky hills sloped near the edge of a lake fed by glaciers melting out of the valleys. The line of march necessarily narrowed, causing congestion and some confusion. Not even Princess Sharina could depend on firm footing.

She'd chosen to walk rather than ride a horse or be carried in a litter. This provided a good example to the troops, all of whom except Lord Waldron himself were on foot. That would've been a good enough reason to do it—

But that military reason simply gave Sharina an excuse to follow her own preferences. She hadn't learned to ride when she was growing up in a peasant village to which horses were rare visitors, and she hadn't liked the animals when as a princess she'd perforce become better acquainted with them.

Walking also permitted Sharina to wear practical garments instead of the court robes which propriety would otherwise have forced her into. She could shrug off what the palace servants thought about her garb, but the common soldiers too would be shocked if Princess Sharina appeared in public wearing a short cloak, a pair of tunics, and sturdy sandals like a peasant woman. The sacrifice she was making to hike alongside them was ample justification for her to wear comfortable, practical clothing instead of silk brocades.

Sharina walked beside Rasile to make it clear to the army that the Corl wizard was a trusted advisor rather than a dangerous alien. Rasile could no more have made the journey on her own legs than Tenoctris could've, so she was being carried.

It wouldn't be uncommon for a noblewoman going on a long journey to ride in a hammock slung between two bearers. Rasile couldn't comfortably lie on her spine, however, so she sat on a sedan chair from which the back had been removed.

The two men carrying her were ordinary Valles chairmen who wouldn't ordinarily have left the city streets. They weren't having any difficulty with the route, however. Apparently cobblestone streets and dirt alleys covered with all manner of garbage were good training for muddy tracks and rocky gorges.

Lord Tadai and the woman who was in charge of the logistics, Lord Hauk's senior clerk, were carried in litters. There were no wheeled vehicles: neither wagons nor carriages would've survived the first fifty miles of this expedition. Pack animals—horses, mules, and donkeys alike— carried the food and minimal baggage of the troops. The Kingdom of the Isles had depended largely on barges and cargo ships for its trade, so the size of the army marching to Pandah had been dictated by the number of animals available in Valles.

"Good morning, Your Highness!" called Lord Waldron, watching from horseback in the midst of aides on foot as the army trudged past. He alone in the army was mounted. "Don't be surprised if there's a delay within the next three miles. The pioneers are corduroying a stretch where the bloody glacier runoff's turned the ground to quicksand, but I'm not sure they're going to reach the south end before the lead battalion comes up with them."

"We can only expect the troops to accomplish what's humanly possible, milord," Sharina called back. "And I'm confident of *that,* since you're in charge."

The horse wasn't merely a concession to Waldron's age— indeed, he'd have been the last man in the army to admit he couldn't march at the pace anybody else did. Attaper had told Sharina in private that the army commander would be running up and down the line of march the whole time, a task requiring that even a younger man be mounted.

The advice was clearly good. The fact that Lord Attaper volunteered it to his rival's benefit was a positive comment on him—and on the spirit Garric had fostered among his officers.

Waldron spoke to his aides and resumed his slow progress down the line, observing the dress of his troops and dealing out praise and correction as required. When he reached the rear guard—under Attaper's command—he'd start forward again. Waldron wasn't the most imaginative of officers, perhaps, but he was competent and utterly indefatigable in carrying out his duties.

Sharina had originally wondered why her brother—and still more, King Carus—left Waldron in command of the army when he'd made it clear from the start that he didn't believe that anyone but a noble from northern Ornifal like himself should be on the throne of the Isles. She'd come to realize what Carus had probably known instinctively, that Waldron's feelings would never affect the determination with which he carried out his duties, and that his oath was as firm as the mountains.

As firm as Garric's oath, in fact; or Sharina's.

The path broadened, though it was slushy with meltwater from the glacier draining from the valley to the left. This range of hills had no name in Sharina's own time: the whole region was beneath the Inner Sea. The present valley was barren rock where it'd melted clear. The sun glinted blue from ice remaining in the deeper recesses.

A monster was frozen into the face of the glacier. Indeed, the tip of a stubby wing already stuck out of the ice.

"Rasile," Sharina said sharply. "What's that? What's the thing in the glacier?"

The Corl wizard had been running sets of beads through her fingers, muttering quiet incantations. The beads were of varying sorts—wood, coral, and a string of stones seemingly picked at random out of a streambed. She followed the line of Sharina's pointing arm, her muzzle twitching.

"A wyvern," she said. She looked at the surrounding landscape as if for the first time. "This is a very old place. Very old indeed. But I do not think it extends very widely."

"But what's the creature?" Sharina said. "Is it dangerous?"

Rasile shrugged on her chair. "It would be if it were alive," she said. "The True People have legends of them. They're predators but not exactly animals; they have some ability to think."

She gave her rasping laugh and added, "There were no wizards among them, though, so they can't be considered truly capable of civilization."

"Will there be more wyverns?" Sharina asked. "Not caught in the ice, I mean."

"I cannot say, Sharina," Rasile said. "But I do not think so. Legend claimed that Barrog, Wisest of the Wise, cleansed the world of wyverns—well, cleansed it of demons, because this is legend rather than history—and imprisoned them all in shackles of ice till the Final Days, when they will be released to fight against men and gods. The True Men, of course."

"Time enough to worry about that when we've beaten the Last," Sharina said, realizing as she spoke that she was very tired. *We're not going to beat the Last. The best we can hope for at Pandah is to win a skirmish, and even that isn't assured.*

A trumpet called from farther up the line. A file-closer with the infantry company immediately ahead of Sharina turned and bellowed, "Hold up!"

Captain Ascor spoke to the signaler at his side, a cornicine whose horn circled his body. That man repeated the call from the front of the line in the richer, less insistent, tone of his longer instrument.

"Your Ladyship?" said Lires. "We're halting again."

Lires had never quite understood the forms of polite address. On the other hand, the trooper had twice been wounded to the point of death in saving Sharina's life. Neither she nor anybody else in her hearing was going to lecture him on the importance of using "Your Highness" instead of some lesser honorific.

"Waldron told us that was likely," Sharina said mildly. She looked up at the hills. They'd left the wyvern behind, but she didn't doubt that there were other—and worse—horrors in the new world the Change had unleashed.

Even without Waldron's warning, she'd have known by now to expect delays. Moving an army by sea was difficult. Ships were slow to get under way. They lost sight of one another and failed to tack on schedule even without storms to confuse matters further.

An expedition by land was far worse. The column moved at the speed of the slowest element, and something was always going wrong at some point or several along the line. Sharina and the Blood Eagles were fairly close to the head of the march; the cumulative delays became worse the farther back in the column you were.

The rear guard would be marching into camp after dark, just as had happened every day since the army set out. Waldron rotated the previous lead regiment to the rear every morning and moved the second regiment in line to the front in continuous motion.

There was a great deal that the epics ignored about moving and supplying an army. The poets talked only of battle—and now that Sharina had seen battles, she knew that the reality wasn't much like the epics either.

Rasile was telling her beads with her eyes closed, muttering in a raspy whisper. Was that a religious exercise, wizardry, or simply a means of relaxation? Of course the answer didn't matter; it was simply the sort of question Sharina's mind spun toward during these maddening halts. She should keep a codex with her to read, though her brother really had more taste for literature than she did.

She looked at the ground. The meltwater was noticeably blue, even in the shallow puddle at her feet. Her face in reflection looked wan, though the color of the water was probably responsible for some of—

Prince Vorsan was standing beside her.

Sharina instinctively braced her hands to push back against the empty air. That was no help at all. The mirrored surface *turned* and she was on the inside, in the hall of polished stone and reflections.

"Why are you doing this?" she shouted at the man who faced her from across the rotunda. She *did* wear the Pewle knife today, as always when she was in the field with the army. There'd been times its heavy blade was the margin between life and death, for Sharina and for the kingdom besides.

She didn't bother to reach through the slit in her outer tunic to touch the hilt now. She was too angry to need reassurance.

"For your own sake, Sharina," Vorsan said. He wore robes of scarlet velvet today, perfectly matching the cabochon-cut ruby on his left middle finger. The ring winked with internal fire as he gestured soothingly. "Surely you must see by now that there's no hope for your world. Leave it and join me."

Sharina stared at the wizard: a soft-looking fellow of average height, not unattractive physically but without the spark that would've made him interesting as a man. She didn't doubt that Vorsan was intelligent and able, but she couldn't imagine spending any length of time in his sole company. Spending eternity with him would be impossible: she'd rather die.

As she probably would, since she *did* see that humans had no hope of defeating the Last.

"Find another companion," Sharina said harshly. "Find somebody who's interested in you. I'm not!"

"Sharina, you don't understand," Vorsan pleaded, taking a step forward. The slim metal servants standing to his left and right moved when he did; Sharina gripped her knife.

Vorsan raised his hands, palms forward. "Please, I only want to help you," he said. "Won't you at least have a little fruit or something to drink while we discuss this?"

On cue, the servitors extended their trays, calling attention to the decanter and crystal glasses on one, and the pyramid of fruit on the other. The grapes and oranges were familiar, but there was also what looked like a rough-skinned pear and some bright green fruits which were the diameter of eggs but perfectly spherical.

"I've said no!" Sharina said, drawing the Pewle knife. "You're a nasty little person! You follow me and you spy on me, and I'm sick of it! Stop!"

The servitors stepped between her and Vorsan, protecting the prince. Despite their weird appearance, the notion of attack by a servant holding a tray of fruit was so incongruous that Sharina suddenly giggled.

She was on the edge of hysteria, she suspected, but it still took the tension out of the situation. She fitted the knife into its concealed sheath carefully, so that she didn't slice either the tunic or herself.

"Prince Vorsan," she said formally. "I must ask you not to trouble me further. Your attentions are unwelcome. If you're a gentleman, you'll respect my wishes."

Vorsan wrung his hands and turned sideways to her with an agonized expression. "I see that I'm a figure of fun to you, Princess," he said. "Well, I can't help that. As foolish as it no doubt seems to you, I who could have anyone, *anyone* I should have thought, with whom to share my paradise out of time . . . I want only you. In all the ages since the Flood, this is the first time I've met someone who was more than the whim of a moment."

"You're trying to be flattering," Sharina said, "but this makes me very uncomfortable. Please leave me alone."

She cleared her throat and focused on the mirror to her right. "I'm going to go now. I hope you'll have the decency to do as I request."

"I only wish I had the strength to do that, Sharina," Prince Vorsan whispered.

Sharina's eyes locked with those of her crystal-clear reflection. She felt the mirror start to shift again.

"I only wish I did," came the whisper pursuing her back to her own time.

ILNA WONDERED IF the cave had an opening besides the one closed by the heavy door: a hole for ventilation slanting out through the rock face above, perhaps, or a tail that looked like a fox's burrow miles away on the other side of the ridge. It probably didn't matter, because there weren't enough people and animals—a modest number of goats and a few pigs—to suck the virtue out of the air.

The cave stank, of course, but so did the homes of all but a handful of the wealthiest peasants in the borough. Everybody else slept with their animals in earth-floored huts whose wattling and thatch slowly decayed.

Gressar, the ginger-bearded village chief, was speaking to Temple, whom he seemed to think was the leader of the party. This irritated Ilna to a degree, but not quite enough for her to make a point of correcting the fellow.

"We've always had the cave for shelter," Gressar said. A single lamp was pegged to the side of the cave at the height a tall man could reach. Originally the pearly flow rock covering the wall would've acted as a natural reflector, but over the years soot had blackened it. "We hadn't needed it, though, since my grandfather's day when the barons of Eaton and Bessing fought and both of them raided the valley."

"Eaton and Bessing were destroyed on the Terrible Day," said another man. "There's no sign of either realm, nor of the free city of Brickkin a day's hike and a half to the south. I searched them out myself."

"And I went with him!" said a third fellow. He nodded with enthusiasm. "I went, and they weren't there."

"But when the barons were gone, the demons came," Gressar resumed, shooting a sour glance at the fellows who'd butted in on his recitation. The Change had probably weakened the village structure; and even before, if this valley was like Barca's Hamlet, no one man would've had the power to give orders unchallenged to his neighbors. "The first night they killed seven people—"

"*And* a dozen goats," the second man said. "Three of them mine."

"Sister take you, Kardon!" Gressar snapped. "If they'd killed you instead of your goats, perhaps you'd be able to keep your mouth shut while somebody's talking!"

"Gently, friends!" said Temple. He didn't sound angry, but he raised his voice enough to give it authority. "We're here to help you out of your problem. Stay calm and it'll be right again before much longer."

"Well, they did kill the goats," Kardon muttered, but he

was at least pretending to be speaking to himself instead of interrupting.

"The demons came back the three nights of the new moon after the Terrible Day," Gressar said. "We knew the signs this time, so we sheltered here in the cave. And we'd rebuilt the door, though not as well as we have since. Still, they didn't force their way in."

"The cats are lazy brutes as well as vicious ones," Ilna said. "They won't go to any effort even to kill."

Temple glanced appraisingly toward her. "The Coerli use their quickness rather than strength," he said. "And they try to avoid enclosures where they'd be at a disadvantage."

He nodded to the villager and went on. "You're fortunate to have had this shelter, Master Gressar, and you've done a very good job strengthening it. But it's time to end the Coerli attacks once and for all."

"It's past time," said a young woman in a savage voice. "It won't bring back my Mira, will it? And you and my worthless husband didn't do a thing to save her, Gressar!"

"Now, Stuna, there was nothing to be done," said the headman with the sort of deliberate reasonableness that you use when you're trying to calm a child on the verge of a tantrum.

It didn't work with children, as Ilna knew from watching over the years, and it *certainly* didn't work with the distraught mother. She gave a wordless shriek and threw herself at Gressar with her hands clawed. He backed a step, then turned and hunched over to escape Stuna's nails.

Two men took her by the arms, looking uncomfortable with the task. When she subsided into tears, they immediately let her go.

"Mira wasn't but four," said a man who hadn't spoken before. "It wasn't her fault, she was just too young to know better. She couldn't find her puppy inside, so she slipped out again while we were closing the door. It's so heavy it swings slow, you seen that. And the demons were already on us, or nearly. There was nothing we could do!"

He kept his face turned away from Temple as he spoke,

which meant that Ilna got as good a view of his features as
the dim light allowed. She'd spent time in one sort of Hell
herself; this man was in a different place, but it was just as
dark.

"Temple?" Ilna said. "The way to my goal is through the
place those beasts come from; *that* my pattern tells me. I
don't know what that place is, but I intend to go there."

"It's a cyst in time," Temple said, while the villagers listened in wonder. "A valley like this one—perhaps this very
one—but in its own universe."

He smiled with a touch of sadness. "It might be much like
the one in which you found me, before the Change brought it
back into the present world. At an unfortunate time, one
might say, but the Last themselves may have been responsible for the timing. There must be a wizard, a Corl wizard
that is, who formed the cyst. That wizard rules the hunting
pack that comes out when the conditions are right here."

"How do you recommend that we enter the beasts' world,
soldier?" Ilna said harshly.

Her fingers were knotting and unknotting yarn. Each pattern she created was more terrible than the last. She knew exactly how the girl Mira died, because she'd watched the beasts
kill Merota. In this valley they'd survived long enough to eat
the child, unlike the band which had only seconds to savor
Merota's slaughter before Ilna took a vengeance more terrible
than their cat minds could've imagined before it happened.

Merota's killers had died, and these would die also. Not
soon enough, as the child's mother had said; but soon.

"We'll go through their doorway," Temple said calmly.
"But first we'll place ourselves in front of it while the warriors are at the far end of the valley. They have to get back
into their enclave before the sun rises, so they'll come to us."

He gestured to the hunters. "And when they do, we'll kill
them," he said. "Since there's no other way to deal with this
band."

"There's no other way to deal with *any* of the beasts," Ilna
snapped. "But why will they all be at the other end of the
valley?"

"Ah," said Temple, nodding. "That's where the men of the village come in. If they're willing to help, that is. Otherwise I'll have to handle that part of the business myself while the three of you block the warriors' way home."

"Our men will help you," said Stuna. She gave a croaking laugh. "Or I swear by the soul of my Mira that I'll kill every one of them as he sleeps. Every one!"

"Lord Temple," said Gressar formally. "Tell us what we have to do."

Chapter

12

METAL CLINKED OUTSIDE the tent, probably a buckle tapping against the bronze cuirass of the officer of the guard. It was a harmless sound, but Cashel felt Sharina stiffen in the darkness.

He didn't speak. Sharina suddenly began to sob. Cashel still didn't say anything, but he stroked her shoulder with one hand and held her firmly with the other. He wished she'd tell him what the problem was, but he wasn't going to badger her. She was having a hard-enough time as it was.

Sharina sat upright. The bedding had been laid on the ground, which'd horrified the servants. She'd held firm, though, insisting that she as regent *was* going on the expedition to Pandah and that she was *not* going to burden the army with a gilded brass bed frame.

"Cashel, somebody's watching me," she said quietly. "His name is Vorsan, Prince Vorsan, and he's a wizard from before the Great Flood. Which apparently isn't a myth. I always thought the Flood was a myth."

Her voice broke with the last word and she started crying again. Cashel put his arms around her. "What did Tenoctris

tell you?" he asked, taking it as a given that she'd talked to
Tenoctris if a wizard was giving her trouble.

"She said not to worry!" Sharina said. "Cashel, he's taken
me into his world. If I look into a mirror or any kind of reflection the wrong way, I'm there in his palace with him!"

"You told Tenoctris that and she just said not to worry?"
Cashel said. What Sharina'd said didn't fit. There was something he didn't know, which was common enough, but this
time it seemed like it was something he could learn.

"I said—" Sharina said, but the fright and anger in her
voice faded by the end of the second syllable. Much calmer
she went on, "Tenoctris said she didn't believe Vorsan would
hurt me. And Rasile said she didn't think we should try to
destroy him, because she couldn't tell the future perfectly."

Cashel rose to a crouch—the tent of even the princess was
a small one; common soldiers simply wrapped themselves in
their cloaks at night—and pulled on his tunics. He was used
to dressing in the dark; a lot of a shepherd's business was
done in the dark and in the worst storms you could imagine.

His quarterstaff lay alongside the mattress stuffed with
horsehair rather than straw like a peasant's. He touched it.
The hickory made him think of the borough; he smiled.

"That means Rasile thought she could tell the future
some," Cashel said. "And maybe there'll be a time she wants
Prince Vorsan around."

"You think I should just let him, well, do the things he
does too?" Sharina said. "I've *told* him to leave me alone,
but he doesn't."

They bumped elbows as she shrugged into her own tunic.
She was trying to keep the irritation out of her voice, but
Cashel heard it regardless.

"No, Sharina," he said calmly. "But I think I ought to talk
to him myself. Do you have a mirror?"

They'd need a light, too. The guards outside the tent had a
lantern he could borrow, but he'd just as soon leave them and
everybody else out of this. Cashel didn't often get angry, but
he was angry now.

He took the flint and steel from the tarred leather cylinder hanging from the tent's ridgepole and struck sparks into a pile of mushroom spores. When the tinder flared, he touched the lampwick to it.

"He has metal men for servants," Sharina said softly. "I heard the sound when I was starting to go to sleep, and I thought . . ."

"I'll talk to him," Cashel repeated quietly. "Do you have a mirror?"

"Here," said Sharina, holding the Pewle knife upright so that their lamplit faces were reflected on the flat of the polished blade. "I think this is . . . suitable."

Cashel saw shadows quiver in the steel; no more than that. Voices murmured outside the tent; rested guards were replacing those who'd been on duty.

"He's there," Sharina said in an urgent whisper. He didn't know whether she was speaking to him or just to herself. "I know he's there!"

"It's smaller than me," Cashel said carefully.

"So's the pupil of my eye," Sharina said. "But I can see all of you. The knife is enough."

"Prince Vorsan," Cashel said, speaking as if the knife blade was the man he was looking for. "My name's Cashel or-Kenset. I'd like to talk to you; it won't take long. You have my word that I won't harm you or yours if you let me in to talk."

A shadow solidified on the metal, seemingly the reflection of someone behind them. It had shape but not texture. "Vorsan, you can trust—" Sharina began.

Cashel touched her cheek with his left hand. "Hush, love," he said, watching the shimmering steel. "This is for men."

The shadow moved and was light, a round room beneath a glowing dome. The man on the other side wore robes of a blue Cashel'd seen only a few times on evenings when he looked into the depths of the sea. Across that backdrop moved clouds of perfect silver, shredding and re-forming like an autumn storm drove it.

Oh, Ilna'd love to see that cloth! Cashel thought; and blushed, because after all it wasn't what he'd come here about.

Vorsan was pudgy. He wore a wreath of silver flowers that matched the embroidered clouds, and on his right and left were the silver men Sharina'd mentioned. They didn't have faces or the kinds of bumps and angles normal people had; it was sort of like they were wax figures and they'd been heated just a little.

Each silver man held a club of metal that seemed to grow right out of his hand.

Cashel cleared his throat and raised his quarterstaff upright—it was too tall for the tent that way—but just held it in the one hand, not threatening anybody. "You don't need those," he said, nodding to the servants. "My word's good."

"Yes, yes, I'm aware of that," Vorsan said, making an expression like he was swallowing something sour. "Still, I'm not a man of violence myself and, ah, I felt it was better to be prepared when I explain the situation to you."

If you think those two metal monkeys'd stop me if I hadn't given my word . . . , Cashel thought; but he didn't speak, because it'd sound like a threat and he wasn't one to threaten folks.

But if I hadn't given my word . . .

"Now, I'm sure you care a great deal for the princess," Vorsan said. "That's correct, isn't it?"

"Yes," said Cashel. "I care for Sharina."

"Well, you see, the point is that you can't protect her from what's about to happen to your world," Vorsan said. "I'm the *only* one who can protect her. I can't seem to get her to understand that. The Last will destroy your world as the Flood did mine, but this time there'll be no respite. Mankind is doomed forever—and the Princess Sharina is doomed as well unless you convince her to come with me. You do see that, don't you?"

"Sir," said Cashel, "I don't believe that we can't win. I'll never believe that Evil wins, not even if it kills me, and I don't think Sharina believes that either. But—"

"I'm telling you the truth, my good man!" Vorsan said. "Do you think I'm mistaken? I created this sanctuary. I'm Vorsan, and I don't make mistakes!"

Cashel laughed. He was still angry, but the little fellow was as funny as a bullfrog puffing himself up and trying to be an ox.

"You've made one mistake I know about, Master Vorsan," he said. He let the laughter stay in his voice. Laughing at the little fellow'd bother him more than shouts would. It wasn't a kind thing to do, but Cashel *was* angry.

"You thought that it'd matter to Sharina even if she thought you were right," he said. "Even if she was sure we were all going to lose and these black ugly Last were going to kill everything else in the world. She'd keep on fighting anyway, because that's what decent folk do when it's that or give in to evil. Which you'd know yourself if you were a man."

Vorsan gave an exaggerated shake of his head. "You can't really believe that?" he said, but though he made a question out of the words, his tone said he really was starting to understand. "The Princess Sharina is unique, so perfectly wonderful—it wouldn't be *right* that she throw her life away so pointlessly. She owes it to the world to be preserved!"

Cashel laughed again. "Do you listen to yourself?" he asked, meaning it for a real question. "Sharina's going to fight for the world, which you'd never do. Just keep out of the way. That's all she wants of you, Vorsan—your space."

"She can't really mean that," Vorsan whispered, looking down at his hands cupped before him. He raised his eyes to Cashel's and went on. "Very well, then; you may leave. Focus on your reflection in the mirror on either side of you."

"One thing more, Master Vorsan," Cashel said. "I gave you my word I wouldn't harm you if you invited me in; and I haven't. But sir—if you trouble Sharina again, I'll be back, without an invitation and without any promises. And I'll end it then, whatever Tenoctris says."

"You can't reach me unless I permit it!" the pudgy man said.

Cashel smiled. "The better part of me doesn't want to prove how wrong you are," he said. "But I'm not as peaceful a man as you maybe think. Good day, Master Vorsan."

Cashel looked into a mirror as clear as the air between him and its surface; and after a moment, he was falling back into Sharina's arms.

THE LAKE WAS a dome of warm mist rising for as far outward as Garric could see from the ogre's back. Air currents opened vistas and closed them, occasionally showing him groves of fruit trees scattered into the distance. The air had an undertone, mildly unpleasant but not one of decay.

"You're smelling asphalt," Shin said. "Bitumen. It's seeped up to fill most of the bowl here over the centuries. Rain doesn't soak in as it would on normal ground, so the surface is cut with freshwater leads."

The aegipan nodded his little goatee toward the lake with a lolling grin. "And islands of dirt and rock remain where the hills were," he added. "They're planted with orchards, I see."

"I've never seen a place like this," Garric said, lifting his right leg from the stirrup and doubling it to stretch different muscles. "It's quite interesting, of course, but I don't see how we can get across it. Can we go around?"

"No," said Shin. "But I believe these men—"

He jogged his chin toward six figures who'd appeared from the warm fog. They were armed, though for the moment they seemed watchful rather than openly hostile.

"—will be able to guide us."

Kore grunted disgustedly. "The stink of asphalt keeps me from smelling anything!" she muttered. "It's worse than being blind, or next to it."

"I'll dismount!" Garric said in an urgent whisper. Kore knelt; the strangers backed away with some shouted disquiet. They must've thought the ogre was crouching to charge.

"We're friends, good sirs!" Garric called and he walked forward, his left arm raised in greeting. "Don't be put off by my mount. She's quite harmless, I assure you."

"Yes, yes, rub it in, why don't you?" Kore murmured in

the background. "It's possible that my humiliation hasn't yet been as complete as it could be. Utterly harmless, yes."

"I'm Garric or-Reise from Haft, traveling southward in hopes of visiting a wise man," Garric said, keeping his tone brightly cheerful. "I'm not wealthy, but I can find a silver piece for the man who leads me and my companions through this—"

He gestured, still with his left hand.

"—lake or tar pit or whatever you call it."

The six men looked a right lot of villains, to tell the truth. Though probably no better disciplined than the troop his party'd met on the northern edge of the teak forest, these were better armed and as growlingly dangerous as a pack of cur dogs.

"You're in Lord Holm's domain now," said the man whose fore-and-aft bicorn hat was decorated with a long feather, now bedraggled but originally pink. He held a cocked crossbow which, unlike the fellow's clothing, looked very well maintained. "Watch your tongue when you discuss his possessions, if you know what's good for you."

"I will indeed, sirs," Garric said, standing arms akimbo with his head high. The most dangerous thing he could do would be to act subservient to these men; they'd be on him like sharks if they decided he could be bullied. "Now, which of you will guide me through to the other side?"

The leader turned to the older man at his side, a fat fellow whose thinning hair was blond but whose beard was russet with streaks of gray. "What do you think, Platt?" he asked. "Do you suppose he's the one?"

"He could be, Leel," the fat man said, scratching his groin with his left hand. "It's not like Milord gave us much of a description, is it? 'There'll be a hero coming; bring him back to me.'"

"Milord's a wizard," said Leel forcefully to Garric. "He can foresee things."

"Then he foresaw us," said Kore, who'd walked up directly behind Garric while he was talking with Leel and his men. "Who but the hero Garric or-Reise could tame a mount as handsome and powerful as myself?"

"She's making them think it's a joke," said Carus, looking critically at the ogre through Garric's eyes. *"But when you think how it came that you're riding her . . . she's a clever lady, whatever she looks like."*

"I've had greater compliments than any a human ruffian is capable of giving me," Kore said, puzzling the locals who hadn't heard the ghost's observation. "But thank you just the same."

"I would be honored to meet Lord Holm," Garric said politely. "Though as I say, my wish is merely to pass through his territory, paying for food and lodging. We'll of course do no harm to anyone on the way."

"Bloody well told, you won't," the leader said, gesturing with his crossbow. The bow was horn-backed wood rather than steel, but Garric didn't need his ancestor's assessment to know that it'd send its square-headed quarrel through a man's chest at short range.

"What is there to harm, Leel?" another man demanded. "They're not working any but the south islands, and you know half the grubbies've run away by now."

"Shut up, Wagga!" Leel said. "Sister bite your tongue out, you fool."

He looked up to judge the position of the sun. "All right, we'll take them back. The big one, whatever it is—"

"The ogre, my man," Kore said with a note of chill. "Your ignorance is pardonable, but your lack of courtesy is not."

"Like I say, whatever," Leel growled. "He can't get across unless he flies. There's a little solid ground and most of the surface is okay for a man if he moves along. But a horse can't make it, and that brute's bigger'n any horse."

"So I am," said the ogre, raising her left hand and spreading the clawed fingers. Their span was enormous, easily that of the ribs of a parasol. "But on all fours, as I will deign to go under the circumstances, I spread my weight more broadly than a horse or even a man. Lead on, sirrah!"

Leel shrugged. "I figure it'll sink to the bottom of the tar," he said. "Which is no business of mine. And you'll—"

He looked directly at Kore for the first time. Leel obviously disliked the ogre, though he didn't seem to be as fearful as many of those Garric had met since he began riding her.

"—have plenty of company down there, much good may they do you. Trying to get through the lake without us to guide you, well—it's been tried."

"Look, Leel," said Platt, scratching his groin again. It seemed to be a nervous mannerism. "It's pretty late already. Don't you think we should maybe wait till morning?"

"No, I bloody well don't," snapped Leel. "Let's get going. Wagga, you lead."

A ratty little man nodded and slipped forward. He carried three javelins in a bundle and wore a hat made of leaves bent onto a frame of willow shoots. Leel gestured Platt ahead of him, said to Garric, "You lot follow me," and stepped onto the yielding, barren surface.

Shin hopped ahead, dancing rather than walking. Garric shuffled onto the path behind him. He noticed the lake's warmth on the backs of his calves before it seeped through the soles of his boots, but it wasn't dangerous in itself.

Dust, vegetable matter, and gravel were worked into the bitumen. The men ahead of Garric moved swiftly, so he fitted his pace to theirs. He was used to marshes, but he'd have been more comfortable if he had a staff to probe and to vault and—if worse came to worst—to spread his weight if he slipped into a sucking cavity. He didn't suppose hot tar would release a victim as easily as the mud of Pattern Marsh in the borough either.

The aegipan turned and raised an eyebrow in question.

Garric grinned, his mood suddenly lightened. "I was just thinking that I'd like a tar bath even less than I did a mud one when I tended sheep," he said. "So I'll avoid it."

"Hey, what if the big one falls through, Leel?" called a man toward the rear of the party.

"Then you find a way around the hole, don't you, Tenny?" said the leader, for the moment a wraith in the mist. "Or you wait here on the lake till the bogeys come to get you."

Tenny snarled a curse, but he didn't raise his voice enough to force Leel to notice him.

"Or again," Kore murmured, "I might decide to spend my final moments savoring a meal of human flesh. We can never be sure of the future, can we?"

The ogre didn't sound concerned. Carus laughed, but Garric wasn't sure the comment had been meant as a joke. On the other hand—

Garric grinned. The thought was amusing even if it weren't a joke, if you looked at the world in a particular way. He'd become enough of a warrior himself to understand that sometimes grim jokes were the only kind available, and those were the times you really needed a joke.

The mist largely cleared, though Garric hadn't noticed a breeze or patch of cooler air to explain it. They'd reached an island. Tar had soaked into the dirt of the margins, forming a black crust. Wagga was trotting across a field of bromeliads with squat, scaly trunks like palmettos. They grew in straight lines and must've been planted deliberately.

"Pineapples," Carus said. *"Saw them on Tisamur my first campaign. You cut the trunk open and it's sweet and sour both at once. Any cold at all kills them, but I guess this steam bath takes care of winter."*

Garric eyed the plants critically as he strode between the rows. They hadn't been tended in weeks or more, judging from the way vines were curling around the trunks. He wondered about the bogeys Leel had mentioned; then he wondered just what Lord Holm wanted a hero for.

They were on the asphalt again. The paths led from island to island. A lead of dark water eight or nine feet wide cut the surface. Wagga and Leel splashed through. Shin leaped it gracefully, landed on his hands, and somersaulted onto his hooves again.

Garric could've jumped across too, but he didn't trust the surface on the other side. Slamming down with his full weight might crack it. The very least he could expect then would be to lose a boot that he'd want after they'd crossed this stinking blackness.

The water was warm, the bottom slimy but less than knee-deep. He hopped up the other side and sloshed forward.

Their bare-legged guides showed no interest in stopping to allow Garric to pour the water out of his boot.

The path across the bitumen jogged repeatedly. Once Wagga led them in a wide circuit. The mist chanced to clear again long enough for Garric to see a single bubble of fresh tar in the midst of the otherwise unbroken gray expanse which they'd just avoided.

They crossed three more islands of normal soil, each planted with fruit trees. The light was failing; the sky was too bright for stars, but all below was in heavy shadow. Neither Garric nor Carus could identify the fruit on the last island, and they didn't tarry long enough in the dimness even to guess at its kinship. Part of the crop was rotting neglected on the ground.

Garric glanced over his shoulder. Kore was close behind, pacing easily on all fours. She'd stripped palm fronds to weave between the long fingers of either hand, increasing their surface area the way the webs of a frog's feet do. She grinned, though her long face touched the expression with savage horror.

"Leel, it's getting *bloody* late!" Platt called. "We should've waited till morning."

"Shut up, you fool, or you needn't worry about bogeys!" Leel snarled back.

Lights winked ahead, then vanished in a curl of mist. "About time," one of the men muttered.

"Look to the left, lad," warned Carus, seeing more with Garric's eyes than the owner did. At first Garric thought he was seeing another island half a mile away. The outlines were too square, though, and when the mist cleared momentarily he thought he glimpsed window alcoves and turrets on two corners.

"Master Leel?" Garric called. "Is that a palace out in the lake there?"

The leader's feathered bicorn jerked around. "Just shut your mouth, fellow!" he said in a tone of desperate anger. "Anything you want to know, keep it to ask Milord, you hear?"

Garric didn't reply. Leel was obviously frightened; there was no point in taking offense at what he blurted.

"He's not a man I'd judge to be easily frightened either," Carus said. *"Well, it could be he doesn't like the dark. Some folk are that way."*

The ghost laughed again. Neither he nor Garric thought Leel was afraid of the dark; but a sword and the will to use it could get you through a lot of situations, frightening and otherwise.

They'd come close enough to see that the lights were pots hanging from poles and leaping with smoky, deep red flames. "Faugh!" growled Kore. "It's tar they're burning."

Garric hadn't doubted her, but the breeze curled smoke toward him and he coughed uncontrollably. Even after he was clear of the wisps, the back of his throat felt flayed.

"Milord!" Leel cried. "We've found travelers! It may be one's the man you seek!"

It was fully dark, now. The flares stretched a furlong both east and west along the shore of the tar lake, though only those toward the middle were hung from poles. People, primarily men but some women and a few children, passed in partial silhouette against the low flames.

The men beneath the hanging lights were armed, several of them carrying shields as well as wearing bits of armor. The man they clustered about wore a striped cape of thin silk and a helmet decorated with the tail plumage of some flightless bird.

"Milord, he rides on a giant!" Platt cried, obviously trying to curry favor. "I guess that proves he's the one you're looking for, right?"

"Milord," said Garric, walking toward the man in the plumed helmet. He bowed, low enough to show deference without cringing. "I'm Garric or-Reise, a traveler from the north and just passing through your remarkable domain."

"Bring him up into the light where I can see him," Holm grumbled. He stepped back to make room, his gauzy cape fluttering. It was obviously for ornament rather than warmth in this steamy bowl.

Garric had thought Holm's apparent height was a trick of the plume and perhaps buskins, but even in thin silk slippers the fellow stood a hand's breadth taller than Garric. He was thin as well, though not particularly healthy: his cheeks were puffy and his hand trembled where he gripped his crossbelt.

Holm's eyes moved from the ogre—squatting placidly on the ground, a coarse mix of gravel and bits of clamshell—to Shin, and finally to the hilt of Garric's long sword. He looked up abruptly and said, "I'm a wizard, you know!"

"Master Leel had mentioned that," Garric said easily. The situation wasn't dangerous yet, but it could very quickly get that way. From the look of Holm's retainers, the fellow supplemented the income of his groves with banditry. The tar lake with its hidden paths would be as safe a lair as any mountain crag. But Holm appeared to have a use for him. . . .

"Leel also said I might be able to do you a favor of some sort," Garric continued. "While my companions and I are merely passing through, we're certainly willing to show our gratitude to you for passage."

"You'll need more than gratitude, you know," Holm snapped. "Unless you can swim the strait—"

He pointed behind him. Garric could smell salt in the air, and waves sounded faintly on a strand.

"—and that's three miles wide. The only ship that can cross it is mine. You see your position, fellow?"

The tossing flames from the tar pots lighted hard faces and weapons close at hand. Lord Holm had twenty or thirty bodyguards—

"Twenty-seven," interjected Carus. *"And Holm himself, if you want to count him."*

—probably as much to control the laborers—the grubbies, Wagga had called them—who tended his orchards as to loot his neighbors. From beyond the ring of armed men, those laborers watched. They were slight folk wearing minimal garments and seemed the same type as the farmers Garric had seen north of the teak forest.

"I've already told you, milord," Garric said, keeping his

voice pleasant but making his control obvious, "that I'm willing to do you a courtesy. If you'll ask politely, we can settle the matter and proceed—I hope—to my purchasing food for me and my companions."

Under normal circumstances life for the laborers under Holm wouldn't be much different than the living they scratched for landlords of their own race. Now, from what Wagga'd said, they were risking the guards' wrath to run away.

"Yes, a goat would be very welcome," Kore said, startling those standing near her. A spearman jumped sideways, tangled his feet, and crashed to the ground in a storm of curses.

"Courtesy, you say?" Holm said. He shot a glance at Leel, then glared at Garric. "Very well. My palace—the palace of my family for seven generations—is out on the lake. Perhaps you saw it when my men guided you across?"

"A fort made of bitumen blocks?" Garric said. "Yes, we did."

"It's a palace," Holm said with a flash of irritation. "It's very well appointed. If the walls are asphalt instead of stone, what of it?"

He cleared his throat. "But that's neither here nor there," he continued. "My laborers are a superstitious lot. They've gotten it into their minds that the shapes which wind twists the fog into are ghosts, so they refuse to go out to tend the orchards. And I must admit—"

Holm made a sour face and looked around him. Guards dropped their eyes rather than meet his glance.

"—that they've infected some of my retainers. What I want as price of your passage across the strait—"

He stared at Garric. He looked something like a dyspeptic owl.

"—is for you to spend the night in my palace. That will break the spell. The, ah, rumor, that is. No more than that. If you refuse—"

Garric curtly waved Lord Holm to silence. If the fool kept on, he was going to say something that couldn't easily be ignored.

"Milord," he said. "I have your promise of passage for me and my companions if we spend the night in that black palace? On your life, you swear?"

"I do," said Holm. "That's all you need do, and I'll give you every help."

"And a goat," said ogre. "A goat tonight. And other food, no doubt, as my master wishes."

"Yes, a goat!" said Holm. The quivering light increased his look of agitation. "Do you agree, fellow? Do you?"

"And one other thing," said Shin, his first words since they'd crossed the tar lake. "We will need a guide. Which of your brave men will guide us, milord?"

"There's no need of that," said Leel. "There's a causeway from here on the south shore straight to the palace. The lake shifts some. They built a causeway so's it couldn't be cut off. Long ago. Long, long ago."

Garric looked at his companions. The aegipan was smiling; Kore rose to her feet.

"Then we agree," Garric agreed. "Master Leel, will you lead us to this causeway, if you please?"

"After they bring the goat, dear master," said the ogre. "I feel a meal should be a good one if it might be my last, don't you think?"

She began to laugh in a booming voice. In Garric's mind, King Carus laughed also with the joy of bloody anticipation.

ILNA STOOD IN the mouth of the cave, looking toward the valley's slope. The sun behind her must be down, but she couldn't yet see stars above the shadowed land.

"We ought to be out there!" Asion muttered from within the cave. "Karpos, you *know* we should."

A child whimpered. Its mother crooned, *"Hush little baby . . . ,"* but Ilna could hear fear in the woman's voice also. All the men in the village were far from the cave and safety, certain victims if Temple's plan didn't work.

"If we were all visible, we might draw some of the Coerli

to us," Temple said calmly. "They won't come after Ilna alone in the doorway, not with easy prey elsewhere. She'll tell us when it's time for us to come out."

The air grew hazy but brightened. In the high sky the alien sun formed the way blood seeps from a pinprick. Four lines of red wizardlight quivered on the hillside, outlining a doorway, and a trio of hunters bounded from their world into that of humans.

A villager beneath the dam at the far end of the valley began winding a bull-roarer through the air, making a rhythmic drone that echoed from the slopes. The leading Coerli had started toward the cave in their usual pattern, but the sound drew their attention to the men of the community gathered in the open. A Corl began spinning his hooked cord, although he was nearly a mile from his intended prey.

A warrior gave a yipping howl and bounded toward the men. More Coerli sprang from the door of light. Those and the further cat men following spread to the flanks of the initial trio, widening the living net.

More Coerli appeared in threes; then the final clot, the younger warriors, chasing after their elders as a rabble. The total number was beyond Ilna's ability to count on the fingers of both hands, but she identified the pattern of the hunters as being the same as what she'd seen the previous night when all of the beasts had left their lair.

"All right," she said to her companions. She didn't look back into the cave. "They're all here. They're running toward the head of the valley."

Temple raised the clumsy trumpet he'd borrowed from the villagers. It was a wooden cone as long as his outstretched arm, fitted with a mouthpiece carved from a goat's thighbone. He blatted a harsh call toward the men beneath the dam.

The bull-roarer stopped with a brief moan. The villager spinning it—Gressar'd been carrying the device when they hiked to the dam this morning—must've just let go of the cord when Temple signaled.

Ilna watched for a moment further to be sure the trumpet

call hadn't affected the pack of Coerli. Then she said, "All right, they're still focused on the men."

Temple set the trumpet upright on the ground. He and the two hunters swung out of the cave and started toward the outlined portal, letting Ilna set the pace. Behind them the women of the village dragged the heavy door closed. One had begun to sob.

Ilna disliked running—and ran poorly, the main reason she disliked it—but it was necessary now. She'd learned that her legs and lungs wouldn't actually fail her if she was willing to keep on despite the pain. She couldn't imagine circumstances in which she'd permit pain to dictate her behavior, so she simply trotted along with an angry look on her face. The expression wasn't a new one for her, of course.

The dam collapsed with a series of hollow *klock*s. Stones knocked against one another as they fell out of alignment and water pressure pushed the whole structure into ruin.

Temple had arranged the project this morning, showing Gressar and his fellows where to place their levers. Ilna hadn't been sure the villagers would be able to execute the plan, but neither had she seen a practical alternative. If the villagers failed, of course, the cat men would kill them.

She smiled faintly. And then they'd kill Ilna and her companions, whose lives also depended on the river's sudden return to the valley it'd been diverted from. She should be able to do for a few more Coerli even in that case, though. Since she neither expected nor desired to live forever, being slaughtered now rather than later didn't concern her greatly.

The planted fields were even more unpleasant to cross going uphill than they'd been when Ilna'd run down them when she'd arrived in the valley. She couldn't say it was pleasant to get to the end of the furrows—she was still jogging uphill, after all—but it was less unpleasant. That was as much as Ilna expected from life, after all.

Her lips twitched in another tiny smile. "Less unpleasant" was *more* than she expected from life.

She glanced over her right shoulder. Pent-up water frothed

and curled as it poured through the displaced stones. The flow built up as it ate away more and more of the dam that'd diverted it, shoving out blocks from both edges, but even so the volume wasn't enough to fill the valley as a solid wall. The cat men howled in surprise and anger, but they had no difficulty in bounding up either slope to avoid the oncoming water.

The villagers who'd ripped the first hole in the base of the dam would've been surely drowned if they hadn't had the raft of massive timbers to clamber onto. Half the houses in the village were in ruins even before the water reached them and undermined their walls: the rooftrees had supplied the materials to make the raft.

There were thirty-one in the labor party, Temple had said: thirty adult males and the woman Stuna. She'd insisted on coming even though she wasn't strong enough or heavy enough to add much to the task. The raft was big enough to hold them all, but the coiling, bubbling water rocked it so violently that several fell off as Ilna watched; they clung to grass ropes which she'd braided from roof thatch while Temple prepared the dam for destruction and the hunters built the raft itself.

"We're here!" said Asion, halting at the gate of light. Close up, Ilna saw a shimmering membrane within the brighter rectangular outlines. "Mistress, what do we do?"

Temple looked at Ilna and raised an eyebrow. She shrugged. He understood the situation better than she did; she'd be a fool to give orders simply to prove that she could. She'd felt the impulse, but at least she'd fought it down before she *proved* herself a fool. This time.

"We wait here and kill the warriors as they try to return," Temple said to the hunters. "When we've killed the last of them, we enter the world on the other side of the portal and finish the job."

Asion looked toward Ilna doubtfully. "Yes," she said, as she determined the pattern she'd use this night. "It's not a complicated problem."

Ilna had time to knot an unusually large pattern this time,

though she had only the short lengths of yarn from her sleeve to work with. They'd do.

The raft wallowed and began to float downstream, rotating slowly in the current. The villagers who'd lost their footing crawled back aboard, saved by the ropes. It'd been unexpectedly satisfying to weave something for a solely physical purpose, a task that had no tinge of wizardry or compulsion.

Ilna smiled like a serpent, a tight-lipped, cruel expression. Whereas the fabric she knotted now had *everything* to do with compulsion. It would draw the warriors to their deaths as surely as a hangman's rope.

The river poured into the valley in a smoother, deceptively calm fashion now that it'd swept away the last of the dam that'd bounded it for so long. Half the Coerli were on the east side, across the broad channel from Ilna and her companions. As if on a signal, they waded together into the water and began swimming toward the raft and its cargo of villagers. The remaining cat men started toward Ilna's party.

Ilna decided her pattern was complete. It was slightly too long for her to stretch it by herself with her arms extended.

"Temple?" she said, handing him one end of the sketchy fabric. "Take this, if you will. When I say to, pull it tight with me."

"We'll change sides then, Ilna," the big man said with a friendly grin. "So that I can hold it in my left hand rather than with—"

He drew his sword. The bronze blade hummed softly.

"—my right."

"Yes," said Ilna, walking behind him and swapping the end she'd been holding for the one she'd offered him.

The river continued to rise, though now slowly. It lapped to the edge of the portal; Ilna felt water bathe her feet, noticeably cool. The loose soil melted and squelched between her toes. She'd wondered if it'd leak into the other world, but she found she could see the panel of light gleaming even through the thin mud.

The door—the membrane of light—behind them made the hair rise on the nape of Ilna's neck. She glanced at her companions to see if they felt it. Karpos probably misinterpreted her gesture, because he said to Temple, "So you're sure they can't come at us through this window from behind, then?"

"If the Coerli enter the portal from the back, Karpos . . . ," Temple said with a deep chuckle. "They'll go to a place neither in our world nor in theirs. They don't know what that world is, but they fear it is a bad one."

He laughed again with honest amusement. "The truth," he went on, "is far worse than they imagine it could be."

Ilna sniffed. "I'd as soon we killed them ourselves anyway," she said.

The cat men who'd leaped into the water were nearing the raft. They swam like dogs, their heads out of water and all four limbs paddling. Perhaps ordinary cats swam that way too—Ilna'd never seen one take to the water.

The beasts didn't seem to mind the swim, but that didn't help them now. Gressar aimed his bow and arrow at the nearest of them. The beast ducked under the water but bobbed to the surface a moment later.

Gressar shot. The bow was crude and short—a farmer's weapon of plain wood, shooting a stone-pointed arrow. It was good enough for the purpose, though: the arrow drove a hand's breadth into the cat man's neck. Blood spouted; the beast thrashed in a circle and sank.

A Corl dived under water and came up to grasp the edge of the raft. Three villagers struck at it together with spears and a club. One of the blows must've gotten home, because the brute drifted away in a spreading red curtain.

A panicked villager flung his spear at a swimming warrior. The weapon wasn't balanced to throw and the man had no skill at the business anyway; the cast missed by an arm's length as the target bobbed beneath the surface. Another man spun out his pebble-weighted minnow net, which settled over the beast's head and shoulders as it rose again. The fisherman dragged his catch toward the raft where another spear, thrust this time, skewered it.

Smiling faintly, Ilna looked up from the pleasant drama

about the raft. She and her companions had their own tasks to perform now: the Coerli on the west of the river were in better order than their swimming fellows had managed.

Karpos nocked an arrow; Asion held the bullet in the pocket of his sling with his left hand. "Whenever you give the word, Ilna," Temple said calmly, his eyes on the oncoming warriors.

Ordinarily Coerli could dodge even sling bullets at close range, but their narrow feet sank deeper in the mud than humans' did. They were splashing well out in the flow to keep clear of the missiles.

Staying out of range had its own problems. They were in waist-deep water, and there was enough current to drag hard at them. Their tails lashed the surface, and Ilna was certain their snarls were fury rather than communication.

She smiled. "We'll let them come halfway closer," she said.

The beasts didn't have a real leader; instead of rushing as one at the command of a maned chief, they snapped and bickered for nearly a minute. The flood buffeted them.

When the attack came, it was almost an accident. A beast lost his footing and splashed forward. Those to either side of him leaped toward the humans, and a heartbeat later the whole band was in noisy motion.

"Now," said Ilna. She drew her pattern taut against Temple's simultaneous pull.

Cat beasts squawked and stumbled. One was spinning out a weighted cord when his eyes took in the full meaning of Ilna's jagged web. His throwing arm spasmed, whipping the capture line sideways to snag the neck of one of his own fellows.

Karpos shot—

Only the fletching of the arrow projected from above the breastbone of the nearest warrior. At this short range, it'd almost completely penetrated the beast's slender body.

—nocked one of the pair of arrows between the fingers of his left hand and shot again—

The beast was tumbling in the slow current; it'd lost its

footing when it froze. The arrow raked it from below the ribs and poked out the opposite shoulder blade.

—nocked the third arrow and shot—

The arrow struck the top of the beast's skull with a *whock;* exiting, the point pinned the long jaws together.

—and reached into his quiver for the remaining three arrows.

Asion's sling was marginally slower to reload, but on targets so close his bullets crushed as well as penetrated. The hunter was a small man, but his arms were enormously strong. The dim red sun darkened the blood swirling from the corpses as they drifted downstream in the flood.

Three beasts remained. The current'd pulled them far enough south that Ilna's web would no longer command them as it should. She said to Temple, "We have to turn to keep the pattern toward them or—"

Temple dropped his end of the pattern and strode forward, shrugging his buckler into his left hand. "This will be simpler, Ilna," he said without looking back over his shoulder.

Then, in a tone of command that reminded her of when King Carus ruled Garric's body during a battle, Temple thundered, "Comrades, don't shoot! I'll finish this!"

He waded into the water. The Coerli were fully alert now. Ilna thought they'd regroup and attack together, but perhaps they were too angry to think the matter through. Or again, perhaps the nearest warrior didn't see any reason to delay: no ordinary man was a match for the beasts' quickness.

Water as deep as his back-bending knees sprayed as the warrior leaped high. It swung a short length of its hooked line to wrap Temple's neck and sword arm from above. The weighted end sailed away instead because Temple's sword was where the beast'd expected a clear path; the cord severed itself on an edge as keen as a beam of light.

Temple hadn't responded to the beast's attack: *no* human was that quick. He'd anticipated it, seeing the pattern of events before they happened and striking at where the beast would be when the blade passed through the place. Just as Chalcus used to do, when he was alive.

The Corl twisted, seeing the death he was flinging himself onto, but all four limbs were off the ground so it had nothing to push against. The sword continued its curving stroke, catching the beast in the short ribs and slicing on through as easily as it'd cut the cord a heartbeat earlier.

The beast flew apart in a gout of blood and stomach contents. Its mouth was open but silent in one half and the legs pumped wildly in the other. Ilna knew how sharp the bronze blade was, but the strength needed to lop completely through a torso was beyond the dreams of most men.

Temple strode forward without slowing. The second warrior lunged low with a wooden poniard in either hand. He scissored them toward Temple's knees like a trap springing, but the swordsman's long arm and long blade had again anticipated the attack: the Corl drove itself onto the sword hard enough to punch the bronze point out through the base of its skull.

The third warrior hadn't verbally coordinated with the second, but the pack were experienced killers who'd worked together in the past: he went high because his fellow had attacked low. As he leaped he slanted his spear downward so that the pair of springy wooden points would grip the human's neck with the barbs on their inner surfaces.

The thrust glanced from Temple's small shield, rising as part of the same motion as had put the sword into the second beast. It was like watching a dance, but considerably more graceful than any dancers Ilna had seen.

The Corl continued on over, landing with a splash in the water behind the swordsman. It dropped its spear and snaked a stone-headed axe from a loop on the crossbelts that were its only garment.

Temple was turning, hunching, bringing the shield down and around. He knew what would happen next—*Ilna* knew what would happen next—but understanding something wasn't the same as being able to stop it. Temple was quick for a human, but the Coerli were as quick as thought, as quick as the shimmer of water.

Motion sparked in the alien sunlight. *Whock!*

The beast leaped straight up, its limbs thrashing. Its head was a bloody ruin. It fell onto its back, then flopped over on its belly and began to drift on the current. Occasionally a further spasm would stir the water, but generally only one limb at a time.

Asion folded the release cord of his sling back against his right palm on the staff. "That was my last bullet," he said sheepishly. "I'm glad I kept it, hey?"

Temple let his buckler swing against the strap that held it while not in use. He stepped to Asion and embraced him, carefully keeping the sword away from both of them. He couldn't sheathe the weapon till he'd wiped the bronze clean of blood and filth.

"I am *very* glad you kept it, Brother Asion," Temple said, stepping back. The torso of the first beast he'd killed lay on the slope above where the water—now slowly receding— had washed. He picked the corpse up by the scruff of the neck and wiped his blade on the brindled fur.

Karpos was cutting an arrow from the body of a beast lying in the fresh mud. "I wonder if the farmers have arrows I could use?" he said. "I don't think I'm going to find more than a couple of my own, what with the current."

Ilna looked down into the valley. The women had come out of the cave. Several of them were running toward the raft, grounded when the initial head of water had passed.

The men were kneeling over several of their fellows whom they'd laid out on the ground. One or more warriors must've gotten aboard the raft and done damage before being killed.

"They've lost everything," Temple said. "They'll have to replant their crops as well as rebuild their houses."

Ilna looked at the big man. His face and tone were both without expression.

"Peasants have a hard life, soldier," she said sharply. "*These* peasants, the ones who're still alive, won't have cat beasts preying on them. That's all I can do for them. Or anybody could!"

"Yes, Ilna," Temple said. "Now, before that sun sets—"

He nodded toward the dim red orb now close above the western horizon.

"—we must go through the portal. Our task isn't done yet."

"All right," she said. "Asion and Karpos, are you ready?"

The hunters got up from the bodies. They moved into line beside her and Temple.

All together, Ilna and her companions stepped through the membrane of light.

"OH!" SAID SHARINA as she saw the citadel of Pandah rising out of the plain. "That isn't what I expected."

"It's bigger than I thought too, Your Ladyship," said Trooper Lires. "I'd heard it was a sleepy little place. Ah, not that we couldn't take it in a week or two. Or maybe even faster if you ordered an assault instead of undermining the walls."

"I'm not going to order an assault," said Sharina dryly, "or make any other military decisions so long as I have competent officers. But I was on Pandah in the past—before the Change, of course—and it *was* a sleepy little island. They grew fruit and garden truck for ships crossing the Inner Sea, and merchants bartered cargoes to local factors."

Pandah now—and, Sharina supposed, in her distant past—had massive stone walls within which rose square towers with arrow slits. Figures moved on the battlements. She couldn't make out details of them, but Lires said, "By the Sister! There's cats there and men both!"

He cleared his throat, turned his head away from Sharina in embarrassment, and then forced himself to meet her cool smile again. Rasile continued telling beads in her palanquin, but her eyes were open and seemingly focused on the city coming into view.

"Sorry, milady," the trooper muttered. "I mean, it's no different from us. I don't know why I said that."

The leading regiments of the royal army were spreading into battle order as they advanced across the plain. The afternoon air rang with trumpets and horns, insistent and never tuned the same. Sharina supposed that made it easy for soldiers to tell their own call from those of other units, but it was gratingly unpleasant to a civilian.

Rasile rose to a squat. Though her palanquin rocked as the bearers paced down the defile to the plain, the wizard balanced on her haunches as easily as a bubble bobs in the air.

She pointed to the southwest. "There is the nest the Last have built around the entrance to this world," she said. "Are you able to see the powers which we wizards focus, Princess?"

"No," said Sharina, following the line of the Corl's arm. Close to Pandah's western walls—so close they partly hid it—was what she'd taken at first to be a shadow. Closer attention showed it to be a structure of odd bumps and angles, higher than Pandah's walls though some of the towers within the city overtopped it. "Rasile, I have *no* talent for wizardry."

Rasile's arms had joints at the wrong points, and her covering of fur—more gray than auburn and worn away in patches—was disturbing. She looked more like a beast in detail than she did when Sharina viewed her as a complete person.

The Corl chuckled in her throat. "Seeing the fluxes is not wizardry," she said, "though the best wizards see the matter they work with. In this case—"

She'd lowered her arm—her forelimb. Now she tapped her clawed fingers twice more on the air.

"—I can see the threads of power spun into two great hawsers, scarlet and azure. But I could not affect them myself any more than you could. The Last are using forces which could not be manipulated by any single wizard; not even by your friend Tenoctris, Princess. Their whole race must possess both the art and the ability to merge their talents the way ants together lift a dead grasshopper."

Skirmishers from the head of the column began moving toward the alien fortress, spreading as they advanced. Small groups of the Last had been working in the plain, demolishing all human plantings and structures beyond easy bowshot of the walls. Now the black figures began moving back toward their citadel.

"They're running!" Sharina said hopefully.

"They're withdrawing until they've judged the strength of the new threat," Rasile corrected emotionlessly. "The walls of their citadel are impregnable. Only the open gates can be attacked, and the Last will close them with their bodies where your warriors cannot use their greater numbers. When you fight the Last one against one they will likely win; and if one of them is killed, another will take its place."

The leading regiments of heavy infantry followed the skirmishers at a measured pace. Horns and trumpets skirled with cheerful enthusiasm.

"Call back your warriors, Princess," the Corl said. "They will die to no purpose. Call them back."

"Captain Ascor!" Sharina said to the commander of her guard contingent. She wasn't going to tell her military officers how to fight, but she would—she *must,* in good conscience—pass on important information which she'd gotten from other advisors. "Summon Lord Waldron to me, if you will!"

The Corl wizard continued to squat on her haunches, telling a string of pink coral beads. Her long face was turned toward the black citadel, but her eyes were unfocused.

"Rasile?" Sharina said. "If we're not to attack the Last, then how are we to drive them out?"

"I'll study the matter now that I've seen their nest," Rasile said. "But the Last are very powerful, Princess. Perhaps we should attack their impregnable walls until they have killed us all."

She laughed again.

Sharina stared at the fortress. Her face felt frozen, and the knuckles of her right hand were mottled where she gripped the Pewle knife.

Chapter

13

THOUGH THE MOON was well risen, Leel took a stick with a ball of tar on the end and lit it from a firepot. "Come along, then," he said to Garric unhappily. "Though you could find it yourself if you weren't blind."

The remainder of Holm's guards had retreated swiftly to a pavilion. The sound of a drinking party came through the velvet sides.

Garric didn't respond. Leel was unhappy at being ordered to lead them, but he was doing the job. Snarling at him—

"Or knocking him flat," Carus interjected with a rueful laugh. *"As I might well've done."*

—wasn't going to make that job go quicker.

"What is it that you think a torch will chase away, Master Leel?" asked Shin in a mocking tone. "Not the thing that haunts this lake, I assure you."

Leel muttered something and spat—though away from the aegipan and his companions. He pulled his torch back from the pot, rotating the tar ball slowly to spread the growing red flames across its surface.

"Mount, master," Kore said. She knelt beside Garric, holding the looped "stirrups" open with her clawed hands.

Garric glanced at her, then scuffed the ground. This gravel strand was as firm as a cobblestone street, but he wasn't sure what the causeway would be like.

He opened his mouth to say he'd walk, then closed it. He'd far better learn whether the surface'd bear him mounted on the ogre now than later when other things might be happening. Particularly since the "other things" were uncertain but certainly threatening. He set his left foot in the loop and gripped the ogre's shoulders to swing himself aboard.

"Tell me, Master Shin," Kore said. "Am I correct in supposing that most warhorses have better sense than the noble heroes riding them? Or is my judgment warped by special circumstances?"

The aegipan laughed. Garric grinned and said, "The epics don't generally discuss the matter, but the figurehead of the hero Klon's ship is said to have given him advice. When I return to Valles, I'll ask Liane to institute a search of the major temple libraries for more information on the question."

Leel stared from Kore to Garric, then down to the aegipan. "Are you crazy?" he demanded.

"Perhaps," said Garric, suddenly cheerful. Shin and Kore were not only companions but friends. "It seems to help, though."

Leel led them through the camp of the laborers, shanties of leaves lashed to twig frameworks. The small dark men watched in nervous silence as they passed. The laborers didn't carry weapons, not even the stones or asphalt torches that were available to anyone here. That must be the decision of Lord Holm and his guards.

Eyes caught by torchlight gleamed from doorways, but Garric only once saw an adult woman. A naked brown child suddenly sprinted on chubby legs from a hut, gurgling laughter. His mother—who didn't look any older than fifteen herself—ran after him, grabbed him by the scruff of his neck, and began to spank him into screams with her slipper even before she got him back into the hut. She kept her eyes turned away from Garric and his companions, as if by ignoring the strangers she could prevent them from harming her.

"Shin?" Garric said. "Do you know how wide this land is? I can smell salt water."

"A furlong wide here, where Lord Holm has moved his household," said the aegipan. "It narrows to half that to the east and west where it finally joins the mainland to enclose the tar lake."

"It's not wide enough," Leel muttered. "If we get a storm

from the south, it'll wash clear over this little spit. That's happened three times since I been with Milord, only it didn't matter because we were a mile out in the lake so the sea didn't even wet the foundations of the fort."

He cleared his throat and corrected himself. "The palace, we're supposed to call it. The palace."

A vagrant breeze drove in from the sea, thinning a wedge of mist. The full moon blazed through the clear air, throwing a line of blacker shadow the length of the raised walkway stretching out into the lake.

"All right," said Leel, pointing with the torch. "There's the causeway. It runs straight to the palace. Just follow it out and you can't go wrong."

Kore drew up at the base of the causeway. In Ornifal men cut ice on the River Beltis in winter. Packed into pits with sawdust between the layers, the blocks remained to chill the drinks of the wealthy at the height of summer.

The causeway was built with asphalt cut in the same fashion from the surface of the tar lake and stacked several layers high to form a road. The top layer of bitumen was mixed with dust and gravel blown onto the lake over the years, so that it became a type of concrete in which tar rather than lime was the binding agent.

The ogre stepped onto the causeway, lowering her weight carefully. Her clawed foot didn't sink in. She paused, cocking an eye toward her rider for direction.

"And in the morning, Lord Holm will carry us across the salt water in his barge?" Garric said. "Is that correct, Master Leel?"

"Milord said he would, didn't he?" the guard growled. He didn't look up to meet Garric's eye. "Anyway, why not? We don't have any cargo since the grubbies won't go out to the islands anymore. We may as well carry you and your beasts."

"All right, let's go across," Garric said. He felt a grudging sympathy for Leel, who obviously didn't trust his master but who was unwilling to lie for him. "If the fog covers the moon again, we're going to have to feel our way."

Shin gave a rippling, golden chuckle and made a motion with his hands. A ball of azure wizardlight swelled to the size of a cantaloupe just ahead of him. It was bright enough to show the seams between the blocks of asphalt. The aegipan danced onto the causeway, singing, *"He who would valiant be, 'gainst all disaster . . ."*

Kore followed at a measured pace. Her claws and the aegipan's hooves clicked on pebbles on the causeway's surface.

Garric glanced over his shoulder. For a brief time he could see Leel's torch as a dull red spark moving west across the neck of land, but then the mist swept in at full thickness and swallowed everything beyond the glow of Shin's ball of light.

"—and follow the Master," the aegipan sang, then broke off into fresh laughter.

The night was thick but not silent. The asphalt surface groaned, and occasionally a bubble plopped hollowly. Such humid warmth made Garric expect frogs and insects, but nothing living made a sound.

Kore paced forward easily. They were silent for some time.

"Can either of you see the palace?" Garric said at last. "As best I can judge, we should be getting close to—"

The air grew noticeably cooler, though Garric didn't feel the breeze that must've driven the change. The sky was clear; stars jabbed down around a moon which was within an hour of zenith. The black bulk of Lord Holm's palace rose a few double paces ahead.

The aegipan made another gesture with his delicate hands, rather like crumpling parchment into a ball and throwing it away; the globe of wizardlight vanished. Useful as the illumination had been, it had given objects an unclean cast when combined with natural moonlight.

Mind, the palace was sufficiently unclean even in the moon's pale purity. Like the causeway, it was constructed of blocks sawn from the lake's surface. That they'd been carefully dressed and carved with pilasters and crude swags made the effect even more grotesque. Kore knelt without being told to so that Garric could dismount.

The windows were tall with pointed arches; the glass set into the openings in leaded frames may've been colored, but Garric couldn't be sure in this light. The double door was of heavy oak and iron-strapped, but both valves stood open.

Torches like the one Leel had carried waited in sconces to either side of the recessed doorway, ready to be lighted. Shin lifted one, stared at it critically, and made a pass over the ball of tar with his cupped left hand. A red spark flashed and the tar began to burn with deep, smoky flames.

Shin offered Garric the butt of the torch, adding with a curl of his tongue, "Or would you prefer to treat me as your servant, Prince Garric? Shall I bear the torch for you?"

"You're not my servant," Garric said, taking the torch. He extended his arm slightly so that the acrid fumes were downwind of all of them. "And I'm capable of carrying this."

"So long as you keep it in your left hand," said Carus. He chuckled. *"I wouldn't like this place even if we hadn't been told we were being sent because nobody else had the balls to come."*

"Foul though I find the odor of this hellpit . . . ," said the ogre. She bent almost double to step through the doorway. "I would know if there were anything alive inside. There is not."

"I would find that more reassuring," said the aegipan as he followed, "if I thought the living were the only or even the greatest danger we might face here."

Garric paused in the doorway to peer at a blotch in the carved molding; it was the discolored knuckle of a bone from an ox or something even bigger. Of course animals—and no doubt men—would've fallen into the tar over the centuries that the asphalt lake had existed. The larger the beast, the more likely that its weight would break through the crust, especially if a skin of rainwater hid it.

He walked into the building. There was no anteroom, just a hall which rose to the height of three normal stories. The domed roof had a large oculus in the center.

Moonlight streamed through that round window and painted the west side of the hall. Tapestries showing horsemen hunting strange beasts across a mountainous landscape covered the bitumen wall; it would otherwise have absorbed the light almost completely. Reflection from the fabric of silk with metal threads illuminated the great room better than chandeliers did the feasting hall of the palace at Valles. That wouldn't help during the new moon, of course.

There were benches around both sidewalls and a high wooden throne with gilt—or perhaps golden—dragon finials at the end opposite the entrance. Garric would've expected a clear space in the center of the hall. Petitioners would stand there during audiences and servants would set up trestle tables for feasts. Instead, a massive black sarcophagus stood directly under the oculus.

Shin and Kore stood at either end of the sarcophagus, staring at it hostilely. Garric joined them, bringing the torch close to get a better view of the ornate reliefs.

"Is it ebony?" he asked, but he was already reaching out to answer his own question. He tapped the lid with his knuckles.

"It's stone," he said in surprise. "It must be jet. It's hard enough to take delicate carvings, at any rate. These are very good."

As Garric eyed the reliefs more carefully, he realized their strangeness as well as the carver's skill. There were two separate bands on the lid, arranged so that the figures' feet were toward the door. In the center of the upper register stood a skeletally thin human figure, probably a man, wearing long robes. His arms were spread to either side in blessing. Though the features were stylized and in any case very small—the face was the size of the end of a man's thumb—Garric thought he detected a similarity to Lord Holm.

The lower register was covered with a profusion of animals, each one identifiably distinct from its many fellows. The beasts fell into at least a dozen different species, each of them similar to an animal which Garric had seen or at least read descriptions of—but none really identical to anything familiar.

The largest of the carved animals were the elephants. These had unusually long, curving tusks, but that could be explained as artistic license. The hump of fat on the beasts' shoulders, though, and the shaggy hair that covered their bodies were like nothing Garric had seen or heard of.

Likewise the lions seemed ordinary enough until you noticed the curved canines projecting beneath the lower jaw, the antelopes had four horns rather than two, and the wolves' heads seemed too massive for even their unusually robust bodies. The circling vultures were far too big also, assuming the elephants and other animals weren't pygmy versions of their present relatives.

"It's an odd place for Lord Holm to keep his father's coffin, wouldn't you think?" said the ogre, who must've noticed the same resemblance that Garric thought he saw. "Of course, one never knows what humans will decide to do. I blame it on their skulls being so small that their brains get squeezed."

"It's not Holm's father," said the aegipan. "At least it's not his father unless Holm is many thousands of years old. Ten thousand at least, I would judge."

Garric stepped back and frowned. "Judge how?" he said.

Shin touched the hilt of the dagger Garric had found in the peel tower and said, "May I borrow this?"

"Yes," said Garric. "Of course."

Shin drew the dagger and slid its point down the margin of the lid. Garric winced to see the blade mistreated, though on consideration he realized that jet wasn't hard enough to dull good steel.

"Do you see how bright the edges of the scratch are?" the aegipan said, gesturing with one hand while the other replaced the dagger in Garric's sheath. It was a remarkable piece of coordination. "Compare them with the dullness of the reliefs. Air doesn't act quickly on jet, but it acts; and this sarcophagus was made millennia ago."

In all truth, Garric couldn't see the distinction—certainly not by torchlight and probably not in the full blaze of the sun. But neither did he see any reason to doubt Shin's judgment, on this matter or on anything else the aegipan chose to state with such assurance.

He looked up at the dome. From where he stood, the rim of the oculus clipped a sooty edge from the moon's silver and gray.

Shin examined the tapestries. They seemed to be well made, but the scenes had no obvious connection with this black palace. Garric wondered if Holm or one of his ancestors had looted them in a raid.

Kore opened the door in the partition wall behind the throne and squatted to look down the passage to the living quarters beyond. She'd have to crawl to negotiate it, and from the blank disgust on her face she saw no reason to do so.

Something sizzled. Garric turned. The light of the full moon blazed straight down on the sarcophagus, flattening the reliefs. A figure formed, coalescing out of the air instead of rising through the stone lid.

Garric stepped back, touching his hilt but not drawing the sword. Kore and the aegipan sidled around the edges of the hall, placing themselves beside Garric and close to the outside door.

The figure, at least seven feet tall even without the pedestal of the sarcophagus to stand on, looked down at Garric and laughed. It was indeed a taller, more cadaverous version of Lord Holm.

"You are the sacrifice?" the figure said. Its voice boomed as if from a vast cavern. "Not before time, I must say. My blood must be thinning for matters to have waited so long."

Garric drew his sword with a muted *sring* of the gray steel blade. He backed another step, trusting his companions to keep clear without him having to waste attention on them.

"Milord," he said to the robed wizard. "I told your descendant I'd spend the night in this palace. I'm not a sacrifice, to you or him or to anyone. My friends and I will go now and leave the night to you."

The wizard laughed again and raised his left hand, knuckles out. On the fourth finger was a ring with a huge red stone. *"Belia!"* he said.

A film of scarlet wizardlight covered the interior of the hall like the membrane inside an eggshell. Kore growled and hunched toward the open doorway. She rebounded from the red shimmer, snarled, and ripped outward at it with both hands the way one would try to tear a silk curtain. Her claws slid without gripping.

Garric lunged, thrusting for the wizard's right kneecap. It was the easiest target and, though it wouldn't be immediately fatal, it'd bring the tall man's vitals within reach of a second stroke.

"Eithabira!" the wizard said, and wrapped himself in wizardlight like a cicada in its chrysalis. The edge that'd sheared hard limestone bounced away. The blade sang a high note; Garric's right hand and forearm felt as though he'd plunged them into boiling water. He damped the vibration by holding the sword against his thigh.

The wizard's laugh boomed again. He clenched his left fist so that the fiery jewel pointed at Garric. Garric made an overarm cut into the sarcophagus lid between the wizard's feet. The jet shattered.

The wizard toppled backward with a hoarse shout. The glimmer of wizardlight vanished like frost in sunshine.

"Mount!" Kore shouted, turning and dropping to one knee. "Mount!"

Garric wobbled. He was as dizzy as if he hadn't had anything to drink in three days.

"Quickly!" said the aegipan, pausing in the doorway to look back. The building rocked, springing several panes of glass from their casements.

The ogre took Garric in her arms and bolted out of the palace. Tremors shook the lake. Shin ran ahead, dancing over the blocks of the causeway as they rose and fell. In the palace behind them the wizard cried out again. He sounded like a rabbit in a leg snare, but very much louder.

"I'm all right now!" Garric said. He thought he was. He started to sheathe his sword but changed his mind. "I can walk myself!"

A great head broke the surface of the asphalt, raising its trunk high as it struggled to mount the causeway. It would've been an elephant if not for the shaggy hair covering its body.

It trumpeted shrilly as Kore raced past with Garric. The pitiless moonlight gleamed as more creatures broke from their ancient bondage all across the lake.

"Quickly!" cried the aegipan. The ogre's clawed strides struck sparks with each leap over the crumbling asphalt surface.

ILNA'D EXPECTED EITHER a landscape like the valley she was leaving or a swamp like the one where Garric'd found cat men preying on the Grass People. In the event, when she stepped through the portal her bare feet scrunched into coarse sand. It was the color of rust, but the small red sun exaggerated the hue.

The terrain was largely barren, but there was water despite the lack of ground cover. What Ilna first thought were sedges—on closer look they weren't—grew in a pool a few double paces to the left, and the swales were studded with what seemed to be ferns springing from woody knobs like cypress knees.

"Well, no doubt which way they came," said Karpos. He nodded toward the track worn into the sand, not so much a line of footprints as a parallel double ridge thrown up to either side of the path. It reminded Ilna of the way ants wore trackways in gritty soil after a rain.

"Not that there was anyway," said Asion, who'd bent down to gather pebbles from the sand. He used his stubby left index finger to sort through possibilities before suddenly flicking four smooth chunks of quartz into the other palm. He transferred them to his bullet pouch.

Less than half a mile ahead stood a structure of glass, all flat planes with the same number of sides as a hand has fingers. The dim sun easing toward the western horizon turned some facets rosy while others reflected the sky or the ground, but the glass had no color of its own.

Karpos sighed and unstrung his bow, then hung the staff across his chest by the slack string. He hadn't had time to retrieve any arrows from the beasts he'd shot.

"I'll lead," he said, swinging out ahead of the rest of the party. He walked beside the Coerli trackway instead of obliterating it, though here the care was reflexive rather than purposeful. As much for courtesy as any better cause, Ilna followed to the side also; Temple was across the track from her.

"Think you can hit a cat with those rocks you're picking up?" Karpos said quietly.

Ilna glanced over her shoulder at Asion. He was watching their back trail with a pebble in the pocket of his sling. He shrugged and said, "It makes me feel better."

"Yeah," said his partner. "I *do* know what you mean."

There were no trees in this place, though unfamiliar plants with straight stems and a crown of short leaves—they sprang from the trunk like the flowers on the stalk of a hollyhock— grew taller than she was, or even than Temple and Karpos. Mats of rootlets supported them, often standing proud where winds had scoured away the surrounding sand.

"I saw something move!" Asion called. "One of them scales on the house, it moved!"

"I thought it was just the light," said Karpos. "But if you say it moved, I believe you."

They reached the structure. From a flat to the opposite point, each pane was as high as Ilna or a Corl. The trail led to one whose bottom edge was along the ground. Sand'd been brushed away in the recent past. Ilna could see into the glass, but its ripples distorted the things inside so that she couldn't tell what they were.

Karpos pushed gingerly with his left fingertips; he held his long knife ready in his right. The glass didn't move.

"Temple?" he said. "Do you know how to make it open?"

"Asion," Temple said. He'd drawn his sword and held his buckler advanced. "Shoot into the center of this pane; that should do it."

He glanced at the rest of them. "I'd expect all the warriors to have been in the raiding party," he added, "but I could be wrong."

Ilna nodded, lifting her hands slightly to call attention to the pattern she'd just knotted. She didn't spread the fabric yet; it'd paralyze her companions if they looked at it.

Asion backed a pace, automatically checking to the sides and behind him; a sling's arc covered a lot of area. He swayed the stone at the end of its tether, settling it in the leather cup.

"Karpos?" Temple warned quietly. He held his buckler out, putting it between Ilna's face and the panel, then turned his own head away. Karpos covered his eyes with his left forearm.

Asion's thong snapped through the air. Glass shattered almost simultaneously in a *crack!*—like nearby lightning. The panel puffed outward in a cloud of rainbow dust which left a few sparkles in the air even after most had settled on the red ground.

"I'll lead," said Temple, stepping into the building. His bronze sword was point-forward at waist level, and the buckler was advanced in his left hand.

"Follow me," Ilna said curtly to the hunters as she entered in turn. The air within was moister than that of the sand wastes outside, and it smelled strongly of the Coerli.

The flooring was fibrous but *rock;* remarkable as that seemed, it wasn't a mistake Ilna's bare feet could possibly have made. The material gave her sensations not of pastures or ripening flax but rather of heat and fire and pressures beyond what anything living could bear.

Could rock feel pain? Ilna smiled. It pleased her to imagine that it could.

The glass walls muted the light, but they let through enough to see by. The building was partitioned inside, but Ilna found she couldn't be sure whether the walls ran up to the roof—or indeed, if there was a ceiling below the roof. Everything was distorted, much as though she'd been trying to see things under water.

"They're up ahead!" Asion called, though he was watching the rear. "Temple, I smell 'em!"

Temple stepped around a corner. Slipped around it, rather;

Ilna didn't see the motion, only the big man's presence *here* and then *there*.

"This is the nursery," Temple said mildly, though he didn't lower his sword. "The kits. None are older than six weeks."

Ilna moved to his left side. Yes, kits; as many as the fingers of one hand. They were in a waist-deep pit sunk into the floor, too deep for them to climb out of on their own. All but one snapped and snarled at the humans, jumping and clinging to the rim of their prison for a moment before slipping back; the remaining one cowered against the back wall.

"Four males, one female," Temple said. "There's at least one female of breeding age also, probably two. They'll be hiding somewhere, probably in the larder."

He quirked a smile at her. "The Coerli aren't like humans, Ilna," he added. "Or at least like you."

Ilna sniffed in disgust. A generalized disgust, she supposed: at the cat men, but at people and at life itself. She shook her head and said, "There's a wizard here, you said. Do you know where he is?"

If she wove something to answer her question, she'd have to put down the defensive pattern she carried. For choice she wouldn't do that.

"He'll be as high up as he can get, I would guess," Temple said, looking upward. "The building had a peak on the outside, so there must be something above the flat ceiling we see."

Ilna followed his glance. *She* didn't see a ceiling, flat or otherwise. The combination of reflection and distortion in the glass panels threatened to give her a headache.

"All right," she said, more harshly than deserved by anything Temple'd said or done. "Take me there, if you will."

"Mistress?" said Karpos uncomfortably. "What should we do about—"

He gestured toward the kits with his little finger rather than the knife in that hand.

"—these?"

"Kill them, of course!" Ilna said. She glared at Temple to

see if he dared object, but the big man's face remained impassive. "But you're not to take the scalps."

"I think it'll be this way," Temple said as though he hadn't heard the exchange. He nodded in the direction they'd been going since they entered the building. Without waiting for a reply, he walked around the pit to the corridor she could see from where they stood.

She followed, listening to the shriek of a kit. It'd dodged Asion's knife by enough that the stroke wounded instead of killing quickly. The sound didn't give Ilna the touch of cold pleasure that she usually got from knowing that the beasts were in pain.

The rooms—the spaces—of the strange building were irregular in fashions Ilna couldn't understand. She must not be seeing them properly; she'd always before been able to grasp patterns, even in the rocks she hated. Her failure suddenly spilled over in a gush of self-loathing that made her dizzy.

"Here're the stairs," Temple said, nodding toward what she now saw was a diagonal panel standing an arm's length out from the wall. She hadn't recognized it as separate until the big man tapped it with the rim of his buckler. "Shall I lead?"

"No," said Ilna, stepping past him with her yarn held up but still not extended. "I will."

"The pantry's beneath the stairs, behind another baffle," Temple said.

"They'll wait!" said Ilna. Her unjustified anger at Temple made her angry with herself.

The steps were both shallower and taller than they'd have been for people; the Coerli had smaller feet but their legs were springier. For Ilna it was almost like climbing a ladder. She kept her eyes upward so that she'd be ready if the cat wizard suddenly appeared at the top of the stairs.

The kits had stopped squealing. She found herself hoping that the hunters wouldn't discover where the females were hiding until after the wizard was dealt with. Her lips pursed, but at least the anger had slipped back into a more usual state of mild disapproval of herself and the world.

Ilna stepped onto a round platform. Until she'd mounted high enough that her eyes were above its rim, she hadn't been sure that the staircase didn't end with the roof itself. In the center of the flat surface sat a male Corl. He had the flowing mane of a chieftain and what'd obviously been a powerful physique many years ago.

Many decades ago. The beast facing her was by far the oldest Corl she'd ever seen. His mane was white and now scraggly, and he'd worn the fur off every joint. The mottled, purplish color of his skin showed through the remaining fur, turning it dirty gray.

Ilna held her pattern taut before her. The beast's eyes were closed.

"Do not bother with that, animal," he said. She'd never before heard the cats make sounds that she could understand. "I know all things, so I know my doom. I will not struggle."

He coughed a laugh. "How can one struggle against fate?" he asked. "Even I, Neunt, the greatest wizard of all time, cannot defeat fate."

Ilna laughed, though there was little humor in the sound. "I've always thought braggarts were fools," she said. "You've proved that better than most, beast, choosing to tell me how powerful you are *now*."

"You can lower that," said Temple quietly, indicating Ilna's pattern with his left index finger. He'd slung his buckler, but he held the sword ready.

Ilna started to snap that she didn't trust others to determine what was safe or wasn't, especially when dealing with wizards . . . but she did trust Temple, she found to her surprise. She folded the pattern into her sleeve without picking the strands apart, then immediately took out a fresh hank to determine the direction they must go next.

Neunt opened his eyes. They were a milky blue in which Ilna could barely see the pupils; if he hadn't made a point of closing them, she'd have assumed the wizard was blind.

"The Messengers gave me the power I demanded of them," he said in a harsh, cracked voice. "Everything I asked for . . . and now you're here and you will kill me, because you are a thing I did not foresee."

He laughed again, but the sound trailed off into wheezing. *He's going to die shortly whether we kill him or not,* Ilna thought. *Though of course we'll kill him.*

"Do you know the Messengers?" Neunt asked when he had control of his voice again. "You do not, I suspect. I did not, I could not—"

Suddenly anger snarled in his broken voice.

"No one could foresee you! No one!"

Ilna looked at Temple. "Kill him," she said. "I'll determine what we do next."

"I will tell you your course," the wizard said calmly. "That's why I waited for you instead of ending my own life as I'd planned. I will tell you how to reach the Messengers, who will give you the power you desire. Every power that you demand, they will provide."

Ilna stared at the ancient Corl, absorbing his words. From the floor below, Karpos called, "Mistress? We've taken care of the females. What do you want us to do now?"

"You can come up here," Temple said, surprising Ilna both with what he'd said and the fact that he'd spoken at all. "This is where we'll be leaving from, I believe."

Ilna looked at him angrily, then snapped to the wizard, "Do you think we'll spare you? I won't. I won't let you believe a lie even if I didn't tell it."

"Of course, animal, of course," Neunt said. "I've failed, which means I deserve to die."

He made a sound that might've been the start of a laugh, but it choked off a moment later. "I failed millennia ago, when I forced my way into the Messengers' presence and didn't protect myself against you. Do you think you will be wiser, animal?"

"I don't care about wisdom!" Ilna said. She heard the hunters mounting the steps behind her. Without looking around she shuffled forward to give them both room to stand safely on the platform. "I want to kill every one of your race, every murdering beast. Do you understand that?"

"What is that to me?" said the wizard, coughing again. "I'll already be dead, will I not?"

He pointed to the floor of the platform. He sat in the middle of a circle etched into the coarse, glassy surface; around the inside were the curving forms of letters in the Old Script.

"Stand within and speak the words," he said. "Nothing more. The powers are focused here as nowhere else."

"We'll have to find a different way," Ilna said, glancing aside to Temple. She was as much relieved as disappointed; Neunt was disquieting in a fashion she couldn't fully explain. "I can't read those letters. I can't read anything!"

"I can," said Temple. He didn't raise his voice; she'd never heard him raise his voice. "Will my voice be sufficient, Chief of the Coerli?"

"Even a child would be sufficient in this place," the wizard said. "It will be as easy as stepping off the edge of this, my sanctum."

He ran his fingers over the grooves of the words of power. "Every bit as easy."

Rousing from his reverie, the wizard turned his milky eyes on Temple for the first time. "But you are scarcely a child, are you?" he said. "I did not foresee you either. My, what a fool I was when I thought myself so clever, so powerful."

"Mistress?" Asion murmured from behind her. "Shall we . . . ?"

He didn't finish the question, but there was no doubt what he was asking. Even the Corl knew.

"You need not kill me, creature," Neunt said. He rose to his feet with more grace than Ilna'd expected from his difficulty speaking. "I do not wish to be defiled by your touch."

With a final bark of laughter, the ancient wizard stepped off the platform.

"Watch him!" Ilna said, expecting a trick. She looked over the edge.

Neunt crashed into the top of a partition which framed one of the rooms. His ribs crunched, and though his broken body flopped down on the side nearer the stairs, sprays of blood dripped slowly down both.

Karpos cleared his throat. "I don't guess either of us gets his scalp, right?" he said.

Ilna ignored the hunter. "What do we do now, soldier?" she asked Temple.

"Now we all stand within the circle," Temple said, as calm as a frozen pond. "And I read the spell."

He gave Ilna a faint smile. "Then it's up to you, Ilna," he added.

SHARINA USED HER fingers to spread a gap in the brushwood screen so that she could look out. The citadel of the Last glowed faintly yellow in the darkness, a little brighter along the edges where the pentagons joined. The color made her think of fungus but—

She grinned at herself.

—that was only because it had to do with the Last. She'd seen walls distempered the same pale shade and found it attractive.

Occasionally Sharina heard the *bang!* as artillery released. When the fitful breeze was in the right direction, she could even hear the slap of bows and the rattle of swords when human soldiers closed hand-to-hand with the black invaders.

The Last were extending their faceted fortifications around Pandah, moving only sunwise rather than in both directions as they'd done before the royal army arrived. They took terrible losses from the artillery's bolts and heavy stones, but slowly, panel by panel, their walls advanced.

The Last undermined Lord Waldron's cross-walls, filled in trenches, and stolidly cut apart infantry sallying in attempts to demolish the fortifications from the inside. The army slowed the inhuman advance, but no human endeavor could halt it.

At Sharina's decision—though with the enthusiastic support of all her officers—the army wasn't cooperating with the brigands of Pandah. Those renegades were barely able to defend their own walls, and they'd do that to the best of their ability regardless.

Sharina sighed. She was looking out at the citadel because

behind her Rasile talked with ghosts and demons. Sharina knew what was happening, of course, and she realized it was necessary . . . but it made her uncomfortable nonetheless.

The enclosure curtained Rasile's wizardry from the eyes of the troops who'd be distressed by it. They knew what was going on—and indeed, anybody who wanted to could watch through the coarse wicker as easily as Sharina now looked out. The troops had laced brush together in much the same way as they made great earth-filled baskets which formed the walls of the encampment.

The Last weren't present in great-enough numbers to attack the camp, not yet at any rate, but Lord Waldron was careful to prepare against unexpected dangers. There was nothing to be done against the *expected* danger, however.

In a few months, despite Waldron's efforts, the Last would complete a ring around Pandah. They could then wipe out anyone still in the city . . . and simply wait and prepare behind polygonal walls which the troops hadn't been able to breach. If the Last filled Pandah before they opened the sides of their glowing black fortress, they'd outnumber the royal army and any possible human army.

Sharina remembered Tenoctris' vision of black monsters appearing on the lens of ice. Even arriving only one or two at a time in the fortified pool here, it wouldn't be long before the black not-men were in overwhelming strength. That would be the end of Mankind.

Thinking that, Sharina turned to look at the Corl wizard. *It's not as though watching the Last grind their way through my world is comforting, after all.* She grinned again.

Rasile stood in a figure drawn with yarrow stalks. She'd spilled them in what'd seemed an aimless fashion to Sharina, but the stiff yellow lengths had fallen into a real pattern: each stalk lay end-to-end with two others.

There was light with her inside the figure, occasionally as bright as a desert sun but more often a dim hint like the moon through overcast. Now it was a faint blue glow coming from something spindly and inhuman. The creature's clawed arms gestured fiercely as it spoke to Rasile.

No sound crossed the figure. Sharina could see the wizard's face: it was as calm as if she were ordering lunch.

The creature lifted its long jaws in what seemed to be a despairing shriek, threatening the sky with its claws; then it faded into darkness. Sharina expected another world, another denizen. Instead Rasile slumped.

Sharina jumped to the Corl's side, careful not to disturb the yarrow stalks. She'd acted without thinking; she might've been jumping into a realm in which only a wizard could survive—

But nobody was safe unless the Last were defeated, and Rasile had a better chance of accomplishing that than Waldron and the whole royal army did. Besides, Sharina wasn't one to worry about her own safety when a friend was at risk. By now the Corl wizard'd become if not exactly a friend, then at least a trusted confidante.

"Their own strength works for me," Rasile murmured. She hunched with her eyes closed. If Sharina hadn't caught her, she'd probably have lain scrunched together on all fours on the ground. "I could never have accomplished that if the Last hadn't concentrated so much power in this place."

"Are you all right, Rasile?" Sharina said. The Corl's body felt hot and her heart was beating quickly, but Sharina reminded herself that the wizard wasn't human. This might be normal for the cat men.

"I'm tired, Princess," Rasile said. She didn't open her eyes, but her voice sounded stronger. "I think even your friend Tenoctris would be tired after that. But I have an answer."

The old Corl straightened. Sharina stepped away as she'd have done if she'd been supporting Tenoctris following wizardry. The initial shock to the system seemed to pass more quickly than would that of comparable physical effort, though sometimes Sharina got the impression that spells left mental scars that never healed.

Rasile took Sharina's hands in her own and examined them closely. The Corl's fingers were short and the palms narrower but longer than a human's.

"Can you swim, Princess?" she said. "Yes, I see that you can."

Her eyes met Sharina's. They were smiling.

"Yes," said Sharina. "I swim very well."

"The Last enter this region through the pool in the center of their citadel," Rasile said, her voice getting a saw-toothed edge to it. "At the bottom of that pool is the First Stone. It is the focus which draws them to this place rather than to another. You must fetch the First Stone up from the pool and bring it to me."

Rasile laughed. "It is well that you do swim, Princess," she said. "Who else could we trust to do this thing without flinching? Your warriors are very brave, no doubt, but they—"

She moved her index finger through the air as though tracing letters. Azure wizardlight trailed away from the stubby claw, each spark taking the flickering form of an armored soldier.

"—wouldn't have stomach for what's necessary, would they? To deal with the Great Wisdom?"

"Cashel would," said Sharina. She tried to keep emotion out of her voice, for fear of learning what emotion she might show if she didn't. "He's not afraid of wizardry. But he's not here; and anyway, he can't swim."

She cleared her throat. "How will I get *to* the pool, Rasile?" she said. "There's only the two entrances and they're both guarded."

"You'll have to be invisible," the Corl said. "And that means—"

A catapult fired. The heavy stone smashed into ricocheting fragments almost as soon as the levers crashed against their stops. One and maybe several of the Last were surely dead, but an endless number of the creatures remained. Like water dripping against a cliff face, they'd eventually wear away the royal army.

"—that you will be blind. Therefore—"

"Blind?" said Sharina. She felt cold and nauseated, as though she'd been punched in the pit of the stomach. "I don't understand!"

"If you cannot be seen," Rasile said, "then you can't see. You will use my eyes."

She stretched. The old wizard seemed to have become more limber as a result of the exercise she'd gotten during the march.

"If you say so," Sharina muttered, looking out at the night again. The thought of being blind still chilled her. "Ah. . . . When will we do this?"

Rasile repeated her throaty laugh. "Not until the morning, Princess," she said. "I must sleep and replenish my strength. And even then, I will be able to accomplish the spell only because of what the Last have created, this strong pillar that I will climb."

Sharina nodded. "I'll get to sleep also, then," she said.

And in her mind, she whispered, *Oh, Cashel. Please come back tonight*.

But she knew in her heart that she would sleep alone.

THE TAR LAKE was a jumble of blocks broken upward as monsters crawled out of it, and the air was thick with the stench of bitumen. Garric would've felt queasy if he hadn't been so angry at being carried like a baby through the chaos. He'd managed to twist in Kore's arm so that he was at least facing forward, but he couldn't pretend he was in control of what was happening to him.

The snarls of beasts rising from the lake were as loud as the howl of a winter storm. Torches were alight on the spit of hard ground ahead, twitching in agitation. No doubt Lord Holm's retainers were shouting, but mere human racket couldn't be heard in this cacophony.

A hairy elephant stood facing them at the end of the causeway. It was much larger than the others Garric'd glimpsed in this place, easily twelve feet high to the top of its humped shoulders. It curled its trunk between its great tusks and lowered its head to meet the oncoming ogre. To either side of the monster the surface glistened with pools of liquid tar; there was no way around.

"Drop me!" Garric shouted.

He'd made the demand repeatedly during Kore's run for the shore, but now the ogre had no choice. She skidded to a sparkling halt and decanted Garric to the ground, surprisingly gentle despite the necessary haste.

Shin was skipping down the causeway ahead of them. He turned a double somersault in the air, landed on his hooves, and sprang skyward like a stone flung from a trebuchet.

The elephant's trunk uncoiled to swat him—but too late. The aegipan landed on the beast's bulging forehead, then backflipped to its shoulders. He grinned at Garric and Kore as he pointed toward the asphalt.

Blue sparks shot from Shin's index fingers. Where each struck the tar, the surface bubbled. Saber-toothed cats hunched upward from both pools. The elephant started backward, swinging its head to one side and then the other.

The cats sprang simultaneously, gripping the elephant's shaggy withers with their claws as their long fangs slashed into its neck. Laughing, Shin sprang free.

The elephant screamed and stepped to its left, twisting as it tried to gore the cat on that side. Prey and hunters splashed into the gleaming asphalt with a burp; a wave surged onto the causeway. Garric jumped over the clinging blackness, reaching the gravel shore before Kore could gather him in her arms again.

"This way, champion!" Shin called. The aegipan's tiny horns shone like sunstruck diamonds. "To the boat!"

"What have you done, damn you?" cried Leel. Holm's henchman stood with an asphalt torch raised high in his left hand and his sword bare in his right. "Have you raised demons?"

Shin pointed. A shaggy creature the size of an ox shambled past Garric and swiped Leel out of the way with a forepaw. Its claws were black and longer than a man's fingers, but it wasn't a bear as Garric first thought: the beast's narrow face and long tongue were those of a leaf-eating sloth.

"This way!"

Garric followed the bounding aegipan. A wolf with massive jaws loped toward them. Garric struck with Carus' reflexive skill, feeling the keen edge bite through bones as heavy as a lion's. The wolf sprang into the air, landed on its feet again, and stumbled into the darkness with its head hanging between its forelegs. Its eyes had glazed.

They'd reached the southern edge of the gravel spit. The air smelled of salt instead of asphalt, and the moon picked out touches of foam on the slow surf.

A barge with a rounded bow and stern was tied up on the end of a timber jetty. Shin darted up the planks well ahead of Garric and the ogre. He hopped to the vessel's railing and perched like a rooster on a fence, calling out in an amazingly loud voice. Garric didn't recognize the language.

Lord Holm and a guard carrying a long-hafted axe reached the jetty. Holm snapped an order. The heavyset guard raised his weapon. Kore grabbed him by the back of the neck and snapped the body outward like a housewife killing a chicken for dinner.

Lord Holm squawked and turned with his thin-bladed sword. The ogre smashed the dead man into him. Holm and the guard fell into the water and sank. Neither came up again.

Shin continued to call from the railing. Garric jumped onto the barge. It rode high; the open hold was empty. There were four sweeps on either side, swung inboard while the vessel was at dock. The looms were long enough to be worked by two or three oarsmen apiece, standing on the port and starboard catwalks.

Kore stood at the end of the jetty, facing the shore. She leaned forward and spread her arms with the claws extended. From the front she'd be terrifying.

People ran toward the barge. The ogre gave a hacking roar, bringing the oncoming mob to a halt.

Garric was trying to get one of the sweeps loose. They'd been lashed to the railing with willow splits and he couldn't figure out the knot in the darkness. He heard children crying.

"Kore!" he shouted. "Let 'em pass!"

"Yes, let them come aboard, Mistress Kore!" Shin said. "They're our crew!"

"Faugh!" Kore said in a thunderous murmur. "I'd rather share with a flock of chickens . . . and they'd be better eating than these swarthy runts, too."

Despite the ogre's complaints, she stepped backward onto the barge without looking. Garric'd realized as Kore carried him down the causeway that her balance was as good as Shin's. He'd always thought of himself as well-coordinated, but he was a toddler compared with his present companions.

The crowd piled aboard the barge. All of them were laborers who'd been working in Lord Holm's orchards. The aegipan harangued them in their own language. The males untied the sweeps with none of the trouble that Garric'd had, while the women settled in the hold. Those with infants clutched them to their breasts.

A pair of long-horned bison lumbered down the beach, kicking gravel. One lifted its head and bellowed like the wind blowing through a hollow log. No more refugees came toward the jetty, and the only torches Garric could see were blobs of tar lying motionless on the ground.

There'd been hundreds of laborers in the camp; fewer than fifty had managed to board the vessel. Perhaps others had escaped to east or west along the strand. Regardless, there was nothing more Garric could do about the situation.

The barge's ragged bow rope was looped around a bollard at the end of the jetty. Garric tried to twitch it clear. When that failed the second time, he cut it with the sword as easily as he'd split the wolf's spine as he ran.

"Push off!" he said. Shin called something, perhaps relaying the order in the laborers' language. At any rate, those at the landward sweeps shoved them against the jetty. It probably wasn't proper procedure—one of the blades split—but the vessel wallowed out from the shore.

A guard ran toward the jetty. He carried a bow and looked back over his shoulder in terror.

"Come back!" he shouted to Garric. "Come back and take me!"

The barge was a dozen feet from the jetty and the oarsmen

were beginning to swing the bow seaward. "Swim to us!" Garric called. "We'll pick you up, but you've got to swim out to us!"

"May the Sister suck your marrow!" the man shrieked. Perhaps he couldn't swim. He nocked an arrow and began to draw his bow.

"Get down!" Garric warned.

The barge rocked as Kore sprang from the railing, smashing the archer to the gravel. Grasping him by the neck and one thigh, she bit into his lower chest. Blood sprayed.

A pair of wolves loped toward her, then paused as they judged her size. The ogre's arms flexed and tore the corpse apart. Laughing, she threw half the body to each wolf.

"Shin, hold the rowers!" Garric said. "We have to wait for—"

Kore loped down the strand on all fours, licking her bloody lips. After the third long stride, she turned seaward.

"Kore, you can't jump this far!" Garric shouted. "Swim—"

The ogre leaped with the momentum she'd gathered. She caught the stern. Though her grip splintered a section of railing, she held and swung herself into the hold. The refugees sheltering there surged toward the bow, silent except for the whimpering of some of the children.

"Swim indeed!" Kore said. "I could've waded, noble master; the water isn't deep here. But why should I get wet?"

The ogre's tongue snaked out to get the last of the blood that splashed her long face. And as the barge glided southward across the sound, the laborers at the sweeps began to chant a cheerful cadence.

THE HAIR ON the back of Cashel's neck rose. Tenoctris held the sword they'd taken from the Last. She pointed it toward a wooden burial marker and called, *"Rathra—"*

She lifted and dipped the blade, marking a segment of an arc. She hadn't bothered to draw anything on the ground before she started chanting.

"—rathax!"

Wizardlight flared, as rich and saturated as a sheet of red glass. It hung in the air between the two points, shimmering and distorting the nighted slope beyond.

"Bainchooch, damne, bureth!" Tenoctris said. She slashed the sword down at each word, throwing another panel of wizardlight into the sky.

As Tenoctris sang the incantation, she turned. Cashel stepped sideways to keep his back always to hers. He held his quarterstaff before him, gripping it a trifle more firmly than he'd have done if he'd been happier about what the wizard was doing.

"Astraleos chreleos!"

They stood on a hillside where short lengths of cane sprouted like a stunted grove. Originally a split in the top of each marker had held a slip of paper with the name of the person whose ashes were buried beneath it, but storms quickly shredded and dispersed those diplomas. The canes could last for years, but when they finally rotted away there'd be a new burial on top of the cremated bones of the earlier ones.

"Buroth, meneus, io!" Tenoctris said, her voice rising to the final syllable. Though her arm and sword hadn't bobbed around even half the imaginary circle, scarlet wizardlight suddenly formed a wall around her and Cashel.

The grass and brambles vanished into a rosy haze. Cashel could see Tenoctris the same as always, but it was just him and her now. She held the sword down by her side and looked out at the sheets of flickering red. Her lips smiled, but it was a hard smile.

Cashel heard distant screaming. First off, he thought it was steam coming from under a heavy pot lid. It kept going on, though, and after a while he wasn't so sure.

The scream cut off short, and the wizardlight was gone. Wind howled, driving flecks of foam from the gray sea hard enough to sting. It was night but too overcast to have stars; if the moon was up, the curtain of clouds hid it.

Cashel's tunics whipped his legs. If he'd been watching his flock in weather like this, he'd have wrapped his sheepskin robe around him . . . unless the storm'd blown up unexpectedly, of course, which'd happened more than once. Then all you could do was to keep moving.

He forced himself to squint out to sea. Trouble travels downwind in a storm like this. Now there was nothing but surf as slow and sullen as dripping sap, but the wedge-shaped head of a sea wolf might slither into view any time.

There could be worse things than sea wolves in this place. He didn't know where Tenoctris had brought them, but it didn't feel like anyplace good.

The beach was broken shells and coarse sand. Driftwood including barkless, salt-bleached tree trunks straggled along the tide line; beyond was low forest. The trees were mostly beech and cedar as best Cashel could tell, but none of them were more than four or five double paces high.

Tenoctris glanced at the sea. "Is it ebbing, do you think?" she asked.

"I think so," said Cashel. "But it can't be much short of the turn."

"We won't need long," Tenoctris said. "A few minutes would probably be enough, but we'll wait an hour before we come back."

She drew in the sand with the point of her sword, twisting the blade now to make a thin line, then a broad flourish. She was writing words of power in letters each as high as Cashel's middle finger.

Cashel looked at the tree line and stepped a safe distance away from Tenoctris to set his quarterstaff spinning slowly. He was getting the measure of the wind, the way it licked the hickory and tried to twist it out of his control.

"There's somebody watching from the woods, Tenoctris," he said quietly. "I can't tell who, but I think there's more'n one."

The beach stretched as far as he could see to left and right. Nothing moved but what the wind blew.

"Yes, there should be," Tenoctris said. She paused and gazed critically at what she'd written. There were as many words as fingers on one hand. The sand was still damp from the retreating tide; the breeze wouldn't fill in the gouged letters for a long time yet, probably till the tide returned to wipe it all out.

Tenoctris reached into the wallet she'd begun wearing on a sash over her shoulder. She brought out the key they'd found at the Tomb of the Messengers, holding it up between her thumb and index finger.

Inside her hand, clamped against her palm by the other fingers, was an ordinary quartz pebble. Cashel could see it from where he stood, but nobody watching from the forest could.

Tenoctris bent down so her hand was right against the beach, behind where she'd drawn the words. She folded the key into her palm and set the pebble onto the sand, then rose with the same hard smile as before.

"This will do, I think," she said. Her voice was a younger, fuller version of the way the old Tenoctris used to speak, but it made Cashel think again that he wouldn't want her for an enemy. "We'll wait on our own world, then return here in an hour."

"Yes, ma'am," Cashel said, bringing the staff upright to his side. "Ah—then what, Tenoctris?"

She laughed. She still held the key concealed in her hand. "Then we finish our negotiation with the Telchines," she said. "On our own terms."

Grinning harshly, Tenoctris began to chant. She was reversing the order of the words of power which had brought them to this bleak shore.

Chapter
14

CASHEL FELT THE wind even before the curtain of wizardlight faded, leaving him and Tenoctris again on coarse sand. The beach was the same as it had been, save that the sea had begun to creep back.

Creatures as gray as the sky were hunched over the words Tenoctris'd drawn on the ground. They were smaller than men, and there were more of them than Cashel could count on both hands.

Tenoctris trilled a laugh. She touched the crook of Cashel's elbow with her free hand—she held the sword in her right—and said, "Oh, Cashel! Can you imagine you'd been an old man and suddenly you were *you,* as strong as you are now? Do you see? That's what's happened to me!"

She sounded like a happy child; well, a happy young woman. Cashel started to think, *Well,* everybody's *a happy child once,* but then he remembered his sister. Ilna'd gotten most of the brains for both of them, but she'd missed her share of being happy. It'd been different while she was with Chalcus, but since he'd been killed she was probably worse off than ever.

It'd been a good while since he last saw Ilna. Cashel hoped he'd see her again soon, and that she'd be in a better place than she'd been when she left.

"What's wrong, Cashel?" Tenoctris said. He realized that he'd been frowning, or anyway hadn't been as cheerful as he usually felt.

"I was just hoping my sister's all right," he said apologetically. Because he didn't want to talk any more about that, he bobbed his staff toward the gray figures and said, "Who are they, Tenoctris?"

"These . . . ," she said, sauntering toward them. She crossed her right wrist on her left to share the weight of the sword on both arms. ". . . are the Telchines. They've been exiled here because they're a nasty, treacherous lot, but they know certain things. In particular, they know the way to the Fulcrum of the Worlds."

Close up, Cashel saw that the creatures wore peaked robes that covered them all the way to the ground. He wasn't sure how they saw out. Maybe the cloth over their faces was woven thinner, but it didn't seem so when he looked at them now.

Tenoctris walked along the straggling line of the Telchines, looking hard at each one as she passed. At the end, she turned and walked back, smiling impishly.

"We've done well, Cashel," she said brightly. "You bring me luck."

Tenoctris patted his arm again; then, without a change in expression, she leaned forward slightly. Using the breadth of the blade, she smoothed away one line of the symbols she'd drawn when they were on this beach the first time.

"You tricked us," whined the creature standing nearest the word Tenoctris had changed. "We came to trade, and you trapped us."

Its voice sounded like that of an injured fox, weak and angry and utterly vicious. Its body didn't move; Cashel couldn't see its lips to tell whether they did or not.

"You're a treacherous liar, Telchis," Tenoctris said coldly. "All your people are. You'd have robbed me and returned to the world from which you were exiled for faithlessness."

"We have kept faith!" the creature protested. "Folk leave goods on our beach and we offer goods in return. They take our goods, or they take back their own if they do not accept our offer."

When he stood this close, Cashel noticed the Telchines' distinctive odor. It was a mixture of old parchment and the acid dryness of dead beetles.

Tenoctris laughed harshly. "I offered the Key," she said. "What did you intend to pay me for the Key, Telchis?"

Cashel held his quarterstaff upright, but his hands were spread at fighting distance on the hickory. He wouldn't insult Tenoctris by placing himself between her and these gray creatures; but if a Telchis did or said anything that Cashel read as threatening, he wouldn't wait for direction before striking. They reminded him of maggots writhing in a possum's corpse.

"Anything," the creature wheezed.

"Anything-g-g . . . ," the troupe chorused. They sounded like feeding time in a fox's earth. . . .

"You would take the Key," Tenoctris said in the cold voice she'd used toward the Telchines from the beginning. "And you would return to your plane, where I could not follow you. And you would pay me nothing. Therefore I caught you here with words of power, and you will tell me the way to the Fulcrum as the price of your lives."

"Not the Fulcrum!" said the creature who'd spoken first.

"Anything but the Fulcrum," his fellows whined softly. "Anything-g-g. . . ."

Cashel looked at the eastern horizon. He thought it'd gotten brighter than it'd been when they arrived, but that might be a trick his mind was playing. He'd like it to be dawn, and he'd like to be out of this place; but he'd stay for as long as Tenoctris wanted him to stay.

"Do you think I'm here to negotiate?" Tenoctris said. "I have no reason to love you, Telchines! The One who exiled you showed more mercy than you can expect from me. Tell me the way to the Fulcrum, or you will stand here till you die and your bodies waste to dust!"

"From the Fulcrum you could shift the worlds," said the chief of the Telchines.

"She could smash the worlds," his fellows echoed. "She could smash our world, even ours. . . ."

"You won't have a world!" Tenoctris said. "You'll freeze and die and your dust will blow across this beach. The Telchines will be only dust and a memory, and at last even your memory will vanish from the cosmos!"

"Tell her . . . ," a Telchis said. Cashel couldn't be sure which one had spoken.

"Tell her the way to the Fulcrum," whispered the chorus like aspens rustling in the darkness.

"I will tell you the way to the Fulcrum," the leader said. His voice was as thin as the cold, cutting wind from the sea. "I must tell you the way. . . ."

For a moment, there was no sound but the wind and the cry of a distant seabird. A voice behind Cashel thundered, *"Lonchar tebriel tobriel!"* A word in the curving Old Script wrote itself in purple flame in the air between Tenoctris and the Telchis.

The sound didn't come from either the leader or all the Telchines together. Despite not trusting the hunched gray figures, Cashel risked a glance over his shoulder.

"Riopha moriath chael!" boomed the voice, and it was the sea itself speaking. The sluggish waves puckered into a lipless mouth. Cashel turned to face it, bringing his staff around in a quick arc. Both butt caps trailed snarling blue sparks of wizardlight.

"Mor marioth!" And the mouth blurred and vanished. The sea remained dimpled for a moment as though oil'd been spilled onto it; then that was gone as well. A moment later the surf resumed its slow march up the beach.

"Yes . . . ," said Tenoctris softly. Cashel looked at her. Her profile was as pale and sharp as a cameo. The words of power were already fading from the air before her. As Cashel watched, the writing shimmered from purple to orange and back very quickly.

Using her foot instead of the sword blade, Tenoctris rubbed out the words she'd written in the sand. The Telchines twisted into the forest like skinks writhing for cover.

Tenoctris reached into her wallet and brought out the quartz key from the Tomb of the Messengers. She held it up to the eyes watching from the trees, then dropped it deliberately beside the pebble she'd left as a decoy.

"Now, Cashel," she said. "We must go to the Fulcrum of

the Worlds. It will be very difficult to get there even now that
I know the way, and—"

She laughed again like a happy child.

"—it'll be *far* more difficult to return!"

A BELT OF thorny brush fringed the stream Garric and his
companions were following toward the mountain. Even
mounted on Kore's back, Garric couldn't see the water, but
there was no escaping the sound of its tumbling violence.
Ordinarily it must've been a seasonal trickle across a
parched landscape, but it was clearly in spate now.

"The glacier filled its valley during winter and retreated a
hundred yards in the course of a hot summer," Shin said.
"Since the Change, the ice has melted faster than ever before. The valley'll be clear in another year except for
shaded crevices; and even there before a second year is
out."

He skipped ahead of Garric and Kore, idly nibbling foliage from a branch he'd broken from the brush. Garric
couldn't imagine that the small gray-green leaves tasted any
better than pine bark, but he'd seen goats strip the bark from
pine saplings. Apparently aegipans were equally catholic in
their tastes.

Shin chuckled. "You're fortunate that it's melting," he
said. "The ice used to cover the entrance to the Yellow
King's tomb. Though no doubt a true champion could've
dug his way down through the glacier."

"Horses don't dig tunnels in ice," the ogre said austerely.
"If you were wondering, noble master."

"I wasn't," Garric said, "but thank you anyway."

The mountain rose like a wall from the plains. Garric
cleared his throat and went on, "How much farther is it,
Master Shin?"

"Not far," said the aegipan. "We're almost to the mouth of
the valley, and it's no more than half a mile beyond."

The strait they'd crossed in Lord Holm's barge the night
before was less than three miles wide; by daylight, they

might've been able to see the far shore before they set out. After they'd landed, Shin—the only one who knew anything about the terrain—told the laborers to row westward where they'd find the considerable settlement within twenty miles. That was where Holm had sold his produce.

The aegipan had led Garric and Kore directly inland across a barren landscape, taking their bearings from the multi-spired peak he pointed out on the horizon. Before midday they'd met the stream and followed it thenceforth.

They hadn't tried to fight through the dense curtain of brush. The barge had been provisioned. Garric had taken half the total in a sling of cargo net, including a cask of water. The rescued laborers were headed for a settlement with food and water; he and his companions were not.

The mountain was a wedge of volcanic rock with a faint greenish tinge. It'd emerged from a surrounding plain of shale which weathering had broken into a loose soil. From the luxuriance of the brush along the creek banks, it was apparently very fertile when it got enough water.

Shin climbed a spur, his hooves sparkling. Kore grunted. "Steep, I would say," she said. "For a horse . . . but let it pass."

She followed the aegipan up the slope. Garric leaned over her shoulder to keep his weight as far forward as he could, much as he would've done if she'd really been a horse. The ogre hadn't stopped grumbling since they took leave of the barge on shore, but she'd kept going despite the added burden of food and thirty gallons of water.

On the other side of the spur was a valley hollowed by the slow force of the glacier. The rock was completely sterile, scoured clean by ice and the stones which its massive weight shoved along with it. At the bottom tossed the creek. The meltwater was white with material dissolved out of the rocks.

Shin laughed merrily. "Are you ready, Garric?" he said. "Perhaps you think that the rest will be easier than what you've faced to get here?"

"I'll dismount, now," Garric said. The ogre had already

begun to kneel. "Shin, just lead and I'll follow you the way we've been doing. Word games were never to my taste, and this wouldn't be a good place to play them even if they were."

Kore stood again and settled the cargo net. It'd be a wrench to go back to riding horses which didn't read his mind. Though that was only an issue if he survived.

The creek didn't fill the valley which the glacier'd hollowed over the years, but the steep slope to either side was complicated with the scree of loose rocks which the ice had dropped when it melted. The aegipan sprang down to the edge of the water, touching the slope three times.

"He places his feet like he was thrusting with a sword," Carus said, watching in delight. *"If he was very, very good with a sword, I mean. As good as me."*

"Hmpf!" Shin said, grinning up at Garric and the ghost in his mind. "Swords are a waste of good metal . . . but if they weren't, warrior, I might show you something."

Carus laughed and appeared to stretch. The ghost had only the memory of a physical body, but that body had been so much of his personality that its presence remained a thousand years after he'd died.

"Oh, aye, lad," Carus agreed with a wry smile. *"I could take a man's head off without thinking about it. Unfortunately, I generally* should've *thought more about it."*

Smiling faintly, Garric climbed into the ravine with his back and his spread arms to the rock wall. He twisted his belt so that the sword lay in front of his right leg where it was less likely to get in the way.

If he'd had to jump the way the aegipan had, he'd have done it. The drop was less than twenty feet here at the mouth of the valley, though the slope was steep enough that you might not hit the side on the way down if you tripped.

Carus chuckled and Garric grinned wider. *Well, I'd have tried to do it. Since I don't need to, I'm not going to break a leg or my neck showing off.*

"I wonder, noble master . . . ," said Kore. To Garric's amazement, the ogre executed a handstand at the edge of the ravine. "What physical act do you imagine you can perform that would impress me?"

So speaking she walked down the slope on her hands, pausing with her short legs quivering in between each of her three long "steps." At the bottom, spattered by the stream, she curled her legs under her again and stood normally.

"Nothing, apparently," Garric said, smiling because he made a point of smiling instead of letting his face slip into the grim lines of his warrior ancestor when receiving a challenge. "Though remembering the discussion we had when we met, possibly there are a few things, eh?"

The ogre bowed. Because her torso was so long, that brought her face within a hand's breadth of Garric's. For a mercy, she'd been eating the mixture of millet and lentils which the barge carried for its crew.

"As you say, noble master," she said. "Will the noble master ride or walk now?"

"I'll walk, thank you, Kore," Garric said. "Though I hope that if I slip, you'll catch me before I fall into the water."

A hundred yards ahead the creek seemed to spew out of a solid wall. When they got closer—Shin dancing ahead while Garric picked his footing cautiously; he didn't dare glance back to see how the ogre was faring—Garric saw that the valley bent sharply to the left. There was a ledge wide enough to walk on, but it was slick with cold spray.

Shin looked back and called, "It's not much farther." He disappeared behind the rock face.

Garric faced outward and sidled after the aegipan with his back to the rock. At home he'd crossed many a log bridge in the rain without thinking about it, but the cost of falling into this foaming meltwater could be much worse than a soaking in Pattern Creek.

It was only after the ledge widened enough for him to walk normally without knocking his left elbow on the slope that Garric looked up from his feet. A thick roof of ice covered the valley a hundred yards ahead. The creek poured from the opening beneath. There was light within, dim but probably sufficient for them to walk without torches.

Garric couldn't tell how far back into the valley the cave went, though.

Frozen into the face of the glacier just above the opening was a monster with wings and a snakelike head. Its leathery hide was a purple-red that made Garric think of maple leaves in the fall.

"A wyvern," said Kore in a speculative tone. "I don't believe I've ever seen one so big before. Have you, Master Shin?"

"Yes," said the aegipan, "but not often. He'd easily be fifty feet from nose to tail if he stretched out."

Any hope that the creature was dead vanished when the great head twitched. Shattered ice fell away with a roar. Some of the chunks which the creek tossed downstream were as big as a man.

"I'd say our timing was fortunate, wouldn't you, Garric?" Shin said. "Rather than a half-hour later, I mean. But come along. We're almost there, and I'm sure you're looking forward to reaching your goal."

He skipped onward, pirouetting every third step. The aegipan must dance simply for fun, because by now he certainly didn't think Garric doubted his agility.

Garric entered the cave. The ogre tramped along behind him. She stood upright, though not much farther ahead she'd have to duck to clear the ceiling.

The creek was deafening in the enclosure, and the air was as dank as winter rain. Illumination through the thick ice had a bluish cast, and it didn't show the loose rocks well. Garric stumbled, then stumbled again. He was glad he was wearing heavy boots.

Shin looked back. He seemed to be laughing, though Garric couldn't hear over the roar of icy water.

They walked on.

RASILE'S CHANT SOUNDED different from the words of power human wizards used, but the cadence was the same. It made goose bumps quiver on Sharina's arms the same way also.

The figure Rasile'd drawn around them, this time using fine white sand rather than yarrow stalks, had twelve sides. Sharina'd had plenty of time to count them while listening to the incantation. Occasionally she let two fingers rest on the hilt of her Pewle knife.

Outside the wicker screen Lord Waldron and his men fought the Last with the desperate courage of men who will die before they give up . . . which meant only that they *would* die. By now the most pig-stupid trooper in the royal army could predict the result of a battle in which the other side's losses were constantly replaced.

"Lady," Sharina prayed under her breath, "You are the Queen of Peace and my business is war; but if it be Your will, aid me so that Mankind not be destroyed."

Rasile's voice rose to a shriek like that of a cat in fury. Wizardlight glared blue above the figure, then vanished. All the world vanished.

Sharina was blind.

"Rasile?" she said. Did she hear terror in her own voice? It was her worst fear: not being able to see, not being able to read. . . .

She reached out and touched the wizard's bony arm. The Corl was unexpectedly warm beneath the layer of fur. "Rasile, I can't—"

Before Sharina could finish the sentence, sight began to return . . . but she was looking herself in the face. The world had a grainier texture. Reds and browns were deeper and more subtle, and her own blue irises vanished into the whites.

"You have your task," the wizard said. "Carry it out as quickly as you can, Sharina, because I am not your friend Tenoctris. There are limits to my power, even in this place."

Sharina opened her mouth to ask questions: "Will you come with me? What happens if I become visible inside the nest of the Last? What if I can't find the pool or the talisman, the First Stone, in the pool?"

That'd be a waste of time, which Rasile had just said was in short supply. Sharina smiled as she walked quickly from

the shelter. Instead of a door, the troops'd extended one end
of the wall over the other.

Sharina's viewpoint moved with her, though she could
still see herself. It took some getting used to, but after
she'd brushed the side of the passage once—sharp ends of
the wattling scratched like a cat's claws—she didn't have
trouble.

The camp was quiet now in the sunlight. Off-duty soldiers
were sleeping; the guards in the towers chatted in desultory
fashion or simply stared in the direction of the Last's stronghold. Sharina could hear a fatigue party working on the
southern wall, but the troops' shelters hid them from the eyes
she was using.

She trotted briskly between the guy ropes and wicker
walls. Her feet kicked up dust, but nothing that couldn't pass
for a whim of the breeze should anyone even notice; no one
did.

Sharina'd been concerned about getting out through the
main gate, but foragers were driving in a score of donkeys
carrying panniers of grain. There were villages of the
Grass People within practical distance, though the food
this party brought back wouldn't supply the army for very
long.

She slipped through the gate. A donkey whickered angrily, but the humans didn't see her. One way or the other,
the army wouldn't need supplies here for very long.

Waldron had laid out his siege lines a quarter mile from
the eastern entrance to the black fortress. The parapet was
manned, but all save three small ballistas had been moved to
reinforce the other flank where the Last were active.

That was a calculated risk: it minimized human casual-
ties unless the Last changed the direction of their attack. If
they sallied from the eastern entrance, many men would die
holding them for the time it took to bring the artillery back.

Waldron had explained and recommended the plan, but
Sharina had made the final decision to adopt it. If things
went wrong and a thousand brave men were hacked to death
in a bloody hour, she'd blame herself.

"Lady, help me," she whispered. Then, "Lady, bring my brother back so that *he* can make these choices!"

There was no gate in the siege lines. Every furlong, ramps sloped up to the guard walks eight feet above the ground, and there were simple ladders at intervals between them.

Sharina walked up a ramp to a salient which once'd held a large catapult; now a squad of infantry occupied it. The men wore cuirasses, but they'd taken off their helmets. Four were dicing while the rest looked toward the enemy and talked about food. They didn't notice Sharina step carefully past them to the wall midway between the salient and the next pair of guards.

She gripped the vertical stiffeners of a basket, then climbed over the parapet. After hanging for a moment, she dropped into no-man's-land and started for the alien fortress.

The ground here was lower and wetter; Lord Waldron had sited their camp on the highest terrain besides the rock of Pandah itself. The elevation was no more than ten feet, but that was the difference between dry bedding and living in a bog.

Sharina splashed for a few steps before she slowed and took more care about how she placed her feet. The eyes she watched through moved slightly to the left of the line she'd been taking, so she moved that way herself.

The Last curtained the entrance to their fortress with a separate baffle built in front of the main wall of the fortress. Two of the creatures stood in its shelter, concealed from the human siege works. They were as motionless as statues.

Sharina paused to let her heart and breathing settle. Her viewpoint edged forward but stopped when Rasile understood what Sharina was doing.

Sharina smiled. At any rate, the wizard must've understood that she wasn't going to be dragged into moving faster than she thought was safe.

When she decided she was calm enough, Sharina walked past the silent guards and into the fortress. The touch of amusement at her wordless argument with Rasile had been more helpful than any number of deep breaths.

From outside, the walls were opaque black in daylight and opaque yellow at night. They were clear with a hint of green from the inside. A troop of forty-odd Last warriors stood near the entrance, ready to respond if humans attacked. They'd turned their backs to the sun and held their arms raised, spreading the membranes between their arms and pelvises. It made them look batlike, though such short vans couldn't possibly carry man-sized bodies through the air. Sharina remembered Tenoctris saying the creatures lived on sunshine rather than food and water.

The Last looked much less human close up than they had at a distance. Their lower abdomens were merely girders to connect their legs and upper torsos.

Sharina strode on, trying to keep at least a double pace away from the Last. Partly she didn't trust her sense of distance while seeing through Rasile's eyes, but she also wondered how good the Last's sense of touch might be. Would the breeze of her passage rouse the interest of the black monsters?

Besides, she didn't want to be close to them. That they were humanoid made them even more disgusting. It was like seeing apes dressed as courtiers, smirking and mowing in a parody of palace manners.

The fortress was roofless; though the walls were transparent, the Last seemed to prefer to absorb the sun's rays unfiltered. The side facing Pandah was higher, jointed together from three or even four layers of pentagonal facets. A score of warriors stood along the southern wall with their membranes spread. At this time of year the sun was high enough to shine into the interior, but come winter it would not be. The battle'd be over before winter, though.

Sharina walked cautiously past the warriors feeding on light. She realized she was instinctively afraid that she'd cast a shadow on them, but they seemed as oblivious of her as their fellows at the east entrance had been.

Perhaps the greatest difference between the opposing camps was that there was always some activity among the human soldiers. The Last stood as black statues while they were waiting to act.

The two creatures on the west end of the line folded their arms, turned, and drew their swords. Sharina froze, though Rasile's eyes moved on a step before stopping to wait for her. The pair strode away from her with a lithe briskness, not quite loping but with none of the jerky angularity that Sharina's mind expected from things that stood like so many marionettes when they weren't moving.

They were going toward the western entrance, preparing to attack the human defenses as thousands of their fellows had attacked over the past days . . . and had died and been replaced, as this pair would die and be replaced.

Just ahead of Sharina was a pool. The Last had cleared its margins as meticulously as a king's robe of state. Nothing impeded the line of sight from it to the southern horizon. There the new white star shone, though concealed for the moment by the noon sun.

For an instant the reflection of a warrior shimmered on the pool's surface; then the creature strode out, black and grim and as implacable as sunrise. As it walked to the line where its fellows stood absorbing sunlight before joining the battle, an identical reflection grew sharper on the water from which the first had stepped.

Sharina took a deep breath and pulled off her singlet. She tossed it on the ground. Would the Last see the garment now that she wasn't wearing it?

It didn't matter: they'd see the splash. Wearing only the Pewle knife on its sealskin belt, Sharina dived into the pool. Her body shattered the image of Prince Vorsan, staring up at her somberly.

Lady, aid me that men may live!

ILNA STEPPED ONTO a moonlit slope, facing a ridge of rock thrusting up from the surrounding grassland. She was alone for only an instant before Temple strode through on her left and the two hunters on her right.

There was no sign of the portal on this side. Her companions appeared out of the air, swelling like drops of water condensing on cold metal.

Asion quickly turned with a stone in the pocket of his sling. Karpos, holding his long knife, looked up the face of the rock without expression. "What is this place, then?" he asked.

"It's the Tomb of the Messengers," Temple said, letting his eyes follow the hunter's toward the peak. He pointed with his left hand to a wedge of shadow just above the line where the soil was too thin for oat grass. "The entrance is at the base, however. There."

"It looks like close quarters," Karpos said. "Not the sort of place I'd look forward to tracking a cat I'd wounded."

"We did the once, though," Asion said with a quick look back at his partner before resuming his survey of the moonlit oats studded with occasional thorn trees. "That striped demon with a pouch that kept stealing our bait way down in the south."

"This could be worse'n that ever was," Karpos said. "Temple, the mistress shouldn't go down in that. Should she?"

"Karpos, you're not to tell me what I should or shouldn't do," Ilna snapped. "And Master Temple, you *particularly* shouldn't be giving me direction."

"I can't answer that question, Karpos," Temple said. He was pretending he hadn't heard her speak. "That's the only way she can reach the Messengers. If that's her goal, she hasn't any choice."

"My goal is to rid the world of Coerli!" Ilna said. "As you should know by now."

She started up the remaining slope toward the long sandstone ridge. She didn't look behind to see if the men were following her, though of course they were. "And," she said, "you should also know that if I wanted your opinions, I'd have asked for them!"

"Well, it'll be all right, I guess," said Karpos, trying to sound nonchalant. "Only I think I better go first, mistress. You know, because I'm . . . well, I've done this before."

"I'm afraid that won't be possible, Karpos," Temple said quietly, "though the thought does you credit. To approach the Messengers requires a kind of strength that you and Asion don't possess. If you were to attempt it, you'd lose your humanity."

Ilna's leg brushed the shrub growing in front of the cave. The leaves were small and plump; bitter to the taste, Ilna was sure, because all the vegetation of this sort was. They had horny tips which she hadn't noticed till they clawed her.

She grimaced, then found her lips curling into a tight smile. The shrub's white flowers showed brilliantly in the moonlight. It was just another proof that attractive things came with a price.

"Look, I guess I can take a chance if I want to!" Karpos said sharply. He was a big man—as big as Garric—but no physical match for Temple. Nonetheless there was a challenge in his tone.

Instead of replying to the hunter, Temple said quietly, "Ilna, you may go or stay as you wish. If these men accompany you, however, they'll be transformed like those who came to question the Messengers and who lacked the power to compel answers. They'll become . . . servitors, I suppose. You know your own mind, but these men have been friends to you."

Ilna stopped at the mouth of the cave. She could enter without ducking her head, but only barely. She wondered how far she'd have to follow the passage. The patterns she knotted for protection wouldn't be effective in the dark either.

The air rising from the depths of the cave carried a hint of spices. Perhaps priests were working rites within? Or the odors could be from a tomb. A waste of expense either way, but nobody'd asked what *she* thought about the matter.

"Look, I'm not afraid!" said Asion. The high pitch of his voice made a lie of the words, but Ilna didn't doubt that he and his partner would act the part of fearless men.

Temple didn't reply. He wasn't arguing with the hunters, of course.

Ilna turned and took eight strands of yarn from her sleeve.

She began to knot them. "Temple," she said, "how deep is this? Should I take a torch?"

"There'll be light before you go much farther," the big man said. "You'll have a long way to go, but being able to see won't be one of your problems."

She'd never asked Temple how he knew the things he did. She disliked people who asked personal questions, and she had no intention of behaving that way herself.

"All right," she said, backing into the cave. She held up the pattern she'd just knotted so they all saw it, then dropped it across the entrance. "You three can wait a reasonable length of time for me. Temple, you probably have a better idea of what that would be than I do. If I don't return, then go on your way. I, ah, I've been glad of your company over the past weeks."

"Look, I'm coming with you!" Karpos said, climbing the last of the slope. He stopped in midstride, short of the entrance. Asion, just behind, would've collided with his partner if he hadn't been as quick and agile as a sparrow.

"No, you're not," said Ilna. "I've put a blocking spell here. It'll work in pitch darkness in case you were wondering, since I've showed it to you in the light."

She cleared her throat. "Temple?" she said. "Asion and Karpos may need a guide if I don't come back. Can you do that?"

Temple shrugged. "I'll lead them if the situation arises, Ilna," he said.

She turned. To her back Temple added, "May the Gods accompany you, Ilna."

"There are no Gods!" Ilna said. Her voice echoed between the stone walls. She shouldn't have gotten angry, but the man had an incredible talent for saying the thing that would reach all the way to the cold depths of her heart.

Ahead, Ilna saw a hint of light. She smiled as widely as she ever did. *What a weaver Temple could've been with an instinct like that!*

Chapter

15

CASHEL WAS PRETTY sure that if he'd been able to close his eyes, he wouldn't have felt any motion at all. He couldn't do that while he was guarding Tenoctris, so he felt a twitch of vertigo when the world stopped spinning beyond the edge of the perfect circle she'd drawn in the middle of an oak grove.

The oaks were gone. The sun'd been directly overhead when Tenoctris began her spell, but now it was close to the southern horizon. Its light brought no warmth.

Cashel and the wizard stood on a beach of rock broken from the ragged cliff, the corniche that the sea battered against during winter storms. The water was too quiet even to show a line of foam, but the low sun lighted it to gleaming contrast with the dull black shingle.

Tenoctris looked about her with a critical expression. "I'm sorry I couldn't come closer than this," she said. "The altar's a focus of great power, but that in itself prevents me from using my art to bring us directly onto it. We'll have to walk."

Cashel smiled faintly. "I don't mind walking, Tenoctris," he said.

He stepped aside and gave his staff a tentative spin, sunwise and then widdershins. Mostly he was loosening his muscles, but it didn't surprise him to see that the ferrules trailed wizardlight in spirals which faded slowly when he put the staff up.

"Something doesn't want us here," Tenoctris said. She looked out to sea, then at the sky. The sunlight was so faint that Cashel, following her eyes, could pick out constellations from knowing their brightest stars.

Cashel spun the quarterstaff again. "That's all right," he said. "Do you know which way we're going, or should we climb that—"

He nodded to the corniche. Though barely higher than he could reach, it was what passed for a vantage point in this barren landscape.

"—and take a look around?"

Tenoctris looked at him. She wasn't angry, but her eyes went all the way to his heart.

"We'll see the altar when we reach the angle of the cliff ahead of us," she said calmly. "It's just around the headland and quite obvious."

They started along the shore. A pair of gray-headed gulls had been looking out from the edge of the sea. One, then the other, flapped into the air and circled to gain height. They shrieked at Cashel and Tenoctris, sounding peevish as gulls always did.

The black shingle wanted to turn under Cashel's bare feet, but other than that he preferred it to the brick or cobblestone pavements he walked on in cities. These stones were rough, but they didn't have spikes or sharp edges.

He glanced at Tenoctris. She wore wooden-soled clogs, though the high uppers were of leather tooled with fashionable designs. She met his eyes, smiled, and said, "Yes, I dressed for what I expected to find."

Her expression sobered. "I should've warned you," she said. "I'm sorry. I'm used to you being able to deal with anything."

Cashel beamed at her. "Yes, ma'am," he said. "I am. Or anyway, I'll try to."

He cleared his throat and said, "I shouldn't've spoken about you knowing where we were. I knew you did."

"You wanted me to get on with our business," Tenoctris said. She wore a faint smile, but he wasn't sure of what was under it. "You were right to remind me of that. We both have things we want to return to."

"Yes, ma'am," Cashel said, thinking of Sharina and feeling warm all the way through. "But I still shouldn't've said it."

A crab longer than Cashel's foot came out of the surf ahead of them. Its shell was the dirty yellow-brown color that sulfur gets when you heat it.

"Those pincers could take your finger off," he said, bending to pick up a piece of shingle. He threw it, hard but not trying to hit: his missile cracked into similar stones a hand's breadth from the crab. For choice Cashel didn't kill things, even unpleasant things.

Instead of scuttling back into the water, the crab charged them side-on. Frowning, Cashel stepped forward, putting himself in front of Tenoctris. A double pace from the ugly creature he shot his quarterstaff out like a spear. The crab hopped in the air, but it wasn't quick enough. The iron butt cap crushed the edge of its shell and all the legs on that side.

The crab landed on its back, scrabbling with its remaining legs to turn over. Cashel stepped closer, judged the angle, and flipped the creature into the water with his staff.

He knew crabs. That one's fellows'd make a meal of it before any of the other predators got a chance to.

"That was funny," he said to Tenoctris. "I've had 'em come for me plenty times before, but not from so far away. Do crabs get rabies, do you think?"

A double handful of crabs came out of the sea, all the same ugly color and just as big as the first. Their clawed feet clicked over the stones as they sidled toward Cashel and Tenoctris.

"I think we'd better—" Cashel said. More crabs appeared. The sea boiled with them. There were too many crabs to count, piling onto the shore like bubbles of filthy yellow foam.

THE COLD BIT Garric's hands and ears. He laced his fingers and twisted them to get the blood flowing. He wondered if Kore thought he was nervous.

He chuckled. Shin looked back and raised an eyebrow. "I *am* nervous," Garric said over his shoulder. "But that's not why I'm wringing my hands, Mistress Kore."

The ogre laughed. The sound made Garric think of bubbles rising through a swamp.

It'd gotten chilly during the night as they crossed the strait in the barge, but since the sun came up only heat had been of concern. It probably wasn't *that* cold here under the ice, but the contrast with the dry wasteland they'd just crossed made it seem a lot worse than it was.

The aegipan paused at a round-topped opening in the side of the rock. The edges were as smooth as those a cobbler made when he sliced leather. It didn't have a door nor could Garric see any sign that a door'd ever been fitted.

"You've reached the resting place of the Yellow King," Shin said. The portal was easily twelve feet high, but through a momentary trick of the light Garric thought the aegipan's slim form was filling it. "Come in, then, Garric."

"And I'll come as well," Kore said. "I'm no longer your steed, man thing. We're agreed on that?"

Garric looked back at her. *Was Kore warning that she was about to attack him?*

No. And if she did, well, you couldn't live like a human being and still distrust everyone and everything you met. If the Shepherd chose that an ogre Garric trusted should pull his head off from behind, so be it.

"Yes, mistress," Garric said. "You've been a good companion and an excellent steed. You're released from your oath. *I* release you from your oath."

"Very well," said the ogre. She set the net of provisions down in the rubble-strewn track. "Then I'm free to become a spectator. I think Master Shin is about to show us wonders."

The aegipan laughed. "Wonders indeed," he said as he walked into the mountain with the others following.

Garric touched the side of the passage: it was as smooth as glass. There was light all around him, but he couldn't tell the source. It was blue, but a purer, clearer blue than what penetrated the ice outside in the valley.

It was wizardlight. And not only the illumination but the passage itself must've been formed by wizardry.

"That shouldn't be a surprise, should it, Garric?" said

Shin without turning his head. "You knew the Yellow King was a wizard. That's why you came here, isn't it?"

Garric's mouth was dry. "I knew the Yellow King was a myth," he said. "That's what I really believed, as you must know. I came because Tenoctris told me to come."

He laughed without humor. "I came because Tenoctris gave me an excuse to walk away from the duties of being king, which I hate because I'm afraid I'm going to do the wrong thing and break *everything*. That's why I came, Master Shin."

"Well, I don't suppose the reasons matter, do they?" said the aegipan cheerfully. "The important thing is that you came."

He stepped into a chamber. Its ceiling rose so high that it was lost in a haze of wizardlight. A helical staircase circled it, rising out of sight. The floor was stone, polished like the walls, and over a hundred feet in diameter.

In the center, facing the entrance, was a huge throne on a three-step base. It'd been carved as a whole from the living rock. On its empty seat was a cushion of yellow fabric. There was nothing else in the great room.

Carus would've drawn his sword in an instinctive response to a situation he didn't understand. Garric kept his hands in front of him with his fingers tented, but *he* certainly didn't understand what was going on either.

"Ah, Shin?" he said. "Are we to wait here for the Yellow King's arrival? Or . . . ?"

"Oh, as for that . . . ," said the aegipan. He turned a double cartwheel to the base of the throne, then mounted it. At each step he appeared to grow larger. When he lifted the yellow fabric—it was a folded robe, not a cushion—he was of a size with the throne.

Shin smiled and bowed to Garric, then settled onto the stone seat. "I've arrived. More to the point, you've arrived to meet me, Garric."

Carus was calculating how to attack the aegipan, but that was Carus. Anything big enough to be dangerous was to him a potential threat. That was a useful trait in a subordinate, but not a good one for the person in charge.

Garric was in charge. He cleared his throat.

"Ah, Your Highness," he said, looking up at the great figure enthroned before him. "I came to ask your assistance in dealing with the Last, the invaders, as you know. I—"

The absurdity of the situation struck him. He laughed, knowing that he must sound a little hysterical. "Will you help us, Your Highness?" he said. "Will you help Mankind, now that you've brought me all this way to ask you?"

"I've been Shin to you during the journey," the great figure said. "I'll remain Shin to you and Mistress Kore, if you don't mind. Shin has a more interesting life than the Yellow King does."

Garric bowed. "I came to like Shin," he said. "I'd be pleased to have him back."

The aegipan rose and walked down from the throne again, shrinking at each step just as he'd grown. At the bottom the neck of the robe slipped over his body. He walked out of the garment.

His tongue lolled in a smile. Garric wondered if he were going to cartwheel toward them.

"Another time, perhaps," said the aegipan, his hooves clicking on the floor.

"The test wasn't of how bold a warrior you were, Garric," Shin went on. "Though you certainly proved that well enough. What I needed to determine was how fit a ruler you'd be for a land in which 'people' means more than members of the human race. You satisfied me ably on that score."

And if I hadn't? Garric thought. He didn't voice the words and Shin didn't answer the unspoken question.

"You know *the answer, lad,"* said the ghost in his mind. *"This one's as hard as I am, and he has no more reason to love us than he does the Last."*

"Perhaps a little more, Brother Carus," said Shin with his mocking smile again. "But that's of no concern now since your descendant has succeeded where a more physical ruler would not have. I'll go to my . . . well, you could call it an altar, on top of this ridge. Those are the steps to it."

He gestured toward the staircase circling the room.

"There's only one problem," Shin went on. "The wyvern we saw breaking out of the ice will make for the highest point also. And while I *could* deal with him, I can't both deal with the wyvern and accomplish what you've asked me to do. In the time that remains, I mean. In the time that remains for humanity."

King Carus began to laugh. His image stood arms-akimbo, looking merrily at the aegipan through Garric's eyes.

"I suppose you wouldn't fancy my chances of arriving here the way Garric did, eh, Master Shin?" Carus said. *"To tell the truth, I don't fancy them either. I figure it'd have ended in a stable with a dead ogre and my head pulled off my neck."*

He nodded toward Kore. The ogre squatted with an elbow cocked on her knee to support her chin. She nodded back, as comfortable in dealing with the ghost as she was with the Yellow King.

"So fair enough, I wasn't the man for that job," Carus said. The lines of his face hardened, though his smile remained. *"But I've fought a wyvern. You get on with your business, wizard. I and the boy here'll keep the beast busy for you."*

"You haven't fought a wyvern as big as this one," said Kore.

Garric shrugged. He didn't need his ancestor to tell him what to do now. "This is the best way to get to him?" he said, gesturing to the stairs circling the wall.

"Far and away the best," Shin agreed. "Even if you were a rock climber. I'll follow you up, then."

Kore stood and stretched. "Follow me instead, Master Shin," she said. "I think I'll go too."

Garric looked at her without speaking.

The ogre grimaced, an amazing expression on her long face. "It's my business what I do, you know," she said. "I'm not your horse anymore!"

She made a dismissive gesture with her right arm. It looked like a derrick swinging.

"Wyvern flesh is quite tasty," she added. "The young ones are, at any rate. I've never eaten one this big myself, but I'm hopeful."

"Right," said Garric quietly. "I'm hopeful too, my friend."

He strode to the base of the stairs. He was nervous. He'd have liked to rush up them, but he was going to need all his strength and wind very shortly.

In truth, he and Kore were probably going to need more strength than they had; but they were going to try.

ILNA COULD NO longer see light when she looked over her shoulder, and the gray glow ahead wasn't strong enough to help her choose her footing. She walked on, her face set and grim; more or less as usual, she supposed.

The worst thing that could happen would be for her to fall into a chasm and break her neck, and she wasn't disposed at the moment to consider that a bad result. She'd go on as long as she lived, but life had held no pleasure for her since she'd watched the cat men kill Chalcus and Merota.

The light was growing brighter. She'd heard things scuttling along the floor beside her for some minutes; now she was able to see distorted shadows the size of dogs. She didn't bother to pretend that they *were* dogs.

"Oh, she's very strong," whispered a voice.

"The Messengers will bow to her," another voice rustled. "Not like us, not poor weak failures like us."

The light was stronger. This time she could tell that the speaker was one of the scuttling things. For a moment it stood and she thought it *was* a man; but then it hunched again. There was nothing human about it, though there might once have been.

Ilna remembered what Temple had said about those who sought the Messengers but didn't have the strength to compel them. Asion and Karpos deserved better of her.

Indeed, there wasn't anyone Ilna could think of who *didn't* deserve better, though there were no few she'd met who she'd send to a clean death without scruple or hesitation. But these despicable creatures were here on their own responsibility, not hers.

She smiled. She wasn't responsible for anybody's presence save her own.

She was descending. Because she'd been in caves before, she expected at least a hint of dampness if not water running along the floor. The air here was as dry as that of the sere grasslands above.

And of course the rock was sandstone, not limestone where natural caves appeared. There was *nothing* natural about this place. Well, she'd known that.

"The Messengers will bow before her!" the little voices chittered. "Oh, what power she has!"

When Ilna didn't look at the creatures, their sounds made her think of rats. Even to her eyes, the way they scuttled was ratlike.

The walls of the cave were wide near the ceiling but bulged in before spreading again at the bottom. There was plenty of room to walk, but Ilna had the feeling that the walls were reaching for her. She hated rock and she hated this cave; but she hated the cat men more. She expected to pay to get the things she wanted.

"What will she demand?" the voices twittered. "Oh, such power! She will rule the Messengers as they rule wretched creatures like us!"

The light had no source and no color. It was gray, the gray of the Hell Ilna'd walked in till she surrendered her soul to evil and gained skills no human could have mastered. In the Hell-light Ilna saw deep into the rock, the patterns locked there in crystalline horror: death and doom and chaos, all drawn in detail.

Oh, yes. She had power. And soon perhaps she would have the power to kill every Corl there was.

The light became fiercer at each step. How deep had she gone? Into the earth, into the mountain? Usually Ilna had a feeling for time—if not for distance the way her brother Cashel did—but the rock confused her.

She'd been buried in this place. She'd buried herself.

And she wasn't alone. The creatures scampered when her eyes fell on them, crawled when they thought she wasn't looking. They wore no-colored clothing and she never saw their features.

"She'll put out the sun/move the stars from their courses/ bring back the age of fire and ice!"

The walls of the passage began to sprout spiky nodules like sea urchins. At first Ilna thought it was lichen, but when she paused for a closer look she found that the growths were crystals extruded from the rock itself. She'd never seen anything like that on sandstone. It was as unexpected as finding maggots in a melon.

She continued on, trying not to look to the sides. Her mouth was set in a line of fierce disapproval, and her fingers knotted and picked out patterns in yarn.

She'd done the same things when she stepped into Hell and became lost to the world. She'd done the same things the *previous* time she stepped into Hell. Her smile quirked. This time at least she knew the way.

The smile faded. Garric wouldn't arrive to save her here, though. That didn't matter. If she destroyed the Coerli as she'd come to do, then *nothing* else mattered.

"She will meet the Messengers!" the voices chirped. The distorted creatures covered the floor of the corridor behind Ilna. Rats the size of dogs, large dogs. . . . "She is meeting the Messengers and they will bow to her! They will bow!"

Ilna stepped into a spherical chamber. It was huge, far too big for her to judge its true size. All the buildings and groves and terraces of the palace in Valles could fit into it.

In the center hung a spinning pink glow. It lit the cavern the way the sun did the surface world.

Ilna noticed that the sandstone walls were banded as far up as she could see. The markings were more vivid than those she'd seen on the bluffs before she entered the passage, but she must be far beneath the surface of the world she'd left.

YOU HAVE COME TO US, said voices in her head, each echoing the other and switching order from syllable to syllable. The sticky pink light trembled in measure with the words. WHAT DO YOU WISH, WIZARD?

Ilna focused on the light with the eyes of her mind just as she would a pattern she intended to weave.

The light *had* a pattern. It shifted as the separate nodes wound around and even through one another. The nodes had shapes, but what Ilna saw of them were the constantly changing parts that they showed to this world for a particular instant.

And the lights were speaking.

WE ARE THE MESSENGERS, the silent voices said. WE HAVE ALL KNOWLEDGE, WIZARD, AND WE OFFER IT TO YOU.

"She is powerful," the gray figures moaned softly. "Never was there one so powerful as she, or almost never."

They spread across the floor of the cavern like mold on rotting fruit, never coming as close to Ilna as her foot would reach if she lashed out. Their smell was overpowering. It seemed to be compounded of old urine and rancid sweat.

How long had wizards been coming here? The squirming mass seemed the size of an army assembled for review; greater than the largest crowds that came to hear Garric speak in the plaza before the palace.

"I want you to kill all the Coerli!" Ilna said. She raised her voice, but it still became lost in the chamber's vastness. "I'm told you can do anything. Can you? I want you to kill them all!"

WE DO NOT ACT, WIZARD, the voices said. WE CANNOT ACT, FOR WE ARE IMPRISONED HERE APART FROM YOUR UNIVERSE. BUT WE HAVE KNOWLEDGE, AND THAT WE WILL SHARE.

A vast sigh stirred the air of the chamber. Perhaps it came from the assembled creatures, things once human but fallen from that state when they reached the Messengers. It seemed, though, that the world itself had breathed out its despair.

YOU WISH TO KILL THE COERLI, the voices said. WE WILL SHOW YOU HOW. . . .

She was no longer seeing the whirling lights. Instead—

A band of Coerli, two handsful less one, ringed a human family. The father held a spear. He lunged at a warrior, who leaped aside with contemptuous ease. Warriors to either side spun out hooked lines. One wrapped around the man's throat and jerked him backward; the other line lashed the spear-shaft to the man's wrist while the beast who'd thrown it pulled in the opposite direction.

The man thrashed and choked until a third warrior stabbed him up through the diaphragm with a flint knife. Then—

A group of Coerli chieftains—grizzled, bearing the scars of age and harsh living—sat on a circle of rocks. Around them stood more of the beasts, too many to count. They were howling in blood-maddened passion. Then—

A female Corl even older than the chiefs stood in a roof-less wicker enclosure. She chanted and marked time with an athame carved from slate. Around her paraded images, ghosts of ghosts to Ilna's eyes.

Most were man-shaped black creatures like the corpses Ilna'd seen when they found Temple. In the distance, though, a nude woman poised at the edge of a pool. The black things seemed to ignore her. Then—

Coerli were devouring their prey. The band's fur was sub-tly different from the spots and striping of the first cat men the Messengers had shown her, though few other humans would've been sure of that. A beast stuck an infant's arm into his mouth and drew it out, stripping the flesh from the bones the way a man might eat a chicken wing. Then—

The Messengers hung in the center of the cavern again, pulsing at the rhythm of blood. Their voices said, BRING HER A KNIFE.

"A knife for the wizard," chorused the rat voices. There was motion in the carpet of hunched foulness. "She must have a knife, and we will bring it."

"I have a knife if I need one!" Ilna said, taking the bone-cased paring knife from her sleeve and drawing the blade. It was fine steel, worn thin but sharp enough to split hairs.

A golden sickle appeared at the entrance to the passage; it shimmered forward from hand to unseen hand. One of the creatures bent closer, depositing the blade in the cleared space around Ilna. He shrank back into the mass of his fellows. The curved blade reflected the light of the Messengers as a putrescent hue that Ilna wouldn't have thought possible from gold.

"I said I have a knife!" she repeated.

BRING HER THE SACRIFICE, the Messengers said. The light they cast clung like treacle to everything it touched. SHE WILL GAIN HER DESIRE. SHE WILL KILL ALL COERLI.

Ilna used her foot to deliberately shove the sickle back into the crowd of servitors. She looked up at the spinning pink blurs. "Why must I sacrifice to you?" she said harshly.

"She will kill them all!" mewled the servitors. "Oh, such power, power beyond any other's!"

YOU DO NOT SACRIFICE TO US, WIZARD, said the voices. THE BLOOD IS POWER. YOU STAND WHERE THE WORLDS TOUCH, SO YOU ACT THROUGH ALL WORLDS.

Ilna heard a rustle. She turned to see the gray once-men handing toward her what she first thought was a bundle of fur. It stirred in the pink light: it was a Corl, a kit no more than four or five weeks old. Its eyes were still closed. When the servitors deposited it in the cleared space, it mewled uncomfortably.

TAKE THE SACRIFICE, the Messengers said. CUT THE CORL'S THROAT. Then they repeated, THE BLOOD IS POWER.

"She will kill it," the servitors whispered exultantly. "She will drain the blood of the Coerli, every one of them!"

A gray creature pushed the kit with an arm or leg, Ilna couldn't be sure which. The little victim yowled and tried to bite.

"Get away!" Ilna said, bending forward. If the servitor

hadn't instantly flung itself back into the crowd of its fellows, she'd have slashed it open with the knife she still held.

Ilna paused, then scooped the kit up with her left hand. She expected it to snarl, but instead it writhed against the warmth of her bosom.

YOU MUST LET OUT THE BLOOD OF THE SACRIFICE, said the thunderous voices. ONLY WITH ITS DEATH CAN YOU GAIN YOUR WISH AND GO FREE.

Over the years Ilna had killed unnumbered animals—mostly doves from her own cote, but sometimes chickens bartered from other householders in the borough. Since she'd set off on her mission of wiping out the cat men, she'd killed them too, old and young; as young as this.

She'd mostly knocked the kits' brains out against rocks; their teeth were too sharp to hold by the head and snap their necks as she did with poultry. She could use the paring knife easily enough, though she'd have to hold the kit so that its blood didn't spurt on her tunics.

Ilna looked up at the Messengers. "I won't make a blood sacrifice!" she said, thrusting her knife into its case and putting it away in her sleeve. She took out a hank of yarn. "Tell me another way or I'm leaving here."

YOU MUST LET OUT THE BLOOD OF THE SACRIFICE, said the voices. YOU CAME TO US. YOU CANNOT RETURN UNTIL YOU CARRY OUT YOUR TASK.

"She must kill the Corl," the servitors cheeped. She heard laughter in the high-pitched tones. "She must comply or she will join us-s-s . . . !"

Ilna held the kit in the crook of her left elbow. Its presence was a handicap, but not a great one; she began knotting a pattern. The gray creatures had eyes. Her skill could reach them, paralyze them as she ran back up the passage that had brought her here. The passage that had returned her to Hell. . . .

She held up the pattern.

HER WEAKNESS HAS BETRAYED HER, the Messengers boomed. SHE IS YOURS.

The pink light vanished, leaving total blackness.

"She is ours!" squealed creatures as numerous as waves in a storm. Warm, probing foulness swarmed over Ilna in the dark.

"RUN FOR THE cliff!" Cashel shouted. The crabs could climb, but at least it'd slow them down a bit. Here on the shingle they were nigh as fast as a man. From the top of the corniche, he and Tenoctris could figure out what to do next. They could try to, anyway. If they let those crabs get hold of them, there wouldn't be anything left but picked bones.

Tenoctris had said something here didn't like them. That was true enough, not that he'd doubted her before.

The low cliff was less than a stone's throw away, but even though Tenoctris was young again, she wasn't much of a runner. It wasn't something ladies did as often as village girls like Sharina, Cashel supposed.

He kept behind her, which was a good thing because she tripped just short of the cliff. She'd have slammed straight into the rock if Cashel hadn't grabbed a handful of tunic right between her shoulder blades.

He yanked her back. Crab pincers carved into his heel. That hurt, which didn't matter; but they could've caught him a few fingers' breadth higher and cut his hamstring, which'd cripple him for life.

There wasn't time to talk or plan or do anything but act. One-handed—the other held his staff—Cashel straightened out his right arm fast and threw Tenoctris onto the corniche the way he'd have flung a heavy stone.

He turned, stamping on the crab that'd caught him. It was good to feel it splash his calloused foot with juices as cold as the sea it'd crawled from, but there were more crabs than he could count coming right after it. He'd raised his staff, thinking he might be able to smash the crabs as they came toward him, but they were way too close and too many.

A crab closed both pincers on his right calf, well above the ankle. More crowded close beside it. There was no time to plan. . . .

Cashel slammed a ferrule down on the crab that was holding him. He jumped upward, using his grip on the staff to lift him as he twisted his body around. If he'd had a running start, he might've been able to swing over the lip of the corniche. Flat-footed he was lucky to grab the top with his left hand. He hung there by one arm, supporting half his weight by the other balanced on the quarterstaff like it was a pillar.

Tenoctris was chanting. Cashel didn't know what she had in mind, but it was going to have to happen quick for it to do him any good. His right leg was bleeding and felt like it'd been whacked with a club. A pincer was still clamped in the muscle though the rest of the crab was mush down there on the shingle.

Crabs crawled over one another, piling up at the base of the cliff, but some were starting to climb. Cashel didn't have enough strength to lift himself over with one arm alone. He could make it if he let go of the staff, but he wasn't willing to do that and let it slip down into that mob of clicking yellow monsters.

It wasn't just that the staff was a weapon that he'd need if he managed to get up the cliff. Cashel and that length of hickory'd been in a lot of hard places together and'd gotten through to the other side. He wasn't going to leave it with the crabs.

He was starting to wobble, though. Strong as he was, he couldn't hold like this forever. He guessed if he had to he'd drop down onto the beach and smash as many crabs as he could before the rest pulled him under.

"Schaked!" shouted Tenoctris, waving the sword she used for a wand. Cashel expected a flash of wizardlight, but instead he heard the bugle of a hound that must be bigger'n he could believe.

Cashel looked over his shoulder. Around the headland came a beast with shaggy red hair and a skull longer than a man's arm. It was as big as *two* oxen. Its canines, upper and lower both, were long, but the teeth farther back in the jaws were built to shear or crush. It loped toward the mass of crabs, spraying back the shingle with its flat-clawed feet.

The crabs began to scatter toward the sea in spreading ripples. The great dog thing bugled again and was on them, lowering its long jaws to scoop them up on the run. It went through the scuttling yellow mass like a scythe through grain, slamming its slavering jaws to crush the crabs it'd caught in the moment previous. Legs, pincers, and parts of shell flew out the sides. Seabirds and surviving crabs would clean the shingle later.

The great beast wheeled, making the beach tremble. It weighed *tons*.

Cashel dropped to the ground. The only crabs near the cliff now were ones that'd been trampled in the first rush. Those still alive either twitched or tried to crawl back to the water; they weren't a danger. He couldn't get up on the corniche any better than he could've a moment before, and this big dog thing could snatch him from where he hung as easy as a man plucks a pear from a low branch.

The beast whuffled. Cashel started his quarterstaff spinning, feeling twitches in muscles that he'd worked hard at awkward angles just a moment before. The beast bugled again; it must eat carrion or else a lot of each meal stayed between its teeth to rot. It loped off in a curve along the edge of the water, sweeping up a second helping of crabs.

"It won't harm us," Tenoctris said.

Cashel took a deep breath. He brought the quarterstaff to a halt at his side, then turned and looked up.

Tenoctris smiled at him from the corniche. "If you'll help me," she went on, "I'll come down. I don't want to jump onto the rock."

"No, ma'am," Cashel said. "And I don't want you to do that."

He leaned the staff against the cliff. Tenoctris wriggled over the edge and hung by her hands; he gripped her around the waist and lowered her gently to the shingle.

Cashel felt himself blush. "I'm sorry about the way I, well, tossed you," he said, taking his staff again.

The dog thing snuffled along the sea's margin now, licking up crabs it'd crippled. It didn't seem to notice the humans. From this angle Cashel saw that its hindquarters were brindled.

"You saved our lives in the only possible fashion," Tenoctris said sharply. "I don't see that as being something you should apologize for."

She grinned. "I always knew you had a great ability to do things by art," she said. "By wizardry. And of course I knew that you were strong the way laymen judge strength. But until I had a healthy young body of my own again, I didn't really appreciate *how* strong you are, Cashel."

"Thank you, ma'am," he said, keeping his eye on the beast that Tenoctris had called to save them. He started to say something more but caught himself.

Tenoctris laughed. "And yes, we'll get on with our own business," she said. "So that you can return to Sharina. Come, the altar's not far at all."

Together they set off again for the headland. Cashel stayed between the wizard and the dog thing. It bugled again, that was all. Maybe it was saying goodbye.

SHARINA ENTERED THE pool cleanly and pulled herself deeper with paired strokes of her arms. She'd expected a shock, but the water was blood warm.

Rasile's viewpoint plunged also, apparently looking over Sharina's left shoulder but seeing farther down than eyes—man or Corl either one—should've been able to do. The water, the distorted fish which nudged close to Sharina before darting away with flips of their tails, and the distant mud shimmered with the red tinge of wizardlight.

The pool was a thousand feet deep, but Sharina was seeing the bottom through the wizard's eyes. She couldn't possibly swim down that far, but she kept stroking toward it. She expected to fail, but she wouldn't quit.

The layer of silt and decay carpeting the pool became transparent in the rosy glow. Sharina saw the tiny blind animals living in it, worms and less identifiable creatures with shells or legs or jointed feelers.

She swam downward. She didn't need to breathe as she should've done. Her spread hands drove her deeper against the resistance of something, but she no longer believed it was water.

The stones on the floor of the pool, eggs of granite that a stream had tumbled smooth in past ages, began to appear through the layer of muck. At first they lay in a scarlet shimmer. Wizardlight brightened around a single stone, a sphere of quartz the size of Sharina's fist. It was very close. It was—

Sharina's arm plunged through the mud she could no longer see and grasped the First Stone. It was cold, then hot; she *felt* her burnt flesh slough away and the bones of her hand turn black and crumble, though she could see with Rasile's eyes that she was uninjured.

She kicked against the bottom and began to swim upward with her left hand alone. The surface was a point of sunlight far above, but still she didn't need to breathe.

The sunlit circle swelled; she could see ripples, the remains of the disturbance she'd made diving in. Six distorted blacknesses were spaced around the margin of the pool, soldiers of the Last drawn by the splash. Even if they didn't see *her,* could they see the turbulence her body made in the water?

Sharina reached across her body with her left hand and drew the Pewle knife. She didn't want to take the stone in her other hand. She might drop it, or worse—she might cripple her left hand also, burn the flesh and bones away. Both her wrists would end in blackened stumps. . . .

She felt a great shock. The pool bubbled; the detritus that'd settled on the bottom over millennia swelled upward in a dark, spreading cloud. What had she done when she removed the First Stone?

She porpoised up through the surface. If there'd ever been a stone curb, the Last had removed it when they'd prepared the pool for their own purposes. Sharina braced herself on the margin with her right elbow and the butt of her knife, then swung out of the water.

The two nearest of the Last sliced at the pool. Their

swords were so keen that the edges scarcely disturbed the water. Neither struck her.

All the Last were alert now, their skin flaps folded. Sharina dodged between two who must've sensed the movement. They slashed toward each other, but their strokes cut only air. Sharina was past, and the perfectly placed blades came within a hair's breadth of each other's black flesh without touching it.

Sharina sprinted for the entrance. Her tunic lay on the ground where she'd dropped it. Her mother, Lora, would be furious with her; Lora'd never understood the concept that reality was sometimes more important than appearance. . . .

When Sharina thought of Lora, it was always at a time like this: when she or Garric was doing something necessary for Mankind which their mother wouldn't have approved of. She grinned despite the situation. *Maybe Lora was a good mother after all. She showed us what to avoid.*

The Last formed a line across the width of the fortress, standing shoulder-to-shoulder. The roiling pool wouldn't provide them with reinforcements for at least some minutes, but stolid black soldiers were returning from the siege lines through the west entrance. They must speak mentally to one another.

Sharina reached the east entrance by which she'd entered. Five of the Last stood across it, filling the space completely. Their swords were raised to slash downward.

No time to think. . . .

Sharina stabbed the warrior in the center through the eye. He convulsed, swinging his sword and shield out to the sides; his legs kicked upward like a frog's. Sharina jerked back as his neighbors struck. The line of warriors forming behind her ran toward the entrance.

Choosing her time, Sharina leaped over the thrashing body. She sprinted out of the fortress and ran full tilt toward the human lines because she didn't need to hide her presence now.

To her surprise, Attaper and a troop of Blood Eagles stood at the base of the wall; they'd climbed down by a sturdy ladder. Rasile stood on the parapet.

"There she is!" Attaper shouted. "Get around your princess, troopers!"

Sharina was seeing with her own eyes, which meant she could be seen. She didn't care about men, not for the moment, but the Last could see her.

She glanced over her shoulder, expecting to find a column of them rushing toward her. There was no artillery to support the troops who'd be pitting their flesh against swords which could cut steel.

The Last weren't following her. Something was going on in the fortress, though; a pair of distorted black bodies flew high in the air and dropped back.

A soldier swung a cloak over Sharina's shoulders and clasped it. It was a military garment and perhaps his own, but Rasile must've told him to bring it for the purpose: none of the other men were wearing them.

Sharina climbed the ladder, balancing without using her hands. She couldn't sheathe the Pewle knife until she'd wiped the purplish ichor off the blade, and she didn't have any way to carry the First Stone except in her hand. The Blood Eagles formed in front of the ladder. They only started climbing when she'd reached the parapet.

Rasile took the quartz sphere. Sharina's right hand felt as though it'd been frozen, but she could see her fingers move when she tried to wiggle them. She stepped to the side so that the Blood Eagles had room to mount the parapet; Attaper was predictably waiting on the ground until all his men were up.

"What do we do now, Rasile?" Sharina asked. She looked around for something to clean her knife on, a rag or a wad of dry grass. There was nothing in sight, and she didn't want to foul some trooper's cloak.

The wizard stepped into a bay from which the catapult had been removed. She spread her yarrow stalks into a figure on the floor of packed turf. "Now," she said, "I will deliver the First Stone to a person who's capable of using it properly, Princess. Because I certainly am not."

"Your Ladyship?" said Trooper Lires, a man who'd regularly stood beside—and in front of—Sharina in bad places.

He was offering a chammy, probably the one he'd used to bring the blackened bronze of his armor to a mirror gloss. "Use this. It'll wash out."

Sharina reached for the swatch of goat hide. Another face was reflected beside hers on the shield boss. She jerked back.

"Sharina, you must come with me now!" cried Prince Vorsan. "There're only minutes remaining for you. You've loosed the creature that the First Stone drew to it. Dear Princess, it's grown beyond anyone's control!"

"Get away from me!" Sharina shouted.

Lires had been looking puzzled, trying to find where Vorsan's voice was coming from. Shocked by Sharina's words, his jaw dropped and he straightened to attention.

"Sorry, mistress!" he mumbled. "Shouldn't have spoke, won't happen again."

"Not you, Lires, the—"

"Sister take you, Lires!" shouted Attaper as he came up the ladder. "You've got a face on your shield and it's talking!"

"Sharina, there's no time to waste. You must—"

The fortress of the Last burst outward with a deafening crash. Plates that no human agency could harm now split and buckled, breaking across rather than where seams joined the individual pentagons.

A cloud of opalescent smoke was rising from the wreckage. Sharina blinked: it wasn't smoke. It was the carapace of a crab bigger than she'd have dreamed possible.

It wasn't really a crab. Tentacles around its mouth writhed, and the single eye at the top of the headplate was larger than the pool from which she'd taken the First Stone.

The creature squirmed toward the human camp. Each pincer was the size of a trireme. One of the small ballistas remaining on this end of the siege lines snapped out its bolt. If it hit, the impact was lost in the immensity of the target.

"Sharina, you must—" cried Vorsan.

Lires spun his shield off the parapet into no-man's-land. "Guess not having that won't make much difference now," he said nonchalantly, drawing his sword. "And the talk was getting on my nerves."

"Sharina, on your life, come!" cried Vorsan from beneath the wall. The shield had landed with the mirrored boss upward. "I don't want to live through eternity without you!"

The creature came on. Sharina glanced at Rasile, who chanted in a four-pointed star and held out the First Stone. Wizardlight played about her, blue and then scarlet.

I wonder if she'll have time to finish the spell, Sharina thought.

She looked at the Pewle knife. She still hadn't wiped the blade, but it didn't matter now. *Lady, be with me. Lady, gather my soul to You when I leave this body.*

The creature lurched forward, far overtopping the parapet.

Chapter

16

THE TELCHINES STOLE the sign that takes a user to the Fulcrum," Tenoctris said, looking toward the slab of black stone which the water lapped. "They didn't dare use it themselves, of course. They just wanted to *have* it."

"Leisin of Hardloom Farm was a miser," said Cashel. It seemed a very long time ago that he'd lived in the borough and hadn't seen any city bigger than the straggle of huts making up Barca's Hamlet. "He didn't exactly steal, but he'd short your wages if he thought he could."

He'd never understood Leisin, a wealthy farmer who didn't eat any better than Cashel himself or even as well. They started with the same cheap fare—whey cheese, oats or barley, and root vegetables—but Leisin didn't have Ilna to prepare and season it with wild greens. Still yet he'd cheat a twelve-year-old orphan who'd spent three summer days resetting a drystone wall that'd collapsed in a storm.

Cashel smiled at a memory.

"Did Master Leisin amuse you?" Tenoctris asked with a guarded expression.

"No, ma'am," Cashel said, embarrassed now. He kept looking across the strait so he didn't have to meet her eyes. There was another headland about a mile distant, rising higher than it did on this side. "I was thinking that though I didn't have my full growth when I was twelve, I was still too big for Leisin to threaten whipping me if I didn't get off his farm without my pay."

"Ah," said Tenoctris. "I suspect Leisin and the Telchines would've understood each other better than you or I understand either one of them."

She glanced toward the strait again; Cashel followed her eyes. The slab rose waist-high above the surface, but they'd need to wade a furlong of water to reach it. There was no way of telling how deep it was.

The salt water'd make his cuts sting, though folks said a salt bath helped them heal quicker too. Cashel thought about the crabs and whether they'd be waiting just out from the shore. He'd know quick enough, he guessed.

"I can carry you over," he said. "It might be best if you rode my shoulders, so I'll have both hands free. If they need to be, you know."

"I'll walk, Cashel," Tenoctris said. She gave him a funny sort of smile. "I'm not an old woman anymore, you know. I won't shrink."

She turned to the sea again. "A wizard standing there can shift the worlds," she said. "Just as the Telchines said. If she's powerful enough."

She raised an eyebrow toward Cashel.

"Yes, ma'am," he said. It wasn't really a question, but it seemed she wanted him to say something. "That's why you wanted to be here, isn't it?"

"Many wizards have wanted to be here!" Tenoctris said. She sounded angry, though why at him he couldn't imagine. "For a wizard with sufficient power and the proper tools, *everything* is possible. She could rule worlds. All worlds, Cashel! Not just this one."

Cashel looked around, moving his hands a little on his quarterstaff. The water was a dirty gray and colder even than the air, which he knew from stepping through leads the tide'd left. The corniche behind them and the hills on the other side of the strait were volcanic and too raw for anything to grow on. The big dog thing that'd saved them must live on what the sea cast up, if Tenoctris hadn't brought it here from someplace else entirely.

He thought of getting out his swatch of raw wool and polishing lanolin into the pores of the hickory, but Tenoctris might think he was pushing her to get on with things. She seemed in a bad mood already.

"You'd have to want to rule things awful bad to be willing to live here," Cashel said. "I guess I'm not the one to say. Though there've been times I wished I could get sheep to show a little better sense."

"I don't think the world has much to fear from you, then, Cashel," Tenoctris said softly. She raised the alien sword and looked at it critically, then lowered its point to the ground again. She was smiling as she met Cashel's eyes again.

"We'll cross to the Fulcrum now," she said. "And I think I'll have you carry me after all. In the crook of your arm. There's no danger in the water, I assure you."

"Yes, ma'am," Cashel said, making a seat of his left arm. She reached around his neck and he gripped the inside of her knee so she didn't roll off.

He splashed in. The water was cold, sure, but nothing that'd be a problem for a short hike. It didn't come up to the middle of his calves. The only problem was he had to walk slower than he'd have liked to because otherwise he'd be splashing onto Tenoctris' legs.

Cashel grinned. He was used to following sheep, so walking slow wasn't a new thing either. He strode on.

GARRIC STEPPED ONTO the high tor. Shin's altar must be the cube of quartz beside the opening that gave down into the cavern. The broken rocks of the ridgeline were beige and russet, and the dry grass in cracks between them had a sere absence of color. The sun was setting in the west, and on the southern horizon the strange white star gleamed like a demon's eye.

The wyvern looked out from the edge of the cliff fifty feet away, peering into the wind that roared up the rock face. From Garric's viewpoint it looked like a gigantic bird of prey. Its tail was rigid, trembling up and down to adjust the creature's balance. Its hide was the color of sullen flames.

The altar was nearly as tall as Garric and apparently equal in all dimensions. From a distance he'd have said it *had* to be artificial, but with the cube in reach he couldn't see any seam between its milky presence and the sandstone it rested on.

Garric started to his left, keeping his distance from the wyvern. It must've heard him, though, because it spun around and for a moment reared upright, spreading its stubby wings to make itself look bulkier. It glared, then stretched its long neck toward Garric and screamed. Its tongue was black, and its teeth were the color of old ivory.

"It doesn't really need wings to look big," Carus said calmly. *"It's the size of a thirty-oared ship already. Well, nearly."*

They were eye-to-eye with the wyvern. In turning it'd halved the distance between them. Garric kept his sword slanted across his body. His dagger was low and out to his left, ready to strike upward.

The wyvern's body lowered as its legs contracted to spring. Garric continued to circle slowly. He was just as tense as the monster, but his feet glided like snakes. His smile mirrored that of the warrior-ghost in his mind.

Kore stepped up from the staircase. Garric'd been wondering if the ogre'd thought better of her offer to fight the wyvern with him, but she'd simply waited to make her entrance when it'd most disrupt the creature's timing.

The wyvern screamed, angry this time instead of threatening; the second opponent had confused its small brain. It hopped sideways along the edge of the cliff; despite its size, it was as agile as a robin.

The ridge shook when the clawed feet landed. Sunset deepened the creature's natural color into that of drying blood.

The ogre slouched to the right, slanting minusculely toward the wyvern the way Garric did from the other side. The beast jerked its head from one to another. It had the narrow face and forward-focused eyes of a predator; with its opponents so close, it couldn't keep them both in its field of view.

"He's not used to being hunted," Kore said with a laugh. "The change'll be good for him."

Shin came up from the cavern and mounted the altar. He moved almost tentatively instead of calling attention to himself with acrobatics.

"Not if things go as I intend," said Garric. He moved closer to the wyvern. If he and the ogre separated too far, the wyvern would leap on one before the other could intervene.

The aegipan raised both hands as if pointing to the sky and began to chant. Wizardlight rippled between his index fingers.

Kore laughed again, then hunched. The wyvern lunged at her, pivoting on its left foot. Its splayed claws gouged the sandstone surface, scattering grit and pebbles.

Kore leaped twenty feet backward from a flat-footed stance. Garric drove in, thrusting into the side of the wyvern's knee. He missed the cartilage because the leg was flexing, but the sword's impossibly keen point ripped into the thighbone.

The beast screamed and whirled on Garric. Instead of dodging back, he slashed across its beak. It lifted its head out of range, spraying blood from where the cut had reached the quick.

The wyvern sprang at Garric, leading with its right foot. He dived to the side. The beast twisted in the air to follow him, but Kore seized its stiff tail in the air. The ogre's weight snapped the tail around, and the wyvern crashed down on its left hip.

Garric got up. The creature buffeted him against the rock with its wing. The pinion was stubby in comparison to the long body, but it was still a ten-foot club of bone and cartilage.

Garric blinked. He'd almost stabbed himself with his dagger when he fell. Had it not been for Carus' reflexes, he'd be bleeding like a stuck pig and dead within minutes even if the wyvern didn't bother to finish him off.

A line of wizardlight sizzled from horizon to horizon, supported on Shin's raised index fingers. Though the sun had almost set, the blue glare lit the ridge as clearly as noonday.

The wyvern lashed its tail, trying to batter Kore loose. The ogre didn't let go at first, but the second stroke flung her to the edge of the cliff. The wyvern lurched to its feet.

If Garric'd been in better shape, he'd have doubled his legs under him and sprung up immediately. Instead he rolled onto all fours, then rose to one knee. The wyvern shrieked and stamped to crush Garric like an olive in the press. Garric thrust into the descending foot, driving half his long blade up into the ankle bones.

The wyvern's claws clenched reflexively, contracting on edges sharp as sunlight. The creature gave a great cry and sprang upward, pulling itself off the sword.

Garric staggered upright and backed away. He was seeing double and he'd lost the dagger, Duzi knew where. It might be sticking in him for all he knew. He didn't think his left shoulder and ribs could hurt more if there *was* a long knife buried in them.

"Frog-brain!" Kore shouted. She waggled her arms out to the side, palms-backward. "Pimple-brain!"

The wyvern turned and pecked down, using its hooked beak like an assassin's dagger. Kore slammed both sides of the birdlike head with the chunks of sandstone she'd concealed in her huge hands.

The wyvern stumbled. Garric minced two steps to put himself in position, then thrust at the right knee again. This time he got home in the joint.

The wyvern tried gracelessly to snap at Garric; Kore hurled the stone in her right hand, bouncing it off the back of the creature's skull. The wyvern tottered.

Garric advanced and thrust again, aiming this time for the left knee. He missed because the wyvern stepped back.

As it put its the weight onto its right leg, the knee buckled. The creature gave a despairing cry and toppled sideways. The ogre stepped out of the way and fell also; a claw had torn deeply into her left leg.

The wyvern crashed onto the sandstone, rolled, and rolled over the edge of the cliff. Garric could hear it screaming in frustrated rage for what seemed an impossibly long time.

The ground trembled when the wyvern struck an outcrop partway down, then trembled again when it hit near the base and was thrown well outward. The third impact was on the track at the bottom of the valley.

Garric sank to one knee again; it took less energy than remaining upright did.

Shin stood like a furry statue on top of his altar. The line of light he balanced had grown to a tube in which a man could stand upright. Astride the horizon at either end was a colossal figure. To the north was an ancient Corl female holding a glowing ball of quartz. To the south stood a young woman who reached toward the ball.

The woman's features were hauntingly similar to those of Tenoctris.

THE CREATURES CRUSHING Ilna down wailed like a fetid wind. The weight came off her. As it did, clear white light flooded the chamber.

She staggered to her feet, squinting against the dazzling brilliance and her tears of rage. The kit wriggled deeper into the crook of her arm. She saw blurred figures approaching and tried to spread the pattern she'd knotted for defense.

Karpos closed his big hand over the fabric before Ilna could stretch it to life. "Mistress, it's all right," he said. "We're here. We'll get you out."

"What are those things?" Asion said in obvious disgust. "They're filthy as possums, by the *Lady,* they are!"

"Temple'll get us out, I mean," Karpos added. "Say, is that one of the cat things you got there?"

"They would've made me one of them," Ilna said.

She opened her eyes; when they were closed, she thought of the future she'd just avoided. The light was that of noon on a sunny day, bright but not unusually so. It was only by contrast to the pink dimness that it'd been so shocking.

Ilna put her yarn away, then tucked the loose fabric of her sleeve over the little cat beast, not so much for warmth as to protect it from the hunters' eyes. She said, "Don't worry about the kitten. It'll be all right."

The light came from Temple's shield. He'd slung it on his left shoulder, so its brilliance blurred from the walls of the cavern instead of blazing directly on Ilna and the hunters. Even when reflected from colored sandstone it kept its white purity.

"How do you do that?" Ilna blurted. "And how did you get here?"

Temple smiled. "I think we'd best leave now," he said. "Since I don't think there's any reason to stay, is there?"

"No," said Ilna, suppressing a shudder. "Nothing's keeping us here."

Temple gestured her toward the passage back to the surface. "I'll follow the rest of you," he said. "That'll be best."

Two of the servitors lay on the stone floor, ripped by Asion's knife. The clean light shrank their bodies to twists of gray rags, and it'd driven the remainder of the creatures into the depths of the cave. Asion wouldn't have needed to strike any of them, but Ilna well understood why he'd chosen to.

She forced herself to look at the Messengers. All she could see was a shimmer in the bright air. They'd cursed her to an eternity of foul oblivion; where had their power gone now?

Ilna turned. "Thank you for rescuing me, Temple," she said. "I should've said that sooner. Thank you all."

"It was a pleasure," said Temple. He smiled. "It was something that should've been done a long while ago. But now . . . ?"

"Yes," said Ilna, striding toward the passage.

"I'll lead," said Asion, uncoiling the strap of his sling.

"I'd like both of you to go ahead, if you will," said Ilna. "I have some business to discuss with Master Temple."

"Yes, mistress," said Karpos meekly. He joined his partner so they entered the passage together. Despite shadows, the shield on Temple's shoulder lighted the way as brightly as it'd been when Ilna came down this way.

"I never thought I'd get out," she whispered. "I thought I was in Hell. Forever."

The kit mewed and rubbed against Ilna's arm. Temple said, "We wouldn't have left you here, Ilna."

He was walking beside her, his right shoulder to her left. She turned and said quietly, "How were you able to come? I'd blocked the mouth of the cave."

When Ilna'd blurted similar words on first seeing her rescuers, they'd been more an accusation than a real question: How *dare* you come here when I forbade it? It embarrassed her to remember that, but her memory was very good. She had many things to recall painfully in the dark hours before dawn, so one more wasn't a great additional burden.

Temple reached under his sash and took out a skein of cords. Ilna knew that if she spread it instead of simply picking out the knots, she'd find the pattern she'd left to close the passage.

"Would this have stopped you?" Temple said.

She frowned. "No, of course not," she said.

"Nor did it stop me," Temple said in the same mild tone as before. He handed the skein, twisted and harmless, to Ilna. Their eyes met as she took it from him.

Temple looked away, up the passage to the hunters several double paces ahead of them. Softly he said, "In a very distant . . . world, let us say, there were humans and Coerli, as there are in the Land. They'd fought and killed each other for generations."

He turned slightly and met Ilna's eyes. "Go on," she said.

The kit kicked away the sleeve that covered it. She touched it with her right hand to calm it. She wondered if it'd been weaned. Probably not.

"A man was born," said Temple to the passage ahead. "The greatest warrior of his time, perhaps of all time. This man decided that the fighting should stop, that humans and Coerli should live together in peace."

"Did anyone listen to him?" Ilna said. She too faced straight ahead. "I shouldn't expect that they would."

"Only a few did at first," said Temple. "But he was a great warrior. He fought those who opposed him and crushed them, killed them often enough. Men and Coerli both. In the end, he had his peace, and his world had peace."

Temple looked at her. "He wasn't a saint, Ilna," he said, his words taking on a harsh burr. "He was nothing like a saint. But he brought peace to his world."

Ilna licked her lips. They and her mouth were dry as lint. "I know a man like that," she said.

"I thought you might," Temple said with a smile. "And perhaps the same thing will happen to him as happened to the warrior I'm speaking of. After he died, people—both humans and Coerli; they thought of each other as people now—put statues to him in their temples. They forgot he'd been a man, a very terrible man when he needed to be. He became a sungod, with a priesthood to tell later ages about how he'd brought the light of peace to the world."

Ilna could see the cave entrance close ahead of them, past the shoulders of the two hunters. "And then?" she asked.

"The Change sewed many times and places into a patchwork," Temple said, still smiling. "Among them was a sacred pool from the warrior's world. When the Last came there, the priests fought them. They prevented more of the creatures from arriving."

Temple grimaced. "They were priests, not warriors," he said harshly. "They didn't have weapons or the skill to use weapons, but they had courage; which in the end was enough."

He looked at her. "They prayed to their God, Ilna," he said. "Not for themselves, but for this Land to which they had been brought to die."

"Let me tell you!" said Asion cheerfully. "I *am* glad to see the open sky again. I surely am!"

"We all are, my friend," Temple said. He gestured Ilna ahead of him, stepped through the narrow entrance himself, and turned.

He gestured. The ridge snapped and shuddered. Dust blew out of the crack in the rock; then the jambs of the entrance smashed together. The whole trembled again as it settled into silence.

"What about the Messengers?" Ilna said.

Temple shrugged. "They remain," he said. "They'll remain for all eternity. But though I'm sure men will find a way to reach their vault again, I don't think that will happen soon."

"Ah, Temple?" said Asion. "What do we do now?"

"I thought that for the time being you might want to stay with Ilna," Temple said with a smile. "And Ilna? I thought you might want to go home. Return to the friends you left after the Change."

Ilna looked at him without expression. The kit mewled and tried to nuzzle her breast. That wasn't going to do any good, but there'd be a milch goat or even a wet nurse in Valles or wherever Garric was.

"Yes," Ilna said. "I'd like that."

Smiling like the statue of a God, Temple raised his arms toward the sun.

"ALL RIGHT, HERE you go," Cashel said, standing beside the black slab. He lifted Tenoctris with his left palm; his right hand, clenched on the quarterstaff, gave her shoulder something to lean back on. "I can't put you up on your feet, though."

Saying that reminded him of the way he'd tossed her onto the corniche. He felt embarrassed all over again, though at the time, well . . . as she'd said herself, he didn't see there being any choice.

"I can stand, thank you," Tenoctris said. She swung lithely upright and walked to the center of the block, her wooden soles clacking.

Running his fingers over the Fulcrum made Cashel wonder what it really was. He'd thought rock when he saw it from the shore, but it had the chill of metal to the touch. It was as smooth as the blade of an axe, and even the color was wrong. He didn't have Ilna's eye for that sort of thing, but he could see the black was too pure to be natural.

Well, that was a question for some other time. Cashel thrust the staff into the sea and wriggled it, making sure it was butted firmly in the bottom. With the hickory for a brace, he took a tall step onto the slab himself. Though he wasn't going to slip, he'd still rather've been back in the cold salt water than walking on this slick surface.

"What would you like me to do, Tenoctris?" he asked.

She'd been looking over the slab carefully, the way Cashel'd check the grain of wood before shaping it into something. Whatever it was made of, it was not only polished but perfectly round.

"I won't need to scribe a figure after all," Tenoctris said. "If I could, even with this—" she waggled the sword "—which I'm rather inclined to doubt, now that I'm here."

Tenoctris drew back her arm and flung the sword into the sea. "There," she said. "I've never liked to use athames. There's an implied threat in them, though they're effective in their way. Do you understand what I mean, Cashel?"

"I think so, ma'am," he said. "But it makes no matter. There's a lot of things I *don't* understand, but it all works out anyway."

She gave him a cold smile. "Simply remain close, then," she said. "That helps more than you may realize. And one more thing?"

"Ma'am?"

"I gave you my locket to hold," Tenoctris said. She held

out her right hand. "I need it back now. I must be whole to accomplish this task."

"Oh," said Cashel. "Right, it'll take me a moment."

He leaned the quarterstaff into the crook of his elbow so he had both hands to work with. The iron cap was likely to skid on the slab, so he held it between the toes of his right foot.

"Are you just going to give me the locket?" Tenoctris said, her voice sharp and rising.

"Yes, ma'am," Cashel said, concentrating on what he was doing. He had to be careful or he'd pull the thin chain in half. "Here you go."

He held out the locket and chain in the palm of his hand instead of dropping it into hers. That'd let her use both hands to put it on without snagging her hair.

"Cashel, I have a demon inside me!" Tenoctris said. "Didn't you wonder where my new power came from? With this locket in my possession, there'll be nothing and no one who can control me!"

"But you'll control yourself," Cashel said. He felt silly holding the locket and her not taking it. She'd even lowered her hand so he couldn't just drop it in her palm after all.

He cleared his throat uncomfortably. "Tenoctris," he said, "I saw the demon. He didn't want to try conclusions with me, and I don't guess he got very far with you either. At any rate, you're still Tenoctris. So here's your locket back, if you need it."

Tenoctris took the locket. "You were a very good shepherd, weren't you, Cashel?" she said.

He smiled. "Yes, ma'am," he said. "And I hope I still am."

He took the wool out and wiped his staff, especially the part he'd stuck into the salt water. He hoped he'd be using it for many years to come; and if he wasn't, well, at least at the end he wouldn't have to be ashamed that he hadn't taken care of his tools.

Tenoctris starting chanting words of power. A disk of wizardlight flickered between her upraised arms and began to extend into a tube.

Cashel put away his wool and watched his friend. He just stood where he was, smiling faintly with his feet braced. To anyone looking at him, he was as solid as the Fulcrum of Worlds itself.

"ALL RIGHT," LORD Attaper said. He sounded irritated and a little bored, but certainly not frightened of the behemoth crawling toward them. "Captain Ascor, get Her Highness out of here fast. Get her back to Valles, I think. I'm afraid you'll have to improvise on logistics."

"No," said Sharina. She nodded to the Corl wizard. "I need to stay with Rasile."

The ground shook as the creature lurched toward the siege lines. Four paddle-like legs drove it, so it as much swam as walked. *It's certainly not a crab,* the back of Sharina's mind noted. Her mouth smiled at the way people think about trivia when they have only moments to live.

"Ascor, I said—" Attaper roared, blasting his anger out at his subordinate because he couldn't, even now, shout at the Princess Sharina.

Sharina stepped between the men, facing the guard commander at inches distance. She was tall for a woman, tall enough to meet his eyes or nearly so.

"Attaper," she snapped, "the world will live or die because of what that wizard—"

She pointed toward Rasile without turning her head.

"—is able to do right now. If she needs help with her art—with her *wizardry,* Attaper—are you going to understand what she's asking for?"

Attaper edged backward. His expression had gone from furious to neutral; when his eyes flicked to follow Sharina's gesture, he frowned in concern. A few of the Blood Eagles were comfortable around wizardry, but their commander wasn't among them.

"Right," said Sharina, turning away. "You do your job, milord, and leave me to mine."

And the crab would do its job or anyway take its pleasure,

and then Sharina wouldn't have to worry about the problems of ruling the kingdom or much of anything else. She stood with one hand on the wicker battlement, facing Rasile. If the wizard *did* unexpectedly request something, Sharina'd be ready to supply it.

Rasile held the First Stone out at arm's length as she wailed her chant. A faint azure circle began to sparkle in front of her. Sharina had the feeling of depth and distance, but the incantation was obviously far from complete.

Removing the talisman had freed the creature. She wondered if it was following the stone. There was no one to ask save Rasile, who'd shortly be as much beyond answering as Sharina herself would be beyond asking the question.

The monster hunched thunderously closer. It could've ripped the siege works apart with its pincers; that it didn't was likely out of contempt for them as a barrier. Sharina glanced up at it coldly, showing the soldiers nearby that she wasn't afraid to face the thing.

She *was* afraid. It was like looking at an avalanche sweeping everything before it. But she was Princess Sharina of Haft, standing with men who'd repeatedly put their lives on the line, literally, for the kingdom they served. She served it also.

"Sharina, I can still save you!" cried the face from the gleaming shield on the ground.

Sharina looked down and said, "Vorsan, if you deserved the title 'Prince,' you'd have saved your own world or died with it!" Like Attaper, she was venting her anger and fear on someone it was safe to attack. "Now, leave me to my duties!"

Rasile stood at one end of a tube that spanned more than merely space. At the unimaginably distant other end hulked a gigantic figure, shadowy but sharpening as the wizard chanted. The blue wizardlight joining the termini sparkled brighter with each syllable.

"I can't live if you die," Vorsan said, but Sharina wasn't looking at him anymore. It looked as though the rock of Pandah itself were crawling toward them. The monster's single glittering eye swept the world from horizon to horizon. It was too high to hit with even a catapult stone.

Attaper shouted, "Loose!" The volley of javelins his troops arced out was as harmless as a spray of rain. For the most part, the missiles glanced off the thick headshield; the few which stuck wobbled like whiskers on a giant's chin.

Each time Sharina looked from the monster to Rasile or the reverse, she felt disoriented. The tube which the wizard held didn't lead in any direction of the world where Sharina stood in the shadow of a creature bigger than anything alive could become.

The figure holding the other end of the tube was equally out of scale with present reality. It grew clearer as the wizardlight brightened. It was human, was a woman—

By the Lady, that's Tenoctris since she made herself young!

The monster's paddle legs tensed, preparing to lift the massive body onto the siege works and beyond. Nearby, soldiers held their swords ready; they'd thrown their javelins.

A small ballista cracked; its crew had reloaded it in time to snap out a final bolt, which drove to its wooden fletching in the headshield. That was a testament to courage and professionalism in the face of certain disaster.

"I'll save you, Sharina," Vorsan called from the fringes of Sharina's consciousness. Then—

Everything turned amber, as though she were viewing the world through a sheet of thin tortoiseshell. The crab thing shrank—

But it didn't. The shield Lires had thrown off the parapet was the size of the sky. An iris opened in its face. The monster flowed into it the way salt vanishes into water.

Soldiers were shouting in amazement and fear, though they'd been stolid in the face of oncoming death. The monster was gone. Remaining was the broad track its advance had carved from where the fortress of the Last had been.

Sharina looked down. The shield lay as it'd fallen, gleaming in the bright sunlight.

"Maybe he's . . . ," she whispered, but she didn't finish the foolish comment. The antediluvian prince *wasn't* all right, couldn't possibly be all right. Even now she couldn't pretend she liked Vorsan, but he'd given her reason to respect him.

"Lady, take unto You the soul of Vorsan, who sacrificed himself for others. Nonnus, be a brother to one who died for me as you died for me."

Rasile's long muzzle worked as she shouted the final words of her incantation, but a hush had fallen over the scene. Neither the wizard nor the troops could break it.

The tube of light became a pulsing sapphire bar, so intense it was almost opaque. Rasile thrust the First Stone into it, while the colossal figure of Tenoctris reached from the other end. Their hands met at the midpoint.

There was a thunderclap. The tube vanished. The Corl wizard staggered forward and would've fallen if Sharina hadn't caught her.

It was midday on the plain outside Pandah, from whose walls men and Coerli stared down in wonder. Nothing remained of the Last who'd been attacking the city, save body parts at the edge of the pit from which the crab thing had emerged.

On the surrounding horizon, scarlet wizardlight trembled.

TENOCTRIS STOOD LIKE a statue, her upraised arms touching a tube of wizardlight as dark as the depths of the sea. Instead of the sparkles and flashes Cashel expected from wizardry, this blaze was dense, almost solid.

Part of him thought he ought to look outward in case something crept up on them, but there hadn't been anything that way since the crabs scrambled back into the water. Even if they returned, they couldn't climb up the slab's slick wall.

Cashel watched Tenoctris instead. What *she* was doing was dangerous and no mistake. He didn't pretend he'd be able to help much if things went wrong, but he'd try.

"Astraelelos!" Tenoctris shouted. *"Chraeleos!"*

At each syllable, the little wave tops flattened in a circle expanding away from the Fulcrum. Tenoctris hadn't grown but she seemed larger; like a mountain, even.

An ancient Corl female stood like a mirror image of Tenoctris at the other end of the tube. She was chanting too, but in her right hand was a ball of crystal with red pulsing fire at its heart.

Tenoctris shouted again, but there was only silence in Cashel's world. The cat woman held the crystal and Tenoctris reached to take it. Their hands met.

Red, roaring wizardlight absorbed the world and expanded. Cashel stood with Tenoctris. Together they looked into the heart of the cosmos.

The wizard's face was calm as a God's. With her left hand cupping the blazing crystal, she pointed her right toward a star. Its white light turned scarlet and swelled from a speck to a shimmering ball.

For a moment the Last continued to crawl across the world on which Cashel had lived. He saw everything. Lines of fierce black figures marched from the icy crater where they'd arrived in the Land.

The light of the red star fell on them and they burned, igniting forests and plains. Those who'd been crossing deserts melted sand into glass as they dissolved. The lens of ice where the Last stood shoulder-to-shoulder exploded in steam as violent as a new eruption from the volcano's cold heart.

Tenoctris lowered her hand. The red star burst, then vanished like smoke in a gale.

She turned and looked at Cashel, smiling faintly. She held the crystal out in her left hand. *Is she asking me to take it?*

"No, Tenoctris," he said, but he couldn't hear the words even in his own head.

Still smiling, Tenoctris pointed her right index finger toward the crystal. It *twisted,* shrank, and was gone.

The scarlet light disappeared with the crystal. Tenoctris fell forward. Cashel caught her and lowered her carefully. Rather than lay her head on the polished black slab, he sat also and pillowed it against his left thigh. A gull high overhead called.

There was a breeze from the west. Cashel wondered if it'd

been there all the time but he hadn't noticed it before. There'd been a lot going on.

"I couldn't trust myself with the First Stone," Tenoctris whispered. She opened her eyes, but just a little bit. "I couldn't trust anybody but you, Cashel. And you didn't want it."

She must mean the crystal. "Well, I don't need it, Tenoctris," he said. "Are you comfortable here? I could take you ashore."

Tenoctris laughed. "No, I suppose you don't," she said. "And after I rest a little while, I'll take us back home. Back to Sharina."

Cashel beamed. "That'll be nice," he said.

The gull called again. Funny. Even the bird's cry sounded cheerful to Cashel just now.

Epilogue

THE PRIEST NIVERS rose from a couch of green velvet so old that the pile was worn to the ground in many patches. "They're returning!" he shouted in a cracked voice.

"If you're planning to invite somebody to dinner, Nivers," said Salmson, "then they'd better like turnips. The rats got at the last of the ham, but it was going bad anyway."

Salmson was officially an under-priest of Franca, the Sky God; in fact he was Nivers' steward. He'd entered with a carafe of watered wine when he heard Nivers awakening from his prophetic trance. Those two and an old cook who mumbled to herself in the dialect of the hinterlands were the only residents of the priestly mansion attached to the Temple of Franca.

"No, you fool!" Nivers cried. "Franca and His Siblings are returning! There'll be blood running on the altars for Them to drink, and the finest delicacies for me!"

He stumbled on the sash of his robe; it'd become untied while he sent his soul in quest of a future better than this ruined present. He went through the ritual at every new moon, but never till now had his dreams reached a destination.

"Come!" Nivers said, hiking up his garments. "Help me find my sandals. The good ones, mind! I have to see the emperor. Palomir will be great again!"

"And pigs will fly," Salmson muttered, but he set the carafe on a stone-topped table and followed his master down the corridor to the suite they lived in. This hadn't been one of Nivers' ordinary dreams fueled by sniffs of lotus pollen. Those fantasies didn't last as long as it took the priest to get up from his couch.

Arched windows here on the third story looked out on the city of Palomir, set like a jewel against the dark mass of surrounding jungle. Light glittered from thousands of spires and peaks. Because the sun was so near the horizon, shadows and refractions concealed much of the ruin of the glass towers.

But just perhaps . . . , thought Salmson. A rat ran down the corridor ahead of him.

GARRIC STEPPED FROM a sunlit mountaintop into the shade of the tarpaulin covering the regent, Princess Sharina, and her council. The camp was behind very impressive field fortifications, but he didn't have the faintest idea *where* it was.

"That's Pandah, but it was an island in my day," said Carus, whose eye for terrain was unmatched in Garric's experience. The ghost's image frowned. *"In yours too."*

"Prince Garric, you've returned!" Lord Tadai said enthusiastically. He was seated across the council table, two doors resting on trestles and covered with baize, so he saw Garric appear.

"I'll bet he thinks you just walked into the tent, though," said Carus, grimly uncomfortable with wizardry even now.

"Garric!" Sharina said, whirling and jostling the table as she tried to get up.

Liane simply kicked her stool over and threw herself into Garric's arms. She wouldn't have done that if she hadn't been very much afraid. . . .

"And she had reason," Carus said. *"Though it worked out pretty well. There's not much a good sword can't take care of when a man swings it."*

Spoken like a common trooper, Garric thought, but he was too happy to be tart. Carus was being ironic, after all. He *did* feel that way—but he knew he'd brought his kingdom down when he'd behaved that way as king.

They were all babbling greetings and congratulations. Garric let it go on for a time because he was drained by the sudden relief from stress. Holding Liane was all he wanted to do, and letting other people talk permitted him to do that.

But I've got a kingdom to run. . . .

Garric gave Liane a final squeeze and broke away. She righted the stool and seated herself primly. Sharina offered a chair—made here in the camp from stakes and wicker like the fascines, though covered with red baize—but Garric didn't want to sit just yet.

"You've marched to Pandah to put down the renegades?" he said, remembering the reports about the island from before he went off with Shin. He hoped he'd kept disapproval out of his tone, but this wouldn't have been the way *he'd* have used such a large proportion of the kingdom's resources.

"To put down a bridgehead of the Last, Your Highness," Lord Waldron said, forcefully enough to show that he'd understood the implied criticism. "We were meeting on how to deal with Pandah itself now that Princess Sharina has destroyed the Last."

"Rasile destroyed the Last," said Sharina. There was something odd in the way she said it, though. Garric didn't know who Rasile was, but he was sure he'd learn soon enough.

"And Tenoctris," said Cashel from beside Garric. "She just brought us back."

Garric turned *fast*. His ancestor's reflex took his hand to his sword, though he didn't draw the blade. His friend stood with a pert young woman whom Garric didn't recognize.

This time it was Sharina knocking her chair over as she leaped up to hug Cashel. Garric moved aside, smiling and glad something'd happened to take folks' minds off the way he'd gone for a weapon when his best friend appeared.

"My way you can apologize if you're wrong," Carus said, this time in dead earnest. *"If something takes your head off because you thought it was harmless, you don't get a second chance."*

"Garric was as responsible for success as any of us," said the woman who'd arrived with Cashel. When he heard the voice, Garric recognized Tenoctris—but *much* younger. "The kingdom's very fortunate in its ruler."

"Your Highness," said Admiral Zettin. "I was just pointing out that we have an opportunity to make an example of Pandah by hanging everyone we find there."

Despite Zettin's brashness he must've seen something in Garric's expression, because he quickly added, "Or all the males, of course, pirates and Coerli both."

"Milord," said Garric. Since Carus took residence in his mind, he'd learned that he didn't have to raise his voice to make it clear when he was angry. "I think we'll make a different sort of example of Pandah. We'll spare everybody, but we'll distribute the males among existing regiments with orders to the non-coms to watch them. And we'll hang the ones who don't take the warning."

"We'll hang a great many of them, I shouldn't wonder," Lord Waldron said, but he wasn't arguing with the plan. He smiled as he glanced at Zettin, a protégé of Attaper's and no friend of the army commander.

"I shouldn't wonder either, milord," said Garric, "but it's important to give them a chance. You have Coerli units with you?"

"We've got cat men," Waldron said, frowning. "I wouldn't call them units, but it seems to work all right for them to swan about in little mobs. They're under the sailor, there."

He jerked his chin in the direction of Zettin.

"Milord?" prodded Garric, because the admiral clearly wasn't going to speak—again—without being asked to.

"Your Highness, the Coerli make excellent scouts and foragers, especially at night," Zettin said, looking at some point beyond Garric's right shoulder. "Their discipline is improving rapidly since we started attaching petty officers, lead oarsmen or the like, to each, ah, war band."

"Not a stupid man," Carus said with a chuckle. *"For all he gets above himself."*

Garric smiled. He stretched, though not as high as he'd like to've done because there wasn't enough room under the tarpaulin.

"Very good, then," he said. "Unless there's something critical for my eyes . . . ?"

No one spoke, though several councillors might've done so if he hadn't stepped on Lord Zettin so thoroughly. "Lady Liane, do you have anything?"

"Nothing vital, Your Highness," the kingdom's spy master said politely. "Our surveyors have reported an Empire of Palomir to the south."

Garric frowned. "Palomir that the Scribe of Breen talks about?" he said, trying to recall just what he'd read in the chronicler from Cordin after the fall of the Old Kingdom. The—nameless—scribe had mixed real millennia-old information with a great deal of myth.

"Yes, I think so," said Liane, pleased that he'd caught the reference. "Palomir appears to be little more than a name in its present form, though. It can wait."

"Then, honored councillors," said Garric, smiling around the group, "I'll retire to my quarters. I'm sure you've all been busy, but I don't mind telling you that I'm about at the end of my resources right now."

A thought struck him. "Ah," he said. "Do I have quarters? I know you weren't expecting—"

"Yes, of course," said Liane, rising gracefully this time. "If I may, I'll guide Your Highness."

Garric bowed and stepped out of the shelter. Blood Eagles fell in around him as smoothly as if they'd escorted him to the meeting.

Coming toward Garric with a pair of hard-looking men was a trim woman he'd been afraid he'd never see again. "Ilna!" he called in delight.

Of all things, Ilna was carrying a mewling Corl kitten in her arms.

THOUGH THE LAST had long been reduced to sparkling coruscance, water continued to boil from the mountain crater. There was a sulfurous tang in the air: the volcano had awakened. Figures slowly melted from the ice which had encased them for uncounted ages.

The giant on the left shook out his long golden hair,

laughed, and drew his sword. He was a beardless youth in all but size, lithe and heart-stoppingly handsome. His eyes were as cold as a viper's.

The female on the right could've been his sister, save that her hair was a deep blue-black and she held a trident. Her laughter echoed the youth's; her voice had the timbre of a hunting cat's.

The figure in the center roused last. He wore a horned helmet, and his white beard spread over a scaled cuirass. He opened his gray eyes and paused for long moments before he raised his double-bitted axe.

"We are free!" he shouted. Thunder echoed the words.

The giant forms swelled and vanished into the storm clouds which rushed from all directions to fill the sky. "We are free!"

The Gods of Palomir had returned.

Turn the page for a preview of

The Gods Return

THE THIRD VOLUME OF
The Crown of the Isles

DAVID DRAKE

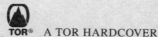

Available now from Tor Books

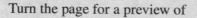

TOR® A TOR HARDCOVER

ISBN-13: 978-0-7653-1261-1   ISBN-10: 0-7653-1261-7

Chapter

1

CASHEL CARRIED RASILE in the crook of his arm up the last few tens of steps to the top of the fire tower, the highest point in Pandah. The old wizard's people, the Coerli—the cat men—held the physically weak and aged in contempt even if they happened to be wizards.

Since the Change, Rasile had been helping the humans who'd conquered the Coerli; her life and health had improved a great deal. Still, the fire tower was a hollow pillar with many tens of steps shaped like wedges of pie on the inside. Lots of younger people, cat men and humans both, would've had trouble climbing it.

Cashel didn't mind. Rasile scarcely weighed anything to begin with, and besides, it made him feel useful.

Cashel's friends were all smart and educated. Nobody'd thought that Garric would get to be king while he and Cashel were growing up together in Barca's Hamlet, but he'd gotten as good an education from his father, Reise the Innkeeper, as any nobleman's son in Valles got. Likewise Garric's sister Sharina.

Cashel smiled at the thought of Sharina. She was *so* smart and *so* lovely. If there was wizardry in the world—and there was; Cashel had seen it often—then the greatest proof of it was the fact that Sharina loved him, as he'd loved her from childhood.

Cashel's sister Ilna couldn't read or write any better than he could, and like Cashel she used pebbles or beans as tellers if she needed to count above the number of her fingers. But there was more to being smart than book learning, and nobody had *ever* doubted that Ilna was smart. She'd been the best weaver in Barca's Hamlet since she'd grown tall enough to work a loom, and the things she'd learned on her travels had made her better than any other soul.

None of that had made her happy. Her travels had been to far places, some of them very bad places. She'd come back maybe missing parts that would've let her be happy. Still, Ilna was much of the reason that the kingdom had survived these past years; why the kingdom survived and, in surviving, had allowed Mankind to survive.

Cashel, well, he was just Cashel. He'd been a good shepherd, but nobody needed him to tend sheep anymore. He was strong, though; stronger than any man he'd met this far. If he could use that strength to help people like Rasile who the kingdom depended on, then he was glad to have something to do.

"I'm setting you down," he said, just as he'd have done if he'd been carrying a bogged sheep up to drier ground. The sheep couldn't understand him and the Corl wizard didn't need to be told. Still, a few calm words and a little explanation never hurt. "It's supposed to be the highest place in Pandah and—"

He looked around. The top of the tower flared a little, but it was still only two double-paces in diameter.

"—I guess the folks who said that were right."

Rasile stepped to the railing. From a distance the cat men didn't look much different from humans, but close up you saw that their hands and feet didn't use the same bones. As for their faces, well, they were cats. Rasile was covered with light gray fur which had a nice sheen since she'd started eating properly again.

Cashel grinned. If Rasile was a ewe, he'd have said she was healthy. Of course back in the borough she'd have been butchered years ago; there was only fodder enough to get the best and strongest through the winter before the spring crops came in.

"I'll never get used to the cities you beast-men live in," Rasile said. She flicked the back of her right hand with the left, a gesture Cashel had learned was the same as a human being shaking her head. "All those houses together, and so many of them stone. None of the True People ever built with stone."

"Well, you don't use fire, so you can't smelt metal," Cashel pointed out. "That makes it hard to cut stone."

He didn't add, "And you cat men aren't much interested in hard work, either," though it'd have been true enough. The Coerli were predators. All you had to do was own a house cat to know that most of the time it'll be sleeping; and when it isn't, it's likely eating or licking itself.

"Anyway . . . ," Cashel continued diplomatically. Rasile didn't mean anything by "beast-men" and "True People;" it was just the way the Coerli language worked. "I don't guess I'll ever get used to cities either. I was eighteen before I left Barca's Hamlet, and it wasn't but three or four tens of houses."

Pandah had been a good-sized place when the royal army captured it back in the summer, but that was nothing to what it'd become now. All around the stone-built citadel, houses were going up the way mushrooms pop out of the ground after the spring rains. There were wood-sheathed buildings, wattle-and-daub huts, and on the outskirts any number of tents made of canvas or leather.

Before the Change, travel for any distance meant travel by ship. The Isles were now the Land, a continent instead of a ring of islands about the Inner Sea, and Pandah was pretty nearly the center. It'd gotten to be an important place instead of a sleepy little island where ships put in to buy fruit and fill their water casks.

The Corl wizard cleared her throat with a growl that had sounded threatening before Cashel got used to it. She paced slowly sideways around the tower, seeming to look out over Pandah.

Cashel had spent his life watching animals and figuring out what was going on in their minds before they went and did something stupid. He knew Rasile hadn't asked to come up here just to view a city she disliked even more than he did. That was why he'd asked Lord Waldron, the commander of the royal army, to put a couple soldiers down at the base of the stairs to keep idlers out of the tower while Cashel and the wizard were in it.

"Warrior Cashel," Rasile said with careful formality, though she still didn't meet his eyes. "You are a friend of Chief Garric. As you know, the wizard Tenoctris summoned me to help your spouse Sharina while Tenoctris herself was occupied with other business."

"Yes, ma'am," Cashel said. "I know that."

"There is no wizard as powerful as Tenoctris," Rasile said, this time speaking forcefully.

Cashel smiled. It was a good feeling to remember a success.

"Ma'am, I believe that's so," he said. He could've added that it hadn't been true before Tenoctris took an ancient demon into her while Cashel watched. Risky as that was, it'd worked; and because it'd worked, the kingdom had a defender like no wizard before her. "Even she says that, and Tenoctris isn't one to brag."

"And now she has accomplished her other tasks," Rasile continued, turning at last to look at Cashel. "It may be that with a wizard of his own race present—and so powerful a wizard besides—Chief Garric may no longer wish to keep me in his council. Do you believe that is so, Warrior Cashel?"

Cashel chuckled, glad to know what was bothering the old wizard. "No ma'am, it's *not* so," he said, making sure he really sounded like he meant it. He did mean it, of course, but with people—and sheep—lots of times it wasn't the words they heard but the way you said them. "Look, Garric's job is fighting against, well, evil. Right? The sort of evil that'll wipe out everybody, your folk and mine both. And the fight isn't over."

The sound Rasile made in her throat this time really was a growl, though it wasn't a threat to him. "No, Warrior Cashel," she said, "the fight is not over."

She gestured toward the eastern horizon. "A very great fight is coming, I believe. But—you have Tenoctris again."

"Ma'am," Cashel said, hearing his voice drop lower because of the subject, "what with one thing and another, I've been in a lot of fights. I've *never* been in one where I wouldn't have welcomed help, though. I figure Garric feels the same way."

Rasile gave a throaty laugh. "I am relieved to hear that," she said. "During the time I accompanied your spouse Sharina, Warrior Cashel, I became accustomed to not being relegated to filth and garbage. While I *could* return to my former life with the True People, I don't feel the need to reinforce my sense of humility to that degree. Wholesome though no doubt it would be to do so."

They laughed together. Cashel looked down at the city, holding his quarterstaff in his left hand. There were all sorts of people below, walking and working and just idling along. They made him think of summer days in the south pasture, sitting beneath the ilex tree on the hilltop and watching his sheep go about their business.

In the past couple years Cashel had gone a lot of places and done a lot of things, but he was still a shepherd at heart. He'd learned there were worse things than sea wolves twisting out of the surf to snatch ewes—but he'd learned also that his hickory staff would put paid to a wizard as quickly as it would to the sort of threats his sheep had faced.

He tapped the staff lightly, clicking its iron butt cap on the tower's stone floor. To his surprise, a sizzle of blue wizardlight spat away from the contact.

Rasile noticed the spark also. Her grin bared a jawful of teeth that were noticeably sharper than those of a human being.

"I told you the fight was not over, Warrior Cashel," she said. "I felt but I did not say that Chief Garric would be wise to keep me by him. I cannot do as much as his Tenoctris does, but I can do some things; and he will need many things done if he and his kingdom, *our* kingdom, are to survive the coming struggle."

Cashel nodded without speaking. From this vantage he

could see birds fishing the pools that now dotted the plains where the Inner Sea had rippled before the Change. Most were the white or gray of seagulls, but there were darker shapes which flashed blue when they caught the sun right: kingfishers, he was sure.

"Would you mind staying here a little longer, Warrior Cashel?" the Corl wizard said. "I would like to work a small spell. Both our height above the ground and your presence will aid me, I believe."

"Whatever you want, ma'am," Cashel said. "And I'd appreciate you just call me Cashel. I'm not a warrior, you know. I'm just a shepherd."

Rasile snorted mild laughter as she squatted on her haunches. She took a handful of yarrow stalks out of a bag woven from willow withies, so fine and dense that Cashel thought it would shed water. The catmen were good at weaving; even Ilna said so.

"You see what you see, shepherd," Rasile said. "But I see what the world sees. If you do not want me to say 'Warrior,' I will not say the word. But the truth does not change, Cashel."

She tossed the yarrow stalks into a pattern on the stone, then began mumbling words of power. Cashel didn't pay much attention to her. He kept watching the sky and the land beneath, the directions that danger might come from.

He was a shepherd, after all.

SHARINA LOOKED AROUND the apartment in which Tenoctris lived and worked. She hoped her shocked dismay didn't show in her expression. The small room had been let into the outer wall of the citadel. The walls wept condensate, and the only window was the small one in the iron-braced door. In all, the place would've been suitable for a prison cell—and had probably been used as one in the past.

Besides being a friend of Prince Garric and Princess Sharina, Tenoctris was the wizard who through advice and skill had done as much to preserve mankind as had any other single person. Though Pandah's population was increasing by the day, she could have any quarters she wanted.

"Oh, dear," Tenoctris said in obvious dismay. She looked like a woman of twenty-two or three, pert and pretty without being beautiful. Apparently Sharina *hadn't* kept her face blank. "I'm sorry, dear. I chose this room because it's what I'm used to. I didn't mean to suggest that you wouldn't give me better or, well, anything. You have to remember that for most of my life—"

She shrugged. Tenoctris had been a woman of seventy when she'd washed up on the shore of Barca's Hamlet, flotsam flung a thousand years forward in time by the cataclysm which ended the Old Kingdom. She now appeared to be the woman she'd been in her youth, but that was true only physically. She'd gained both knowledge and wisdom over a long life. She retained those virtues and had now added power that few wizards ever could have claimed.

"—I was considered rightly to be a wizard of very little power. I prided myself on my scholarship, again I think rightly, but—"

Tenoctris grinned. Her cheerfully wry expression would've been enough by itself for Sharina to identify her, no matter what features she was wearing.

"—scholars aren't lodged or fed as well as wizards who can split mountains with an incantation and a gesture."

"Well, speaking as an innkeeper's daughter rather than as Princess Sharina," Sharina said, keeping her tone light, "I'd rather a friend of mine had better lodging. But I understand the attraction of the familiar. I wish I had the same freedom in what I wear."

She tweaked her silk robe. It was a relatively simple garment compared with full court dress weighing as much as a cavalryman's armor, but contrasted with the tunic she'd ordinarily worn in Barca's Hamlet—both an inner and an outer tunic for unusually formal occasions—it was heavy, hot, and confining.

A squad of soldiers talked in low voices as they waited outside in the passage. They were Blood Eagles, members of the royal bodyguard. Sharina had come to accept that, because she was a princess and regent in her brother's absence, she would always have guards.

She grimaced. It wasn't that she wanted to be alone—nobody in a peasant village expected privacy, especially in the winter when even a wealthy household heated only one room. She wasn't used to people actually *caring* what she did, however, day in and day out. Well, there was no help for it; and the dangers were real enough.

Sharina smiled faintly. Though she doubted men with swords would be any help against the wizardry which had been the worst danger to the kingdom these past two years.

"What's your opinion of Rasile, Sharina?" Tenoctris asked abruptly. She fluttered her hands, also familiar—though it seemed odd to see a young woman making the gesture an old woman used to make. "I know she's a powerful wizard; *that* I can judge. What sort of person was she to work with?"

Sharina took time to frame her reply. The room's low-backed chair was stacked with codices. The bed likewise, though there was room enough for a slim person to sleep along the outer edge. And the three wicker baskets of scrolls, though of a height to be sat on, struck Sharina as too flimsy for that to be a safe option.

There was room to squat, however. She squatted, just as she would've done back home while popping open peapods for dinner.

"Rasile doesn't waste words," she said. She grinned. "Or mince them. Which I actually appreciate. She's brave, calm, and good company."

Sharina met the gaze of the old/young wizard who'd seated herself on the edge of the low bed, putting their eyes on a level. "She wasn't you, Tenoctris," she said. "But you couldn't have left me with a better helper."

"No, she isn't me," Tenoctris said with a quirk of her lips, a smile that wasn't quite humorous. "She's a great deal more powerful than I *ever* was. And equally precise, which is why she hasn't precipitated a cataclysm the way so many powerful wizards have done in the past. Also, I don't think she cares much about her power."

"She isn't as powerful as you are now, though?" Sharina said carefully. She wasn't trying to be flattering, but she needed to understand the tools that preserved the kingdom. Tenoctris and Rasile were among those tools, just as surely as she and her brother and all those who took the side of Good were.

She was Princess Sharina. She *had* to think that way if she was to do the best possible work in the struggle with evil, and there was no margin for anything but the best possible work.

"Cashel is accompanying Rasile at this moment," Tenoctris said, looking squarely at Sharina. "I thought that might be a good pairing for the future, if the kingdom's safety required a wizard with suitable protection to act at a distance from the palace and army."

Sharina didn't mean to turn away, but she found her eyes were resting on the top codex of the pile on the chair. It'd been bound with the pebbled skin of a lizard. There was no legend on the cover, but on the edge of the pages was written *Hybro* in vermilion ink. The word didn't mean anything to her.

She pursed her lips. "You mean the sort of thing you and Cashel did just now, while I led the army against Pandah," she said without emphasis. She looked at the wizard again. The young, pretty, very powerful wizard. "That went very well, I believe."

"Yes," said Tenoctris flatly, "it did."

She paused. "I always found Cashel impressive," she said. "I find him even more so now that I have—"

She twisted a lock of hair to call attention to her gleaming, sandy-red curls.

"—more capacity for appreciation."

This time it was Tenoctris who looked away. She cleared her throat and continued, "Sharina, I have powers that I wouldn't have, couldn't have, dreamed of in the past."

She smiled wryly. "In a very *long* past life. I hope that this power hasn't caused me to lose my judgment, however. Specifically, it hasn't caused me to miss what Cashel is: a rock which will stand though the heavens fall."

"I never doubted you, Tenoctris," Sharina said. She didn't know if that was true. Her lips were dry.

"If you're wise," Tenoctris said, smiling again, "then you never doubted Cashel. You never should doubt Cashel, Sharina. Though the heavens fall."

Sharina rose, feeling a trifle dizzy. That was common after squatting, after all. "I'm sure Rasile will find him a good companion and protector," she said. "If there's need, of course."

There would be need. Sharina was as sure of that as she was that there would be a thunderstorm. She didn't know when or how violent it would be—

But she knew that the storm was coming.

ILNA'S FINGERS KNOTTED short lengths of cord as she looked at the four people across the desk from her. She was angry, but that—like the fact the sun rises in the east—wasn't unusual enough to be worth comment.

Directly before her were a pair of plump young women, Carisa and Bovea, foster nurses employed by the Lady Merota bos-Roriman Society for Orphans; they were crying. A man of thirty named Heismat, originally from Cordin, sat to their left. He'd wanted to stand, but he'd obeyed when Ilna ordered him onto the third low stool. Despite his bluster and the angry red of his face, Heismat's eyes were cold with fear.

Ilna smiled, though nobody could've mistaken the expression for humor. Heismat knew he was in trouble, though as yet he didn't understand how serious the trouble was. It was hard to convince some people that they shouldn't knock children around, and even more people thought a Corl kit was an animal rather than a child.

Mistress Winora, the manager of the Merota Society, stood beside the door with her hands crossed at her waist; her face was expressionless. Winora was fifty, the widow of a merchant from Erdin who'd been killed in the chaos that followed the Change. She'd kept the books and managed the Erdin end of the business while her husband traveled, so she—unlike Ilna—had the skills required to run the day-to-day operations of the Society.

Carisa and Bovea were among the many other women who'd lost their spouses recently. There were even more orphans than there were widows, so it'd seemed perfectly obvious to Ilna to put the two together to the advantage of both, paying each pair of nurses a competence sufficient to care for a handful of children. She'd done so in the name of Merota, who'd been an orphan also until Ilna and Chalcus took charge of her.

Ilna's fingers knotted, forming a very complex pattern. It calmed her to knot and weave, but she had a specific purpose this time. She was *very* angry.

Merota and Chalcus had died during the Change. If you believed in souls, then Ilna's soul had died with them—with her family. Ilna didn't believe in souls or gods or anything, really, except craftsmanship. And she believed in the death that would come to all things, though perhaps not as soon as she would like.

"Look, I'm sorry," Heismat snarled. He glared at his knotted hands. He'd been a laborer before the Change and had come to Pandah to work in the building trade. "I *said* I was sorry, didn't I? I didn't mean to do it!"

"Mistress," blubbered Carisa. Heismat was her boyfriend. "It was only because he was drinking, you know. He's a good man, a *good* man, really."

"Mistress Winora, how is the kit?" Ilna asked. Her voice was thin and as cold as the wind from the Ice Capes.

"She'll live," Winora said. Her face was bleak, her tone emotionless. Winora regarded this as failure on her part. "She'll probably limp for the rest of her life, but we may be lucky."

Ilna nodded. "Worse things happen in this world," she said.

It wasn't Winora's fault. It was the fault of Ilna os-Kenset, who'd created a situation which allowed a child to be injured instead of being protected as was supposed to have happened.

Worse things happened, as she'd said. She'd done far worse things herself. But this *particular* thing wouldn't happen again.

"There were other instances of Master Heismat hitting the kit," Winora said. "They weren't as serious, and I didn't learn about them until after this event. I'm sorry, mistress. I wasn't watching as closely as I should have done."

"People make mistakes," Ilna said quietly, her eyes on Heismat; he fidgeted under the cold appraisal. She thought, *At least you're aware that it was a mistake.* If Winora had said the wrong thing—and it wouldn't have had to be very wrong, because Ilna was extremely angry—she'd have been next in line as soon as Ilna was done with Heismat.

"Mistress, please," Carisa said, mumbling into her kerchief wadded in both hands. "Heismat's a good man, only the cats killed his whole family. *Please,* mistress."

The rhythmic *ching! ching!* of iron on stone sounded from the courtyard. A mason was carving letters and embellishments for the lintel with strokes of a narrow-bladed adze. Ilna had been angry to learn that money was being spent on what she considered needless ornamentation when a painted sign would do.

She'd checked her facts before she acted, though; someone who got as angry as Ilna did learned to check the facts before acting. Lady Liane bos-Benliman, the fiancée of Prince Garric and, less publicly, the kingdom's spy master, had ordered the carving. Liane was paying for the job from her own funds.

Ilna still thought the carving was an unnecessary expense, but she'd learned a long time ago that what she thought and what the world thought were likely to be very different. And Ilna also knew that she made mistakes.

Sometimes it felt like she made only mistakes, though of course that wasn't true anyplace but in Ilna's heart. She'd thanked Liane for her generosity.

"Mistress," said Heismat, glaring at his hands. "I didn't mean it, only I come home and there the beast—"

"Cloohe, mistress!" said Bovea. "Little Cloohe, and it's my fault, I'd shut her up when we saw it was getting on and Heismat wasn't home yet, but she must've slipped out while I was dozing."

"I seen the, the cat, and I thunk of my own three that the cats kilt and I couldn't stop myself, mistress," Heismat said brokenly toward his knotted fists. "I'd drunk a bit much. I *knowed* I shoulda kept away, but I wanted to see Carisa and, and I didn't think. I seed the, the kit, and I just flew hot."

"Mistress, it was the drink," Carisa said. "It's my own fault not to keep Cloohe locked up better when it got so late and Heismat not back."

"I've already split the women up and put them with stronger partners, mistress," Winora said in the same dry tone as before. "They're among the best caretakers we have. Though of course I've warned them that you may choose to dismiss or otherwise punish them."

Ilna shrugged. "I'm concerned with preventing a recurrence," she said, "not vengeance. I tried vengeance long enough to determine that it wasn't a satisfactory answer."

How many of the Coerli did I kill after they'd slaughtered Chalcus and Merota? Many, certainly. More than even Merota, who counted any number you pleased without using tellers, could've kept track of.

Ilna smiled. Bovea, who happened to be looking at her, stifled a scream with her knuckles.

"Mistress, I'm sorry," Heismat said, stumbling over the words in his fear. "I swear by the Lady it'll never happen again. *Never!*"

"It were just the drink, mistress," Carisa pleaded. "He's a *good* man."

Ilna looked at the girl; without expression, she'd have said, but from the way Carisa cringed back there must've been something after all. "As men go," Ilna said quietly, "as human beings go, I suppose you're right. Though I'm angry enough as it is, so I don't see what you think to gain by emphasizing the fact."

Carisa blinked. Her hand was over her mouth. "Mistress, I don't understand?" she mumbled.

Ilna grimaced. There were *sheep* with more intelligence than this girl—who was Ilna's age or older in actual years.

Still, Carisa was a good mother to orphans, which is more than Ilna herself could say. While Ilna was caring for Merota, a cat man with a stone mace had dashed the child's brains out.

"Master Heismat, look at me," Ilna said.

Heismat's face twitched into a rictus. His eyes slanted to Ilna's left, then above her; he knuckled his balled fists.

"Master Heismat," Ilna said. She didn't raise her voice, but her anger sang like a good sword vibrating. "I'm offering you an alternative to being hanged and your body dumped in a rubbish tip, but I assure you that I *will* go the other way if you don't cooperate."

"Mistress, I'm sorry," the laborer said. Tears were dribbling into his sandy beard and the rank stain darkening his gray pantaloons showed that he'd lost control of his bladder, but he was looking directly at Ilna as she'd demanded. "It'll never happen again, I *swear!*"

Ilna raised the pattern she'd knotted. It was quite a subtle piece of work, though no one else in the world would've understood that. Her patterns generally affected everyone who looked at them. That was true here as well, but only Heismat had the *background* to be affected. His memories were the nether millstone against which Ilna's fabric would grind out misery and horror.

She smiled because she was *very* angry, then folded the pattern into itself and placed it in her left sleeve. She'd pick the knots out shortly.

"All right," Ilna said, rising. "Mistress Winora, you'll have business to go over with the nurses."

She looked at Heismat, who was blinking in surprise. "Master Heismat," she said, "you're free to go also."

She considered adding, "And I hope I never see you again," but that would've been pointless and Ilna tried to avoid pointless behavior. Given that all existence struck her as fairly pointless, the whole business was probably an exercise in self-delusion, another thing that she'd have said she tried to avoid. The train of thought made her smile.

"But what happened?" Bovea said. Heismat and Carisa were keeping silent, probably stunned by what they thought was their good luck. "Nothing happened, did it?"

"Bovea, be silent!" Winora snapped as she stepped aside from the door. "You're in trouble enough already, girl."

Ilna stopped and looked back. "Nothing happened unless Master Heismat takes a drink," she said, "which he's promised not to do. If he goes back on his word, he'll experience the slaughter of his family through the eyes of one of the Corl hunters involved. *Every* time he takes a drink."

"But . . . ," said Carisa. Heismat simply sat with his mouth open. "A drink? You don't mean he can't have a mug of ale? Mistress, the water's not safe in Pandah with all the people coming in and the wells so shallow!"

"I mean any drink," Ilna said. "Anything with alcohol in it. As for the water in Pandah, I quite agree. Your friend can find a place where the water's safer, I suppose."

She smiled.

"Or he can die," she added, eyeing the laborer critically. He stared back at her as blankly as a landed fish. "We all die eventually, and there's nothing in Master Heismat's behavior that makes me wish he was an exception."

Carisa lifted her apron and began sobbing into it. Ilna touched the latch lever to open the door; Winora put out her hand.

"Mistress?" Ilna said sharply. She didn't mean the anger; not exactly, at any rate. She very much wanted to be shut of this affair, and Winora was prolonging it.

"Mistress, do you wish me to continue in my position?" the older woman said. She met Ilna's eyes, but she was obviously frightened. *She's terrified!*

"Yes," said Ilna. *Am I as terrible as that?* "You caught the business as quickly as reasonably could be done."

She felt her lips lift in a cold smile again. Ilna *was* that terrible, of course; but not to this woman whose only mistake was that she hadn't been perfect, that she hadn't foreseen *all* the things that could go wrong. A Corl kit had been crippled; worse had happened to a child named Merota because of Ilna's own mistakes.

"And you told me at once instead of trying to hide it," she added. "That was wise."

"Thank you, mistress," Winora said, shuddering in relief. She glanced over her shoulder, drawing Ilna's attention also. Heismat had his arms around Carisa and was trying to murmur reassurance to the blubbering girl. He probably *was* a good man, as humans judged such things.

"It would have been a mercy to have killed him instead," Winora said without emphasis.

"Yes," said Ilna. "But this way he's a better example to others."

She opened the door. Gilla, Mistress Winora's chief assistant, was standing in the hall with her back to the panel. When it opened she jumped aside and said, rattling the words out all together, "Mistress-Ilna-this-gentleman's-come-to-see-you! I told him you'd said not to be disturbed and you wouldn't be, not while I had life and breath!"

"Thank you, Gilla," Ilna said. From the way the plump woman was wheezing, she had very little breath left. Ilna felt a touch of real amusement that didn't reach her lips. Still, it lightened her mood. "Lord Zettin? As a matter of fact, I was hoping to see you today. Can we speak for a moment further after you've finished your business?"

"Mistress," said Zettin, "it's your business that brings me here. I was furious when I learned that my staff had turned you away! Is there some place we can get privacy?"

He looked around. Faces ranging from infants' to that of the aged charwoman ducked away from his angry glance. The building served not only as the foundation's office but as a temporary barracks for orphans who hadn't yet been assigned to a pair of nurses in the community. A high nobleman like Lord Zettin would've been an object of wonder even if he hadn't been wearing a dazzling parcel-gilt cuirass.

"My business doesn't require secrecy," Ilna said, feeling her lips pinch over the words. It offended her that anybody might even think she was trying to hide something. "But we can sit in the garden, and I'm sure—"

She looked at—glared at, she supposed—Gilla.

"—that Mistress Gilla will see that we're not disturbed."

"Yes, mistress!" Gilla said. "Whatever mistress says! Ah, would mistress and her guest like some refreshment while you confer?"

"That won't be necessary," Ilna said firmly, leading her visitor through a reception hall in which six female clerks now worked on the foundation's accounts. In truth her mouth was dry from anger at Heismat, but she didn't want servants interrupting her with carafes and tumblers. This wouldn't take long.

She didn't bother asking what Zettin wanted. If *he* was thirsty, he could wait the length of a brief discussion also.

Lord Zettin was thirty-one or two, quite young for someone in so senior a position. Before the Change, he'd commanded the fleet and the phalanx of pikemen which the oarsmen formed after their ships were drawn up on the beach. He'd gotten the job not only because he was keen and clever—which he was—but because Ornifal's wealthy nobility considered the position a lowly one.

It *had* been lowly when the Dukes of Ornifal claimed to be Kings of the Isles but had little control beyond the shores of their island. When Garric became Prince Garric and the real ruler, the fleet and phalanx became important—and Admiral Zettin showed himself to be skilled as well as clever.

The Inner Sea became a continent at the Change and grounded the fleet. Zettin now commanded the kingdom's new scouting forces, another job that established officers didn't want. The scouts were a mixture of hunters, shepherds, and cat men; they moved fast in small units which didn't bother with the baggage train of the regular army. From the scraps of conversation Ilna had heard from Garric, Liane, and Sharina, Zettin was again doing very well.

The house Ilna had taken for her foundation came with a

courtyard garden. It had been not only ill-tended but awash in garbage—its most recent occupants had been renegade Coerli, and their immediate predecessors were bands of human pirates.

So far as Ilna was concerned the courtyard could've stayed a wasteland, though of course the garbage had to go. Members of the new staff had made it a priority, though, and the orphans seemed to have thrown themselves into the work. In less than a month the apple trees and the cypress had been pruned, and the planting beds were bright with zinnias, tiny blue asters, and even a late-blooming cardoon. The flowers must've been transplanted; they certainly couldn't have grown so fast from seeds.

Ilna sat on one of the two stone benches framing a small round table. She deliberately chose the seat in the sunlight rather than that shaded by the cypress. Her fingers were picking out and re-forming the pattern they'd knotted for Heismat. She didn't need to be able to strike Zettin with despair or paralyzing fear, but she could. So long as she was in the sunlight, he was certain to see whatever she lifted before his eyes.

"I apologize for my staff, Mistress Ilna," Zettin said, sitting straight up on the opposite bench. *A good thing he isn't in the sun; that breastplate would be blinding.* "They didn't realize who you were and mistakenly thought that they shouldn't interrupt the morning briefing."

Ilna opened her mouth. Before she could get a word out, he continued, "Mistress, I know I've seemed to be arrogant and not to, well, show the courtesy I should. But please believe me, I've always had the kingdom's interests at heart. If I push hard and don't always listen as well as I might, that's the cause. Believe me, I never would've allowed you to be turned away!"

Ilna frowned, not at what the nobleman was saying but because he was saying it to her. *He thinks he's offended me.* That was reasonable; he must by now be used to his pushiness offending people. What *wasn't* reasonable was Zettin bothering to apologize, as though she was powerful enough to hurt him.

"I stopped by on my way here," Ilna said. "I asked for you personally because you're the only person I know in the scouts. I have a favor to ask—"

"Anything, mistress!" Zettin said. "Anything in my power. Just ask!"

"I was trying to," Ilna said, glaring at Zettin. He was a slim, good-looking man who was careful of his appearance; his dark-blond hair and mustache were neatly trimmed, and there were no smudges on his armor.

Zettin's mouth worked on a sour thought. He brushed his left hand over his face and said, "Mistress, my apologies. Again."

She paused, suddenly struck by a vision of the Ilna os-Kenset which this nobleman saw. She *was* powerful. A word to her childhood friends Garric or Sharina would send Lord Zettin off to command a garrison regiment or as envoy to a distant, minor court.

Ilna wouldn't do that, of course; she hadn't been angry, and politics disgusted her anyway. If she *had* felt a need to punish the man, she'd have done it directly as she'd done to others in the past. Quite a few others, now that she considered the matter.

"Yes," Ilna said. "During my travels immediately after the Change, a pair of former hunters named Asion and Karpos helped me. They're here in Pandah, but they're uncomfortable in cities."

She smiled wryly at herself.

"They're even more uncomfortable than I am," she said. "They'll take reasonable orders. They wouldn't make good soldiers—"

That was a mild a way of putting it; Ilna grimaced. In fact it was mild enough to be a lie if you looked at it closely, and Ilna hated lies.

"—but I think they'd be useful as scouts for you. They . . ."

She paused again and swallowed. She suddenly found herself choking on emotion, an unexpected circumstance and a very uncommon one besides.

"Asion and Karpos," she resumed forcefully, "earned my

respect and gratitude. I suppose you take courage for granted, but they also showed cool heads and great skill many times. I'd like them to be in a good situation."

Zettin nodded crisply. "Yes, of course," he said. His eyes drifted toward bees buzzing about the calendula, then met hers again. In a sharper tone he went on, "Can they work with Coerli?"

"Yes, that won't be a problem," Ilna said. "I'll tell them to dispose of the cat-scalp capes they made while they were with me."

Zettin barked a laugh, then looked shocked. He muttered, "Sorry, mistress, I didn't mean to laugh. . . ."

He stopped.

"I *intended* it as a joke," Ilna said tartly. "It's true, of course, but Asion and Karpos have too much judgment for me to need to tell them that."

"It would've been all right," Zettin said, the cool professional again. "The Scouting Corps has all-human units—and all-Coerli units too, for that matter. But the mixed units get better results, and it's one less thing to worry about when assigning billets."

He cleared his throat. "Ah, mistress?" he went on. "You won't be needing the men's services again yourself? Because I can see to it that they're stationed near Pandah if you'd like."

Ilna shook her head. "I don't know how long I'll be here," she said. "I've already stayed much longer than I cared to."

She heard the bitterness in her voice and scowled; she was showing weakness.

"I don't know what I'll be doing in the future," she said, keeping her tone neutral. "Dying, I suppose, but before then . . ."

She spread her hands, palms up.

"Well, no doubt something will appear."

Zettin appeared for a moment to be glaring at the cardoon's purple face. He drummed the fingers of his left hand on the bench beside him, then turned to Ilna with a look of resolution.

"Mistress," he said firmly. "I'm about to bring up a personal problem, nothing whatever to do with the business of the kingdom. The only reason I dare to mention it is that you implied that you want to get out of Pandah?"

"Go on," Ilna said. Her fingers were taking apart the pattern they'd knotted; when she'd reduced it to loose yarn, she'd again recast it. Weaving gave her something to do while she listened. . . .

"My sister Zussa has married into a wealthy family, but they're in trade," Zettin said. "I want to be very clear about that."

Ilna sniffed. "I suppose my family was in trade also," she said, "before my father, mine and Cashel's, drank up his share of the family mill. Please get to the point, Master Zettin."

She *would* not call him or any man "Lord."

"When her father-in-law died last year," Zettin said, smiling faintly, "her husband Hervir took over the family's spice-importing business. The firm was based in Valles, but after the Change Hervir put in motion plans to move it to Pandah. He's, ah, quite a forward-looking young man."

Also, he's smart enough to take advice from a well-connected brother-in-law, Ilna thought.

Zettin had noticed the deliberate slight of "Master," and had been amused by it. Before this conversation she would've said she didn't care for Zettin particularly, putting him in the same category as all but a handful of the people she knew. To Ilna's surprise, the fellow was edging toward that select handful.

"Hervir heard that a source of saffron had appeared on the north coast of Blaise since the Change," Zettin said. "As you probably know, in the past saffron came only from two or three valleys in the mountains of Seres. Saffron from Blaise could come up the New River almost directly to Pandah."

"Go on," Ilna said. It was simpler to be politely noncommittal than to snarl that *of course* a peasant from Barca's Hamlet knew nothing about a spice so expensive that it was weighed out with carob seeds, just like jewels.

"Hervir had been planning to set up the new headquarters in Pandah himself, but when he heard about this opportunity, well . . ." Zettin shrugged. "Hervir and I haven't always seen eye-to-eye."

He flashed Ilna a wan smile that made him look unexpectedly human. Zettin usually had points sticking out in all directions; everything he said or did seemed to be a way of getting advantage. For the first time in the two years since Ilna met him, that wasn't the case.

"Or perhaps," he said, "we do see eye-to-eye—we're too much alike to be friends. Regardless, I respect Hervir whether or not I like him. He sent Zussa here to prepare the new headquarters and set off himself to Blaise with his secretary, six guards, and a belt of money. He planned to buy a riverboat on Blaise and sail down to Pandah with the saffron."

Zettin paused, looking across the table. Because something was obviously expected of her, Ilna said, "Go on," again.

This time the pattern her fingers were knotting wasn't a weapon. The lines in yarn were a reflection of the universe, though Ilna herself was never conscious of their meaning until she concentrated on what her fingers had woven without her conscious mind's control.

"Two days ago the secretary and guards arrived in Pandah," Zettin said. "Hervir wasn't with them, nor the money either. The secretary—his name's Ingens and he's been seven years with the house, a perfectly reliable man Zussa says—Ingens says that Hervir went off alone at night with the chest. He was meeting a man with the saffron, supposedly. He never came back."

Zettin spread his hands with a grimace. "Now," he said, "I don't want you to think that I believe in fortune-tellers, but Madame Raciana, Hervir's mother, does. She went to a fellow, a charlatan I'm sure, who swears that Hervir was spirited off by wizardry. She's prodding Zussa to get one of my wizard friends in the court—"

He grimaced apologetically. "I'm sorry," he said, "but

that's what they think. One of my wizard friends to rescue her son. And Zussa, I'm sorry to say, is making my life a misery until I act. Mistress, I know you're not a wizard, but, well, you have that reputation."

He paused with a cautious look on his face. *To see how I'm taking that,* Ilna realized. The statement was true, so she certainly wasn't going to snarl at Zettin for what he'd said. And it was possible that the belief that Ilna os-Kenset was a wizard also was true. Not the way Tenoctris was, or the cat woman Rasile; but there were things Ilna did that only wizards could do, and she did some things that even wizards could not.

"Go on," she said aloud.

"If you could come with me and tell Raciana that there's no wizard's work involved, that Hervir was knocked on the head and robbed," Zettin said earnestly, "then she'll let me take care of the business the way it should be. I'll send a troop of my scouts under a good officer up to where Hervir disappeared. They'll get to the bottom of the trouble, I'll warrant."

"I'll certainly go with you," Ilna said, rising. She began to reduce the oracle to short lengths of twine again. "I'd like to talk to this secretary."

She smiled coldly at the nobleman as he rose with her. She could see her reflection in the breastplate, distorted across the gilded images of sea gods cavorting.

"But I won't tell Madame Raciana that her fortune-teller is wrong," Ilna said, "because to my surprise that doesn't seem to be true. Master Hervir really was taken by wizardry . . . and I think I may have found a sufficient reason to leave Pandah."

LIANE SAT IN the roof garden, her back to the west so that the sun fell over her shoulder onto the *Books of Changes* from which she was reading to Garric. She turned a page.

" 'Piety lies conquered,' " she continued. Her voice was like polished amber, smooth and soft and golden. " 'Starry

Justice leaves the bloody earth for the far reaches of the heavens.' "

She paused and grinned at Garric. "If Pendill's to be believed," she said, "things were as bad by the end of the First Age as they are now. Perhaps we should feel encouraged that they haven't gotten even worse?"

Garric laughed. He sat in the tiny grape arbor; Liane had moved a wicker bench for better light, but they were both out of the direct sight of everyone else in—well, in the whole world. That was unusual for anyone who lived in society, and almost unheard of for a prince and his consort in a palace full of servants, office-holders, and courtiers.

"I think we've improved from that," he said, luxuriating in the fact that he wasn't for these few moments being ruler of a kingdom under threat. "Piety hasn't given up the fight yet, and as for Justice—I was a peasant, and a peasant'll choose the king's law any day over the local squire's justice. I think the kingdom's moving pretty well in the direction of having a rule of law, though I don't pretend to've convinced everybody."

"If you're dealing with human beings," said King Carus, the ghost in Garric's mind, *"you won't convince everybody that the sun rises in the east. And there's no few of 'em who'll try to brain you if you won't agree that it really rises in the west."*

Garric chuckled in unison with his ancient ancestor. Carus had been the last ruler of the Old Kingdom; he'd spent his reign battling usurpers as well the monsters which entered the waking world as wizardry rose to its thousand-year peak. In the end a wizard had destroyed both Carus and himself, had destroyed the Old Kingdom as well, and had very nearly destroyed Mankind.

"The thing is, lad . . . ," Carus said. Garric saw the ancient king as a man of forty or so, leaning on the battlements of a half-glimpsed tower. He wore a bright blue tunic and red breeches more vivid than the roses clinging to the masonry. *"I was as quick to knock heads as the next fellow. Quicker, I dare say, and certainly better at it. I'd have brought the king-*

dom down myself without any wizard's help. None of which I understood until I saw you ruling the right way, of course."

Garric's lips pursed as he considered the matter. Liane knew about the ghost in his mind, but she wasn't party to their silent conversations. Therefore he said aloud, "You can't rule with a sword alone. But until the Golden Age returns, you can't rule without a sword either. I'm very fortunate in having an ancestor who was the greatest warrior of . . ."

He paused again for thought. Carus grinned, and Garric's grin echoed the ghost's. "The greatest warrior ever, I think," he said aloud.

"It does seem," said Liane, closing the book, "that there's more peace if everyone's convinced that Prince Garric and the royal army will destroy anybody who breaks that peace."

She reached down for the portable desk in which she kept current files but straightened again without touching it; the details of government could wait for the time being. "That's particularly true of the Coerli. I'm frankly amazed that the integration of them into the kingdom has been so smooth."

"The Coerli aren't comfortable unless they're in a hierarchy, but once they've got one they'll live with it even if they're not on top," Garric said, smiling faintly. "There's a lot of human beings the same way. Just about every professional soldier in this army, for example."

Liane set Pendill down, though she didn't open the traveling desk to put the book away properly. "I'm still glad it worked this way," she said. "If it hadn't, we would've had to wipe the Coerli out."

She stepped into the arbor and settled beside Garric. It was a muggy day, but her soft warmth was welcome.

"You said something about a sea serpent in the south?" Garric said. It disturbed him to realize that he couldn't completely relax anymore, not when there was still work to be done. There was always work for a prince to do. . . .

"In Telut," Liane said. She would've risen to get the report covering the matter from her desk; Garric tightened his arm slightly to keep her where she was; she relaxed against him again.

Liane used her notebooks as props, but she normally didn't bother to open them while discussing the matters they contained. Though the archives of the kingdom's intelligence service were well indexed and staffed by skilled clerks, Liane really ran it out of her head.

Her father had been, among other things, a successful merchant. She'd used his contacts and business training to weave a web of spies through the Isles. That was now as necessary as the royal army, but it worked only because Liane, demure and cultured and beautiful, sat like a spider at its center.

"Refugees from the city of Ombis on Telut," she said slowly, wriggling against him, "said an army, an armed rabble under a chief calling himself Captain Archas, summoned the city to surrender. They closed the gates."

Garric gently rubbed the back of Liane's neck, massaging the sudden tension from it. Her voice softer again, she continued, "Two of the refugees swore they saw Archas call a huge serpent out of the sea. But Ombis hasn't been within ten miles of the coast since the Change."

"What do your own agents say?" Garric said, more to show he'd been listening than because he didn't think Liane would get to that question on her own.

"They haven't reported," she said. "A Serian who crossed the Seaway says that Ombis was completely destroyed, however."

"We'll take care of it," Garric said calmly. He'd learned in childhood that keeping his tone calm was more important than what you said. That insight was even more valuable when dealing with humans than it had been with sheep. "I don't know how yet but we will, whether it's real or a hallucination. We have Tenoctris and the army and anything else it might take. We have the whole kingdom's resources. Evil *won't* win."

"No, Garric," Liane whispered. "It won't."

After a moment she said, "When we were studying Old Kingdom epics at Mistress Gudea's Academy, I thought they were terribly boring. I didn't want to *read* about adventure, I